The Haun

Alan Titchmarsh

The Haunting

HODDER &
STOUGHTON

While every effort has been made to contact and acknowledge the copyright
holders of extracts used in this book, this has not always been successful.
Full acknowledgement will gladly be made in future editions.

First published in Great Britain in 2011 by Hodder & Stoughton
An Hachette UK company

1

A CIP catalogue record for this title is
available from the British Library.

Hardback ISBN 978 0 340 93688 7
Trade Paperback ISBN 978 0 340 93689 4
eBook ISBN 978 1 848 94693 4

Typeset in Plantin Light by Hewer Text UK Ltd, Edinburgh
Printed and bound by CPI Group (UK) Ltd, Croydon, CR0 4YY

Hodder & Stoughton policy is to use papers that are natural,
renewable and recyclable products and made from wood grown
in sustainable forests. The logging and manufacturing processes
are expected to conform to the environmental regulations
of the country of origin.

Hodder & Stoughton Ltd
338 Euston Road
London NW1 3BH

www.hodder.co.uk

For Nick, whose confidence inspires,
with so many thanks.

Contents

1	The Streamside, Hampshire – 16 April 1816	1
2	St Jude's School, Winchester – 16 April 2010	11
3	The Fulling Mill, Hampshire – 17 April 1816	16
4	The Riverbank, Hampshire – 16 April 2010	20
5	The Manor House, Withercombe – 17 April 1816	26
6	St Cross Apartments, Winchester – 17 April 2010	35
7	The Manor House, Withercombe – 17 April 1816	41
8	Mill Cottage, Itchen Parva – 17 April 2010	49
9	Rakemaker's Close, Old Alresford – 17 April 2010	54
10	The Bluebell Inn, Withercombe – 19 April 1816	60
11	Mill Cottage, Itchen Parva – 29 May 2010	64
12	The Streamside, Hampshire – 16 April 1816	72
13	The Old Mill, Itchen Parva – 29 May 2010	81
14	Winchester Cathedral Library – 5 June 2010	85
15	The Fulling Mill, Hampshire – 20 April 1816	93
16	Mill Cottage, Itchen Parva – 4 June 2010	98
17	The Streamside, Hampshire – 16 April 1816	108
18	St Jude's School, Winchester – 7 June 2010	112
19	The Streamside, Hampshire – 16 April 1816	118
20	The Old Mill, Itchen Parva – 7 June 2010	124
21	The Portsmouth Road – 16 April 1816	129
22	The Hotel du Vin, Winchester – 12 June 2010	136
23	Portsmouth – 16 April 1816	143
24	Mill Cottage, Itchen Parva – 13 June 2010	148
25	72 Godolphin Street, Portsmouth – 16 April 1816	154

26	Mill Cottage, Itchen Parva – 13 June 2010	161
27	72 Godolphin Street, Portsmouth – 16 April 1816	165
28	Mill Cottage, Itchen Parva – 19 June 2010	170
29	The Old Mill, Itchen Parva – 19 June 2010	178
30	72 Godolphin Street, Portsmouth – 16 April 1816	185
31	72 Godolphin Street, Portsmouth – 16 April 1816	189
32	The Old Mill, Itchen Parva – 19 June 2010	193
33	72 Godolphin Street, Portsmouth – 16 April 1816	197
34	Mill Cottage, Itchen Parva – 20 June 2010	204
35	72 Godolphin Street, Portsmouth – 17 April 1816	210
36	The Streamside – 20 June 2010	215
37	Portsmouth – 17 April 1816	221
38	The Old Mill, Itchen Parva – 20 June 2010	228
39	Winchester – 17 April 1816	236
40	The Manor House, Withercombe – 21 April 1816	243
41	St Jude's School, Winchester – 21 June 2010	248
42	Mill Cottage – 24 April 1816	254
43	Mill Cottage, Itchen Parva – 21 June 2010	261
44	Hatherley – 22 April 1816	269
45	St Jude's School, Winchester – 22 June 2010	277
46	Mill Cottage – 27 April 1816	284
47	The Old Mill, Itchen Parva – 22 June 2010	292
48	Hatherley – 30 April 1816	298
49	Winchester – 26 June 2010	303
50	The Manor House, Withercombe – 1 May 1816	312
51	Mill Cottage – Christmas Day 1816	322
52	Mill Cottage, Itchen Parva – 17 July 2010	327
53	The Old Mill, Itchen Parva – 18 July 2010	335
	Acknowledgements	341

The only supernatural agents which can in any manner be allowed to us moderns, are ghosts; but of these I would advise an author to be extremely sparing.

Henry Fielding, *Tom Jones*, 1749

I

The Streamside, Hampshire
16 April 1816

Fish say, they have their stream and pond;
But is there anything beyond?
                Rupert Brooke, 'Heaven', 1915

It was not a day for death. For a start, the weather was all wrong. It was one of those perfect days, the sort that occur only a handful of times each year. Usually in spring. Air as clear as crystal; the sort of day when the whole world seems to sparkle and glisten – freshly laundered by a shower of rain, buffed up by the gentlest of breezes and then polished to perfection by clear sunlight. It is there only for those who are prepared to see it – the sort of people whose senses are heightened by having spent much of their time out of doors rather than having had their finer feelings dulled by decades of desk-bound toil. Those poor mortals whose eyes are forever cast downwards are likely to let the moment pass, and by the time their gaze is raised heavenward, it is to discover the source of the rain that dampens further their mood or the squall that tears at their clothing.

On this April day, at a quarter to nine in the morning, Anne Flint took advantage of her mistress's absence in the hope of changing her life. Tentatively she lifted the latch on the heavy oak door and slipped from the great house without a backward glance.

The events that had occurred since she had risen at five o'clock had made her more determined than ever . . .

A bucketful of ashes can be quite heavy. If you are small. And slight. And slender of wrist. Anne struggled down the staircase of the Manor House as quietly as she could, slipping out of the back door and down to the vegetable garden where old Mr Moses, who used to be the groom, now tended a few desultory rows of cabbages, swedes and turnips. She emptied the bucket gradually along the path that led to his dilapidated shelter, whose coppery-coloured roof tiles slithered towards the ground in a tumbling pyramid. There would be no danger of encountering him. He did not rise until half past eight at the earliest and it was not yet half past six. The bucket emptied at last, Anne retraced her steps to the house and made to store it in its usual place in the cellar. She ducked between the dried hams that hung from the iron hooks studding the vaulted ceiling and slowly climbed back up the cellar steps. As she did so, she heard the firm footsteps of Mrs Fitzgerald walking down the passage. Anne took the precaution of picking from a stone shelf behind the door a bottle of vinegar and a box of salt.

At first she thought she might escape being seen by hiding behind the open cellar door, but that strategy was invalidated by the housekeeper herself who, thinking that the door had been left open by mistake, closed it and revealed the junior housemaid, salt and vinegar in hand, standing flat against the wall and looking sheepish.

'What are you doing there?'

'Just coming out of the cellar, Mrs Fitzgerald.'

'You are out of the cellar. Why is there any need to stand behind the door like a shadow?'

'I was just—'

'Idling. Again.'

'No, ma'am. I was . . .' Anne held up the box and the bottle to show the fruits of her mission.

'They are doing no good at all in your hand. They need to be applied to the brass.'

'Yes, ma'am.'

'Off you go. Get your bowl and your cloth. There's plenty to clean before breakfast.'

Anne cast her eyes downwards, partly out of shame, and partly weariness. Her bones ached, her fingers were sore and her spirits low. There seemed no respite from this daily round. The sooner you had completed one chore, there was another in its place. Oh, she knew she was lucky to have work at all, and she was not shy of it. It was just that this was not the sort of work she wanted to do. Not now.

Mrs Fitzgerald, of robust constitution, four feet eight inches of rough black linen and a collar of starched white cotton, read the situation. 'And there is no earthly point in you dreaming about being a lady's maid when you cannot even polish the brass or lay a fire.'

'But I can, ma'am. I do.'

'To your own satisfaction, perhaps, but not to mine.'

Anne bowed her head. 'No, ma'am.'

'Now off you go. Bowl and cloth from the cupboard, the salt and vinegar you have.'

'Mrs Fitzgerald, do you think I might—?' She did not have time to complete the question.

'If you are asking to be let out of the house again, the answer is no. I have never objected to you taking a few minutes off from time to time. You know that. But you were gone for two hours yesterday, and such an abuse of privilege is not to be countenanced. You will work through.'

'But—'

'Enough. Bowl. Cloth. Salt. Vinegar. Go!' And with that the housekeeper turned on her heel and headed off down the passage in the direction of her linen cupboard. Anne leaned back against the wall and closed her eyes. When would it ever end?

For two whole hours she rubbed at the door handles and finger plates, the brass and irons and fenders and anything that looked as though it should have glinted. She rubbed until her fingers ached; the vinegar was merciless at discovering cuts which then stung as though attacked by a wasp.

The longcase clock in the hall struck the half-hour. She glanced up at the black hands on the dial far above her head. Half past eight o'clock. Anne could bear it no more. Silently she walked along the passage that led to the linen cupboard and the pantry. There was no sign of Mrs Fitzgerald in either. She walked back and put her head round the doors of the kitchen and the scullery. The housekeeper was nowhere to be seen.

Swiftly Anne opened the cellar door and tripped down the steps, replacing the salt and the vinegar. She rinsed her hands in a bowl of water that stood on the stone sink under the cellar window and dried them on the ragged hank of cloth that hung from the nail to one side.

Wearily she mounted the cellar steps and closed the door behind her. Along the passage she went, listening at the foot of the stairs for voices. They were faint – somewhere upstairs Sir Thomas was talking to Mrs Fitzgerald. She could make out no words but instinctively knew the tone of each voice in the household. Sir Thomas's was deep and rumbling, Lady Carew's gentle and soft, Mrs Fitzgerald's had an Irish lilt and a hard edge to it. The two sons, when they came home, were hard to distinguish from one another, but neither of them was in residence at the moment – Master Edward was away with the militia, and Master Frederick in London at his uncle's chambers. She liked Master Frederick. He was kind to her.

But she had no time to think of them now. In a few minutes Mrs Fitzgerald would come downstairs. If Anne was to leave and make her assignation it must be now or not at all. Her heart beat rapidly in her chest at the prospect and she found it difficult to breathe. How foolish would it be to disobey Mrs Fitzgerald's orders? Supposing no one came? What then? She looked again at her hands: reddened and cracked, two of her nails were badly torn. Several of her fingers had chilblains. These were not the hands of a lady's maid; they were the hands of a labourer. And now that she had stopped for a moment it seemed that her whole body ached.

She took a woollen shawl from the hook in the kitchen, threw it around her shoulders and slipped out of the door. Mr Moses saw her go but did nothing more than knock out the contents of his clay pipe on his gaiters and carry on hoeing between his turnips. What a housemaid did was none of his business. He liked a quiet life and would not be drawn into gossip and speculation.

Beyond the wrought-iron gate in the high wall of mellow brick to the side of the house lay a narrow path of bare earth that snaked its way beneath the overhanging branches of hazel and quickthorn. Anne gathered up her skirts and brushed her way between the towering stems of cow parsley and campion, pulling at a stem of grass which she popped into her mouth and chewed. It tasted of spring: fresh, green, full of promise.

Slowly she walked now, listening to the birds that sang from the branches above, their notes carrying for miles around on the still, sharp air. The sound of horses' hooves and the ring of the wheels on a distant farm cart died away, until she was aware of nothing but the sound of finches and sparrows in early morning reverie and the rustle of her dress through the undergrowth. A long stem of goosegrass caught at her shawl. She pulled at it as it wound its way around her arm, eager for company and unwilling to be cast aside. 'Get away you! I aint for 'oldin' back. Not today . . .'

She knew exactly where she would go. Following the path until it forked beneath a sturdy oak that had seen the births and deaths of ten kings and three queens, she took the turning to the left that led down a grassy bank. At the bottom of it ran a stream, bordered by swords of sweet flag and youthful meadowsweet, yet to send up its foaming froth of creamy flowers. The stream was not a river. Not yet. That distinction it could lay claim to just a couple of miles down the narrow valley, when it would join other juveniles that would add to its breadth and depth. Now it was barely six feet across and ankle deep, shimmering as it ran in whispering eddies over the smooth pebble bed. At the girl's approach, minnows darted into the shadows.

Anne flopped down on the bank and squinted as the sun, slanting through the osiers, caught her in the eye. She threw back her head and felt the warmth on her cheeks and forehead.

For a few minutes she did nothing more than breathe; filling her young lungs with the freshest of air; not that stale, indoor kind, laden with dust and the acrid tang of polish. Then, pulling her feet up close, she undid the long laces and slipped off first one boot, then the other, before reaching up under two layers of calico to find the ribbons that secured her stockings. She slid them from her legs and lowered her slender white feet into the clear water below. They were pretty feet – not the sort to be found on older housemaids.

She gasped at the coldness of the water, then smiled to herself as a pleasing numbness crept through the feet that for most of their days were encased in the black boots and thick stockings that were part of her daily uniform.

How wonderful it was to be free of them. To be free of everything. To be herself, her own person. Maybe it would be half an hour before anyone missed her. Wondered where she had gone. Asked 'Has anyone seen Anne? Where is that girl?' Maybe, just maybe, today would be the day that she did not go back. That she would finally make her escape from the drudgery that was her lot, day in, day out.

The prospect was too exciting to contemplate. She would take her mind off it. As she dangled her feet in the water and swished them backwards and forwards, the better to wash away the wearying aches of her domestic life, she reached into the pocket of her apron and pulled out a small book. A piece of purple ribbon marked her place. It had been too short to be of any use for tying hair or stockings, so had been tossed aside. Anne found it in one of the bedroom fire grates early one morning.

There was very little of it, but she liked the feel of it: the smoothness of its texture as she ran it through her fingers, the strength it exhibited when she snapped it taut between the thumb and forefinger of each hand. With a small pair of scissors borrowed from her mistress's dressing case, she cut the ends into neat chevrons and used it as a bookmark. She had not got very far with the book, but her reading was improving daily and, unless she persisted, admonished Mrs Fitzgerald, she would never make anything of herself. Anne wondered what there was to make.

She had never had what Mrs Fitzgerald referred to as 'an heducation'. That was for children of families with fathers and mothers who could make sure they were sent to dame schools, or else arrange for instruction at home. Anne had no family. At least, none that she knew of. She had begun to read at the orphanage, encouraged by a kindly beadle. They were rare, by all accounts, but she did find Mr Hawkins kindly. At first.

He would sit beside her and take her through her alphabet, would read with her for a while each day – from the Book of Common Prayer, whose words were mysterious and confusing but which, nevertheless, accustomed her to putting sounds to those often long and strange-sounding words. She did not mind too much that he sat so close to her, even though he smelled rather stale – a mixture of old ale and pipe tobacco. Only when he began to touch her did she suspect he was not the kind man she had at first imagined him to be.

It began innocently enough – an encouraging pat, a hand on her shoulder, then her knee; but soon he began to touch her where she knew he should not have touched. It frightened her.

From then on she tried to avoid meeting him; certainly made sure she was never left alone with him. Then he stopped teaching her. Would not even look at her. It was only a few months later that she was sent into service. Now she would have to manage for herself. And she would. She might be alone, but she was determined that would not always be her situation. One day she would meet a handsome young man and fall in love. Those were the sort of stories she liked to read now. She had found one while cleaning the attic in the big house; took great care to ask if she might borrow it. Mrs Fitzgerald had looked at the faded title on the dusty spine and frowned. 'Romantic. Well, if you must. At least it might encourage you in your hendeavours. But do remember that it is just a story. Life is seldom quite so hexciting.'

But Anne liked the story. It took her several months to read, and then she was allowed to borrow another and another and her reading became more assured. She could read a book a week now. The one she carried with her on this April day told of a highwayman and a young girl. How he came and swept her off her feet. She was not at all sure that she wanted to be swept away by a highwayman – by all accounts they were rough, unwashed brutes – but it excited her to imagine what it might be like to live a little dangerously. Her heart missed a beat at the prospect.

Reality soon reinstated itself. No one at all looked like sweeping her off her feet. She was fifteen now, not bad looking, with her red-brown hair and fair complexion. At least Sam told her that. Said that she was 'very presentable'. But what did he know? Sam would never get anybody. Certainly not her. Sam was the yard boy in the stables. He could read and write, it was true, but it would take someone special to win her hand. Not someone like Sam with his warts and his big feet.

She sighed heavily. What hope was there? Who could possibly want to win her hand? She picked up the book and read: 'The wheels of the coach rattled across the cobbles of the courtyard until the p-o-r-t-c-u-l-l-i-s of the castle was reached.' She wondered what a portcullis could be. Perhaps it was some sort of doorway.

She made to read on, but it was too fair a day to be engrossed in a book. This was her moment of freedom; her escape from the things she was made to do into a world of her imagination. Carefully she laid the purple ribbon between the pages of the book and slipped it back into her pocket, glancing round to see if she was still alone.

The meadow was quite empty as far as she could see. The person she hoped to meet was nowhere to be seen, but neither was there here anyone to chastise or to scold her. She allowed herself to dream for a while. In spite of Mrs Fitzgerald's opinion to the contrary, she liked to believe that exciting things could happen, even to her. Especially now. She tied the laces of the two boots together, slipped a stocking into each of them and hung them around her neck. She withdrew her tingling feet from the water and rubbed them on the soft grass to dry them. Already she felt better than she had when she left the house. She had always felt most at ease out of doors, but there were no jobs for girls in the open air; no jobs worth having, anyway. Not for someone who might one day soon be a lady's maid, and certainly not in winter when the wind whipped at your ears and the rain soaked through to your drawers.

Slowly her dreams began to fade. The sun rose in the sky. It seemed as though this would be a day just like all the others. She had better return and face the music. She would stick at her job for as long as it took, and one day she would be able to leave service and bring up a family of her own. One day. Today she would have to settle for what few moments she had left to let the sun caress her pale skin and the scent of May blossom fill her head with dreams. Perhaps that was all they would ever be, after all. It seemed as though the day that had promised so much would not be quite so special after all.

As she clambered up the steep bank from the stream, she did not see the figure by the oak tree. It blended into the shadows . . .

2

St Jude's School, Winchester
16 April 2010

Happy is the country which has no history.
                                    Early nineteenth-century proverb

'It's boring, sir.'

Harry Flint looked over the top of his glasses, the better to see the youth who was addressing him. 'What do you mean, boring?'

The boy shrugged. He was not one of the brightest in the class, but then neither was he a total no-hoper, nor one of the tiresome troublemakers who did their best to interrupt every lesson.

'Just . . . well . . . what has it got to do with us? It's history.'

Harry took off his glasses, slid from the desk on which he had been sitting and walked across to the window. He looked out across the school yard to the fields and meadows beyond. It was one of those perfect days, the sort that occur only a handful of times each year. Usually in spring. Air as clear as crystal; the sort of day when the whole world seems to sparkle and glisten – freshly laundered by a shower of rain, buffed up by the gentlest of breezes and then polished to perfection by clear sunlight.

'What's it got to do with you?' He asked the question softly, rhetorically. But he nevertheless received a reply.

'It all happened ages ago. All this stuff about kings and queens. It doesn't make any difference to us.'

The boy's words hung in the air. Harry repeated them slowly. 'It . . . doesn't . . . make . . . any . . . difference . . . to . . . us.'

He turned to face the boy and the rest of the class. A sea of wary faces gazed at him. They could sense his mood was changing. Better to sit quietly and wait until the moment passed; until things blew over.

The questioning boy glanced at the clock, hopeful of being saved by the bell. No chance. There were still five minutes to go before they would be released from Flinty's grasp and could hurtle out into the playground to hit one another.

'Just because something happened a long time ago – in this case around two hundred years ago, Stephens, it does not mean that it does not affect you today, or that it is unimportant. The past . . .' Harry glanced about the room, searching for a face that might offer him a crumb of encouragement . . . 'Wilson, what does the past do?' he asked of a studious lad who might hopefully come to his aid.

'It informs the present, sir.'

The rest of the class let out a low moan and the boy Wilson looked suitably abashed.

'It informs the present and enables us to place our lives in context.'

Feet shuffled under desks.

Harry sighed heavily. 'The reign of George the Third, while from your point of view as far away from your own lives as . . .' he sought for a suitable analogy . . . 'as Harry Potter or Spiderman, is nevertheless a part of your history. Not everything that happened all those years ago is dull, or unimportant or irrelevant.'

He scanned the room once more, hopeful of a glimmer of interest or a spark of enthusiasm. None came.

'Here was a king who lost America, who is remembered as

being mad – which is far from the truth; whose grasp of agriculture and encouragement of architecture and the arts was matchless; who was subjected to the most fiendish treatment at the hand of doctors to cure him of ailments they didn't fully understand, and who died blind and deaf, handing over his kingdom to a self-indulgent son who squandered his own talents and gave us the Brighton Pavilion.'

A hand went up halfway back in the classroom.

'Yes, Palmer?'

'Sir, can we go to Brighton?'

Before Harry could answer, the air was riven by a metallic clanging. The boys began to clear their desks of books.

'Bloody philistines,' murmured Harry. He raised his voice. 'We'll continue this fascinating discussion on the fate of King George the Third on Monday and look at the relationship between the Prince Regent and his subjects in greater detail. 'Thank you gentlemen.'

'Thank you, sir.' The answer emerged through the mixture of chairs scraping against the wooden floor, books being dropped and feet clattering out of the classroom.

Harry sank down into the chair behind his desk, looking across the room towards the window and thinking that they had a point. He wasn't a bad teacher, he thought. Most of the time. It was just that every now and again he got carried away and assumed that every last one of them was as excited about history as he was. Well, had been. The repetition of facts over the years had wearied him. Maybe they had a point. Maybe it wasn't relevant any more. Who cared whether George the Third was married to Charlotte of Mecklenburg-Strelitz or Caroline of Brunswick? What difference did it make to a bunch of lads who were more interested in their MP3 than George III?

Perhaps he had been doing the job too long. Well, it wouldn't be much longer now. This would be his last term. When the summer holidays came they could say goodbye to Flinty – and George the Third, too, for that matter. And what then?

If only he knew. That was the thing about the future: it was all so uncertain. So uncomfortable. Not like the past. You knew where you were with the past. Things slotted into place perfectly. Neatly. He liked neatness. Orderliness. That was his problem. That was why he was on his own now . . .

It was no time to brood. The rest of the afternoon was clear – free periods. And it was Friday. Thank God for that. He would go out. Leave the classroom behind and shake off the grey mood brought on by an ungrateful bunch of twelve-year-olds who . . . No; he would not run them down. Who could blame them? Truth to tell he could understand their lack of enthusiasm for a life of which they had no comprehension. The life of someone who lived two hundred years ago. He might keep droning on about the past inform-ing the present, but did he really believe that after all these years of repeating it like some religious litany? Well, yes. He did. Let go of that and where are you? The whole world would crumble. Of course the past affects the present. And yet . . . and yet . . .

Harry glanced up at the coat of arms fixed to the wall above his desk. It was of a swan on a blue ground with the school motto beneath it: *Nitor donec supero* – I strive till I overcome. 'Some hope,' he thought.

The boy Palmer was dawdling around the door of the classroom.

'What is it Palmer? No home to go to?'

'Yes, sir. It's just that . . .'

'Well?'

'If we could go to Brighton and see the Royal Pavilion it might just come alive.'

'Palmer, if I take you to Brighton to see the Royal Pavilion, the only thing that would come alive would be the amusement arcades. True?'

The boy shrugged. 'Suppose so.'

'Go on. Off you go. It'll soon be the weekend and then you can make Winchester come alive.'

Palmer brightened. 'Have a good weekend, sir.'

'And you Palmer; and you.'

He slid his own books into the leather holdall and walked towards the door. It really was a lovely day. Time to blow away the cobwebs and get a breath of fresh air. Where to go? Down by the river. He loved the river. Being near to it always made him feel better.

As he left the classroom he glanced again at the school coat of arms and smiled ruefully. St Jude. How appropriate. The patron saint of hopeless cases.

3

The Fulling Mill, Hampshire
17 April 1816

As Ovid has sweetly in parable told,
We harden like trees, and like rivers grow cold.
Lady Mary Wortley Montagu,
Six Town Eclogues – 'The Lover', 1747

The first they knew of it was when the hammers slowed. 'Another damned branch must have come down,' shouted William Palfrey, the miller, to his wife Agnes. 'I'll go and see to it. Send Jacob along; I'll need help to clear it like as not.'

The life of a fulling miller was not, he reminded himself, an easy one. Or as straightforward as it might seem. Prices of raw material continued to rise, and of the finished product – the thick and rich felted cloth – well, they continued to haggle over it every hour of every day. And the bloody thumping . . . not that he noticed the pounding of the hammers any more. They were just a part of life. Flour: that's what he should be milling. Thirty to forty loads of wheat a week old Gaskell was grinding. But all that dust . . . Still, at least he was away from the town, making a living on the banks of a river. No one would prise him away from it. Not until he was taken in a box.

The miller made his way down the three flights of rickety wooden stairs and pushed open the battered door adjacent to the mill stream. The storm two days before had interrupted their work more than he would have liked. It was fine now, but branches that the earlier spell of weather had dislodged often took a day or two to find their way down to this stretch of the river. Sometimes they would arrive while the winds were still blowing; but on many occasions they would be caught up in the overhanging branches of a willow or a sycamore and their progress downstream delayed. It was not unusual for the hammers that pounded the cloth to slow down a week or more after a storm; but that was nature for you. Unpredictable. Always.

The sturdy wooden framework that William and his son Jacob had erected across the river usually caught these wayward branches before they could find their way into the mechanism, but they would gather around them more and more debris and slow down the flow of water that powered the hammers. It was a simple matter to pull them free, but it usually took more strength than William possessed – fighting against the flow of floodwater – and he called upon his son for the requisite muscle power.

William walked around to the mill leat to see what was causing the problem. At first he could see nothing at all – the morning sun shining on the rippling surface of the gin-clear water dazzled him. He put up his hand to shade his eyes. The water seemed to be flowing over the top of the barrier quite evenly; there was no branch sticking up, as there usually was, to show where the blockage had begun. He held on to the corner of the archway under which the water flowed in order to look along the barrier. It was then that he saw, not the broken branch that he expected to see, but instead a pale hand protruding from a waterlogged sleeve.

Once William and his son Jacob had fished the body out of the river and hauled it up onto the bank, they stood silently for a few moments looking at it, their own silence broken by the steady rush of water over the oaken beam. This was not a vagabond or a drunk who had fallen in and drowned – they had seen a few of these over the last twenty years; enough to make them sanguine about the appearance of a dead body. No, this one was different. The person on whom they gazed was no vagabond, and no heavy drinker either. Her clothes were those of a housemaid. Her hands pale and soft. Her damp auburn hair clung to her pallid cheeks and her green eyes stared vacantly at the sky as she lay like a broken china doll on the soft grass of the riverbank.

On such a day as this, when the birds sang and the sunlight dappled the water through fresh green leaves, how could such a young life be brought to an end? This was a day of beginnings – of eggs being laid and chicks being hatched; of questing shoots from bean seeds and starry white flowers of wild garlic. It was not a time of year associated with death and decay.

'What shall we do?' asked Jacob, his face as pale as that of the young girl on whom he gazed, and his voice betraying a fear that was rising in him as rapidly as the water had risen in the river two days previously.

William ran a gnarled hand over the snow-white stubble on his chin, then rubbed both hands dry on the front of his rough worsted breeches. 'We'd best tell Sir Thomas. He'll know what to do.' The miller stared again at the lifeless body. The skin was translucent, dusted with pale freckles and framed by the hair, which now glowed like amber in the morning sun. The girl's lips were gently parted to reveal white teeth, and her slender feet, glistening with water droplets, were garlanded with bright green weed.

'Milfoil,' murmured William. The irony of the name did not escape him. It was the girl who had slowed down the mill on this occasion, not the strands of green waterweed entangled with her feet.

He recognised the fabric of her dress. It was the sort of thing he always noticed – the quality of the material; the way it was cut. Her dress was of a thick gingham, a small check. Pale blue. She must be one of Sir Thomas's housemaids. This was the uniform of the more lowly members of the squire's domestic staff. But how had she come to be here? It was at least two miles to the big house. Up there the water was shallow; the river nothing more than a gurgling stream. And where were her boots and her stockings? Had she been paddling and lost her footing?

There was little point in wondering. William Palfrey knew that these were questions to which he was unlikely ever to have an answer. Deaths were deaths and there was seldom any mystery surrounding them when they occurred on your doorstep. They were invariably down to old age, disease or misfortune. One of the three. Only the last of these gave him pause for thought. The misfortune of slipping was tragic but straightforward. But if the girl had not fallen or slipped . . . He shook his head, the better to clear his head of unwelcome thoughts. An accident; a dreadful, sorry accident. Nothing more.

'Saddle the horse,' he instructed his son. 'I'll go find Sir Thomas.'

4

The Riverbank, Hampshire

16 April 2010

We should show life neither as it is nor as it ought to be, but as we see it in our dreams.

Anton Chekhov, *The Seagull*, 1896

He should not really be here. He should be marking. Or preparing. Or ... well, something constructive, rather than sitting on the banks of a river on an April afternoon. Oh, to hell with it. No one would find him here. They would assume that he was hard at it, head down in the public library or somewhere else suitably dreary; conscientious Harry Flint, no life except for that which he finds in his books. 'The History Man' with none of the sex appeal and street wisdom that such a title – thanks to Malcolm Bradbury – had come to signify.

He could feel one of those Peggy Lee 'Is That All There Is?' moments coming. They were occurring more frequently now. The onset of his forties seemed to coincide with pointless self-analysis, mainly as a result of the unexpected solitude that life had thrown his way.

He breathed deeply, in the hope of dispelling negative thoughts and the fog that seemed to fill his head. Chalk dust might be a thing of the past thanks to interactive whiteboards, but these days there were other things to cloud a teacher's mind. Futility and frustration, for a start. And loneliness.

It was two years now since Serena had left him. Bored, she said. Fed up with taking second place to his books, and tired of a lack of fire in their relationship. Her announcement hit him like a sledgehammer.

They'd met at mutual friends': she a high-flying lawyer; he the steady schoolmaster. It was she who kept long hours – coming home from work close to midnight when he, after a day's teaching, had finally given in and gone to bed. She who, when she was at home, sat at a desk in their joint study and pored over pink beribboned bundles while he cooked and cleaned, put a glass of wine at her elbow and tried not to get in the way.

How could he be the one who had caused it all to fall apart? By being too easy-going? Too tolerant? Wasn't that what marriage was all about – give and take?

He really hadn't seen it coming. She'd admired his quiet self-containment at first. And his wit. And his memory for quotations. Well, he liked to think so. She had, after all, intimated as much. Hadn't she? At first, when their love was fresh and exciting? He remembered her telling him that he made her laugh, though for the life of him he could not imagine why.

They married quickly, within two months. He'd rather have waited longer, just to be sure (though he never told her that), but her vitality and enthusiasm had got the better of him. The difference of their worlds – and of their outlook – was what had brought them together. Each fascinated by the other. In the end it was what drove them apart. Stupid that neither of them could see that it was things in common that acted as marital glue. A common sense of values, at least.

Serena's world was light years away from his own. The parties they went to at her friends' were riotous affairs – men with loud voices and women with low-cut dresses and high-pitched laughs. It was not that Harry was a prude – far from it – or that he didn't like laughing. He did. But they were just not his sort of people. When he answered their questions about teaching, and history, he was aware of their gradually diminishing attention. Of their eyes drifting over his shoulder to see if there was anybody more interesting in the room. How often he reflected on this now; convinced himself that it was his dullness that had led to the demise of his marriage. 'Who could blame her?' was the echo that now reverberated in his loneliness.

Serena was true to her word. It was over from the moment she delivered her verdict. Six months after they married, she moved out, and he had neither heard nor seen anything of her since. He tried contacting her, but texts and phone messages went unanswered. And so, eventually, he gave up trying.

It wasn't meant to have happened. The reason he had waited until he was nearly forty before he got married was because he wanted to be sure. Didn't want to make a mistake he would later regret. The same mistake as his parents. They had seemed to be so happy when he was a boy. It later became apparent that they had stuck together solely for his sake, their only child. He imagined that all parents had periods of separation. After all, his father travelled; had to spend weeks away in order to earn a living. His best friend's dad was in the army. Same sort of thing. It was bound to put a bit of a strain on any marriage, but if you loved one another you stuck together. And they did. For a long while. Only when he went off to university did they tell him they were going their separate ways – his father to New Zealand and his mother to marry a Scotsman.

Now they were both dead – his father from an early coronary and his mother in a car accident. At least they had both been civil about their split. Had kept in touch with him and with one another. But it made him wary. Careful. Determined not to commit himself until he was absolutely sure that 'this was the one'. It had been Serena who'd convinced him that they were made for each other. Told him not to be such a stick-in-the-mud. That what they had was fun – worth pursuing. Why worry about tomorrow?

They spent a weekend away in Paris just a month after they had met: walking along the banks of the Seine, looking at the bookstalls and the flower kiosks, lunching in small cafés, dining in cosy restaurants and lying in in the morning until almost noon, to be woken by the bells chiming out over the silvery rooftops of Paris. What a dream it all was . . .

God, what a fool! A complete illustration of 'marry in haste, repent at leisure'. It irritated her eventually: his ability to find a phrase or an aphorism for every occasion. It had amused her at first. She found it quaint. In the end it just rankled.

There were times when he saw things clearly. Understood perfectly why it had happened. Blamed himself entirely. And yet there were other moments – increasingly frequent as the months went by and another page was torn off the calendar – when it all seemed so unfair.

He reached down and picked up a pebble. It was round and smooth in his grasp, a comforting sort of thing to hold. He raised his arm and tossed it into the swiftly flowing water where it landed with a deep-toned 'plop'. A few seconds more and the ripples that it set up had disappeared. A pebble dropped in the water of life – a few ripples to signify its existence and then . . . life goes on as if nothing had happened. Except that in his case it didn't seem to.

Handing in his notice had taken courage. That's what he liked to think. His capacity for stupidity might have been borne out by an unwise marriage, but this decision was, in a way, a rebellion. Proof that he was not boring. Or predictable. Or unadventurous.

He had no idea what he would do, but he was not without funds – he had enough to survive on. The only kind thing that Serena had done was to say she would not ask him for any money. She earned more than him, she had conceded; and, being a lawyer, had no appetite for litigation on her own part. 'A waste of time. The only people who win are the lawyers. I'm not that sort. And I don't want to hurt you.'

As if she hadn't already. But he was grateful for that one crumb of generosity of spirit. At least he had not misjudged her capacity for fairness – of a sort.

So what now? He had already made the decision to move. Within the month the new owners would take over his flat. Time he got a move on. Literally. But where to? Not far. He liked it here in this part of Hampshire; it was pleasantly rural but accessible. London, when he needed it – which was rarely – was not far away, and the south coast could be reached in under an hour.

But leaving the flat they had shared was the first step, and an inevitable one. There was too much of her there. The decorations had been her taste: heavy and rich, with dark-coloured walls and a predilection for French furniture. Not his style at all, but he had gone along with it. More fool him . . . recrimination followed hard on the heels of recrimination. He must snap out of it. It was eating him away. Soon there would be no more than a bitter, hollow shell of Harry Flint remaining.

He would begin today. On this bright April afternoon. Spring: a good time to start a new life. A good time to move on.

He got up from the grassy bank and walked towards the car. He would go into town and look in the estate agents' windows. 'Tomorrow is the first day of the rest of your life.' Now if he had trotted out that tired old saw when he was married, he could have understood why she had pushed off.

It was time that he found out who he really was. What his destiny might be. He almost laughed out loud at the ludicrousness of such a thought. But he would make a start. He would grab a fistful of suitable particulars from every estate agent down Winchester High Street and then go home and sift through them. With any luck there would be something suitable and then he could get down to work. Not school work, but the tracing of the ancestry that had occupied him since a few weeks after Serena had left.

That, and studying the lives of the saints, managed to fill most of his otherwise idle hours. He could not remember how he had first become interested. It was not as if he was particularly religious. Respectful, yes. Hopeful, even, of finding some kind of solace within the Anglican liturgy. The interest in saints had been a spin-off – he was curious to discover how ordinary people had managed to lead such extraordinary, even fantastical lives. But as interests go, martyrdom and genealogy were not likely to set the world, or another woman, on fire.

A part of him thought that it was rather a pathetic way of getting over a failed marriage. A touch too introspective. But then, as he regularly told those unwilling boys who sat in front of him every day with glazed expressions: 'The past informs the present and enables us to place our lives in context.'

He was beginning to wonder if he really believed that any more.

5

The Manor House, Withercombe

17 April 1816

So quick bright things come to confusion.

William Shakespeare, *A Midsummer Night's Dream*, 1595–96

Sir Thomas Carew, baronet, the local magistrate, met the miller in the hall of the Manor House at Withercombe. His face was grave and his voice raised to little more than a whisper. The body, he instructed, should be taken there immediately. He would inspect it, and only then could it be transferred to the back room of the Bluebell, the local inn, where the coroner's court could convene and give its verdict. He also gave his opinion that the miller's cart would be the most suitable form of transport. That would create a minimum of fuss, and it was as well to be circumspect at this stage, lest any cause for alarm be given. There would be no need to inform anyone else just yet. Best keep it to themselves. Sir Thomas himself would instruct the local coroner without delay. The chances were that the young girl had lost her footing and fallen in the water, hitting her head and then drowning. It would likely be as simple as that.

William Palfrey had returned to the mill and the same grey cob that he had ridden to the Manor House was hitched up to his cart.

Jacob sat up front with his father, glancing back every now and then to check the security of the sad load as they rattled along the lane towards the Manor House. She was covered in a sheet of coarse felt – a poor, uneven bolt that his father had rejected as unfit to be sold on. And yet it was judged fit to be her shroud, this pretty young woman whose life had been cut woefully short. Jacob noticed that the cloth had slipped a little to one side and revealed one of the girl's pale, delicate feet.

'Pa, stop!' he called, still looking backwards. The miller pulled on the reins and halted the cob in its tracks. Jacob jumped down from the box and adjusted the cloth, tucking it under the girl but taking care not to touch the cold, still body with his fingers. He could feel her weight against his hand. His heart beat more loudly in his chest and he felt even more queasy. When he had adjusted the fabric to his satisfaction, he climbed up beside his father and nodded to him. No further words were exchanged between them, as William Palfrey flicked at the reins and bid the horse walk steadily on.

And still the sun shone. Still the birds sang from the tree-tops and copses as they passed, and the river flowed gently by, unconcerned by the events of the morning; events that had filled poor Jacob with fear and given him a reminder of the first bitter taste of mortality.

He was fifteen and, like most boys of that time, was no stranger to death. He knew that babies died, hours or days or weeks after being born, quite often in these parts. And old folk in their fifties and sixties, too. He had seen their bodies laid out when he called with his father to pay their last respects. There were epidemics, too, when no one was safe, not even the strongest youth. But on a warm spring day, when there was nothing evil going around and no reason for a young maid to fall foul of miscreants and footpads by his stream, in his valley, it all seemed so wrong. The one thing that struck him most forcibly was that he had never seen such a beautiful corpse. And she really was quite beautiful. The sort of girl he would have been proud to have courted. Maybe even married. The thought distressed him even more.

His father noticed his expression – the tightness of his lips and the tears that were forming in the corners of his eyes.

'No reason to upset yourself,' he murmured as softly as he could while still being heard over the gentle clatter of the horse's hooves on the rough and stony lane.

'Beautiful,' whispered Jacob. 'So beautiful.'

'Aye. 'Tis a sad day when girls of her age are taken from us.'

William tried to lighten his son's mood, though he knew it would be to no avail. 'We can leave her with Sir Thomas. She will be in good hands there. At home. Where she belongs.'

'How did it happen, do you think?'

'Lost her footing, I shouldn't wonder. As simple as that. The river stones are slippery at this time of year – the weed has begun to grow on them. It is easy to lose your footing, and there are larger rocks on the riverbank. She probably hit her head on one of them and then—'

'So her boots and stockings would be by the river? Where she fell in?'

'Like as not.'

'I will go and look for them when we get back.'

William nodded his assent.

They arrived, after twenty minutes or so, at the Manor House, and the miller drove the cart round to the stables. The cob's hooves clattered loudly on the cobbled courtyard and the wheels emitted a metallic, rasping sound. On hearing them, the groom came out from a small wooden doorway to meet them. Timothy Jencks was a small, fine-featured man whose face, today, showed none of the good humour for which he was renowned. Normally the life and soul of the Bluebell Inn, his now grave expression suited the solemn task that lay ahead of he and the miller – that of carrying the lifeless body into the stables where Sir Thomas would inspect it and decide what should be done next.

William and Jacob got down from the cart and Jacob took the horse's reins to hold it steady. The miller and the groom greeted each other with a nod.

'Sorry business,' said the groom.

'That it is,' agreed the miller.

Jacob stood transfixed while the two men eased the felt-covered body from the back of the cart and bore it across to the stables, still enveloped in the coarse grey fabric. They did not struggle. She was not a heavy load and that, in itself, affected Jacob even more deeply. She had left this life like a wisp of thistledown, and seemed to weigh little more.

They had lain the body on a long, rough table that was usually used for the mixing of grain and mash for the horses.

No sooner had they done so than Sam, the yard boy, had put his head round the corner of the grain store and asked, 'What's goin' on, guv'nor?'

'Never you mind,' retorted Jencks. 'You get about your business.'

The youth was not to be deterred. 'That there a body?' he enquired.

The miller nodded.

'I've told you,' Jencks reiterated, 'there's muckin' out still to do and enough harness to keep you occupied until yon time. Be off. Nothing to do with you. Sir Thomas will be here presently and will not want you around.'

It was not that Sam did not hear the words, rather that what he saw overwhelmed him so much that he was drawn towards the body by a force that he was unable to resist.

The felt covering had left part of the girl's dress on view. The corner of coarse blue gingham hung down over the edge of the long table and the boy walked forward and took it reverently in his hand. He pressed the material between his thumb and forefinger. 'One of ours,' he murmured.

'Just you go and . . .' Timothy Jencks's words of warning went unheeded as Sam lifted the edge of the damp grey felt, the better to see the face of the body that lay in front of him.

What his eyes beheld caused the colour to drain from his face.

Before he could say anything, and before Timothy Jencks could administer a further reprimand, a commotion in the stable yard caused the three men to turn round.

'Take these dogs away! I distinctly asked Stuart to shut them in.' Sir Thomas, endeavouring to make his way across the cobbles, was being impeded by three dogs that, not unreasonably, had assumed they were in for some sport on this fine spring morning. Sir Thomas was, after all, clad in the coat and breeches he wore when he went shooting. The events of the morning were unexpected as far as his hounds were concerned as well as for himself. Sir Thomas was irritated, and his flushed cheeks contrasted even more than usual with the white mutton-chop whiskers that framed his face. Two springer spaniels and a pointer cavorted at his heels intent on the sport they had promised themselves and from which they were not going to be diverted. They had caused their master to lose his temper and now his footing on the uneven cobbles of the yard. It was Jacob who caught him before he toppled over. Sir Thomas gave the youth a nod of gratitude.

'Reaper, Stalwart, Oscar – AWAY!' At the sound of the thundered admonishment, the dogs hastened off in the direction of a footman who was now running across the stable yard to make good his earlier omission. His face was almost as flushed as Sir Thomas's.

Regaining his dignity, the magistrate, local squire and lord of the manor bowed briefly from the neck at William and looked enquiringly in the direction of his groom, who motioned him towards the table on which the body lay.

Sam was still standing alongside it, causing Sir Thomas to glance at his groom as though to admonish him.

'I'm sorry, Sir Thomas, he just . . . well . . .'

Annoyed that yet another member of his household was demonstrating how little dominion he had over his charges, Sir Thomas intervened. 'Sam, come away! This has nothing to do with you.'

The boy remained transfixed. 'Sam! Do you hear me? Go about your business.'

Sam looked round, his face still white, and said, quite simply, 'Not her.'

'Boy, I am not going to tell you again—'

Uncharacteristically, Sam interrupted his master. ''Tis not her. 'Tis her dress, but not her.'

Confused as well as annoyed, Sir Thomas asked, 'Not who?'

'Not Anne. Anne Flint. 'Tis not her . . .'

Sir Thomas stepped towards the table and looked down at the fair, pale face that looked upwards but past him with vacant eyes.

'Good God!' he muttered softly. 'No. Indeed it is not.'

He remained silent now, looking down at the body, as though unable to believe his eyes. Then he became aware of the miller who was standing at his shoulder.

'I thought,' said William, 'that she must be one of your maids. Her dress is of your household I think, sir.'

'It is. It most certainly is, but . . .' Sir Thomas looked directly at the miller. 'One of my housemaids went missing yesterday. She left the house in the morning. Mrs Fitzgerald had just scolded her. Lady Carew is away. I was upstairs instructing Mrs Fitzgerald and it was she who saw her go. She did not make to admonish her, or stop her leaving. She had worked hard that morning, and although on occasions she would slip down to the stream for some fresh air, Mrs Fitzgerald usually turned a blind eye. She was a good girl; a girl who loved the countryside. It was only because the previous day she had been gone longer than she should that Mrs Fitzgerald had to admonish her. Most days she always came back in time to continue her work and these . . . dalliances with nature, I suppose you could call them, seemed . . . well . . . important to her. I think her family must have been on the land. Not that she knew of her family—'

'Orphan sir?'

Sir Thomas nodded.

'But this is not her?'

'No.'

'And the girl has not returned?'

'No. She has not.'

Sam looked agitated. 'Something must have happened to her.'

Sir Thomas, realising that the boy was perturbed, made to console him. 'Yes. Something must. But this . . .' He looked down again at the body on the table.

Sam interjected, ''Tis her dress, sir.'

'We do not know that, Sam,' snapped Timothy Jencks. 'It is one of our housemaid's dresses, but that does not mean it is Anne's.'

Sam shook his head defiantly. 'Look . . .' He stepped closer to the body and pointed to the short length of purple ribbon that protruded from the apron pocket. 'This is hers. She used it to mark her place. In books.' Tentatively, and as though it were no longer a part of his body over which he had control, he slid his hand into the pocket of the dead girl's apron and withdrew the purple ribbon.

He turned to Sir Thomas with a look of desperation on his face. 'No book,' he murmured. 'Only the ribbon.'

Under other circumstances, Sir Thomas would have uttered an exclamation of the 'Bless my soul' or 'Good heavens' variety. But on this occasion he said nothing, just carried on staring at the face of the girl in the servant's dress.

'So,' enquired the miller softly, 'we do not know who she is?'

'Oh yes,' said Sir Thomas. 'We know who she is.' He remained gazing at the girl's face as though transfixed. 'Are you acquainted with the Earl of Stockbridge?' he asked.

'I know of him, sir, of course. From the big house at the foot of the downs.'

'Hatherley.'

'Yes, sir. Hatherley.'

'The earl has three daughters.'

'Yes, sir.'

'This is the youngest of them. Lady Eleanor. Or rather, it was . . .'

Sir Thomas broke out of his reverie and carefully replaced the coarse cloth over the face of the dead girl.

'I should have known,' muttered William.

'I beg your pardon?'

'Her hands – they was soft. Not at all like those of a housemaid.'

'No,' said Sir Thomas. 'Not at all.'

William, as a matter of habit, rubbed the palms of his hands down his breeches and shook his head. 'So what was she doing wearing a dress that belonged to your maid?'

'I have absolutely no idea, Mr Palfrey. No idea at all.'

Sam turned away from the group and stumbled out into the yard. If this was Anne's dress, where was Anne?

6

St Cross Apartments, Winchester
17 April 2010

Travel, in the younger sort, is a part of education; in the elder, a part of experience.

Francis Bacon, *Essays*, 1597

Harry did not sleep well. Perhaps it was through worrying. Well, there was no perhaps about it, really. Worrying was a way of life to Harry Flint. Mithering, as one of his northern aunties would have called it. 'Come away and stop mitherin',' she'd berate him as a child. He couldn't help it. He could have studied for a PhD in mithering and come through with flying colours.

But he had, he considered, just cause on this bright Saturday morning. In the space of the next few weeks, he would need to find himself a new place to live and a new job. Most people would do things in the right order – find a job and then find a place to live. Harry would uncharacteristically throw caution to the wind and do things the other way around. Besides, he did not want to think about another job. Not just yet. How could he when he did not know what he wanted that job to be? No: somewhere to live was his top priority. With the sale of the flat going through and by drawing heavily on what his parents had left him, he would be able to afford a small place without having to commit himself to a mortgage. He should count himself lucky. He did count himself lucky. Sort of . . . He showered and made himself a pot of coffee before sitting down and looking out of the window.

The fair weather of the previous day looked set to continue. A good day to look at houses. He reached across the table and pulled towards him the two piles of estate agents' particulars that his trawl of the High Street had yielded the previous day. He had done a preliminary sifting the night before – taking out all those properties that did not fulfil his requirements. Why was it that estate agents insisted on giving you details of houses that were patently unsuitable either in terms of price or accommodation? His brief had been quite specific – detached, two to three bedrooms and a small garden – and the budget he had quite clearly indicated. The larger pile he picked up and dropped in the waste-paper bin – everything from one-bedroomed flats to eight-bedroomed mansions set in twenty acres and varying in price from £200,000 to a couple of million. Was innumeracy a prerequisite of being an estate agent? Perhaps that might be a suitable career. He shuddered at the thought. The smaller pile he spread out on the table in front of him.

There was nothing that set his heart on fire. But he would have to settle on something, or else go into rented accommodation. He sat up and looked around him at the flat. Three of the four walls that surrounded the large sitting room were clad, floor to ceiling, in books. Books on history, books on art, books on Georgian architecture and furniture. Pevsner's *Buildings of England* – a complete set that had taken years to put together – sat beside James Lees-Milne's diaries. Biographies of Payne and Hawksmoor, Wyatville and Kent, nestled between works on old Sheffield plate and Worcester porcelain. The Kings and Queens of England occupied two whole shelves (Cromwell relegated to a neat pile on the floor) and volumes on Ramsay and Lely, Zoffany, Romney and Lawrence competed for shelf space with Sowerby's *English Botany* and Grove's *Dictionary of Music*.

How could he face putting all these into store and going into rented accommodation? He would apply himself. It was spring; the house market traditionally moved faster in spring. Surely there was something out there?

He was torn. He really wanted to get on with the project that eased his mind, that of researching his roots. Finding out what had gone before seemed to offer more in the way of stability than what lay ahead. He knew it was rather a feeble security blanket, but brushed aside any thoughts that it might in some way be compensating for an unfulfilled present. So far he had been moderately successful, having traced back five generations:

?
|
Merrily Flint = Elizabeth Henry
1816–1880 1820–1887

Liza Flint   Henry Flint = Judith Bunyard
1837–1838   1838–1888 1841–1916
|
Thomas Henry Flint = May Schofield
1867–1916 1869–1917

Robert David Flint   Henry Richard Flint =
1900–1942   Mary Ellen Denaby
1898–1940 1899–1940
|
Michael Henry Flint = Betty Maidment
1930–1993 1942–1999
|
Henry (Harry) Flint
1971–

Now it had started to become tricky. Where had his great-great-great-grandfather – the delightfully named Merrily Flint – come from? The internet drew a blank at this point. Perhaps now parish records in dusty ledgers were the only gateway to his past. That would mean foot-slogging. And much slower progress. Not today. It could wait a little. There were more pressing matters to be attended to. Like a roof over his head.

He looked back at the table and the four properties that had made his shortlist. A semi-detached cottage – 1920s – in Alresford. Out of town but still accessible. Not in a bad state of repair, but he could not say that it really excited him.

A detached bungalow in St Cross. He looked again at the details. A bungalow. He really was not ready for a bungalow. He could still climb stairs. Why on earth had he kept that in? He lobbed it, along with the Alresford semi, into the bin.

A town house with views of the cathedral. Now this really was something. On four floors. Georgian. With a manageable walled garden. Perfect. His heart began to pound. Until he looked at the price. It was way beyond his means. But couldn't he get a mortgage to make up the difference, if it was just what he wanted? The fly in the ointment was not one that was easily overcome: banks and building societies were not overly keen on giving mortgages to the unemployed. Bugger! He threw it into the bin after the semi and the bungalow, knowing that brooding on it would only give him grief.

There was one property left. Two sheets, paperclipped together. He eyed up the particulars. It was detached, true, so that fitted the bill. It had a small garden. And it was Victorian. Not Georgian but . . . well, it was reasonably priced and the rooms would accommodate both him and his books. He checked the address. It sat right alongside the A31.

Harry flopped back in his chair. So that was that. Nothing. Not a single affordable property that he could feel comfortable living in. He picked up the details to throw them after the others, removing, as was his habit, the paperclip. Like pins, they were never thrown away – a trait he had inherited from his mother. The second sheet, he assumed, would be directions to the house on the A31, even though any fool could have found it driving from Winchester to London.

As he removed the clip, the second sheet was revealed and his heart skipped a beat. The front page showed a small detached thatched cottage. It was not in a good state of repair, but something about it spoke to him. The garden in front of it was overgrown, the cottage itself barely visible through a haze of apple trees and brambles. The thatch was in reasonable condition but the dwelling had clearly been unoccupied for some time. It was likely to be damp. The rooms would be small. Reality took hold. There was unlikely to be enough space to house his ever-increasing library. He totted up the number of rooms: a small hallway, two receps, kitchen, cloakroom, two bedrooms and a bathroom upstairs. Not really enough to make the place a viable proposition.

He turned over the sheet of paper and checked the price and the level of council tax. Well, it was affordable. Then he saw an additional paragraph and a small map: 'In addition to the cottage there is a small stone-built outhouse on two floors which was once a miller's storeroom. It has potential to be converted into a granny annexe subject to planning permission.' Or a library, thought Harry.

The map was the final *coup de grâce*. It showed the location of the cottage and indicated quite clearly its curtilage. The garden which surrounded it, overgrown though it might be, ran down to the banks of the River Itchen.

He dropped the sheet of paper on the table and began to feel a little sick. Then he looked at the name of the property: Mill Cottage, Itchen Parva.

The feeling of possession was overwhelming. Then he checked himself. A romantic-sounding name was insufficient reason to take on a liability. But then the name was not the reason. The river was the reason. The name just – well – added to its emotional pull.

He glanced at his watch. A quarter to nine. The estate agent would not open until at least 9.30. He drummed his fingers on the table and told himself not to be so childish. What was the likelihood of them being able to arrange a viewing today? Well, the property was empty. Perhaps it would not be a problem.

It was bound to be under offer. Picture-book cottages like this, with river frontage, did not hang around. Why had they even bothered to give him the particulars?

For the next forty-five minutes he tried to occupy himself. He made the bed, put in a load of washing, went through the post – three bills, two circulars and a Lakeland catalogue. He couldn't settle to the latter; he must be tense.

As the bracket clock on the chest of drawers struck the three-quarter hour, its notes ringing like an alarm call through the still Saturday morning air, he dialled the estate agent's number.

7

The Manor House, Withercombe
17 April 1816

His daughter went through the river singing, but none could understand what she said.

John Bunyan, *The Pilgrim's Progress*, Part II, 1684

Sir Thomas knew just what to do. Sam, on the other hand, did not. He stumbled across the stable yard without knowing where he was going. His head swam, his stomach churned and a deep sense of bewilderment swept over him as he walked past the open doorways where Leger and Botolph, Thistle and Alderney pushed out their heads and munched the sweet hay, torn from the wooden racks that Sam had filled that morning. They remained oblivious to the state of mind of the boy who took care of their every need.

He rounded the corner, out of sight of the three men, and sat down on the edge of the water-filled trough. His head in his hands, he tried to get some kind of purchase on the events that had unfolded. Where was Anne? Why was someone else wearing her clothes? And why was this someone else a lady, and a dead lady at that?

The whole scenario was beyond his compass. The clock above the stable struck nine. The horses were fed and mucked out. Timothy Jencks was fully occupied dealing with his master, the miller . . . and a dead body. Sam stood up and looked around him. All was quiet. Without hesitating he walked, then ran along the edge of the yard and out through the ornate iron archway at the end of the stables into the parkland beyond. Through the dappled edge of the wood he ran, on and on, the dull metal buckles on his shoes gathering strands of grass and clover. After a few minutes he was at the edge of the stream – Anne's favourite spot, he knew – and he flopped down, panting. His stomach heaved, perspiration poured down his brow and he flung off the leather jerkin and drank from the cool water of the stream, suddenly remembering what had happened there and then regretting his actions. He had drunk from the water that had drowned a girl.

He threw back his head and the tears came unbidden to his eyes. For a few moments he could do nothing but sob. He liked Anne. He liked her a lot, even though she spurned him and told him that she could never be his. They were too young, she had said, and not suited.

Too young? And now where was she? Who was she with? He hoped and prayed that she was safe. Impatiently he wiped the tears from his eyes on the rough cambric of his shirt.

He got up and walked along the edge of the stream, looking for something that might show where she was, or where she had been. But there was nothing – nothing but the flash of a kingfisher and the plop of a young trout darting for cover. There was no sign of Anne or even of her former presence.

For fully half an hour he sat, perched on a smooth boulder above the stream, his thick brown hair falling over his eyes and helping to shield them from the sun. He put on his leather jerkin and got up to go. As he did so, he saw something dark amongst the sword-like leaves of flag iris at the streamside. It was not a stone. It had a rectangular rather than a rounded outline. He bent down and picked it up. It was a small leather book, rather battered and faded on the spine. He opened it and read the title: *The Highwayman's Bride*. It was Anne's book. It must be. She had had an obsession with highwaymen over the last few days. Said that one day she would be swept off her feet. He was sure that she would really have preferred to be swept off her feet by a respectable groom rather than a surly highwayman. Surely she could not simply have been taken? Kidnapped? And what of the earl's daughter wearing her dress? What was Anne wearing? So many questions and not one answer. But he had the book. Anne's book, he was sure of it. He would go back to the house and show Timothy Jencks and Sir Thomas. They would know what to do.

The body was carried by servants to a small anteroom in the Manor House. The Bluebell Inn was no place for a lady of rank, Sir Thomas had decided. The body was laid on an oak table and covered with a white linen shroud – more suitable than the poor-quality grey felt the miller had supplied. That was rolled up and handed back to him. Jacob loaded it with reverence on to the back of the cart, wondering what they would do with it when they returned to the mill.

Sir Thomas would go in his chaise to inform Lord Stockbridge. They would harness the horses immediately and hope that on their arrival he would be there. Sir Thomas considered sending Timothy to fetch him, but felt it would be better to do the job himself rather than to entrust it to his groom. That might be seen as being too offhand.

He thanked William and Jacob for their trouble and sent them on their way in the cart with the roll of felt tied on securely. They made the journey home in silence, both of them musing on the likely outcome of this remarkable mystery.

The yard was silent when Sam returned, with the book safely tucked into the pocket of his jerkin. He could not find Timothy, and both Alderney and Leger were absent from their stalls. The doors of the coach house were also open and the chaise was gone. Sam deduced what had been going on in his absence, and hoped he would escape a scolding on Mr Jencks's return for leaving him to harness the two greys on his own. Perhaps when he showed them the book they would forgive him. He did hope so.

Sitting on the rim of the old stone horse trough once more, he took it out and fingered the rough leather binding, then opened it and flicked through the pages, vainly hoping that it would offer some kind of clue to the whereabouts of a girl without whose presence he felt bereft. He regretted teasing her so much, but then she was more than capable of standing up for herself – baiting him about his big feet, and his warts. He couldn't help either, but he wished now that she had been more approving of him. He missed her. Quite desperately.

As the chaise rattled its way to Hatherley at the foot of the chalk downs, Sir Thomas Carew mused on how he could best approach the matter. There was clearly no tactful way in which you could tell a man that his daughter had been found drowned. As the chaise swayed from side to side, and Timothy made encouraging noises to the horses, Sir Thomas looked out across the Hampshire countryside and, like Jacob Palfrey just two hours earlier, wondered how such a tragic accident could occur on such a glorious spring day.

Eventually the chaise turned into a long drive lined by lime trees, shimmering in their lush April finery. Sheep grazed in the parkland to either side, looking up in that vaguely interested way they have as the chaise rattled its way towards the front door. The house itself was a model of elegance, built during the brief reign of Queen Anne, with tall, white-painted windows and a pleasingly porticoed front door.

Timothy Jencks was relieved to find a servant in front of the house. Without Sam beside him, he did not want to leave the horses unattended while he went to the front door, and he could certainly not ask Sir Thomas to look after them.

The servant – an elderly man in a waistcoat and breeches – looked up as the chaise approached. Timothy gave him a wave of acknowledgement and instructed: 'Sir Thomas Carew of Withercombe to see the earl. Be he in?'

The servant nodded and mounted the stairs to the front door, opening it and disappearing inside. Within a few moments the horses had come to a standstill and the servant had returned from the house wearing a dark green footman's coat. He opened the door of the chaise and Sir Thomas alighted with some difficulty, clutching the servant's arm by way of assistance. He was a large man, and the exertion of entering and disembarking the chaise invariably left him discomfited. He mopped his brow with the silk handkerchief pulled from the tail of his black coat (his hunting clothes having been exchanged for something more suited to this sombre occasion). This was an encounter that he most certainly did not relish.

'Lord Stockbridge is in the library, sir, if you will follow me.'

Sir Thomas nodded and did as he was bid, climbing the steps – with the welcome aid of his cane and the iron handrail – and stepping into the cool, chequered-floored hall. He took a few moments to compose himself before crossing into a large room lined with oak bookcases.

The earl was as small and slight as Sir Thomas was large and round. Among the tables, books, folio cabinets and globes, he was not at first visible. But then Sir Thomas saw him. He was standing by the fireplace with his back to the flames. Upon his face was a look of foreboding that Sir Thomas could do nothing to dismiss.

'Your lordship.' Sir Thomas bowed respectfully from the neck.

'Sir Thomas.' A less demonstrative bow from the earl.

Sir Thomas hesitated. 'I come, I am afraid, with grave news.'

The earl's expression did not alter. Neither did his stance. He remained absolutely still, with both hands thrust under the tail of his dark blue coat, his eyes fixed, gimlet-like, on Sir Thomas.

'It is your daughter, Eleanor.'

Still no reaction from his interlocutor.

'She is at the Manor House at Withercombe. I am afraid that she was discovered this morning by the miller from Itchen Stoke.' Sir Thomas fought for the right words. The finality of the word 'death' eluded him. 'She is, I am afraid—'

'Dead?'

The earl's candour momentarily caught the baronet off guard. He nodded. 'I am afraid so.'

The earl's interrogative glance obviated the need for any further question.

'She was found early this morning in the river alongside the mill. There was nothing the miller and his son could do. It was too late.'

The earl turned away now. 'I see,' he murmured. 'And . . . ?'

'We brought her . . . that is, her body . . . to the Manor House. She lies there, awaiting your instructions.'

The silence sat uncomfortably on them. Then the earl asked, quite slowly and with little trace of emotion, 'Do you have a daughter, Sir Thomas?'

'No, sir. Only sons.'

'You do not know about daughters?'

'Alas, sir, of them I have no experience.'

The earl nodded slowly.

Sir Thomas shifted his not inconsiderable weight uneasily from one foot to another, unwilling and unable to interrupt the thoughts of Lord Stockbridge.

'They are not easy, Sir Thomas. They make demands. When they are very young they are rash and rebellious and when they are older they are intransigent. They do not listen to reason in these modern days. They have minds of their own.'

Sir Thomas half smiled sympathetically. He would have loved a daughter. To spoil. To make a fuss of him. To tease him as daughters did.

'They are a drain on one's finances, a cause of grey hairs, a thorn in one's side, and yet . . .' The earl paused, unable, for a moment, to continue. 'They are any father's delight, exasperating though they may be. Her uncle is due to come and see her today. Back from Italy. She was the apple of his eye, too.'

A rumble of thunder was followed by the sound of heavy rain through the open window. A sudden deluge made further conversation difficult. Lord Stockbridge stepped towards the open window, closed it and turned to face Sir Thomas once more. 'Eleanor was always headstrong. Adventurous. Yesterday she went out walking on her own, despite my remonstrations. I could do nothing to stop her. But then I had no reason to believe she would come to any harm. She is fifteen now . . .' He paused, then whispered, 'Was fifteen . . . Her late mother . . .' Then he stopped, unable to continue.

Sir Thomas knew that he could not escape the next obstacle in his declaration. 'Milord, there was one strange circumstance.'

The earl fixed his gaze upon Sir Thomas once more.

'Lady Eleanor was wearing . . . maids' clothing. The clothing of my housemaid, Anne, who has, I am sorry to say, gone missing.'

The earl did not respond, but upon his face was a look of such incredulity that Sir Thomas was totally silenced.

8

Mill Cottage, Itchen Parva
17 April 2010

I in these flowery Meades wo'd be:
These Christal streams should solace me;
To whose harmonious bubling noise,
I with my Angle wo'd rejoice.
> Izaak Walton, 'The Angler's Wish' from
> *The Compleat Angler*, 1653–55

'Sold, sir.'

'What do you mean, sold?' asked Harry incredulously. 'You gave me the particulars only yesterday afternoon.'

'Sellers' market, sir. Things are moving fast at the moment. Spring, you know.' The young estate agent looked as though he had been born just a few weeks ago, though his attitude was more akin to that expected of a long-standing member of the House of Lords. He stood there in his tweed jacket, corduroys and check shirt, with woven Turk's head cufflinks, fresh from an estate management course at the Royal Agricultural College and looking as though he owned half of Cirencester.

What Harry really wanted to say was: 'Look here, you little shit, stop giving me all this crap.' Instead he settled for: 'I am well acquainted with the seasons and know that April is in spring. What I don't understand is why – barely fifteen hours ago – you would give me the details of a property that you now tell me is sold.'

'Well, it is not exactly sold, sir, but it is under offer.'

'Which means?'

'Which means that somebody has said they will buy it.'

'But they haven't bought it yet?'

A slight flush appeared in the young man's cheeks. 'They have not yet exchanged contracts. That will occur once they are happy with the survey and their solicitor's searches. We expect completion within the month.'

Harry was lost for words. Eventually he asked, 'Is there any chance I can have a look at it?'

'As I say, sir, it is under offer.'

'And if the offer falls through?'

'Very unlikely, sir. This is, after all, a highly desirable property . . .'

'A highly desirable property that needs a master builder to get it habitable and a JCB in the garden which at the moment is as impenetrable as the Forest of Arden.' Harry held up the particulars and pointed to the photograph of the picturesque ruin.

The bell on the door of the estate agent's office broke into their conversation with a resounding 'ping' and a middle-aged couple entered. The young man looked relieved and seized the opportunity for respite that the couple offered. 'Excuse me a moment. Sir? Madam?'

'We wonder if we could arrange a viewing of the bungalow in Oliver's Battery?'

'Of course.'

'Might I have the keys then? So that if your current sale falls through you have something in the way of back-up?' Harry spoke in a voice that brooked no contradiction. The better part of twenty years of teaching small boys had offered ample opportunity to refine an intimidating tone; a tone that would strike someone so recently of school age as being incapable of contradiction. It did the trick. With Pavlovian predictability, the young man said, 'Of course, sir,' and handed over the keys.

It was, undoubtedly, a rash thing to do.

He would have been better advised to have left his name and number and asked that Master Cirencester should call him if the cottage became available.

To see it now would simply pile on the agony. And agonising it most certainly was. Perhaps if he had viewed it in filthy weather, in wind and rain, on an autumn day, he would have seen it for what it was – a tumbledown pile of stones topped by a battered straw hat. But it was not filthy, wet weather, and it was not autumn. It was a perfect spring day. Bees and brimstone butterflies beset him as he fought his way through the brambles in the wake of prospective buyers who had gone before. At least they would have come off worse with the thorns and scratches. Dog roses feathered his path, pushing their paper twists of buds heavenward. Ancient and tortured apple trees that would have provided inspiration for Arthur Rackham towered over him, their stooping boughs encrusted with pale green lichen and their branches festooned with blossom as pink and white as coconut ice. It was hard not to be sentimental when this painting of a cottage garden by Helen Allingham sprang to life before him. How could something so neglected and ignored be so beautiful?

He stopped where he stood, barely ten feet inside the gate, knowing that this place had ensnared him even before he reached the cottage itself.

'Come on, come on,' he thought to himself. 'Get a grip.' Here was heartache in spades and barrowfuls. Should he be successful in buying it, he would become its slave; should he fail he would be cast into a slough of despond.

Reaching finally the peeling front door that was the colour of a summer sky, he pushed in the key and turned it. For a door so battered it opened with ease and in silence, and he peered into the two rooms to right and left. Both had fire-places, and small windows that let in a surprising amount of light. He explored upstairs – a primitive bathroom and two small bedrooms with dormer windows. In spite of the age of the cottage it did not smell of damp and decay. It was just . . . well . . . empty. Waiting. Expectant.

He let himself out of the back door and battled his way through the undergrowth. He ducked under a low-slung washing line and picked his way across to the outhouse, a large brick-built and gable-roofed structure that sat to the west of the cottage. Inside, its walls were of bare brick; a plain wooden staircase led to what must once have been a hay loft. He felt the walls: bone dry. Not a trace of damp. Try as he might he could not stop himself from imagining what life would be like here. And then he remembered the river.

He let himself out of the outhouse, locking the door behind him, and set off in search of the bottom of the garden. At first all he could hear was birdsong: a robin, and then a yellow-hammer, then sparrows – rare house sparrows chattering in a bay tree – and blue tits and chaffinches . . . 'Farther and farther all the birds of Oxfordshire and Gloucestershire' – well, Hampshire at any rate. This was Edward Thomas's own county; he would have known the same sounds: birdsong has a timeless quality . . . and so, it seemed, had the cottage. A blackbird gave voice to its ear-splitting alarm call as it shot out of a mattress of brambles where a nest full of pale blue eggs lay safe from harm.

And then, through the enveloping welter of birdsong, he heard the sound of the river. A gentle whispering at first, and then more assured. Finally, he reached the grassy bank that sloped to the water's edge, and gazed on the clear stream as it waltzed gently by. The Itchen was perhaps twenty feet wide here and three feet deep. A proper river. A river prized for its brown trout. He pulled the particulars from his pocket and read the line that caused within him an even greater yearning to remain: 'Twenty yards of single bank fishing rights.'

He went home disconsolate, dropping off the keys and asking to be called if the current buyer had a change of heart. Five hours later he took the call that he had told himself would never come. The previous buyer had got cold feet; Mill Cottage was his if he wanted it. Harry confirmed that he did. The young estate agent could hardly believe how nice he was.

So it was that Harry Flint became saddled with a crumbling thatched cottage in an overgrown wilderness on the banks of the River Itchen. The funny thing was, it already felt like home.

9

Rakemaker's Close, Old Alresford
17 April 2010

Save us from our friends.

Fifteenth-century proverb

Harry could see from the look on their faces that they thought he was quite mad. What they said confirmed his suspicions.

'It's falling down, dear!' was Pattie Chieveley's verdict.

Her husband, Ted, was more comprehensive in his condemnation: 'It's a heap. You'll be a slave to it. It will drain your bank account. Your books will go mouldy. Why don't you buy a new flat somewhere? With no garden to worry about? And thatch? I mean, do you know what the fire risk is like? And your insurance premiums will go through the roof – not that there is one.' Ted Chieveley made to smooth down what little sandy hair was left on his domed head, feeling that the desperation rising within him must have made it stand on end.

Harry smiled. 'I know. Daft isn't it? But the place . . . well . . . it just spoke to me.'

The Chieveleys had become, in a way, surrogate parents to Harry. When he had joined St Jude's five years previously, Ted had been the headmaster. For a year before his retirement, he watched over the new history man in a fatherly kind of way. The two had got on, sharing a fondness for Georgian England and the literature of the time. Ted, too, had once taught history and, as retirement loomed, he looked forward to indulging his interests and perhaps buying a small Georgian house near the cathedral close in Winchester. In that he was of similar mind to Harry. But, as Harry, too, had discovered, the harsh reality had turned out to be somewhat different.

Harry had known that the Chieveleys would not approve, encouraging and helpful though they had been to him over these past rocky months. They were anxious for his wellbeing when he was clearly down in the dumps, and tried at such times to jolly him along. Right now they were worried. Worried that he had completely lost the plot and was about to commit his life savings to a lost cause.

'Have a Scotch,' muttered Ted. 'Might restore your clearly puddled brain and make you see things more clearly.' He moved to the sideboard that occupied an entire wall of the small sitting room in the modern semi; it was a family heirloom that they had steadfastly refused to get rid of when they moved to more modest accommodation three years ago.

Ted poured his wife a small Martini and he and Harry a generous measure of 'Famous Grouse', handing his honorary son the crystal tumbler with a further admonishment. 'It'll be Equitable Life all over again, and this time you'll have no one else to blame.'

'I wasn't with Equitable Life,' protested Harry.

'No, but we were.' Ted took a gulp of the amber fluid and flopped down in an easy chair. 'Put not your trust in insurance salesmen,' he muttered bitterly.

Pattie picked up the conversation. 'Well, if you're sure it's what you want . . .'

'I am,' said Harry. 'I know it's in a bit of a state . . .'

'Ha!' Ted almost choked on his whisky.

Pattie gave him a withering look and he refrained from further criticism.

Conscious of the fact that they worried about him, and aware of their kindness and consideration, Harry did his best to allay their fears. In the aftermath of his divorce, they had been the two people to whom he could turn at any time and on any occasion. Ted was inclined to pessimism, but when push came to shove he knew how to get Harry out of the doldrums – either by handing him a rod and taking him down to the river for a spot of fishing, or hauling a bottle out of the Sheraton sideboard and offering him a dram. His other 'cure-all' was 'a nice hot bath'. It seemed, to Ted, a panacea for most if not all ills. 'What you need is a nice hot bath' – invariably topped off with another dram. In-depth analysis, while well within Ted's intellectual compass, was not something he applied to domestic issues, being a firm believer in the old saw 'a trouble shared is a trouble dragged out until bedtime'. Only when he saw that his own ministrations were failing signally to have any effect on his patient did he defer to 'the little woman' and let Pattie take over as ministering angel.

Pattie was a touch more astute than her husband. She might look like the archetypal doormat of a wife, but appearances were, in this instance, deceptive. Sharp-eyed and sensitive to mood, she knew just when to let her husband ramble on and just when to stop him in his tracks. When he started on one of his hobbyhorses – the raising of university tuition fees ('woefully overdue; university is not for everyone; perhaps now we'll be able to get an English plumber if they get themselves a trade instead of a degree'), or the reduction in numbers in the armed forces ('at least we won't have the bloody resources for another Afghanistan'), she would whistle softly under her breath the theme to *Love Story* and Ted would swiftly get the message, pick up his rod and head for the river or shut himself in the boxroom that passed for a study.

Ted had retired at sixty-five, hoping that his pension fund would see him through a comfortable twilight. Equitable Life had had other ideas, and now he supplemented his income by a few half-days each week stocking supermarket shelves. Many considered it beneath his dignity. A retired headmaster? Working in a supermarket? The very thought! What would his ex-pupils think? What sort of message did that send out? Harry thought it spoke volumes about the man. There were times – not infrequently – when Ted drove him nuts. But on such occasions he reminded himself of what the Chieveleys had done for him and just where he would be without them.

The only other close friend he had was a different kettle of fish altogether. Rick Palfrey taught maths at St Jude's. Where Harry was introverted and introspective, Rick was best described by words beginning with 'out'. Outgoing, outspoken and, on occasions in Harry's opinion, outrageous. He had to be in the mood for Rick but, like the Chieveleys, he had helped Harry come through the tough times. When Serena had been at her most unreasonable, it had been Rick alone who had managed to make Harry smile, and occasionally even laugh, by telling him exactly what he thought of this 'black-eyed bitch' who had taken his friend for a ride. While never totally agreeing with Rick's somewhat harsh assessment of his former wife, he had found his point of view refreshingly uplifting.

'What does Rick think?' had been Pattie's next question.

'Haven't told him yet.' Harry took a slug of Scotch by way of fortification.

'You'll need more courage than a glass of Scotch will give you when you do tell him,' murmured Ted, draining his glass.

'I'm seeing him tonight. For a curry.'

'Cobra then,' offered Ted.

'What dear?' Pattie Chieveley looked puzzled.

'Cobra beer. Good with a curry.'

'Really? I'm surprised you know about that, Ted. I can never get you near the place. I tell you, Harry, weaning him off steak and French fries is a life's work. The nearest he gets to exotic food is pear belle Hélène, and it took me twenty years to get him to try that.'

Ted rose from his chair and walked towards the sideboard. 'I know about it from the supermarket. It keeps me in touch with market trends. Not that it means I have to follow them. I know what I like. A good steak. Nothing wrong with that. As long as it's Aberdeen Angus – not that stuff the Argies send over.' He glanced at Harry. 'Another one? To give you courage?'

'No. I'd best be off.' He looked at his watch. 'Meeting Rick in an hour. At the Taj Mahal.'

Pattie smiled. 'That's a long way to go, dear.'

Harry said nothing, but tilted his head on one side and gave a mock frown as if to answer her.

Ted looked blank for a moment, then asked, 'What was I doing? Oh, yes.' He refilled his own glass. 'Well, I just hope he succeeds where we've clearly failed.'

'What do you mean?' asked Harry.

'In putting you off.'

Pattie got to her feet. 'I think you've said quite enough, Ted. Harry's clearly set his heart on the place and, if that's what he wants, I don't think we should try to change his mind.'

Ted shrugged. 'All right. You know best.' He glanced at his watch. 'Good God! Is that the time? It'll be on in half an hour . . .'

'What will, dear?'

'Strictly Come X Factor On Ice.' He winked at Harry. 'Just

got time for a nice hot bath . . .' And he left the room beaming from ear to ear.

'He was joking, wasn't he?' asked Harry.

'Of course, dear. It'll be another glass of Scotch and then he'll curl up with *Mansfield Park*. He gets a bit impatient with these television presenters, but he knows where he is with Fanny Price.'

10

The Bluebell Inn, Withercombe
19 April 1816

No! No! Sentence first – verdict afterwards.
Lewis Carroll, *Alice's Adventures in Wonderland*, 1865

They had no idea Sam was there. Inside the Bluebell Inn, the coroner was addressing a jury of twelve men drawn from the local hundred – the division of the county of Hampshire over which he presided. Right now they were ranged around the body that lay on the scrubbed pine table. Sam could just make out its shape between their thick-coated bodies. It had been transported from Hatherley to the inn with due ceremony, and soon it would be taken back to Lord Stockbridge for burial, the men would emerge and Sam would hear their verdict on the girl who had met her fate in the river.

He sat, for the present, on a wooden bench at the side of the brick-built inn, where the cool spring breeze whipped at his neck and chilled his calves through the coarse weave of his stockings. The clear, bright weather of the past few days had been replaced by more typical April fare – blustery, with showers that washed the dust from the roughly pleated nettle leaves that sprang up around the water pump. Idly he kicked at them, flaying their fresh growth until there was little left except the shredded fibrous stems and a stinging sensation in his ankles. He hardly noticed.

It was three days now since Anne had disappeared, and there was still no sign of her, nor any word as to her whereabouts. He had asked the local coachman for news on his daily return from London but, in spite of calling at towns and villages along the lanes that led from Winchester to the capital, the coachman had seen or heard nothing. From Hyde Park Corner to Basingstoke, from the Wheat Sheaf at Popham Lane, through Popham and East Stratton to Lunways Inn and the Worthys, a total of sixty-two and a half miles, the coachman had encountered no one who answered to the description of Anne Flint. He would ask his fellow coachmen who plied the route to Reading and to Poole down in Dorset, but he was not hopeful.

'Red hair you say?'

'Reddish brown.' Sam was aware that he had never had to describe Anne before. Was not sure how to put his feelings and his observations into words. 'It shone, like. In the sun.'

The coachman nodded; a movement which caused him some difficulty in the stiff-collared coat which encased him up to the neck and which made any sudden movements not only difficult but unwise. His face was creased and cracked through years of exposure to the elements atop his coach, and his thin, dark hair flattened down against his forehead by the brim of the tall felt hat he now carried in his hand.

Sam continued, in an effort to offer more clues as to her identity. 'Her skin was . . . well . . . pale like. Freckles.'

'Pretty?' asked the coachman, with a twinkle in his eye.

Sam nodded, and felt the colour rising to his cheeks.

'Travelling clothes?' enquired the coachman.

Sam shrugged. He knew that he was describing the Anne that he had last seen. Now he could only be sure of her face, and her hair. What her attire would be he did not know, for the earl's daughter had been wearing Anne's clothes. He did not say this to the coachman. Did not want him to connect Anne with the girl who met her end in the chill waters of the river.

'An' you think she mun be bound for London?'

'She used to talk about it, being a lady's maid and all. London would be the place to go to do that, wouldn' it?'

'There is always t'other way, o' course. Down to the shipping.'

'She never mentioned that. Not going abroad. Anne had never been nowhere. Not other than the orphanage.'

'Ah, young girls, my lad. They has dreams. They does the most unaccountable things as we poor men can barely compre'end.'

Sam looked downcast, then asked, 'But you will look out for her?'

The coachman nodded. 'I will keep an eye open, that is as much as I can say.'

And he went about his business, attending to the newly harnessed team of horses.

It made no difference how many times Sam scratched his head, his thoughts became no clearer and Anne no nearer. He wondered if he would ever see her again.

After half an hour, the jurymen came out of the back room of the inn. They said little as they walked around into the taproom for much-needed refreshment. The sour-faced coroner in his black coat and breeches, with the white scarf at his neck, nodded curtly towards the local constable who had assembled them and, without further ado, mounted the steps of the Basingstoke coach whose fresh team pawed at the flinty ground, impatient to be off. Within a few moments his baggage had been secured on the box, the door had been slammed behind him, the horses were whipped up by the now tall-hatted coachman, and the wheels of the coach rattled away down the lane in the direction of Worthy and Lunways Inn,

East Stratton and Popham and the Hampshire byways that led to Basingstoke. The local coroner had no time to spare: illness in the surrounding towns – among coroners as well as commoners – meant that his load had increased of late. He looked forward to a time when he would be able to stay closer to home. All this travel disagreed with his liver.

Sam sneaked round the side of the inn and leaned on the frame of the open door, the better to hear the conversation that emanated from the taproom and to shelter from another sudden shower that threatened to soak him to the skin. At first the low growl of voices was indistinct above the patter of the rain on roof and road, but little by little some phrases drifted more clearly from the inner gloom and through the open door: 'A sad affair' was one. Then, 'His lordship should have kept a closer eye. Not done for young women of good birth to be abroad on their own.' And a phrase that he would never forget as long as he lived: 'Death by misadventure.'

Mill Cottage, Itchen Parva

29 May 2010

We make our friends; we make our enemies; but God makes
our next-door neighbour.

G.K. Chesterton, *Heretics*, 1905

When the last packing case had been brought into the cottage,
Harry told himself that it did not look too bad. Rick told him
what it really looked like.

'A heap of shit.'

'Do you mind? This is my life savings. An investment. And
if that's the best you can come up with, you can push off now.'

Rick dumped the box he was carrying on to the floor of the
kitchen. 'Hey; if that's all the thanks I get for giving up my
Saturday, then I'll push off.'

'Well . . . this place is probably sensitive. It's seen a lot over
the last three hundred years.'

'And the rest,' muttered Rick.

'So just you give it a bit of respect. Anyway, where did you
put the beers?'

'Where they were meant to be put three hundred years ago
– in the larder.' Rick nodded towards the door in one corner
of the kitchen.

'See,' said Harry, with an air of triumph in his voice. 'You
wouldn't find one of those in a modern house.'

'No,' agreed Rick. 'We have what we call refrigerators nowadays. You'll come round to our way of thinking in a couple of

centuries.' A look of exasperation crossed his face. 'I know you teach history, but surely you can appreciate modern technology. Where's your fridge?'

'Left it at the flat – the new owner bought all the white goods and the new one hasn't arrived yet. Modern technology, you see: the firm I bought the fridge and the cooker and the dishwasher from had a problem with their computers and they can't confirm delivery until Monday.'

Rick made a sound something between a harrumph and a grunt and leaned on the draining board of the stained butler's sink while Harry went into the larder and came out with two bottles of beer. 'Opener?' he enquired.

Rick fished into the pocket of his jeans. 'Here you are. Never travel anywhere without it.'

For a few moments the two were silent, all but draining their bottles of beer from the neck. Then Harry said, 'Well, there we are then. Done it for better or worse.'

Rick was reluctant to dampen his friend's spirits any further. 'Mmm' was all he said, and then, 'So where's this river then?'

Harry nodded in the direction of the garden. 'Down there. Want a look?' He pushed open the kitchen door and led the way through the thicket of brambles and bindweed, through the emerging thistles and dog roses that had now decorated their leafy stems with single flowers of palest pink.

'God! Where are we going?' asked Rick. 'Up the Amazon?'

'Not quite,' retorted Harry. 'Down the Itchen.' Holding his hands and the beer bottle over his head, Harry wove through the undergrowth in the direction of the bottom of the long garden. Eventually he caught a glimpse of the sparkling water and asked, 'Can you see what it is yet?'

'What from here?'

After much jostling and slashing at the tangle of stems with a well-placed boot, the two men arrived on the river-bank; and for the first time Harry heard Rick in complimentary mode. 'Bloody hell,' he said. 'This is lovely. Is it all yours?'

'Twenty yards of it.'

'Well, I can see why you did it now. Got your rod?'

'Somewhere in there,' he gestured towards the house.

'Lovely. Bloody lovely. I'd be down here every day. Shame I don't fish.'

Harry laughed. 'It'd be wasted on you. The peace and quiet would drive you mad. Good for picnics, though, when I've cleared the garden. You can bring Rachel and Tilly down if you want.'

'Oh, I see. It's a garden. I hadn't realised. I thought it was the local nature reserve.'

Harry looked about him. 'Yes,' he mused. 'It'd be a shame to spoil it all. Perhaps I'll just make pathways through it and let the wild flowers keep on growing.'

'Docks and nettles, thistles and bindweed?' asked Rick.

'Not them. But the dog roses, and the osiers on the bank.'

'They'll get in the way of your casting.'

'Oh yes. I hadn't thought of that. Well, we'll see . . .'

Rick turned to look back up the garden. Between the dense canopy of hawthorn and goat willow he could see the mellow brick of an adjacent house. 'Who lives there?'

'Don't know yet. Haven't called on the neighbours.'

'Smart house. What I can see of it.'

'It's the old mill,' said Harry. 'Bigger than this.'

'Oh, the big house?' asked Rick, with mock reverence.

'Sort of. But just a mill – nothing grand. A fulling mill.'

'What's a fulling mill?'

'Its where they used to make felt. The water powered the hammers, which beat the fibres into thick cloth.'

'I see. Bet they're a bit stuck up,' grumbled Rick. 'Having the bigger house and all that.'

'They might not be. It doesn't always follow—'

Their musings were interrupted by a woman's voice.

'Hello?'

Neither of them could see where the voice was coming from and they craned their necks in the direction of the sound.

'Over here.'

Between the dog roses and the hawthorn they could pick out the movement of some form of life. Quite what it was it was hard to see through the dense undergrowth, but they made their way towards the sound until they had a clearer view. The voice belonged to a woman. She was dark-haired, quite pretty, about thirty-something, Harry judged, in that way men have of instantly summing up a woman's qualifications. But it was Rick who was first to greet her.

'Hello! You the neighbour?'

'Yes. Are you?'

'No. That's him.' He muttered under his breath: 'Worse luck.'

Harry butted in, hoping that his new neighbour had not heard the aside. 'Just moved in – yesterday and this morning.'

'Yes, we saw. I thought you might like . . .' There was a pause, during which the woman spotted the beer bottles. 'Oh, I was going to offer you a coffee.'

'Thank you, that's very kind,' offered Harry. 'Only . . .' He held up a beer bottle.

'Yes, I see. Too late.' The woman laughed; a light, rippling laugh. It came as a pleasant surprise. Harry hadn't heard that kind of laugh for a while.

'So you live in the big house,' asked Rick, his voice betraying just a trace of sarcasm.

'Oh, not that big actually.' She smiled. It was a lovely smile, Harry thought. So did Rick.

'I'm Harry. Harry Flint. This is—'

'Rick Palfrey. Just helping him move in.' They were about ten feet away from her now, but the dense thicket of brambles prevented any closer contact.

'Alexandra Overton. My friends call me Alex.'

Harry nodded.

She saw the slight confusion on his face. 'I mean, you can call me Alex. Everybody does.'

'Yes.'

Rick stepped in to ease the conversation along. 'Been here long yourself?'

'About two years. Just about got the place sorted out. Your turn now.'

Harry smiled ruefully. 'Yes.'

'Look, this is silly. Why don't you come round. I'm making a spot of lunch; we might as well say "hello" properly.'

'Oh, I . . .' Harry hesitated.

'Brilliant!' said Rick. 'Have you got any soap? It's one thing Harry seems to have lost on the journey and my hands are black.'

She grinned. 'Oh, I think I might find some.'

They made their way back through the wilderness and, once they were out of earshot, Rick said, 'You're in there!'

'What? Don't be ridiculous.'

'She's lovely. What a bit of luck.'

'It is a bit of luck, yes, having a nice neighbour but—'

'Well, you never know.'

'Rick, I am not on the lookout, in the market or . . . well . . . anything like that. I'm very happy on my own. Anyway, it's all too recent to start thinking about—'

'Relationships?'

'Yes.'

'All the same, it's nice to know that it's close at hand when you need it. And it has been two years . . .'

'Look, I've already told you to push off for being rude about the house. If you're going to start fixing me up with my next-door neighbour, you really can go and take a running jump.'

'All right, all right, only trying to cheer you up. How long has it been now?'

'Not long enough.'

'I just think it's time you started mixing with younger company. I mean Ted and Pattie are all very well, but a guy needs to mix with his own age group as well.'

'I do mix with my own age group. I mix with you.'

'Yes, but in case you haven't noticed, I'm married. And I've never really had any of those other kind of feelings, so there's no point in you raising your hopes there.'

Harry shot him a withering glance.

Rick parried. 'No; not even at your most engaging would you persuade me to have a back garden. Anyway, I've seen the state of yours . . .'

Harry picked up a towel and threw it at him. 'Silly sod. Anyway the next-door neighbour's husband wouldn't be very pleased.'

'Not sure there is one.'

'What do you mean?'

'No wedding ring.'

'Good God, you don't miss much, do you?'

'Old habits . . .'

'Don't let Rachel hear you.'

'Oh, she knows.'

Harry leaned on the jamb of the front door of the cottage. 'Can we just get one thing straight?'

'Mmm?'

'I have enough to occupy me at the moment. I have a new house in urgent need of repair, the prospect of unemployment which can't go on indefinitely, a bank balance that is pretty much on its knees and a future that is uncertain, to say the least.'

'But what about your spare time? What are you going to do with that?'

'Trace my ancestry.'

Halfway down the front garden path, Rick stopped. 'You're going to what?'

'Trace my ancestry. Well, I have. Partly. You should try it yourself. Find out who you are.'

'Look sunshine, I know who I am, and I have no interest in finding out about those who came before me.'

'Pity. You might find it interesting.'

'On the other hand, I might find out lots of things that I'd rather not know.'

'Ha!' Harry let out an exclamation of scorn.

'What?'

'Now who's not being adventurous?'

They had left the cottage and were walking across the patch of freshly cut grass that led across to the Old Mill, and Harry was anxious that the conversation should take on a more anodyne tone. 'Can we just stick with the weather and local geography at this first meeting please?'

'Entirely up to you mate. I'm just a hanger-on, remember?'

As they approached the front door, it opened, and Alex Overton stood in front of them smiling and welcoming. At her side was a small child of about six or seven. A girl. She smiled at them and then spoke. 'Hello,' she said, 'I'm Anne.'

12

The Streamside, Hampshire
16 April 1816

Early one morning, just as the sun was rising,
I heard a maid sing in the valley below.
Oh, don't deceive me; Oh, never leave me!
How could you use a poor maiden so?
'Early One Morning', traditional

Anne Flint reached the top of the stream bank and looked
about her. There was still no sign of anybody. Perhaps today
would not be the day after all. The sun was rising steadily now
and the blue sky growing paler. A breath of wind began to
ruffle the narrow leaves of the osiers.

She realised that she had better return home. To a short
break Mrs Fitzgerald would turn a blind eye, but a longer
absence would be frowned upon, unless she did not go back
at all. She decided it was better not to think about it. Mrs
Fitzgerald had warned her about what was expected of young
housemaids. Too many of them, she said, had no sense of
responsibility. Did Anne know that most housemaids stayed
in their job much less than a year? Some of them only for a
few months? Then they thought they would better themselves
and go off to London. What a waste that was. Did Anne really
want to end up at a hiring fair? Standing in a line with all the
other maids up from the country and hoping for a position in
a busy town household? Had she not seen the engravings in
Sir Thomas's library? Those by Mr Hogarth of *The Harlot's*

Progress. Did she really want to end up like Moll Hackabout? Did she know what life was like in a bawdy house? Anne wondered why Mrs Fitzgerald was so well informed, but the thought of it made her shiver and she sat down and began to put on her stockings.

She most certainly did not want a life like that. Whatever it was. But neither did she want to be wed to coals and ashes all her life. She wanted to be a lady's maid, then she would not have to spend most of her day on her knees, emptying out the grates and scrubbing stone floors. As a lady's maid she could wear fine clothes – well, finer than the worn blue gingham that was her daily uniform now. That would show Sam, wouldn't it? Sam, the yard boy. If she became a lady's maid before Sam became a groom, that would teach him. And then she felt suddenly guilty. Guilty at the selfishness of her thoughts. Sam was not a bad person. He was quite kind to her really, but oh, he could be so irritating. And infuriating. She thought that was the right word. She began to put on her boots, glancing up as a blackbird shot through the osier, its alarm call ringing out in the clear morning air.

It was at this point that a figure caught her eye. Someone was standing under the oak tree at the top of the bank. Her heart leapt. Was it some vagabond, come to rob her? Or a highwayman? But there was no horse. Just the solitary figure in a long, black cloak. As the figure approached, she could feel her heart thumping in her chest. She wanted to back away, but there was only the stream behind her, and her boots were not yet laced up. She remained fixed to the spot, unable to move, her position fixed due to a mixture of fear and undress.

'I startled you. I'm sorry.'

The words surprised her. Not only for their apologetic tone – nobody ever apologised to a housemaid – but also because they were spoken by someone she had thought would not be coming to the streamside after all, in spite of her promises to the contrary. She could see more clearly now as the figure approached and removed the hood that had covered its head. This was certainly no highwayman. Nor anyone who looked likely to rob her.

'I was watching you. You seem very happy this morning.'

Anne bobbed out of courtesy. 'Yes ma'am.'

'What did I tell you, Anne? You are not to call me ma'am. It makes me feel so old.'

The girl in the cloak was of her own age. Her hair was a similar colouring to Anne's, and her complexion equally pale.

'Sorry . . . er . . . miss.'

The girl laughed. 'It is becoming warm.' She undid the ribbon that fastened her cloak and let it fall, catching it over her arm as it did so and revealing a plain dress of soft pink.

Anne gasped a little.

The girl looked at her questioningly.

'Sorry . . . only . . . it is such a pretty dress,' apologised Anne.

Eleanor shrugged. 'It is nothing special. Just a day dress.'

'Better than mine.' Anne looked down at her own tired gingham.

'But yours is practical. Better for walking in the country-side. Better for running away in.'

Anne smiled shyly and her cheeks began to colour.

'Do you mean?' She hesitated. 'Like . . . today?'

The girl looked Anne in the eye. 'Only if you are sure.'

Anne's heart beat faster. 'Oh yes. I am sure. Is he . . . is Mr La . . . ?' She hesitated over the pronunciation, took a deep breath and said slowly, 'Is Mr Lavallier . . . ?' But then she faltered once more and her unfinished question hung on the air.

'Yes. He is coming. He will bring a spare horse from Winchester. Then we shall all three return there to board the Portsmouth coach at noon.'

Anne could not speak.

'Would you like to walk a while?' The girl indicated the narrow pathway of beaten earth that ran beside the stream.

Anne nodded. As they began to walk she said, 'I have not ridden before. Not properly, like.'

'I suspected so. That is why we have but two horses. You shall ride with Mr Lavallier and I shall take the other horse. We will keep you safe, Anne; you need not fear. And then you will be a lady's maid at last!'

The girl looked about her. 'What a perfect day! Are you nervous, Anne? I have to confess that I am very nervous. It is just as well that I have you for company or I suspect I should take fright and go home.'

'I am not very good company,' Anne confessed.

'Compared with what I have left behind, I think that you are. My elder sisters think that I am far too young to have any life at all; that it is all very well for them to be engaged in searching for a husband, but every day they tell me that I am still too young. More importantly, my father is of the same mind.'

'Are they right, do you suppose?' asked Anne.

'Some girls of my acquaintance are already engaged to be married. Do you think fifteen is too young to become engaged?'

Anne could not recall ever being asked for her opinion on anything. Opinions were what other people had and expressed to her. She had not really formulated any of her own. She had thoughts, and feelings right enough, but they had never been sought by anyone else.

'I think that I am not quite ready to be engaged to be

married.' She thought of Sam and her opinion was confirmed beyond contradiction.

'That is just how I felt.'

'But not any more?'

Eleanor looked about her nervously. 'He cannot be far away now.'

In the weeks that had gone before, Anne had come to look forward to her meetings with Eleanor Stockbridge on the riverbank. At first she was not sure that she would like her. Thought that she would be all lofty and above herself. It was a surprise when, on bright spring days, Eleanor took off her shoes and dangled her feet in the water alongside Anne's. They had talked of their lives and their aspirations – each of them quite, quite different and each, in their own way, convinced that they would never break out of the routine that had become their daily lives.

For one brought up an earl's daughter, Eleanor had little of what Mrs Fitzgerald would have called 'side'. She was refreshingly down to earth and seemed to genuinely take to the humble housemaid. When she caught Anne by the stream reading a book, she would look over and help her with the words over which she stumbled.

When the weather was foul they would talk only briefly, sheltering under the high wall just across from the stables. And, as the weeks progressed, Eleanor hatched a plan to elope with her intended – Mr Lavallier – a man she had met at the Basingstoke Assembly and whose father had plantations in far-off lands.

It sounded so romantic and, as their friendship grew, Eleanor determined that Anne should flee with them as her lady's maid.

At first the idea frightened her. But then, as the weeks wore on, the prospect of returning to her chores day after day seemed to offer little in the way of compensation.

'He is a very handsome man,' Eleanor assured her. 'And a gallant one. But he dare not ask my father for my hand lest he be refused. My age and the distance from England of his interests would make my marrying him out of the question.'

Anne recalled the moment when the intended scheme was first described to her. Eleanor spoke softly, as though fearful of being overheard, even though they were quite alone by the stream and well away from any kind of society. 'We plan to run away together.' She saw Anne's eyes widen and quickly asked, 'You do understand, don't you? There is absolutely no chance of my father agreeing to the match and we do so love one another. I really cannot bear to be separated from him any longer.'

'What will you do? Where will you go?'

'To Portsmouth at first. Then we shall set sail for the West Indies. Do you not see Anne? This is a chance to experience things. To escape and live a real life.' Eleanor could see Anne's eyes widening. 'And you, too. Would not you like to experience things?'

'Oh yes ma'am . . . I mean . . . I would like to be a lady's maid.'

Eleanor laughed, a light, rippling laugh. 'A lady's maid?'

'Yes. So that I could wear better clothes and not have to kneel down cleaning out fire grates every morning and fetching water and scrubbing steps and . . .' She realised that her thoughts and words were running away with her.

'You could be my lady's maid.'

Anne's face lit up at the thought, but then reality sank in. 'You should not tease me ma'am . . . that is . . .'

'I do wish you would call me Eleanor.'

'Oh, but I could not. I am a housemaid and you are—'

'A lady?'

Anne nodded.

'But I would rather be your friend, Anne. I need a friend. And you have become a good and true friend.'

Anne's head began to spin. A few weeks ago she had hardly a friend in the world, apart from Sam, and he didn't really count. And now here was a girl from a good family – the kind with whom she was in service – asking if she would be her friend. A look of concern crossed Anne's face. 'But Mrs Fitzgerald says we can never be friends.'

'Who is Mrs Fitzgerald?'

'The housekeeper. She says the most we can hope for is friendliness, but not friendship.'

'But that is so unfair.'

'But true.'

Eleanor sighed. 'Perhaps.'

'Do you have a lady's maid? Anne had asked.

Eleanor had looked downcast. 'Yes. Weaner. She is very old. Almost forty.' Then she brightened. 'You could be my lady's maid. As we are the same age it would be much more congenial. I could call you "Flint" if that made you feel better. "Flint." Much better than Weaner – it sounds not nearly so dour, don't you think?'

'I . . . I . . . am not sure what "dour" means,' Anne had answered nervously.

'It is one of those words that means what it sounds like – miserable and curmudgeonly.'

'What is cur-mu . . . ?'

Eleanor laughed again. 'We would have such fun together, you and I. You could teach me about the country and I could teach you about society – not that I think very much of it.'

'Where do you live?' asked Anne.

'Hatherley. Underneath the downs.'

'But that is several miles away.'

'I know. And I should not have walked so far in these shoes.' Eleanor lifted the hem of her dress and revealed a pair of silk shoes with short heels. 'Not really made for walking in, but I left in something of a hurry.'

'Were you in trouble?'

'Not exactly. My father was being tiresome and I needed some fresh air. I did not mean to walk so far but my thoughts were carried away and before I knew where I was . . . here I was.'

'Then we shall both be in trouble,' confessed Anne, smiling.

'Yes.' Eleanor sat down on the long trunk of a fallen willow that had been brought down by winter gales. She lay her cloak across the rough bark and motioned Anne to sit beside her. 'You must tell me where you came from, and I shall tell you all about me and then we really will know one another better.'

'But Mrs Fitzgerald—'

'Oh, I can assure you that Mrs Fitzgerald's temper will be nothing like as bad as that of my father. And anyway, we have to work out how you can come and be my lady's maid.'

Her voice was so kind and so gentle that Anne's worries about Mrs Fitzgerald melted away and she sat alongside her new-found friend on the willow trunk and began to talk of her life at the Manor House.

Eleanor listened attentively to the story of the orphanage, and the unpleasantness with the beadle, and then related the events of her own brief life at Hatherley until Anne felt that they had known one another for a long, long time – not just two hours. Two hours! It must have been as long as that, judging by where the sun was in the sky. She must return; they would be wondering where she was and Mrs Fitzgerald would scold.

'But you will come back? Tomorrow?' Eleanor had asked.

'Tomorrow? I . . . I'm not sure . . .'

'Oh, but Anne, you must. You must help me. I cannot run away with Mr Lavallier on my own. You must come with me.'

All that was several weeks ago; and now here was Eleanor with her cloak over her arm, waiting for her lover to gallop to her rescue and spirit her away to foreign lands. But they would not be travelling alone. Anne would be going with them. She pulled her shawl closer about her and waited . . .

13

The Old Mill, Itchen Parva
29 May 2010

The lads in their hundreds to Ludlow come in for the fair,
There's men from the barn and the forge and the mill and the fold,
The lads for the girls and the lads for the liquor are there,
And there with the rest are the lads that will never be old.

A.E. Housman, 'A Shropshire Lad', 1896

They sat at either side of a scrubbed pine kitchen table eating cheeses, salami and rough, warm granary bread. The coffee did not materialise, but a bottle of wine did – the better, said Alex, to celebrate a new arrival.

'Where are you from?' asked Anne. She was a bright child with bright eyes and leaned on the table with both elbows.

'Hey! Don't be nosey,' admonished Alex. 'And take your elbows off the table when you're eating.'

'But I'm not eating. I'm talking.'

Alex raised her eyes heavenward and shot an apologetic look at Harry.

He smiled across at the child.

There was nothing at all self-conscious about her. She was engaging in a totally unaffected sort of way. Disarming.

He answered her as best he could. 'I've come from St Cross – the other side of Winchester. I teach at a school in town. But not for long.'

'Have you been sacked?' asked Anne.

Rick and Harry both laughed. 'No. I've decided to leave.'

The child looked thoughtful and Harry noticed how the sunlight streaming in through the window glinted on her auburn hair. 'What about you?' he asked. 'Where do you come from?'

'Here. The Old Mill in Itchen Parva.'

'And before that?'

'Southampton.'

'And which do you prefer?'

Anne looked quite serious as she stood up from the bench on which she had been sitting. 'Here. I like the country. Much nicer than the town. I like the river too. It speaks to me.' And then, having concluded the conversation to her satisfaction, she asked, 'Please may I leave the table?'

'Of course,' said Alex. 'Off you pop – but stay away from—'

'I know, I know . . .' The child picked up a large stuffed dog, whose fur had seen better days, and tucked it under her arm before going out of the door and into the garden.

The two men looked after her. 'Quite grown up,' murmured Harry absently.

'More grown up than the thirteen-year-olds I have to teach,' confirmed Rick.

'A teacher then?' asked Alex.

'Yup. Both of us. For our sins . . .'

'Subject?'

'Maths,' said Rick.

Alex glanced at Harry.

'History.'

'Oh, much more my bag,' confessed Alex.

Rick suppressed a smile and Harry kicked him gently under the table. 'How about you?'

'Oh, I help out at the local day centre. Voluntary stuff. No time for anything permanent; single parent and all that.'

'Oh?'

'Yes. Widowed. Two years ago. That's when we moved. Not a happy time, but I tried to protect her from the worst.' She paused. 'Anyway, enough about that. Not the best thing to talk about on first introduction. Makes me sound either desperate or despairing and I'm neither.'

Reacting to the uncomfortable turn in the conversation, Harry made to change the subject. 'Know much about this place?' he asked.

'The mill? I know that it's very old, that it was a fulling mill; that it is a full-time job looking after it and that there is nowhere else that I'd – or should I say we'd – rather be.'

'Isn't it a bit big for you?' asked Rick.

'You'd think so. But we don't rattle. And I do have rather a lot of books.'

Harry sat up.

'Not you as well,' groaned Rick.

'I'm sorry?'

'This guy here is Hampshire's answer to the British Library.'

Alex's eyes lit up. 'Really?'

Harry replied defensively, 'He exaggerates. I just have . . . well, rather a lot of them.'

Rick warmed to his subject. 'I've told him to get an e-reader but—'

'Don't you dare!' scolded Alex. 'What sort of books?'

'Oh, all sorts.' Harry felt embarrassed. This was not the sort of conversation he had envisaged over lunch with a new neighbour. Not that he was ashamed of his books, but he would rather have kept the conversation anodyne, bland even. For now, at any rate. Just until he saw the lie of the land. I mean, they had only just met, and here was his life being laid bare. Typical of Rick that he should have waded in. He pushed back his chair. 'Anyway we'd better get out of your hair. Everything's in but there's still a lot of unpacking to do.'

Harry got up from the table. Rick followed reluctantly. 'Thanks for lunch,' said Harry, trying as best he could to sound bright. 'I'll get you round for a drink. Both of you. As soon as I can find a clear surface to put a glass down and somewhere to sit.'

'That would be lovely. Well, you know where we are if you need anything. If you've forgotten anything. Or can't find it. Tin opener, washing-up liquid, that sort of thing.'

Harry nodded. 'Thanks.' He shook hands with her rather formally and looked out of the window to where the child was lecturing the flea-bitten stuffed dog. 'Good to meet you. And Anne.'

14

Winchester Cathedral Library

5 June 2010

The English Bible, a book which, if everything else in our language should perish, would alone suffice to show the whole extent of its beauty and power.

Thomas Babington Macaulay, 1800–1859

Harry had been to the cathedral in Winchester often before. Though not a regular worshipper – or even a casual one, come to that; he never felt totally at ease with the commitment – he would stand at the back of the nave during evensong and let the liturgy flow over him, taking his mind, if not his corporeal self, to some other place. But until now he had not discovered the library. Its entrance was far from impressive, and those not looking for it would pass by the doorway, little knowing what treasures lay above their heads. He felt slightly ashamed that neither had he set eyes on the famous Winchester Bible. 'Call yourself a historian with an interest in the saints,' he muttered to himself, 'when you have not taken the trouble to go and see one of the most important religious texts in existence?' The insult added to the injury was that common one of ignoring the treasures on your doorstep as you travel the world in search of riches.

Today was probably not the day to do so. It was a day when he should have been painting a wall, repairing a window or slashing down brambles, but having had a week of that in the evenings, and a particularly tricky time in the classroom thanks to an outbreak of bloody-mindedness on the part of the boy Palmer and his cohorts, he said 'bugger it', and ambled around the cathedral's lofty nave and transepts, coming across the stairs that bore a simple sign indicating that they led to the 'Library and triforium'.

Tentatively he climbed, turning right at the top into a small, narrow room with an oak-framed glass case running down its centre. Nobody else was there, and what he saw made him gasp. He had always imagined that the Winchester Bible would be a large black tome, heavily figured and fitted with bronze clasps – a sort of souped-up family Bible; the kind on whose end-papers eighteenth- and nineteenth-century families jotted down their hatches, matches and despatches. The four volumes that lay open in the glass case in front of him could not have been further removed from the dreariest examples of King James's commission. The language of the Bible he had always loved. And the Book of Common Prayer, while not at his bedside, he regularly took down from his bookshelf and read out loud for the euphony of its language. The Magnificat: 'My soul doth magnify the Lord. And my spirit hath rejoiced in God my saviour. For he hath regarded the lowliness of his handmaiden.' And the Jubilate: 'O be joyful in the Lord all ye lands; serve the Lord with gladness, and come before his presence with a song.' Aural beauty. But what he beheld on this June day was something altogether removed from the everyday litany of the devout; something whose visual beauty he had never seen matched in any other book.

Avidly Harry read its history. Commissioned in 1160 by Bishop Henry of Blois, and taking some fifteen years to complete, the handwritten Bible was copied out by a single scribe and utilised the craftsmanship of six different illuminators for its exquisitely painted initial letters. About 250 calfskins were used in its production. Harry stared at it in wonder, dazzled and entranced by the illuminated letters, the rich blue lapis lazuli from Afghanistan, entwined with brilliant gold leaf. When Harry had drunk in enough of its riches, he turned and took the few steps necessary to enter the room opposite. Here he found the collection of a bibliophile who presided over the cathedral five hundred years later: Bishop Morley.

This was Harry's kind of room: flanked by tall dark oak bookcases topped with orbs and pointed finials, the single-vaulted room was not large, and yet it spoke to him as venerable libraries always did. These ancient volumes, bound in their own emotive raiment of calf- and goatskin, marbled boards and gutta-percha, diced Russia and vellum, offered their riches to all who would accept them. There is, thought Harry, a similarity between libraries and God. Then he dismissed the thought as being overly pious.

There was an atmosphere here, not just of learning, but of centuries of complex history – a tightly woven fabric of lives entangled with events. It was difficult to empathise with those whose sense of the passing of time was not remotely developed. To Harry, his place in the overall scheme of things was at the same time overwhelming and fascinating. To hold a book that had been held two, three, four, even five hundred years before by a scholar, a gentleman, or any member of society, was to him akin to grasping the Holy Grail. It linked him with generations past; with a developing civilisation, and he could not stop his mind running over the minutiae of their daily lives – what were they wearing? Where did they live? What did they do? Who were they?

It was not just the Winchester Bible that engendered such

feelings within him. How could anyone not feel a thrill on holding
a herbal from the sixteenth century, when it contained the sum
total of medicinal knowledge at that time? He knew that what to
him was an ancient volume of superseded knowledge was, to his
forebears, the perceived difference between the life and death of
a member of their family, however rudimentary such 'cures'
might seem today. How could that leave anyone unmoved? How
could anyone fail to thrill when their fingers turned the pages of a
first edition of *Pride and Prejudice*? He had held one, once. Read
the title page and memorised its words and layout:

PRIDE
AND
PREJUDICE
A NOVEL
IN THREE VOLUMES

BY THE
AUTHOR OF SENSE AND SENSIBILITY

VOL. I

London:
PRINTED FOR T. EGERTON,
MILITARY LIBRARY, WHITEHALL.
1813

There was the added frisson that its author – not named
within the book, the writing of novels being an unsuitable
occupation for a lady – lived locally, in Chawton, just a few
miles away, and was buried here in the cathedral itself. How
could such a geographical link not stir the senses?

Harry shook himself out of his reverie. He had wondered if the cathedral library might be the sort of place where he could do more research into his ancestry, or at least that might offer him more of an insight into the place where he now lived. Perhaps it would connect him with the time when the revered Miss Austen's story was written. The time prior to 1816 he had yet to research. His genealogical journey had been under way for only a few months, and in the few spare moments he seemed to have between teaching and managing what had been an unexpectedly eventful domestic life. Perhaps now he could take more time over it. Delve more deeply into his ancestry and the history of his new home. The tracing of his Georgian forebears might come to nought on this day, but at the very least he could gain a greater knowledge of the landscape in which he now lived. That sort of information, he was told by the curator, could be found upstairs in the Triforium Library – Bishop Morley's books were mostly of the seventeenth century; the later volumes were stored separately. Did he have an appointment? He regretted that he did not, but the kindly woman smiled at him, led him up the stairs and opened the glass cases of the less impressive upper library and allowed him to take down the volumes that might be of use.

His own father and grandfather had moved away but, before them, when generations of families had been less peripatetic, three generations of Flints had all resided and worked in this part of Hampshire. His grandfather, Henry Richard, had been a printer in the East End of London. Along with his wife, Mary, he had been killed in the Blitz. Henry's brother, Harry's great-uncle Robert, had died two years later in 1942 in the battle of El Alamein.

The Flint family had not fared well in the two world wars.

Harry's great grandfather, Thomas, while too old to serve, had been travelling as a cook on a ship which was sunk in the Battle of Jutland in 1916; his wife May had died just a year later – of a broken heart, was the family story.

Prior to this, all the members of his family that he had been able to trace had worked on the land. Henry Flint had been a farm labourer; his sister Liza had died at just one year old during a flu epidemic. The Flints had not gone in for large families; an heir and a spare seems to have been the family motto, though that scheme had clearly petered out with Harry himself, who was an only child. To all intents and purposes, the same was true of Henry Flint, his great-great grandfather, since his sister had died so young. But Harry's trail dried up when it reached Henry's parents, the delightfully named Merrily, born in 1816, and Elizabeth Henry, whose surname had clearly been handed down to first-born sons from generation to generation.

Merrily had been described in the birth certificates of his children as a 'shepherd' and his wife as a 'domestic servant'. But who were Merrily's parents? This was the task ahead of him. Finding Merrily's own birth certificate was the key, and it would mean scrutinising parish registers and perhaps the records in the National Archive. But right now it was the Mill Cottage that interested him. Who had lived there and what had they done?

The library's shelves, at first glance, would yield little of use to someone in search of local history – thesauri and religious tracts, Latin texts and collected writings held faint appeal – but a polite word with the curator produced a couple of volumes that she thought Harry might find useful. For over an hour he pored over them, their pages giving off the scent of ages and the tang of bottled time and gradually allowing him to build up a picture of the goings-on around his humble Mill Cottage at Itchen Parva.

There had been another village back then; well, more of a hamlet really – a scattering of cottages. Withercombe, it was called. There was a Manor House, and a fulling mill. Many of the buildings had disappeared over the years, fallen victim to fire or flood, pestilence and general neglect, and the Manor House to that malaise which dominated Britain in the 1950s and 60s, that of knocking down large old houses in the belief that they were unsustainable dinosaurs of little intrinsic or lasting value.

The buildings that remained had been absorbed into a newer village. Gradually he linked together the disparate pieces of this geographical jigsaw, discovering as he did so that the Old Mill next door to him, and his own cottage, had once been leased by a family called Palfrey. He leaned back in his chair and smiled to himself. Bloody typical; he had done all this work to trace his own ancestry and ended up finding out more about Rick's family than his own.

At least, he presumed they were Rick's ancestors. He had, after all, teased Harry mercilessly that – for all his interest in history – he himself was nothing more than an off-comed-un' – a foreigner, a grockle, an emmet. Strange how many insulting words a mathematician could find to hurl at you when he put his mind to it. It mattered not that Harry's forebears had been from these parts – the direct line had been broken by Harry's parents, and Harry had been born in 'foreign parts', insisted Rick, whose own family he knew had never left the county, even if he had little or no interest in their detailed history.

Harry's chagrin was mollified by the fact that he would take great delight in telling Rick that the house in which Alex

Overton now lived had once been occupied by Rick's ancestors. With that pleasing little nugget jotted down in his notebook, he left the cathedral library and headed for home.

15

The Fulling Mill, Hampshire
20 April 1816

The angels were all singing out of tune,
And hoarse with having little else to do,
Excepting to wind up the sun and moon,
Or curb a runaway young star or two.

Lord Byron, 'The Vision of
Judgement', 1822

'What does that mean then?' asked young Jacob Palfrey of Sam the yard boy. 'Misadventure.'

'Means what it says, I suppose. She 'ad an adventure and it went wrong.'

'What sort of adventure?'

'I know not. They took her back to Hatherley after the inquest. They will bury her there, I expect, with the rest of her family. The ones that's dead.'

Three days after finding the body, Jacob was still feeling out of sorts. 'S'all wrong,' he kept murmuring to himself. 'T'aint right.'

Sam had soldom bared his soul to Jacob before the fateful day, but the events of that bright spring morning had thrown them together and they took what little comfort they could from chewing over the matter almost every day. Sam, like Anne, had to choose his moments to escape with great care, lest Timothy Jencks the groom took exception to his absenting himself for too long and exacted retribution in the form of an even greater workload.

'No sign of your Anne then?' asked Jacob.

'She weren't my Anne.'

'Not for want of tryin' though, eh?' A rare smile broke out on Jacob's lips. Then he remembered the fear he had felt that morning when they fished the body out of the river and his face took on a serious expression once more.

'I did find one thing,' confessed Sam, reaching into the pocket of his jerkin. He pulled out the small book. 'She were readin' this.'

'Where d'you find it?'

'In the sweet flags by the stream. Where she liked to go. She must have dropped it. Or it fell out of her apron pocket.' He turned the book over in his hands, as if somehow it might give up secrets other than those held within its covers.

Jacob held out his hand and Sam passed him the small volume. Slowly he read the title out loud: '*The Highwayman's Bride.*'

'She like to dream about things,' said Sam defensively. 'Doesn't mean she was ever going to run away.'

'You don't think that's what she done then? Just upped and left?'

Sam shook his head.

'Why not? You say she did not like her job, so what would stop her running away?'

Sam paused for a moment and looked at his feet. 'She would have told me.'

Jacob smiled again, half mocking, half indulgent. 'So there was something between you?'

'No. There was not. But I am sure she would not have gone without saying something. Or leaving me a note. She could write as well as read.'

'So what else could have happened?'

'She could have been taken against her will.' He put his hand out and Jacob returned the book. Sam put it back in his pocket.

'By a highwayman?'

'Maybe.'

'None in these parts at the present.'

'Or a blackguard.'

'Do you think she knew someone?'

'Not sure. She did say she had a friend.'

'A man friend?'

'She would not say. Liked having her secret. But she never said that she would leave. She wanted to be a lady's maid—'

'She would have had to have left to do that, wouldn't she?'

'Maybe.'

'You know something else?' asked Jacob.

Sam hesitated and then said, 'By the stream . . . there were hoofprints in the mud . . .'

The clock over the stable struck the hour.

'I'd best be away afore Mr Jencks catches me.' He picked up the pitchfork that leant against the wall.

'Think you she is dead?' asked Jacob bluntly.

Sam shook his head vigorously and began to walk back towards the stables.

'You has no way of knowing.'

Sam spoke without looking back. 'I knows she ain't dead. I just knows.'

Back at the fulling mill, Jacob Palfrey asked his father what he thought.

'Maids like that is forever running away. Most goes to London. They has fairs there – hirin' fairs. They likes girls up from the country. Feels they can mould them and bend them to their will. Need not pay them a fair wage neither.'

'You do not think she may be dead then?'

William Palfrey looked up from his work on the cloth. 'No body yet,' he said.

In his attic room in the fulling mill that evening, Jacob Palfrey sat down at the rough oak table tucked underneath the eaves and, by the light of a single candle, filled in his diary for the day in a slow and methodical hand. There were few lads in the village who had learned to write. Though Anne worked at her letters regularly, Jacob and Sam were the only ones who had leapt at the chance when the governess from the Manor House had offered to teach any others who cared to master the art of penmanship. The twice-weekly lessons had lasted little over a year and, as a result, the finer points of grammar had escaped him, but Jacob found some satisfaction in being able to set down his thoughts. His diary, though primitive, was his way of expressing those feelings that he would find impossible or unwise to admit to others:

Apr. 20 Still no sign of Anne. Sam do say she might have been taken by who he know not. He seen hoofprints in mud by the stream and found her book in the sweet flags. I say she may have run off with a lover tho Sam not wanting to believe this. Father think she has indeed run away and that we will see her no more. Father to Winchester with three bolts of cloth and to watch hanging of man called Jacques for stealing two sheep. Another man Eastwood imprisoned 1 month for killing a sailor at Ship Tavern. Fine bright day again.

His daily life thus recorded, he left the pages open so that the ink might dry, blew out the candle and pulled the rough woollen blanket over his head, the better to keep out the wind which was now whistling between the roof tiles.

16

Mill Cottage, Itchen Parva

4 June 2010

On firmer ties his joys depend
Who has a polish'd female friend . . .
While lasting joys the man attend
Who has a faithful female friend.
                Cornelius Whur, 'The Female
                                Friend', 1837

Harry could have left it longer than a week. In some ways he wanted to. But Alex had been so hospitable on the day of his moving in that it seemed churlish to postpone returning the compliment. He had knocked on her door on the Friday after returning from school and asked if she would like to come round for lunch with Anne on Saturday. Lunch, she said, was not possible; she had promised Anne a trip to Winchester and lunch in Pizza Express.

'Perhaps another time then,' Harry had said, happy to let the appointment slide, his initial obligation having been fulfilled.

'I could do supper,' she'd replied. 'Anne's going to a sleepover and I'll be on my own.' Then she realised the potential imposition and did not want him to feel that he was being cornered. 'Or we could both do lunch next Saturday . . . oh, no, sorry: school spring fair. Oh dear . . .'

'Supper tonight then. That's fine. But I can't promise you anything very special.'

'I wouldn't expect anything special.'

'No; what I mean is . . .' He saw her wry smile. 'Right. Well, about seven thirty?'

'Perfect; I'll have had a chance to get back and smarten myself up.'

Harry wondered why he had done it now. Why hadn't he waited a few weeks? It wasn't as if he really wanted to get to know her. He really was just being neighbourly, wasn't he? Not that Rick would let him get away with that.

'Wow! You're quick off the mark,' he'd said in the staff room that Friday lunchtime on asking Harry what he was doing at the weekend. 'I was going to ask you round for supper with Rachel and me, but since you're out on the town . . .'

'I'm not out on the town; I'm having a quiet supper in.'

'Just the two of you?'

'Well, yes, but . . . do you have to read into it more than is actually there?'

Rick shrugged. 'Just showing an interest, that's all.'

'Putting your oar in, more like.'

'Well, I hope you'll both be very happy.'

Harry shook his head. 'You don't give up, do you?'

Rick turned to face him. 'I just want to see you happy, that's all; and mixing with company your own age.'

'Like you?'

'Yes; but not just me. Female company.'

'Will you—'

Rick cut him off. 'It's been long enough, you know. You don't have to stay single for the rest of your life.'

'I might want to.'

'Bollocks. I know the Witch of Endor wasn't every man's dream, but can't you remember what it felt like at the beginning? Before she turned into the missus from hell?'

'Yes.'

'It was good, wasn't it? Something special. Blew your socks off.'

Harry did not speak, but Rick could see that he had touched a nerve. He put a hand on Harry's shoulder. 'I just want the old you back, that's all. The one with a twinkle in his eye. The one I could have a laugh with.'

'And you can't now?'

'Well, yes . . . but . . . you know what I mean. Just loosen up a bit, Harry. Risk lowering your defences. Just a little.'

'Men aren't supposed to talk about things like this,' muttered Harry.

'No. But men aren't supposed to spend all of their lives being miserable either. Serena might not have been the woman you thought she was, but that doesn't mean that all the rest are the same.'

'No. I suppose not.'

'Look at me and Rachel.'

Harry raised an eyebrow.

'All right, so we might not see eye to eye all the time . . . We do have the occasional . . . difference of opinion . . .'

Harry risked a gentle cough; Rick and Rachel's arguments were legendary.

Rick ignored the interruption. '. . . but I couldn't be without her.'

He paused, and in the silence realised that he had said enough. 'Well, whatever. Have a good time and I'll see you on Monday. You can fill me in then . . . on your hot date.'

The exercise book, though well aimed at the figure retreating through the door, missed its mark and, instead, caught Deirdre Tattersall, the religious studies teacher, on the left breast as she entered the staff room. She did not say anything, but her look could quite easily have turned Harry into a pillar of salt.

And now it was a quarter past seven. He went through a mental checklist: white wine in the fridge (he plumped for a Chablis as being fairly safe – champagne might appear to be too celebratory and to load the evening with excessive significance) and a bottle of Merlot open by the log fire. He'd managed to get it to stop smoking by lifting the grate off the tiny hearth with four house bricks – not pretty, but at least he could now breathe.

He looked about him and smiled to himself at the modest transformation of the previously bare sitting room. It was hardly Designers' Guild, but it did now looked lived-in: cosy without being twee, manly without being austere. He had found a home for a few dozen of his books on pine shelves he had constructed in the narrow alcoves at either side of the fireplace. Three small table lamps dotted about the place gave it a warm glow without showing up too many of the flaws in his barley-white emulsion technique. He had found second-hand curtains in Winchester that fitted the tiny windows and arranged the furniture that had come with him from St Cross in a way that meant he did not have to fall over it when he crossed the room. A couple of Mary Fedden watercolours – what passed for his pension scheme – decorated the two unadorned walls, and a scrubbed pine table under the end window turned that into a dining area. The old sofa could do with a couple of bright throws to hide its threadbare arms but they could come later.

The fire crackled in the grate and broke in on his thoughts. It was followed by the bouncing ring of the little shop bell that hung by the front door, whose simple wire mechanism snaked its way to the outside of the cottage via a series of small but elaborate pulleys. Harry would have checked his appearance in the mirror, had there been one. As it was, he settled for running his hand through his hair in the hope that it would be enough to make him presentable. The clean navy blue shirt and chinos would have to do the rest.

He opened the door. Alex's first words were unexpected: 'How sweet!' she said.

And then, thinking that he might assume she was talking about his appearance, she added, 'The bell, I mean. Just like a sweet shop.'

'Oh . . . it was here when I came; I just had to fiddle a bit with the mechanism. I think it's probably pretty old.'

Alex held up a bottle of champagne. 'I thought we ought to celebrate.'

Harry's circumspection was swept away. This was a cause for celebration and Alex was determined not to let the moment pass without popping a cork to mark the occasion. She saw the look of slight embarrassment on Harry's face.

'A new house. You can't really toast that with plonk, can you?'

'Er . . . no. Lovely. That's very kind.'

'It is chilled. I've had it in the fridge all day. Goodness this is nice. What a transformation. And you've only had a week.'

Alex had entered his house, and his life, it seemed, like a whirl-wind. She barely drew breath as she remarked on this picture and that pair of curtains, the fact that the walls had been painted and the floor covered with an old Persian carpet. 'It's as if you've always been here. How very clever. Most men can't do that. They move their furniture in and it looks like a second-hand shop.'

Harry found himself grinning.

'What is it? asked Alex. 'Oh, I'm sorry. Listen to me, going on like a steam train. I've hardly drawn breath. Must be nerves.'

'No. Not at all. I'm glad you like it.' Harry found two wine glasses. 'Sorry about these; the three champagne flutes that survived the move across town were in a box that one of the removal men dropped on the kitchen floor.' He handed Alex a glass of fizz. Somehow it seemed to glitter rather more than usual. 'Cheers!'

'Here's to you and your new house . . . cottage . . . palace!'

'I'll settle for cottage. And here's to you – my first guest, if you don't count Rick. And not many people do.'

'Is he a pain?' asked Alex with a look of genuine concern.

'No, not really. He's a good mate. Thick and thin and all that. And mainly thin. Anyway, no time to talk about him. Thank you for coming.'

'Thank you for asking me.'

They sipped at their wine in one of those awkward momentary silences, then both spoke at once and laughed at their mutual nervousness.

Harry motioned her to sit down on the sofa to one side of the fire, while he sat in the armchair opposite her but not too far away. It was impossible to be at a great distance from anybody or anything in the tiny sitting room.

For the first time, Harry had a chance to look properly at her. Her hair was thick, shiny and dark, lightly brushing her shoulders. Her deep brown eyes shone in the firelight and the honey-coloured sweater she wore over cream trousers showed off her figure not in an obvious way, but flatteringly nevertheless. He noticed the slenderness of her bare ankles above the suede loafers, and the thin gold chain around her neck. He did not remember her being quite so good looking, but then reminded himself that he had only seen her in her garden and over her kitchen table on a Saturday morning. It's not that she was what Ted Chieveley would have called 'all dolled up', just that she had smartened herself for the evening out; made the most of what she had. As far as Harry was concerned, that was clearly considerable.

All these thoughts he put to the back of his mind; telling himself that it was all academic. Alex was being neighbourly, nothing more, and it was pointless speculating about anything to do with relationships. They had only just met, for heaven's sake. And he knew nothing about her. Absolutely nothing. Other than the fact that she was a widow with a small child. He made polite small-talk for a few minutes while Alex settled herself into the sofa, and then excused himself while he got up to bring in the smoked salmon starter.

The conversation did not need to stop; the kitchen was barely six feet from the sitting room and they chatted away while he covertly removed clingfilm, sliced lemons and arranged brown bread on a wooden platter.

Gradually, from being an effort, the conversation became more relaxed. They talked easily together about where they lived, the state of the garden, Harry's plans for doing up the cottage properly, where he would put his books and what he would do when he had finished teaching – about which he had precious little to offer.

He had bought a chicken pie for the main course. 'Sorry,' he said. 'It's not home-made.'

'Who cares?' she said. 'It's very nice to be sharing it.'

He felt an unfamiliar kind of warmth coming over him, and then banished the thought as fanciful.

As they sat down to eat it he said, 'We've done nothing but talk about me. What about you?'

'Oh, goodness. You don't want to know all that . . .'

'Yes I do. How do you come to be here?'

Alex thought for a moment. 'What was it that Harold Macmillan said? "Events, dear boy, events."'

Harry smiled. 'Yes; we've all had a few of them.' And then he waited for her to carry on.

'We lived in Southampton. I was married to a lawyer. We'd been married for eight years and then . . .' She paused momentarily. 'He died. It was all very traumatic. Anne was five at the time so it was upsetting for her but I knew she'd get over it. She didn't understand fully and that at least was a blessing. It was all very messy.'

Harry looked at her quizzically but said nothing.

'I was a lawyer, too,' she continued. 'We were in the same chambers. I gave up work when Anne was on the way. That's why I have so many books, too. Not as interesting as yours. Torts and Litigation instead of Titian and Lautrec.'

'Very good,' said Harry appreciatively. 'And after . . . after he died, you came here.'

'Yes. I needed a fresh start. I felt we both did.'

'And Anne has settled in all right?'

'Yes. Small children are surprisingly resilient. To some things. I think she was young enough not to be too scarred by it, you know. But I worry about her. She's quite quiet sometimes, and I wonder if there is something that she's not telling me; not sharing with me.'

'And what do you . . . how do you . . . ?'

'Fill my days?' I do a bit of work down at the local day centre, though its future is a bit uncertain. Local government cutbacks and the like. And I concentrate on Anne; making sure that she grows up without being spoiled. I'm very aware of being a single mother and all the baggage that comes with it – and the things people think.'

'What do you mean?'

'Oh, you know. That I must be on the lookout for someone. No one's husband is safe.'

'Seriously?'

'Oh, you wouldn't believe. I spoke to a very nice man outside the school gates a few months ago. Nothing untoward. Just pleasant chat about children and things while we waited for ours to come out. He was there most afternoons. The next thing I know he doesn't come for her any more; his wife does and gives me a lecture on staying out of her life.'

Harry's expression made Alex laugh. 'It's true, unbelievable as it sounds.'

'So you're not—'

'On the market?'

'No, I didn't mean . . .'

Alex smiled. 'Oh, one day maybe. I've had a gentle dabble on the internet but . . . oh, now I am beginning to sound desperate. And this is not the conversation I wanted to have tonight. Not at all appropriate. I'm so sorry.'

'No. I'm sorry. I shouldn't have asked. It's just that—'

'It came up. I know. Look, I'd better be going.' Alex got up from the table and made to leave.

Harry got up, too, and rather surprised himself by saying, 'I'd rather you didn't. I really don't mind what anybody thinks. And I certainly don't think . . . well . . . anything at the moment. Except that there's a pudding in the fridge and it would be a shame not to eat it.'

He was surprised to see a tear roll down Alex's cheek. She sat down softly on the sofa and said 'Oh dear. I'm so sorry. Too intense. Too sensitive. Too everything . . .' and she smiled at him as another tear sprang unbidden from her eye.

Harry sat down alongside her and put his arm around her shoulders.

'I'm afraid I'm not very good at this,' she said. 'Not very good at anything much.'

'You're a bloody good next-door neighbour,' he said. 'Shall we settle for that for a while?'

17

The Streamside, Hampshire
16 April 1816

It is better to suffer wrong than to do it, and happier to be sometimes cheated than not to trust.

Samuel Johnson, *The Rambler*, 1750–52

The sound of horses' hooves filled Anne's heart with a mixture of hope and fear. She pulled her shawl tight about her and turned, with Eleanor, to see the horseman galloping down the meadow beneath the oaks. Within seconds she felt the hot breath of the black stallion on her naked arms, thrilled to the whinnying of the grey mare reined in at its side and saw the sparkle in Eleanor's eye as she beheld the man she loved, leaning down from his horse and cupping the back of her head in his hands.

'You came!' she said.

'Of course I came. Did you doubt me?'

'Not for a minute. And yet . . .'

The horseman slipped from the saddle, took Eleanor in his arms and kissed her fully on the lips. Anne could but look on embarrassedly, wishing that for a moment she were somewhere else while the two lovers completed their intimate greeting.

Eleanor eased away from the youth in the dark green coat. 'This is Anne. I told you of her.'

Roderick Lavallier bowed smartly from the neck and said with a glint in his eye, 'Of course. Are you ready for adventure, Anne?'

Anne nodded. She was incapable, at the sight of the kind of man she had dreamed of, had read about in her books, of anything more than a weak smile.

'Then we must go.'

Anne looked at him as he turned again to Eleanor. He was tall and angular, with high cheekbones and bright blue eyes; his thick brown hair tied back with a glistening black ribbon. Sir Thomas's sons, thought Anne, were handsome enough, but Roderick Lavallier made them seem plain by comparison. And, oh, the way he dressed! His dark green coat was caped at the shoulders and his riding boots and breeches were spattered with mud from the ford he had crossed at the bottom of the field. In the white silk stock at his neck, a single pearl glistened.

'You must change,' he instructed the two women.

They looked at him questioningly.

'If Anne is to ride with me as you suggested, Eleanor, then she must wear your clothes. It would not do for a gentleman to be seen riding with a maid. In such a case we might well be stopped.'

The two women looked at each other and then Eleanor laughed. 'Over here, Anne. We must exchange our dresses behind the osiers. No one shall see us. We need change nothing more, and Richard has brought another cloak for you, have you not?'

The man nodded. 'But hurry. We must catch the coach to Portsmouth within the hour.'

The next few minutes passed in a haze for Anne. Eleanor helped her remove her dress and Roderick Lavallier obligingly attended to the horses and looked in the other direction to avoid any embarrassment. The two women were of almost exactly the same build, and for the first time in her short life,

Anne Flint found herself wearing a rich pink day dress and gloves, topped with a riding cape. Such was the excitement that she could hardly bring herself to speak.

Eleanor, on the other hand, giggled and chattered as she buttoned up Anne's gingham dress on her own body and tied on the apron. She, too, then wrapped a shorter cape around herself and said brightly, 'Look, Anne, we have become each other. Is this not strange?'

It was, indeed, strange, and suddenly Anne began to wonder what she had become a part of. Now that her dream had become reality, the seriousness of her situation began to dawn. But there was no time to change her mind. Roderick Lavallier was holding the reins of the two horses and asked impatiently, 'Are you ready? For we must go.'

He lifted Eleanor on to the side-saddled grey and handed her the reins. Then he turned to Anne. 'Hold my shoulders,' he instructed. Anne did as she was bid, and felt Lavallier's arms around her small waist. She could not recall when her heart had beat faster, and she did think that at any moment she might swoon into a deep faint.

The gleaming stallion threw its head to one side, tearing the reins from his master's grasp. 'Steady Jupiter!' murmured Lavallier, recapturing the leathers, and before she had time to decide whether or not fainting was a likely eventuality, Anne was lifted up on to the saddle, and instinctively held tightly on to the stallion's neck. It pawed at the ground and gave an impatient snort. For the first time in many years she felt real fear, but then Lavallier was up astride the horse behind her. 'Hold very tightly to the pommel,' he instructed, and then turned to Eleanor. 'Are you ready?' he asked.

'I am ready, my love' she cried, with excitement in her every word.

He flashed her a wicked grin, dug his heels into the glistening flanks of the black stallion, and the three of them galloped off up the river valley and out towards Winchester.

18

St Jude's School, Winchester

7 June 2010

Thou hast most traitorously corrupted the youth of the realm in erecting a grammar school.

William Shakespeare, *Henry VI Part* 2, 1590–92

'Walk, don't run Palmer! Save the speed for sports day . . .' The last sentiment was delivered sotto voce, not least because Harry felt that sarcasm should be a teacher's last resort. Sad that he was beginning to have recourse to it more and more. The boy Palmer disappeared into the distance of the school corridor with no perceptible reduction in horsepower and Harry turned into the staff room and flopped down into a chair. It could be worse. They could be in Brighton with Palmer wreaking havoc on the prom. It'd be mods and rockers all over again.

'Had enough?' enquired a bright voice. It was Rick. 'You should try maths with twenty-two seventeen-year-olds whose testosterone levels are off the Richter scale. Thank God we're single sex or I dread to think what they would be doing to each other in the break.'

'At least you can give them problems to solve that will occupy them for a few minutes. It's more difficult when Palmer and his cohorts are trying to persuade you to let them act out the Gordon Riots because that way they will be easier to understand.'

'Poor bugger.'

'Heaven knows what they'll want to do when we get to the assassination attempt.'

'Strong coffee then?'

'Very.'

Harry wondered how long it would be before Rick probed about the 'weekend assignation', as he called it. His question was answered almost immediately.

'Well? How did it go?'

Harry glanced at his watch. 'Twenty-three seconds. A personal best.'

'Oh, come on. Any spark there?'

'Subtlety not the strong point this morning, then? It went very well, thank you.'

'That it? No blow-by-blow account?'

'No blows exchanged. She was just . . . well . . . very nice.'

'Oh, bloody hell. I was expecting a bit more than very nice, to be honest.'

Harry glanced around. The staff room was large, with small groups of teachers scattered in different areas. The arrangement made it easier to have relatively intimate conversations without being overheard, provided you took the precaution of keeping your distance from those of a particularly curious disposition. 'I think she was a bit scared, if you must know. A bit nervous.'

Rick looked surprised. 'What, with you? Mr Unthreatening?'

Harry ignored the jibe. 'I think she's been hurt a lot. Since . . . you know, since she lost her husband.'

'Did she say how he died?'

'No. And I didn't ask. It didn't seem right, and the moment never came.'

'And did you tell her all about you?'

'No; we never got round to that.'

'Ah, one of those who likes to talk about herself . . .'

Harry jumped in. 'No. I don't think so. Just a bit lost, I suppose. A bit like me.'

Rick put down the two coffee cups on the table. 'God, you two must be fun when you get together.'

'Well, it was fun at the time. It just got sort of . . . well, a bit introspective. I think she finds relationships hard. I don't think she's really ready for one, to be honest. Told me a dreadful story about some mother at the school gates giving her hell for chatting to her husband.'

'Potential cougar?'

'I hate that term. Anyway, the object of our meeting was just to be sociable.'

'You make it sound like a Women's Institute AGM.'

Harry took a sip of his coffee. 'When I've anything to report, you'll be the first to know.' And then he remembered. 'Oh, and I've some news for you on a different topic.'

'What's that?'

'Your ancestry.'

Rick sighed. 'You do lead a heady life, don't you?'

'No, listen. This'll surprise you.'

'Oh, yes?'

'The old mill – it used to be a fulling mill—'

'I know; you said.'

'Well, the family who were the tenants, back in the early 1800s, their name was Palfrey.'

'Bugger me!'

'If you are as native to these parts as you claim to be, then it looks as though Alex Overton is living in your old family home. Unless, of course, it's a different branch of Palfreys.'

'How did you find this out? Did she tell you?'

'No. I did some research at the cathedral library. There's

not much there in the way of local history but, as luck would have it, there were a couple of books that made reference to Itchen Parva, and the mill and the Palfreys.'

Rick brightened. 'Could I claim it back, do you think? Or at least claim rights over the people who now live in it?'

'Doubtful.'

'Well, well, well . . .' He fell silent for a few moments and the two of them continued to sip their coffee. Then Rick said, 'Perhaps I should get that old trunk down from the attic.'

'Which trunk?'

'Oh, there's an old trunk my granddad gave me – full of old bits and bobs. Never really bothered to look at it. Probably just old notebooks and stuff.'

'What? You've had this all the time and you never thought to tell me?'

'It doesn't interest me, Harry. I live in the present and it's the future that concerns me, not the past. There's no point in living there. Look where it's got you.'

Harry took all manner of light-hearted insults from Rick as a matter of course, but this one stung more than most.

'Not very kind.'

'No. I'm sorry; I didn't mean to – well . . . I mean, I just think you should start putting all that behind you. Crack on. When you leave this God-awful school, put all this historic stuff behind you – literally. That's where it belongs. Make a new life based on where you are now and what you are now. Stop living in the past.'

'I can't.'

'Why not?'

'Because it haunts me. There's something there that I can't put my finger on. Something that is of the present. Oh, I don't know. It's all so confusing. Maybe you're right. It hasn't actually got me anywhere, has it?'

Rick shook his head sympathetically. 'Have you thought of – ' he looked around to make sure no one could hear – 'internet dating?'

Harry nodded. 'Tried it a couple of times.' He shuddered. 'Strange who turns up when you say your interests are history, genealogy and the lives of the saints.'

'I'm not surprised. Why don't you . . . embroider a bit?'

'There's no point in lying.'

'I don't mean lying – just, well, souping it up a bit. You could say you were into Formula One racing.'

'But I'm not.'

'Watch a couple on the telly. They just go round and round a track. Not much to learn or to answer questions on. As sports go, it seems to attract lots of dishy birds. I mean, look at that Bernie Whatshisname. And those drivers are forever getting their leg over.'

'I'm not interested in getting my leg over.'

'Well, it must be more fun to talk about bad guys who are alive rather than good guys who are dead.'

'But I'll end up having to spend every weekend at Brands Hatch.'

'Yes, but think of the evenings.'

Harry laughed. 'You're incorrigible.'

'But not lonely,' said Rick. 'And you are. You should be out enjoying yourself instead of tucked away in libraries. And what's the worst that could happen? One duff date.' He glanced around. 'You see Deirdre Tattersall over there – religious studies?'

'Yes?'

'Found a guy on the internet. Read all his stuff. Seemed just her type – said he was tall, dark, handsome. Wrote that he WLTM petite blonde. Well, that's Deirdre. Almost . . .'

'And?'

'She turns up to find this short, fat guy with no hair left who was no fun at all, in spite of the fact that he'd said GSH – Good Sense of Humour – on his details.'

'Did she complain?'

'Oh, she told him straight, there and then. You know Deirdre.'

'What did he say?'

'Oh, he apologised about his height. Said that when he was honest, nobody turned up at all.'

'What about the GSH?'

'He said he thought it stood for Gas Central Heating.'

Harry spluttered into his coffee.

'There you are, you see. Worth a laugh.'

'I think on balance I might be better sticking with the next-door neighbour.'

'You see, I knew you'd come round to my way of thinking. When are you going to see her again?'

'I don't know. But I think before we go any further, she needs to know a bit more about me. She's told me all about herself—'

'All?'

'Well, more than I've told her. And she was good company.'

'There you are then.'

The bell signalling the end of the break resounded through the school, and the members of staff stood up as one to take their crockery to the communal sink.

Rick and Harry drained their mugs. 'Mind you,' said Rick. 'You do have one big failing, I'm afraid.'

'What's that?' asked Harry.

'No Gas Central Heating.'

19

The Streamside, Hampshire
16 April 1816

A horse misused upon the road
Calls to heaven for human blood.
William Blake, 'Auguries of
Innocence', 1803

Having gone for what seemed like minutes without drawing a single breath, Anne now found herself panting as the horses galloped side by side along the bank above the stream. The pounding of the beast beneath her, the sound of its roaring breath and the shine on its rippling ebony coat, coupled with the closeness of a man – as close as she had ever been held in her entire life – mingled raw fear with exhilaration. She could not bring herself to look up at him, but occasionally glanced to her left where Eleanor, with her cloak flying, was riding the grey mare; the eyes of horse and rider as bright as each other.

She could smell Roderick Lavallier now, a fragrant but manly smell; a mixture of leather, linen and cologne that made her stomach churn. She could feel his arms encasing her as he held the reins, and his breath upon the back of her neck.

'How long do you think?' asked Eleanor, shouting above the sound of the pounding hooves. The mare, not as strong as the stallion, was struggling to keep up.

'Around four miles – it will not take us long and then we shall be aboard the coach and you can rest.'

Anne struggled to keep her balance. It was all she could do to cling on to the pommel of the saddle and remain still so that she would not be a burden to him and not disturb the horse. In the event it was not Anne who disturbed the horse but nature.

As the track alongside the stream widened, the mare had come almost right alongside the stallion. Aware of her close proximity and of her tantalising scent, the stallion, Jupiter, turned his head to the left and bit the mare on the neck. With an ear-splitting whinny, the mare careered sideways then stopped in her tracks and reared up. Eleanor, whose horsemanship was by no means slight, fought to control her mount, and at first it looked as though she would succeed. Lavallier reined in the stallion and turned sharply to go to Eleanor's rescue. As the black horse approached, the grey reared up again, fearful of a further attack, and this time Eleanor was thrown. She let out a sharp cry as she tumbled from the saddle, her leg becoming entangled with the stirrup leather.

At this point the stallion lunged towards the mare again, but the mare took avoiding action. Her head thrown to one side, she galloped down the bank towards the stream, trailing Eleanor behind her like a rag doll, and stopping only when she had reached the water.

'Eleanor!' Lavallier's voice cut through the air as he raced towards her. Anne could do nothing but cling on for dear life. Reaching the stream, Lavallier leapt from the saddle and dashed to Eleanor's side as she lay half in and half out of the water, her head resting on a boulder that was becoming increasingly stained with blood.

Lavallier looked up in desperation. 'Help me!' he cried to Anne.

With difficulty Anne slid down from the now snorting horse and ran to his side as speedily as her unfamiliar dress would allow. She said nothing, but gazed in horror at the lifeless form of Eleanor on the bank of the stream. It had all happened so quickly. Maybe it had not really happened at all. Perhaps if she shook her head she could go back for some minutes, or even an hour, and stop it from happening at all. But no; she was here, looking down on her friend whose eyes were wide open and focused on nothing at all. The smile had vanished from her lips and her cheeks were drained of all colour. Her lover looked up at Anne beseechingly, his face a mixture of horror and disbelief.

'How could it have happened?' he asked.

Anne could do nothing more than stare. And then she began to shake and the tears to trickle down her cheeks.

'Anne, you saw, did you not? It was nobody's fault. The horses . . .' His voice faded and he turned again to look at Eleanor. Her eyes were still open, her face expressionless. Her cloak and her shoes had been lost in the chase and she lay in her servant's clothes among the sweet flags and the rushes.

'Oh my love,' murmured Lavallier softly. 'Oh my love, my love!' He stood up quite slowly, not for one moment taking his eyes off the body. 'We were to have been married . . .' but the tragedy of the situation prevented any further explanation.

By now Anne's body was wracked with sobs. 'What shall . . . we . . . do . . . ?' she asked, through staccato breaths.

Lavallier was bent over the body now. Tenderly, he stroked Eleanor's cheek and then, with the finger and thumb of his right hand, he gently closed her eyes. 'Goodbye my love,' he whispered. He stood up, looking down at the body, and in that moment a change came over him. Anne saw it quite clearly.

The face, which had borne so much love and tenderness, now hardened. The firm jaw was set; the eyes cold as ice.

Roderick Lavallier drew his cloak around him. 'We must go. There is nothing we can do here.'

'But where?' asked Anne.

'To the coach, and then to Portsmouth. You must come with me.'

'But I cannot,' Anne exclaimed through the sobs.

'You must. You cannot stay here. What would people think – when they found you?'

'I . . . I do not know but . . .'

'They would accuse you of murder, Anne. You are wearing Eleanor's clothes. They would think you had robbed her and killed her and then taken her clothes and dressed her in your own to confuse.'

The rising fear Anne felt was evident in her voice. 'But I did not . . . I was not—'

'It will make no difference, Anne. You are a servant; Eleanor was a lady. The law takes little heed of servants.'

A sea of confusion swam through Anne's brain. What could she do? What Roderick Lavallier said would be construed was true, even though the reality was completely different.

'We should go to the squire. Sir Thomas will know what to do,' she offered.

'And how will we explain our circumstances? Shall we admit that we were to run away to Portsmouth and then sail to the West Indies? Shall we explain why you are wearing Eleanor's clothes and she yours? What do you think will be the squire's response to such a revelation? And how will Eleanor's father Lord Stockbridge treat me? And you? For abducting his daughter you will be hanged, Anne, and I shall be transported.'

'But not if you explain.'

'I am in no position to explain. The best we can hope for is prison, and the worst, death by the gallows. That is our choice. Our only recourse is to continue with our journey and for you and I to travel as husband and wife.'

The conversation was interrupted by an air-piercing shriek. The stallion had made one more attempt to attack the mare, which had aimed a well-placed kick at its hocks. With a loud whinny the stallion took off across the meadow and the mare, content that she had seen off her assailant, bent down to drink the cool, clear water from the stream.

'We have no choice now, Anne. We have only one horse. We must travel together or you must return and face the consequences.'

'But what about Eleanor?'

'We can do nothing for Eleanor now, God rest her soul.'

'But can we not take her somewhere?'

'And risk being accused of her murder?'

'But to leave her here . . . alone and—'

'She has gone, Anne. She is not Eleanor any more. She is a body, and bodies are found every day in town and country.'

His coldness horrified her. To think that just a few moments ago she had thrilled to his touch, been overpowered by the scent of his cologne and his clothes. She had felt safe – swept off her feet. She knew it was not for her own sake, but nevertheless she had been embraced on horseback by this handsome buccaneer of a man – the kind she had so often read about in her books. Her book? Where was her book? There was no time to think of it now. Her mind had no room for such diversions. The man she had thought to be a dashing hero, the lover of her only friend Eleanor, now frightened and revolted her in equal measure.

How could he have changed so suddenly, so completely? She had no further time to think. Lifted into the saddle of the grey mare, she felt his arms around her waist once more, only this time a different kind of thrill ran through her body; a thrill born of fear and terror.

20

The Old Mill, Itchen Parva

7 June 2010

SAINT, n. A dead sinner revised and edited.

Ambrose Bierce, *The Devil's Dictionary*, 1911

'I just wanted to apologise,' said Alex.

'There really is no reason why you should,' offered Harry.

'Oh, I think there is. I was far too intense and you probably wanted to run a mile.'

'It's very considerate of you to say so, but you are really quite wrong. I'm very flattered that you bothered to tell me anything.'

'And we never talked about you.'

'Just as well, really. Rick thinks I've nothing interesting to say.'

'This Rick seems to be quite a large part of your life. You're not joined at the hip, are you?'

'Sometimes I wonder,' muttered Harry. 'No, not really. He can be a real pain in the arse but he's got me through quite a lot.'

They were sitting in the kitchen of the old mill early in the evening of the day on which Rick had lectured Harry.

'Anyway, I was able to tell him something for a change. I went to the cathedral a couple of days ago. Do you ever go?'

'Once a month or so. I like going to evensong. I find it . . . helpful.'

'Oh.'

'Yes. I don't admit to it very often. I find it puts people off.'

'No, it's not that,' Harry assured her. 'I stand at the back myself sometimes. Just to listen. To let it wash over me. It's, well, comforting.'

Alex did not add any more, fearing that any conversation about religion would be a turn-off.

Harry continued, 'I went into the library, looked at the Bible . . .'

'What did you think?' she asked.

'It blew me away. Those illuminated letters. They could have been painted and gilded yesterday, instead of nine hundred years ago.'

'I know. It just reminds you that we are not necessarily more intelligent – or gifted – than those who went before us. We just have different priorities. But what's all this got to do with Rick? I can't imagine he's into illuminated manuscripts.'

'No. I found a couple of books that talk about this place – the Old Mill.'

'Really?' Alex's eyes brightened. 'What did they say?'

'That the people who lived here at the beginning of the nineteenth century were called Palfrey – Rick's family name.'

'Good heavens! And is he local?'

'Yes; and never lets me forget it.'

'So this place was probably lived in by his ancestors?'

'Could have been. He's promised to look in an old trunk his grandfather gave him. I ask you; he knows I'm interested in history – especially family history – and he's never mentioned it. Bloody typical.'

'Let me know what you find. I'd love to know more about this place.'

'You don't find it boring, then? History, genealogy – that sort of thing?'

'Not at all. It's fascinating. I love knowing what's gone before; who's gone before.'

Harry hesitated, then asked, 'I don't suppose you're interested in Formula One, are you?'

'Not in the slightest,' said Alex.

'Thank God for that.'

'Should I be?'

'No, no; it was just something Rick said. A silly joke.'

'Well, let's stop talking about Rick and start talking about you. How do you come to be living on your own?'

Before Harry had time to answer, a small face appeared around the doorway. 'Can I come and say goodnight?'

Anne Overton was wearing a pair of pyjamas with a pattern of small horses prancing all over them and clutching the stuffed dog he had seen before which was possessed of even less fur than he had remembered.

'Of course you can.'

'Goodnight Harry,' she said.

'Goodnight Anne.'

She walked up to him and looked up into his eyes. 'Can I give you a goodnight kiss?'

Harry was momentarily thrown off guard and then recovered himself enough to say, 'Yes; of course you can.'

He bent down and felt a small pair of lips kiss him softly on the cheek. For a moment he felt quite overcome with emotion. How silly. A small child kisses you on the cheek and you become all sentimental.

Her mission accomplished, Anne said 'Goodnight then', and turned and disappeared through the doorway.

Harry looked at the empty doorway, unsure of what to say, then he glanced at Alex and saw that her eyes were glistening. 'She doesn't often do that. You're very honoured.'

He wanted to ask whether she meant, 'She doesn't often do that to the men I have around' or just, 'She doesn't often do that to anybody', but he resisted the temptation and smiled gratefully as Alex poured him a glass of red wine.

'So?' she asked. 'Are you going to tell me?'

It was midnight by the time he left, and there was that awkward moment at the door when the form of parting has to be decided upon. The discomfort was minimised by Alex who bent forward and kissed him on the cheek. 'Thank you for coming. For your company.'

'Thank you for listening,' he said. 'I'm sorry if it all sounded so pathetic.'

'Not pathetic,' she replied. 'Just sad.'

Harry shrugged. 'That's me. Sad old man . . .'

'Oh, that's something you need to work on,' said Alex with a glint in her eye.

'What's that?'

'The self-esteem. There's no reason for it to be quite so low, you know. You're quite good looking and, if you don't mind me saying so, quite bright as well.'

'Well, thank you. It's a while since I had such a compliment.'

'I can keep them coming if you like.'

'That's probably enough for me to be going on with. I don't want to get above myself.'

'Somehow I don't think you could.' She hesitated. 'Shall we do it again?'

'That'd be nice. Only . . .' Harry hesitated. 'I'm very conscious of . . .' He gestured upstairs to where Anne would be sleeping.

'Well, she's going away for the weekend. To stay with a

schoolfriend in Bournemouth – they've got some kind of holi-day apartment overlooking the sea.

'Oh. And are you busy? I mean, say, on Saturday night?'

'Not at all.'

'We could go out if you like. Dinner? Theatre? Movie?'

'Dinner sounds good. We can talk more then. I rather like talking to you, Mr Flint. And listening, of course.'

For the first time in as many months as he could remember, Harry Flint went to sleep with a smile on his lips on the night of the seventh of June – the feast day of St Robert of Newminster, according to his diary of the saints. St Robert was born in Gargrave, North Yorkshire, and became one of the founders of Fountains Abbey before being made Abbot of Newminster in Northumberland. All of which would have seemed of little consequence except that in 1147 some monks accused him of 'excessive familiarity with a pious woman.'

It came as a relief to Harry to discover that St Robert was completely exonerated.

21

The Portsmouth Road
16 April 1816

Let the ungodly fall into their own nets together,
and let me ever escape them.

Psalm 141 v. 10

Anne sat silently on the seat opposite Roderick Lavallier within the coach as it bounced along for twenty-nine and a quarter miles to Portsmouth. Thundering through St Cross and past the Twyford turning, Anne could hear the trunks and valises rattling above her head until the horses slowed a little past the Fair Oak Inn. She could hear the coachman and the guard up on the box exchanging pleasantries and gossip above the din. How she wanted to leap out and run away, but such an opportunity did not present itself; the coach kept moving and Anne was firmly sandwiched between a silent dowager in deep purple whose black bonnet covered most of her face, and a large bewhiskered man in a caramel-coloured coat who smelled of beer despite the early hour. Oblivious to the motion and discomfort of the coach, the fat man slept soundly and snored loudly, except when a particularly large pothole in the road caused the coach to lurch with such force that he was jolted awake. At this he snorted, rubbed his nose on a particularly grubby scarlet kerchief, and then promptly fell into a resonating slumber once more. The coach picked up speed again as they rattled on to Titchfield and Fareham, Porchester and Wimmering.

For most of the journey, Anne tried to avoid Lavallier's eyes, and gazed out of the window as the pastoral scenery lurched by. He made no conversation, finding himself seated beside a mother and her young daughter who had clearly exchanged words before they boarded the coach, for they uttered none the entire journey. Lavallier had warned Anne not to speak once they had dismounted at Winchester, lest it become obvious to all about her that this was no 'lady' but a girl of lowly birth with her long Hampshire vowels. He further instructed her to pull up the hood of her cloak so that her face remained hidden from view.

So it was that the entire journey was undertaken without a single word of conversation; those who would have spoken were not minded to do so, and the rest were content to remain silent. The only sounds that filled Anne's ears were the jangling of the harness, the clatter of the wheels, the stertorous breathing of the man in the caramel-coloured coat and the rhythmic sound of horses' hooves over cobbles and dirt tracks, through mud and mire. At each small cluster of cottages, and at each village on the way, the guard's bugle would be sounded, and Anne's nervousness be heightened as the strident notes rang through the air.

And now the hardness of the ground beneath the hooves told her they were not far from their destination. Anne's one act of defiance was to lower her hood once in the coach, despite a glowering look from her captor. Through its window she could see the towering form of Portsdown Hill as they went past Cosham – at least, she imagined that was what it must be, having heard its lofty eminence spoken of by Mrs Fitzgerald. And then came the realisation that she would not see them all again: Mrs Fitzgerald and Sir Thomas, Sam and Mr Jencks, Mr Moses and his vegetables, they were now all a part of her past and heaven knows what the future held, or where that future would be. She felt a tear forming in her right eye, and rubbed it away impatiently. This was no time to be feeble; she would have to show her mettle if she was to escape from this dreadful man and not end up being shipped to the West Indies where she had no doubt she would become little more than a slave.

She was sure now that Lavallier was a dreadful man, a dishonourable one, and conscious that she knew nothing of him and his background, save that Eleanor had said his father had sugar plantations. But how could she believe even that, having observed the way he had behaved when he discovered that Eleanor was dead? Dead! That word, so filled with anguish and finality, and which she had never imagined could ever be applied to Eleanor, the one friend she had who was so brimful of life in the all-too-brief spell that they had known one another. She must think. She must use all her wits and guile – the two things Mrs Fitzgerald had considered, where Anne was concerned, to be in perilously short supply.

She glanced about her in the coach. Roderick Lavallier flashed her an admonishing look and motioned her to pull up the hood of her cloak, which she had managed to slip to her shoulders for the better part of the two-hour journey. The other passengers were also aware that their excursion was coming to a welcome end. The large man in the caramel-coloured coat was stirring and wiping his eyes with the grubby kerchief. Some form of rapprochement was taking place between the mother and daughter; the elder managed a weak smile, while the younger rested her head on her mother's arm, where it received a stroke for its trouble. The purple dowager was peering out of the window towards the sea. The sea! They were almost there and there was now no time to make any plan for an escape. Over Portsea Bridge they bumped and on through Hilsea, past Halfway Houses when the towering masts of ships began to slice into the skyline. The horses slowed now to a steady walk, and the noise from the streets grew louder as they entered 'the most considerable naval arsenal in the British dominions': Portsmouth.

Now she could hear the coachman shouting at passers-by, and see the shiny black hats of the tars as they jostled with one another outside inns and shipping offices. To have arrived here by coach on any other occasion would have thrilled her, and she felt, beneath the welter of fear that enveloped her, an anger that she had been robbed of what under other circumstances would have been an exciting adventure. She had never even travelled in a coach before, let alone as far away as Portsmouth, and now here she was, overwhelmed by the sight of masts and towering hulls, flapping sails and men scuttling like monkeys up the rigging of four masters and schooners, barques and brigantines. She could identify none of them, though their romantic-sounding names were as familiar to her as her own, thanks to the books that had held her captivated by candlelight each night in her bed.

The coach turned into the yard of an inn, and much commotion now surrounded them. With little delay, the four horses that had brought them from Winchester were unhitched by the ostlers and another fresh team made ready. Almost before the door of the coach had been opened, the passengers' luggage was being handed down from the roof and removed from the boot by the guard.

The fat man got out first, oblivious to those around him, puffing and panting as he turned his body round, the better to extricate himself from the tight confines of the coach. The purple dowager looked the other way, her face a picture of disdain, and the mother and daughter – now fully reconciled – smoothed down each other's clothes for the disembarkation.

Lavallier motioned Anne to remain in her seat until the others had vacated theirs. Only when the interior of the coach was quite empty, and they heard the voice of the coachman shouting, 'All change!', did Lavallier rise from his seat and step out through the door, offering Anne his hand to help her down the two steps which had been lowered for their convenience.

As she alighted into the salt-laden air, the whole of Portsmouth seemed to envelop her. Seagulls screeched above their heads, adding their plaintive wails to a cacophony of sound composed of rolling casks and cartwheels, hawkers crying their wares, hauliers and carters exhorting everyone to move aside and sailors drunk and sober, uniformed and roughly clad, swarming like bees up and down the gangplanks and docksides. It was as if the whole of the city were out on the streets, each vying with the other to see who could make the most noise.

Reeling as though she had been dealt a blow about the head, and with a sickly feeling in the pit of her stomach, Anne found herself being steered along the dockside by Lavallier's arm, which he clamped securely about her waist. A porter followed them with a barrow on which Lavallier's trunk and two large carpet bags were precariously balanced. Anne was conscious of the fact that she had no belongings of her own, save what she stood up in, and for the first time was grateful that she had been allowed to keep her own boots, Eleanor's feet being a good deal larger than her own. They peeped out incongruously beneath the rich pink dress and the all-enveloping cloak, which Anne took some comfort in drawing closely about her.

Her captor, for that was how she now regarded him, propelled her forwards, avoiding the tarred ropes and hawsers that held the ships secure, past the pedlars and the sellers of sweetmeats, between groups of women with rouged cheeks and reddened lips who wore brightly coloured and ill-fitting clothes. They shouted at the sailors and used many words that Anne had not heard before, and a few that she had.

At the end of the dock they turned up a side street which seethed with even more humanity, spilling from doorways of ships' chandlers and coffee houses, shops selling exotic objects and richly coloured carpets, butcher's and baker's, greengrocer's and fruiterer's, with their produce piled high in colourful pyramids. Anne had never seen so much food in one place.

Before she had time to take it all in, Lavallier motioned her through a small archway and into some kind of office. It, too, was busy, with men exchanging money for pieces of paper – men in tall hats and long coats; all of them serious looking and clearly not without means. Anne felt even more nervous.

'Sit here,' instructed Lavallier, pushing Anne down on to a hard wooden chair in one corner. Above the polished wooden counter she read the heading on the large black board to which the men behind the counter kept referring: 'SAILINGS', it said, in large gold letters, while underneath it were chalked the names of ships – *Leviathan* and *Osprey*, *Venus* and *Mermaid*, *Dolphin* and *Blue Moon*, the times and dates of departure indicated alongside them. It was all so exciting. So romantic. So totally terrifying.

Lavallier untied the cord at the neck of his cloak, unbuttoned the coat beneath it and sought in his coat pocket for a slender bundle of papers which he took out and examined. As he did so, he took his place behind a gentleman whose transaction was clearly nearing completion. All the while he would glance regularly in Anne's direction. She could feel his eyes almost boring through her. Then, the man in front of him raised his hat to thank the official behind the counter. As he departed, Lavallier took his place and began to engage the official in conversation. Anne seized her brief opportunity. Without a backward glance she got up from the chair and slipped silently out of the doorway. Pulling her cloak tightly about her to avoid its being caught in the many obstacles that stood in her way, she wove her way swiftly up the alley, past the vendors and the passers-by, under canvas awnings and between carts and crates and barrows until she emerged, eventually, in a small square. It was quieter here; the bustle had subsided and the houses were tall and elegant with large windows, iron railings and porticoed front doors.

Still she did not linger, but crossed the square and zig-zagged her way through more alleyways and narrow passages until, at last, she had left the seething mass of humanity and, more importantly, Roderick Lavallier, behind her. She had shaken him off. She had escaped. She stopped for a moment to catch her breath, leaning on a wall in a quieter square, while her chest heaved and perspiration beaded her brow.

The moment of triumph was brief. She had, indeed, rid herself of her captor, but now the only thing of which she was entirely certain was that she was alone in a strange and frightening city, and that she was totally and utterly lost.

22

The Hotel du Vin, Winchester

12 June 2010

Life is packed with coincidences; so many
that you would not believe. But it is only the merest few
that we notice, and we think even these can be explained away.
But they cannot. They are there to haunt and,
to those who will attend, to instruct.

Author's own

The first argument was who would drive. It was only a small one. A difference of opinion born of the consideration of each for the other. Harry won, or lost, depending on whose side you are on, and picked her up in his old Volvo estate at half past seven.

Alex's first question surprised him and made him laugh: 'How long did it take you to get ready?'

'About three times as long as normal,' he admitted.

'Me, too. Actually, more like four.'

Her openness was refreshing, but it did nothing to ease his state of mind. Were things moving too fast? What did he expect of this relationship which, as yet, hardly qualified for the term. Did he want it to be a 'relationship' at all?

Banishing these thoughts from his mind, and anxious to keep things on a lighter social footing, he asked, 'Did Anne get off to Bournemouth all right?'

'Just about. She's not keen on cities. She's a born country child – never happier than when she's picking wild flowers, or netting minnows in the river, or just out in the garden with "Mr Moses".'

'Mr Moses?'

'Her dog. That threadbare animal that she carries under her arm.'

'Funny name for a dog.'

'She found him down by the river – someone had dropped him in the rushes. We left him on the garden fence for days to see if anyone would come and pick him up, but they never did, so Anne said she'd give him a home until his rightful owner turned up.'

'How long ago was that?'

'A couple of months.'

'So Mr Moses is now a part of the family?'

'The most important part. She talks to him. Tells him things.'

'What sort of things?'

Alex looked thoughtful. 'She doesn't say. But at least it means she's articulating her thoughts, rather than bottling them up.'

'You're not a bottler then?'

'I thought we were going to talk about you tonight, not me.'

Harry took the criticism kindly and swung the Volvo into the car park behind the Hotel du Vin. They did not link arms as they walked along the brick path at the back of the hotel. Harry thought how good it would have felt to hold her hand, and then admonished himself for such a pathetic thought. But it had been so long since he had enjoyed any kind of liaison with a woman that even the prospect of hand contact gave him a kind of thrill.

They were ushered to a corner table and inconsequential conversation followed over the menu and the wine list. Alex plumped for the goat's cheese tart and then the monkfish, Harry for lobster bisque and steak. They compromised over the wine: no bottle, since Harry was driving, but a single glass of claret for him and a glass of rosé for her.

As their glasses chinked, Alex said, 'Your turn then. You know all about me – well, enough – now it's my turn to find out about you.'

'This could be the shortest date in history,' muttered Harry.

'Speed dating?'

'Something like . . .' Harry told the story of his brief but frenetic courtship with Serena, of their equally brief marriage and hasty divorce, and did his best to sound neither maudlin nor self-pitying.

'She sounds dreadful,' offered Alex as he wound up his story.

'No; not dreadful.'

'Well, you were mismatched then.' Alex considered for a moment. 'Did you really think you could make it work?'

'It did work, at first. We were blissfully happy. But just not for long. The differences rose to the surface and before we knew where we were, it had all crumbled.'

'But you must have felt uncomfortable about some things from the beginning?'

'Only her friends. I never really got on with them. Hooray Henrys, you know . . . I've always found them a bit tiresome. But it was Serena I'd fallen in love with. You can't dislike someone because you don't like their friends.'

'No, but you can judge them a bit by the company they keep.' She said it gently but firmly.

'Yes; I suppose you can . . . on reflection.'

Alex asked: 'Is she with anyone now?'

'No idea.'

'So you don't see her then?'

'No. Not since the divorce came through. It's almost as if she never existed. As if our marriage never happened. I wonder sometimes if it was all a dream. But then that's Serena. Once she's made up her mind about something, there's no going back.'

'Or looking back?'

'No.' He thought they had talked enough about his misfortunes. 'How about you? Do you ever look back and think "what if?"'

Alex leaned back in her chair. 'Oh yes. About so many things.'

Harry thought it would probably be a mistake to probe further. This was meant to be a happy evening out. He had already dragged the conversation down with his own tale of woe; better to be upbeat.

'Goat's cheese tart?' It was the waiter's voice. 'And the lobster bisque?'

They fell upon the food as though they had not eaten in days.

'You probably think I'm a real no-hoper,' confessed Harry. 'Bringing a girl out to dinner and talking about his ex-wife, and then ordering "surf and turf" – I mean how unimaginative.'

'Are you?' asked Alex.

'I hope not. And if I am, I'm determined to change. That's why I'm making a new start. In a new house and with a new career. If I can find one,' he added as an afterthought.

'Well, I don't think you're a no-hoper at all. Just a bit bruised. That sort of thing saps your confidence; I've seen it happen enough times to know that – with both men and women.'

'Do you have lots of friends?' he asked.

'Not any more . . . I mean, not since we've moved.'

'Choice or circumstance?'

Alex looked uneasy, and then said softly, 'A bit of both', before asking, 'How's your soup?'

It was half past ten by the time Harry pulled into the short gravel drive of the Old Mill. The rest of the evening had been devoted to lighter fare – the kind of music they each liked, whether Venice was better than Florence, whether Florence was better than Rome, the relative merits of home-made bread, and were Nespresso coffee machines really any good or was it just because George Clooney advertised them?

The last topic gave Harry the excuse to ask Alex back for coffee, rather than having it in the hotel. She accepted happily, but on their arrival back at the Old Mill she said, 'Look, why don't you come and have coffee with me; my place is proba- bly warmer for a start. I've got an Aga.'

'Show-off,' countered Harry.

'Oh, you'll get one, I guarantee. Once you've been through your first winter here by the river, you'll realise how nice it is to be warm.'

Harry grinned cheekily and said, 'I'm quite warm right now, thank you.'

'I'll take that as a compliment,' replied Alex. 'Come on.'

She opened the door into the Old Mill kitchen, lit by a single lamp on the windowsill, and then walked through a low arch- way into the sitting room, where the dying embers of a log fire glowed softly behind a tall wire guard. Alex took two small logs from a wicker basket and dropped them on to the grate. There was a brief shower of sparks before the fire flickered into life and small flames licked at the dry birchwood.

Harry had not been in this room before, and he looked about him and smiled at the warmth and friendliness of it all.

There were two soft but lumpy sofas facing each other in front of the fire, their elderly loose covers partially hidden by throws of heather-coloured tweed. Scrubbed pine bookshelves flanked the fireplace and a grandfather clock with the painted face of a full moon ticked sonorously in one corner, while a fully furnished doll's house sat in the other. Odd chairs held piles of books, and a bunch of old-fashioned roses stood on the low table between the sofas, the soft pink, purple and crimson petals of the fat flowers now cascading onto the magazines beneath the lustre bowl that held them. There was nothing too studied about the place; it was naturally stylish and supremely comfortable.

'Very nice,' he murmured – to himself, so he thought.

'You like it?'

He was startled to think that the words had been spoken out loud. 'Very much.' And then, 'Oh, you've got a Mary Fedden.' He gazed at the picture hanging above one of the stripped pine bookcases.

'Just a tiny one.'

'With a cat and a lemon and a mug.'

'I like her stuff,' said Alex. 'Fresh. Even though she's now very old.'

Harry gazed at the picture. 'How strange.'

'Why strange?'

'Because I've got a couple.'

'Why should that be strange?'

Harry shrugged. 'Well, I just don't know anyone else who has one.'

Alex smiled at him. 'Nor me.'

She made the coffee and brought it to the sofa where Harry was sitting. 'Music?' she asked.

'It should be me doing this,' countered Harry.

'Well, make the most of it.' Alex went to an iPod that rested between two speakers and within moments Ella Fitzgerald was singing about being 'Mad About the Boy'.

'Oh, no!' exclaimed Alex. 'That wasn't meant to happen. How unfortunate.'

Harry grinned. 'Fortuitous, I'd say.'

Alex flopped down on the sofa beside him. 'What are you doing tomorrow?'

'I don't know. I haven't really thought. I did have plans to crack on with tracing . . .' And then he realised he was not remotely interested in his ancestry. Not right now. He wanted to talk about her. About them. About now rather than yesterday.

He turned to her and asked, 'What about you?'

'Free day. I can do what I want.' Alex looked at him and smiled, and before he knew what was happening he had his arms around her and they were lying back on the sofa kissing.

Somewhere in the back of his mind he heard Rick's voice saying, 'I told you so.'

23

Portsmouth
16 April 1816

Loss of virtue in a female is irretrievable; that one false step involves her in endless ruin.

Jane Austen, *Pride and Prejudice*, 1813

'Lost your way, dear?'

Anne was shaken out of her trance-like state by the voice in her ear. She turned to discover the kindly, smiling face of a woman who looked rather elderly, but whose mode of dress was that of a much younger woman, and one unfamiliar with the generally acknowledged virtue of self-restraint. Her petticoats were full and voluminous, her dress of a satin once fashionable but now passé and, if one were judging by the generous sprinkling of stains, infrequently laundered. Around her shoulders lay an elaborate wrap that had seemingly once belonged to a member of the fox family blessed with three heads and five feet, and upon her head sat a collection of feathers which, had they been seen in the road, would have been identified as an unfortunate thrush who had come off badly in an argument with a coach-and-four. Her hands, encased in black net gloves, carried a reticule and a threadbare parasol with a heavy knob of a handle.

Anne looked at the woman's face. Her cheeks were the colour of a Quarrenden apple and her lips as red as blood. Several soot-black beauty spots decorated the skin around the mouth and eyes and the whole vision rendered Anne lost for words.

'What's a nice girl like you doing on her own in Portsmouth?' The individual arrangement of teeth added sibilance to the question.

'Lost,' blurted out Anne, without thinking.

'Oh, we're lost are we? And do we have any money?'

Anne shook her head.

'Oh dear! Well, it's a good job you bumped into old Phoebe then, ain't it?'

Warning bells rang in Anne's head. She had heard about the likes of 'Old Phoebe' and knew exactly what they were about. Mrs Fitzgerald had made sure of that.

'No. I mean—'

'Well, does you need help or doesn't you?'

It seemed futile to claim to the contrary, when it was patently obvious to anyone, including Old Phoebe, that she did indeed.

'What sort of help?' Anne heard herself ask.

'Shelter; a room for the night. A position.'

'A lady's maid,' countered Anne defensively. 'That's my position. I'm going to be a lady's maid.'

'Of course you are, dear. Eventually. But in the meantime you'll need a roof over your head and some food and the wherewithal to find yourself that position, won't you?'

Anne could not bring herself even to nod. She kept glancing over her shoulder in the direction of the shipping office – or at least the direction in which she assumed the shipping office was, her passage from it having been convoluted and confused. She was convinced that at any moment Lavallier would round the corner, scoop her up and whisk her off to the *Osprey* or the *Godolphin* or the *Leviathan* and thence to distant territories where she would be lost to her familiar world forever.

'Someone looking for you, dear? Someone who worries you?'

Anne nodded and Old Phoebe saw the terror in her eyes. 'There's dreadful men abroad. Men the likes of which I will have no truck with. My men are nice men. Every last one.' She reached into her battered velour reticule and pulled out a square of fine linen, edged with lace. It did not glow with the whiteness of her mistress's handkerchiefs at the Manor House, thanks to the exacting laundering standards of Mrs Fitzgerald, but it was kindly proffered and Anne managed a very weak smile.

'Wipe your eyes, dear, and come along with Old Phoebe. You need only stay as long as you want. I will not hold you there.'

Anne shook her head violently. 'I need to get back to the Manor House.'

Old Phoebe looked sympathetic. 'Which Manor House is that then?'

'At Withercombe.'

'Withercombe . . . mmm . . . is that a long way away?'

'It is in Hampshire.'

'So is Portsmouth, dear, but this is a large county, and you'll need the coach fare to get back there.'

'But I have no money,' protested Anne. 'Not even a farthing.'

' 'Tis of no account, ducky. 'Tis of no account. Them as comes with me seldom has. Not at first, anyway. But they soon becomes more comfortable.'

Anne dabbed at the tears that rolled down her cheeks, and tried not to cough as she inhaled the strong, stale perfume that emanated from the handkerchief. She remained fearful that Lavallier would appear at any moment, and knew that if he did then he would see off this old lady with little trouble, spinning her some yarn about an absconding daughter or servant and spiriting her off through the dark and threatening alleyways into the hold of a ship bound for the other side of the world.

What was the alternative? At least if she went with Old Phoebe she would be in her own county and able – if the old woman was to be trusted – to earn enough money to be able to afford her fare home. If the worst came to the worst, then she could always run away again. The thought filled her with a renewed sense of dread. But here she was, and there seemed little alternative; no respite at all from the fear that filled her heart and her bones.

'What would I have to do? To earn some money to pay for the coach back to Withercombe?'

'Just be nice. To my gentlemen.'

'But I've never—'

'No dear, of course you haven't. And Old Phoebe ain't the sort to make you do things against your will.' The old woman looked about her; she was becoming impatient now and seemed keen to be on her way. 'Make your mind up, dear, only I have things to do . . .'

For a brief moment, Anne considered declining the old woman's offer and continuing her journey through the busy streets of Portsmouth, but a gaggle of passing sailors, clearly the worse for rum, tumbled by at that moment. One of them grabbed at Anne's skirt and asked, 'Ready for a good time, lady? Better than the usual, aint ya?'

Phoebe put a protective arm around her new charge and swung at the tar with her stout parasol. The handle caught him smartly about the left ear and his companions fell about laughing at his misfortune.

'No need for that, you old bizzom,' retaliated the sailor, his face bearing a hurt expression. 'Just a polite inquiry . . .'

Anne looked at the old woman. 'All right then. But just for a short while. Until I get enough money . . .'

At this Old Phoebe smiled, the better to demonstrate her

benevolence and unique dental arrangement, and put her arm through that of her new charge. 'You just stick close, and we'll be there in two shakes of a sailor's leg, if you sees what I mean.' She looked Anne up and down as she bustled her across the square and down another alleyway. 'Nice dress, dear. We'll have to find you one or two more like that.'

Anne shot her a worried glance.

'Oh, don't you mind. You won't have to pay for them; we'll find one or two nice gentlemen who'll be only too happy to provide you with pretty clothes.'

'For being a lady's maid?' asked Anne hopefully.

'Of a sort, dear. Of a sort . . .' And their journey continued down alleyway after alleyway until Anne's head reeled with the sights and sounds and smells of a milieu that was as foreign to her as that on the other side of the world.

24

Mill Cottage, Itchen Parva
13 June 2010

To begin to live in the present, we must first atone for our past and
be finished with it, and we can only atone for it by suffering . . .
Anton Chekhov, The Cherry Orchard, 1904

Ordinarily, Harry did not mind when Rick turned up unan-
nounced; his presence gave a frisson to the day, insults a
speciality. Parrying them, while often irritating, sharpened his
wits. But when he arrived on the doorstep at 9 a.m. on the
Sunday, Harry was less than welcoming.

'Do you know what time it is? What day it is?'

'Yes to both.' Rick look strangely uncomfortable, as though
he were about to deliver some unwelcome news.

Noticing his friend's demeanour and regretting his initial
hastiness, Harry made to sound more welcoming. 'Come in
then. Coffee?'

Rick nodded. He was clearly preoccupied; his brow
furrowed, his manner distant.

'Are you all right?' asked Harry.

'Yes. I'm fine.' Rick made to sound more relaxed, but his
body language contradicted his efforts. 'What about you?'

'Couldn't be better,' responded Harry, as he held the kettle
under the tap.

'But you look as though you're about to deliver bad news . . .'

Rick shrugged. 'Sort of. Not exactly bad. Well, it could be,
but there's probably nothing in it.'

Harry looked concerned. 'Let me be the judge of that.'

Rick sat down at the kitchen table. Harry noticed that he was avoiding eye contact.

'Come on, then; out with it.'

'How's the lady next door?' asked Rick, looking up at last.

'Very well, thank you. Why do you ask?'

Rick reached into the inside pocket of his leather jacket and pulled out a large sheet of folded newsprint. 'You know that trunk I was telling you about; the one that my granddad kept, with all the stuff he hoarded about the family? Well, I thought I'd get it down and have a look at it.'

'And? Don't tell me you've finally taken an interest in your roots. I told you it was worth doing.'

Rick continued. 'I didn't really get very far. Grandpa clearly just put things in it when they cropped up, so the newer stuff is on the top.'

'That figures.'

'I started to work through them, and I found this.' He unfolded the sheet of newspaper and handed it to Harry.

At the top of the left-hand page was a picture of the Old Mill and below it were a few brief lines on its history, remarking that it had been in the Palfrey family for several generations until it had been sold to another family in the 1960s. Now it was on the market again for the first time in a generation. Harry checked the date of the clipping – 2008; two years ago. As well as showing a picture, it also listed the full particulars of the house.

'So when did your grandfather die?'

'Last year. I've only had the trunk a few months. Not really had a chance to go through it, to be honest. It was only you going on about it that made me go up to the attic and get it down.'

Harry made to hand the clipping back. 'There you are then – you're on the trail of your family history. Your granddad clearly knew all about it.'

'Yes. I suppose that's why he kept the clipping.' Rick did not take it from Harry's grasp. Instead he said, 'There's something else. On the other side.'

Harry turned over the page and, as he did so, felt his heart thump. There, in the centre, was a picture of Alex Overton on the steps of the Crown Court in Winchester, accompanied by two men in suits. The headline caused him to sit down in the chair next to Rick as he read: 'SOUTHAMPTON WOMAN CLEARED OF ASSISTING HUSBAND'S DEATH'.

Harry looked up. He was pale now. The colour had drained from his cheeks.

'I thought you ought to see it,' said Rick. 'I thought you ought to know.'

'Yes,' said Harry softly. 'Yes, of course.'

The dense silence was interrupted by the whistling of the kettle. It was Rick who got up from the table and poured the boiling water into the cafetière.

'You're not meant to let it boil,' murmured Harry.

'Just for now I don't think that's important. The important thing is that she was cleared.'

Harry looked up and held out the clipping. 'Would you read it to me? I don't think I can bring myself to . . .'

Rick took the newspaper clipping and read as levelly as he could:

'At Winchester Crown Court, the Hampshire lawyer Alexandra Templeton . . .' He looked up. 'She must have changed her name after the case . . . was today cleared of assisting in her husband James's suicide. Templeton (36), himself a lawyer, had been suffering from premature onset

Alzheimer's disease for two years. His death, from an overdose of sedatives, had been the subject of a police investigation in which his wife Alexandra (35) was accused of having aided his suicide. The Judge, Mr Justice Westmacott, in his summing up, said: "This was a sad case of a bright and intelligent man suffering from the cruellest of diseases and being cared for throughout by a wife for whom he had the highest regard and whose selfless attention to his needs was never less than admirable. From the evidence we have heard, I am confident that Mr Templeton decided to take his own life and that he was in no way assisted by the woman who had loved and cared for him, not only throughout the happy years of their marriage, but also towards the end of his life when Mr Templeton's health declined. He clearly felt that he could no longer be a burden upon his wife and family or upon society. His note to that effect would appear to be his own work and that of himself alone. There is no evidence to suggest that Mrs Templeton was in any way a party to her husband's taking of his own life. She leaves this court without any stain upon her character and has the deepest sympathy of those here today. This is a sad case that should, in my opinion, never have come to court. I can only hope that Mrs Templeton and her daughter can be allowed to continue their lives in peace and that in time the unfortunate and tragic circumstances of the past two years will be replaced in the collective consciousness of those involved by recollections of happier times, and that both Mrs Templeton and her daughter will, in the fullness of time, be able to face the future with optimism and, eventually, some happiness. This is a situation in which more and more of us find ourselves, and it behoves us all to treat such circumstances with sympathy and understanding."'

Rick carefully folded up the paper and laid it on the table.

For a few moments neither of them spoke, then Harry said, 'She was exonerated.'

'Totally. It could have happened to anybody. I just thought you ought to know.'

'But if she was clearly innocent, why did the case come to court?'

'I wondered about that. I asked my mum if she could remember anything about it. She said there was something about a neighbour who told the police that Alex had something to do with it.'

'Jealousy?'

Rick shrugged. 'Who knows?'

'But why didn't we know about it?' asked Harry. 'We don't live that far from Southampton?'

'Probably school holidays – we could both have been away. And it didn't make the nationals.'

Harry thought for a moment, then he asked, 'Why do you think your grandfather kept it?'

'It must have been just coincidence,' said Rick. 'I suppose it just happened to be on the other side of that piece about the family home. I mean, what else could it be? He wouldn't have known the Templetons. I imagine it just so happened that she was looking for a place – a move to the country, as it said – and the Old Mill came up at the same time. She'd have had enough money from her husband's estate to buy it, presumably, and she wouldn't want to hang around in Southampton where everybody knew her, would she?'

'I suppose not.' Harry looked as though the weight of the world were upon his shoulders.

'I didn't show it to you to worry you, or to make you feel any differently towards her. I just thought you ought to know, that was all.'

Harry ran his hand through his hair and leaned back in his chair. 'It's a bit of a jolt, that's all.'

Rick poured the coffee into two mugs. 'She hasn't mentioned it, obviously?'

'Well, no,' said Harry. 'It's not the sort of thing you go around advertising to someone you've only known a couple of weeks, is it?'

'No.'

'And, anyway, there's no reason why she should. She was exonerated. Cleared of any involvement.'

Rick stirred in two sugars. 'There were obviously some who weren't convinced, I suppose; which accounts for the move and the change of name.'

'Are you saying—?'

'No. No! Just thinking out loud, really. Just concerned for you.'

'Well, don't be.'

Rick took a sip of coffee and then asked, 'Do you think it's her maiden name – Overton – or just one she picked at random?'

'How should I know?' Harry's voice was louder now and his manner more assertive. 'I'm sure she'll tell me when she's good and ready. Until then . . .' He threw his hands in the air and looked questioningly at Rick.

Rick got up to go. 'Yes; well, I'm taking Tilly to see *Mary Poppins The Musical* this afternoon; Rachel's off playing tennis.'

Harry looked at him incredulously.

'S'what fathers have to do,' said Rick. 'See you later. And . . . I'm sorry. You know . . .'

Sheepishly he closed the door behind him, leaving Harry with thoughts as confused and tangled as the garden that ran down to the banks of the river.

25

72 Godolphin Street, Portsmouth
16 April 1816

If a man be gracious and courteous to strangers, it shows he is
a citizen of the world.

Francis Bacon, *Essays*, 1625

The doorway was not, at first, obvious. It opened off a side
street some way from the smart square where Old Phoebe
had encountered her newest prospect. Anne was confused
and frightened. Torn between running off and encountering
the menacing Lavallier once more, and committing herself to
the charge of the old woman of dubious repute, she was
endeavouring to convince herself that she had little choice but
to follow the kindlier of the two, though deep down she knew
that this, too, was a risky prospect.

But what could she do? Withercombe was over thirty miles
distant. Was that far? It certainly seemed so. The coach had
managed it in just a few hours, but on foot? And in the clothing she wore? She chastised herself for being feeble. She was
not feeble; she had reserves of courage – that's what they were
called in the book she had been reading. The book. What had
happened to the book? She must have dropped it when she
was changing by the riverbank. It was too late to worry about
it now. But she had needed every ounce of her courage to run
away and she had not hesitated, had she? Well, only a little.
Why could she now not just say 'goodbye' to the old woman,
thank her for her trouble and be on her way? But which way?

In which direction was Withercombe? And how would she pay for refreshment without a farthing to her name? And then they were at the doorway of the shabby house and Old Phoebe was pushing her up the three steps into the gloomy interior. She began to be fearful. Old Phoebe read the signs and made to reassure her: 'Worry not, my dear. It may not be as grand as the house you have been accustomed to, but we are very welcoming at number seventy-two.'

The old woman cleared her throat extravagantly and then called out, 'Mr Pontifex! Where are you, Mr P? New visitor to meet you.'

Old Phoebe pushed Anne before her into the gloomy passage, past other curtained doorways, and as they neared the end of it, a small head peeped out around a dusty crimson swag of velvet. It was bordered by black velour pom-poms which fringed the face of a man with elfin features and made him look like something from a travelling sideshow. For a moment Anne wanted to laugh out loud, but fear overcame her once more as she beheld this strange, goblin-like creature.

'Mr Pontifex, this is Anne.'

Mr Pontifex brushed aside the curtain and stepped out into the hallway. In the half-light Anne could see that he had an angular and crooked body and was quite unable to stand upright. It was as though his entire frame had been twisted like a stem of honeysuckle around a hazel branch. His head was a shiny pale dome, fringed by wispy white hair, and his nose was pointed. Anne half expected his ears to be pointed, too. Had she been back at Withercombe, she and Sam would have been amused at this odd, gnome-like creature, but here, in these strange and intimidating surroundings, she found herself unable to speak.

'Ah! Hello!' said the goblin. For a moment he uttered

nothing more; just looked Anne up and down with great curiosity. Old Phoebe broke in on both their thoughts.

'This is Anne. Lost, I'm afraid, and without any means of getting home. So, Mr Pontifex, I took her in. Offered her shelter and sustenance before she heads off on her way back to . . . where did you say it was, dear?'

'Wither—'

'Somewhere in Hampshire,' cut in Old Phoebe, clearly not in the least concerned as to the precise identity of Anne's domicile.

'Do you think we can look after her, Mr P?'

The little man smiled and Anne saw that he had even fewer teeth than Old Phoebe. 'Of course!' he croaked in a voice as squeaky as the hinge on the farm gate. 'Nothing easier!' His eyes did not leave Anne, and his bony hand reached out towards her. She flinched a little as he took the fabric of her dress between his fingers. 'Nice; very nice.' Then he looked at Anne questioningly. 'Your own gown?'

'Yes,' replied Anne, hastily. Then she hesitated, before reaffirming, 'Yes.' The wisdom of telling the truth at this moment was something about which she was uncertain.

Pontifex nodded. 'I see. Only you don't sound . . .' He shrugged, deciding for whatever reason not to pursue his line of questioning. Then he brightened. 'Refreshment – that is what you will be requiring. After your long and tiring day.'

Anne did not like to say that it must have only been midday, since it did, indeed, seem to have been hours since she had slept, eaten or drunk.

'Follow me, Miss Anne . . . this way.' He led the way further down the passage and ushered Anne through another curtain doorway into some kind of back parlour. As they entered, Old Phoebe slipped the complicated fox fur from her shoulders and unpeeled her net gloves. 'Yes,' she confirmed, 'we have had a bit of a morning of it, Mr P. Muffins and porter if you please.'

At this Pontifex raised his eyebrows and muttered, 'Bread and porter with pleasure,' and scuttled out through another door.

'You just sit down and make yourself at home, dear, while Old Phoebe changes into her house clothes, yes?'

Anne said nothing but perched on the end of an overstuffed chaise longue as the old woman swept out after Mr Pontifex and left her to take in her surroundings.

It was not a large room, but it had tall windows in the end wall; windows that were masked by several layers of unmatching fabric, each drawn up into a swag with a generous array of tassels. The drapes reduced to a great degree the amount of light that filtered in, but Anne could still make out the main features of the room that seemed filled to bursting with furniture and artefacts. The walls were hung with large pictures – not like those at the Manor House: oil paintings of Sir Thomas's ancestors, and scenes of hunting and fishing – but pictures of young ladies whose pale bodies were draped with translucent muslin or clad in chemises like those worn by the fine young ladies who occasionally visited the Manor House with Master Edward and Master Frederick. They were reclining at ease on sofas very much like the one upon which Anne found herself sitting.

Tall stands, enveloped in heavy but threadbare squares of velvet, carried potted palms with browning fronds, not nearly as lush as those in Sir Thomas's hothouse; and chairs and tables, none of them matching, were dotted in haphazard fashion about the room, which was peppered with candlesticks of brass and mahogany. An abundance of shawls seemed to have been strewn at random over every stick of furniture to disguise its humble origins. The overall effect was one of grubby and rather pretentious gentility. Anne's first thought was that she would have felt the sharp edge of Mrs Fitzgerald's tongue had she left any of the rooms in the Manor House in this deplorable state. Even the ashes had not been cleared from the grate in the black iron fireplace. Perhaps that would be one of her first jobs.

Mr Pontifex and Old Phoebe had been gone for several minutes now. Anne's anxiety continued to build and she took deep breaths of the sour-smelling air to try and clear her head.

A night. She would stay for one night only. Maybe two. Quietly, without meeting anyone but Old Phoebe and Mr Pontifex. She would do some cleaning and washing – clear the grates and shake out the dusty rugs here and in the other rooms of the house. She would stay just long enough to raise the money for her coach fare. Then she would return with haste to the Manor House, hoping that they would forgive her foolhardiness and that Mrs Fitzgerald would consider that the events she had endured were enough to have brought her to her senses and that there was no need to scold her further. She realised now that it had been a mistake. She was not at all ready to leave her present life and seek adventure. The first taste of it had been enough to convince her that her lowly role was sufficient for her needs – for a little longer, anyhow. What was the point in being a lady's maid when it led to folly like this?

Then she thought of Eleanor lying by the stream, and her eyes began to fill with tears. She was almost the same age, still alive, while Eleanor – where was Eleanor now? They must have found her, surely? Noticed that she was wearing Anne's clothes. What must they have thought? Sir Thomas would have been told. And Eleanor's father. It was all so horrible. How could they possibly know the truth: that it was all a dreadful accident and that she – Anne the scullery maid – did not really mean it to happen? She had simply been swept along by it all. It was only because she wanted to be a lady's maid that these disasters had occurred. She had gone into it with a spring in her step and excitement filling her heart, but now it had all ended. Her life had changed forever, and all in a matter of a few hours.

She remembered Lavallier and the way he had looked at her; the menace in his eyes. It made her shiver. She was not certain of the present time of day or of when he was due to embark upon his voyage, but she knew that if she stayed here with Old Phoebe for a single night that he was certain to have boarded his ship and sailed for wherever he was bound. Tomorrow she could safely walk the streets again, discover the times of coaches to Withercombe . . . no, not Withercombe – the coaches did not stop at Withercombe. She would take the coach to Winchester, she remembered now. From there she would have to walk. But in which direction? Again, with a stab of anguish, she realised just how little she knew of the wider world. She knew neither where she was nor how to return from whence she had come. Her life, to date, had been bound up with the Manor House, with Sam and Mrs Fitzgerald, and now here she was, sitting on a dusty sofa in a strange and oppressive room in a frightening city whose noise and bustle, mood and manner caused her to be bewildered and fearful in equal measure.

'Here we are then.'

Anne started at the interruption to her thoughts. Mr Pontifex had re-entered the room, bearing a wooden tray upon which sat three small pewter tankards and three slabs cut from a loaf of bread. A curled lump of ochre-coloured cheese and a knife accompanied them.

Old Phoebe followed in his wake. The fox fur and layers of shawls had been replaced now by a voluminous amber-coloured cloak of faded silk that enveloped her like a shroud. It had puff sleeves that made its inhabitant look even more voluptuous, and upon her head sat a mobcap of black lace. Her cheeks were freshly rouged, her beauty spots as black as pitch, and she seemed to float upon a vapour of stale roses.

'Luncheon!' she exclaimed, greeting the arrival of the bread and cheese and porter with a level of enthusiasm that Sir Thomas would have reserved for his eight-course dinner on Christmas Eve.

Anne looked up at the two of them – the woman appearing in a vision before her like some extravagantly decorated cottage loaf, and the man who seemed to be nothing more than a dried-up spider. As his bony hand reached out towards her, proffering the foaming tankard of porter, she wanted more than anything to leap up from her seat and dash down the passageway and out of the door. Instead, her hunger and thirst overrode all other sensibilities. She took from the beaming spider the tankard, and drained its contents in one. A feeling of warmth immediately enveloped her and she managed a weak smile in the direction of the plump old woman.

'Bread and cheese, dear?' asked Phoebe. 'Got to get your strength up, haven't we?'

26

Mill Cottage, Itchen Parva

13 June 2010

Three things are not to be trusted; a cow's horn, a dog's tooth and a horse's hoof.

Fourteenth-century proverb

Harry had seriously thought about calling Alex and coming up with some excuse to avoid their spending Sunday together. The prospect of an entire day with her – a prospect which, the night before, had seemed so full of promise after many barren months in terms of female company – left him feeling ill at ease. Should he bring the subject up? Would she be aware that he knew? Had she assumed all along that he had known about it and just been too polite to say anything?

He had the phone in his hand at one point, but put it down again, cursing himself for his lack of faith in her. But it wasn't that. Or was it? Did he trust her? What business was it of his? Well, quite a lot, actually, if he was going to make something of this relationship. How could he go into it unsure of whether or not the object of his affections had helped her husband to kill himself? The judge seemed pretty sure she had not. And even if she had, she would have done so on compassionate grounds. Wasn't it more cruel to watch someone you loved, who wanted to die, sitting there suffering day after day?

No. He could not go there. He would have to trust his instincts: Alex was the one person he had met since his separation from Serena with whom he felt totally at ease. Not partially, not just a bit, but totally, completely and utterly. Truly, madly, deeply. Stupidly. He chastised himself for allowing himself to fall for her so heavily in the space of a couple of weeks. But he had fallen. He knew he had, in those moments when he dared to be honest with himself. He could not even remember feeling quite this consumed by his feelings for another person, even with Serena. Oh, he was bowled over by her – entranced by her *joie de vivre* and freedom from care. He had thought himself in love, but perhaps it was just infatuation. And yet it seemed futile to make comparisons: disrespectful to his own emotions and to those of others. How easy it was to find excuses for earlier behaviour through the safe distance of elapsed time, to let oneself off the hook by assuming that the passage of the years automatically granted greater wisdom.

Whatever else he felt about Alex, there was a deep and underlying respect. But why? In so short a space of time? He tried to analyse his feelings – knowing all the while that it was pointless to do so, and yet needing to explore, to divine what was at the root of his . . . admiration for her. For that is what it was. He admired her determination, her generosity of spirit, her relationship with her daughter. Her taste. They seemed to like the same things. She didn't even blench when he mentioned his interest in tracing his ancestry or the lives of the saints and that, surely, was the supreme test. If a woman like Alex could cope with an aspiring anorak like him, then she had to be little short of an angel. If she had any faults, what were they? That she was too friendly? Too ready to strike up a relationship? But then, after what she had been through, wasn't she as desperate as he was, underneath, to find someone to share things with?

Desperate: that dreadful word. So damning, so . . . desperately true. His thoughts went round in circles: if she had helped her husband, didn't it prove that she was someone who cared, who minded, who wanted to do her best for whoever she was with? Even if that meant helping them to die? He wanted to banish such thoughts. These were not the sort of emotions that should be occupying him this early in a relationship. He should stop brooding. Call her and ask her what she wanted to do; when she wanted to meet. To ring her now and call it off would not only be distrustful, it would be cowardly.

Anyway, he would not call her on the phone. He would go round.

It was eleven o'clock. He found her down at the bottom of her garden, sitting in an old canvas chair on the banks of the chalk stream, gazing at the water. For a moment she did not see him, and he looked at her, sitting there in the June sunshine with a white cotton skirt that she had pulled up to expose her shapely legs to the early summer sunshine. She wore a simple navy blue vest that flattered her curves and he felt, again, that flip in the pit of his stomach. Her dark hair shone in the dappled light filtered by the overhanging osiers.

She seemed to be miles away, cradling the mug between her hands and staring into the clear depths of the gently rippling stream. He hardly wanted to break the spell; instead to stand watching her for hours. To be invisible; to be in her company without her knowing. To watch her and know her movements until they became as familiar to him as his own. To admire the curve of her neck, the fall of her hair, the deftness of her fingers.

And then a moorhen called – a loud 'chook' that rang through the still morning air – and at the same time a twig snapped under his foot. She turned and saw him and smiled. 'I wondered whether you would be up yet,' she said. And he knew then that whatever had been before did not matter. Somehow, for some reason, it could all be explained. There would be a reason, a good reason; and on this sunny Sunday morning, the best thing of all was that he was here with her in a part of the world that he loved and which had somehow welcomed him home.

She made him lunch – a simple affair of pâté and crusty bread, fresh strawberries and local cheese. He opened a bottle of muscat brought from his tiny cellar. 'Too sweet,' she said with a glint in her eye as she saw the label.

'Just right for summer days,' he countered, and when she tasted it she knew he was right. He lowered it into the water at the stream's edge to keep it cool, and when they had lunched and finished the bottle, they wandered indoors and up to her bedroom. It seemed the most natural thing in the world. There was no nervousness, no fear of each other's bodies. The ease that was so in evidence when they talked was mirrored in their love-making – gentle and tender. For some while afterwards, they lay in each other's arms, the dormer window open, letting in the sounds of birdsong and gently whispering willow wands.

She turned to him and smiled. 'I wouldn't want you to think I did this with every man I meet,' she said.

27

72 Godolphin Street, Portsmouth
16 April 1816

Change in a trice
The lilies and languors of virtue
For the raptures and roses of vice.
Algernon Charles Swinburne,
'Dolores', 1866

The room that Old Phoebe had shown Anne into was a small affair on the fourth floor of the narrow house in Godolphin Street, reached by ever narrowing stairs; so narrow that the old woman had a deal of difficulty in forcing herself up them. When they reached the room, Phoebe exercised a neat minuet with Anne upon the modest-sized landing to allow her guest to enter the room ahead of her. There would have been little chance of them both occupying it at the same time.

'You rest here a while and wash off the cares of the day,' she had instructed. Adding, 'I shall be back in a little while.'

It was still light outside, but the multitude of drapes across the casement cast the space into a deep gloom. It was sparsely furnished: a chest of drawers over which yet another fringed shawl was thrown was topped by a china basin and ewer. This was clearly where Anne was meant to 'wash off the cares of the day', but the water had a brown colour to it and Anne thought the better of any contact with it. Behind it hung a small and clouded-looking glass.

A hard button-backed chair was pushed into a corner and,

from where she sat on the brass bedstead, Anne could see that the bottom had come away and that brown horsehair was falling out of it. Two wooden candlesticks, perched on the mantelpiece of the small cast-iron fireplace, added to what little light there was, and their flickering flames made frightening shadows on the wall. The room smelt musty, as though it had not been aired for years. Mrs Fitzgerald would not approve of such neglect. The dust beneath the bed was almost half an inch thick, and the counterpane that covered it was clearly a stranger to the laundry. It was stained and there were burn marks upon it, as though someone had been carelessly smoking a pipe while reclining. Anne's ministrations would clearly be needed in this room as well.

She glanced up at the piece of crude needlepoint hung in a mahogany frame over the bed, and read it out loud under her breath: 'Yea, the sparrow hath found her an house, and the swallow a nest where she may lay her young.' It seemed a strange sort of sentiment and it made Anne shiver. She did not like to remove any clothing, but her feet were aching now so she untied and slipped off her boots and rubbed her toes with her hands to improve the circulation. Eventually some kind of feeling returned to them, and almost simultaneously she realised how tired she was. Exhausted by the day's emotions and the fear they had struck into her heart, she pulled up the hood of the cloak she still wore so that it covered the back of her head, then lay back upon the lumpy palliasse. She had not eaten since the slice of bread and cheese she had had for breakfast – that offered by Mr Pontifex had looked far from appetising and she had politely declined to partake of such dubious nourishment. Plain though the kitchen fare was at the Manor House, Mrs Fitzgerald had always prided herself on the fact that it was wholesome and fresh. Any that was not went straight down to the pigsties. The memories of her former life – the life that was yesterday – came flooding back to her. But the tankard of porter that she drank so eagerly to slake her thirst had made her drowsy. She struggled now to keep her eyes from closing. Soon the room faded from view and she was lost in a deep but fitful sleep.

It was, she imagined, only several minutes later that she awoke. Surely no more. For a few moments she could not recall where she was, but then, with a fearful dawning, she remembered what had happened. Her head seemed to be filled with some kind of fog, and her bones ached, but the sleep, although uneven, had replenished some of her strength. She sat up on the bed and blinked repeatedly, the better to focus her vision. The candles still flickered on the mantelpiece, but they were slightly taller now than they had been when she had fallen asleep.

She looked down at her body and started. It was no longer clothed in the soft pink dress that had been Eleanor's, but in a loose-fitting chemise, topped with a threadbare silken gown – a more modestly cut version than that worn by Old Phoebe when she had shown her up to her room.

Quickly she slipped from the bed and crossed to the looking glass. Fuzzy though the reflection was, she could see that her hair had been rearranged and tied in place with a ribbon. She put up her hand to feel the bow, as though she could not rely on her vision alone to convince her of the transformation. Her cheeks looked pink and her lips were a darker shade of red than normal. Her heart beat loudly in her chest now. Who had done this to her, and why? Then everything that Mrs Fitzgerald had warned her about – when she was admonished for her ambitions to flee her position and escape to another grand house as a lady's maid – came flooding back to her. She sat down heavily on the bed, with the dawning realisation that it was unlikely that she would be expected to dress like this if Old Phoebe and Mr Pontifex had wanted her to empty the grate and polish the furniture.

Unbidden, a phrase from *The Highwayman's Bride* came into her mind: 'In the bawdy house he had his wicked way with her.' Her heart was beating rapidly now. While never completely sure what 'his wicked way' would be, Anne felt certain that it was not something that she would enjoy, neither was it something that she was in any way ready to experience. Then the images of Moll Hackabout in Sir Thomas's library came flooding back to her. Was this what she looked like? Was this about to happen to her? She had never really wanted to be a highwayman's bride; she knew it was all a silly dream that simply thrilled her when she read about it. And she was certain that she did not want to be – she hardly dared even think the word – 'a harlot'.

She dashed towards the basin and found herself retching into it. Then she sat down upon the bed again and mopped the edges of her mouth with a small square of linen she found beside the basin. How could she have been so foolish as to have come here? What did she imagine that Old Phoebe and Mr Pontifex wanted of her, other than that she would be expected to . . . she fought to avoid putting into words the thoughts that swam around in her head.

But she was aware of sounds now. The house that had once been so quiet seemed now to echo with distant murmurings. They were not the voices of the old man and woman. They were younger voices; voices with more energy and vigour, both male and female. And the house now somehow smelled differently. There was a sweetness to the air which she had not registered on first arriving. A sickly, smoky vapour that seemed to envelop everything and which made her feel light-headed. And then there were footsteps upon the wooden stairs outside her room. A single pair of footsteps. Silence descended again. Anne breathed heavily, wondering what could possibly happen next. After a few moments, she saw the tarnished brass knob turn, and the door of her room began to open.

As it swung wide she had a clear view of her visitor. The figure who stood before her, a glass in his hand and a smile on his lips, caused her heart to leap.

'Well, well,' he said softly. 'If it is not Anne Flint.'

28

Mill Cottage, Itchen Parva
19 June 2010

I long to talk with some old lover's ghost,
Who died before the god of love was born.
John Donne, 'Love's Deity', 1633

It was a decision taken by both of them the previous Sunday evening, that to live too much in each other's pockets at first would not be a good thing. Not so much for them – their own total comfort in each other's company left no room for doubt and, with one reservation on Harry's side, they were as sure of each other as they could be. No. It was for Anne, whose own world had been troubled enough by her father's death two years ago. At last she was now beginning to enjoy some semblance of order and stability in her seven-year-old life and that, they both agreed, was something that must be preserved, even if it meant taking their own developing relationship at a slower pace. At this point Harry was on the verge of clearing up the one area of unease in his mind and raising the subject of James Templeton's death, but the moment passed and he let it go. Why spoil a perfect weekend asking questions that did not yet need to be asked. That bridge would be crossed eventually, but there seemed to be no valid reason why it should happen today.

His school week had passed by uneventfully, with Palmer and his cronies being no more obnoxious than usual, and from here he could begin to see light at the end of the tunnel. The end of term was but a month away by now and, for the first time in many months, he began to feel quite excited about the prospect of his new life. There were other things to think about, rather than just his family tree. As yet he was not sure what they were, but in their nebulous form they occupied his mind and gave him a feeling of well-being. Admitting to himself that they amounted to his being in love was something he pushed to the back of his mind, for no other reason than that he did not want to spoil the moment by over-analysis. He rather liked this floaty feeling; it had been some time since he had experienced it, and the sensation had a degree of novelty but also, he suspected, fragility.

On this rather cloudy Saturday morning, Alex and Anne had promised to keep out of his hair while he set about the one bit of house reorganisation that he had decided was necessary. The upstairs bathroom was at the end of the landing and, should he ever have guests, the inevitable meeting on the landing with sponge bag and towel could be avoided only if he made a doorway into the bathroom from his own bedroom and fitted a bolt to both that and the outer door. That way he would have what amounted to an en-suite arrangement, but on leaving he could slip back the bolt of the door to the landing to show that the bathroom was vacant. It seemed a simple enough job; the wall was not load-bearing. All he would need to do was knock out a portion of the lath and plaster wall, insert a new doorway, plaster around it and fit another door. Simple. But filthy. And in the small space where there was barely room to swing a cat, it was something that he would have to do alone.

He had sheeted up the passageway and all other doorways so that he was cocooned in the bathroom itself. Having pinned up a sheet on the opposite side of the wall to prevent the bedroom being filled with dust, he opened the bathroom window to let in much needed fresh air, and then hacked away at the old wall, its brittle plasterwork tumbling in great clods on to the dust sheets below. Having taken the trouble to invest in a face mask and goggles, the resulting discomfort was not as bad as he feared, but the combination of lime and horsehair filled the air with a fine dust that seemed for a while every bit as impenetrable as fog.

Through the gloom he heard a voice calling. 'Bye Harry!' For a few moments he was encircled by plaster dust, having given the wall a particularly hefty bash, and could not answer. It would be Alex and Anne, saying goodbye on their way to the village fete. They would understand if he didn't respond. Right now he could not get to the window due to a particularly strong lath that was bent out of the wall and to which he was taking his saw. When he did finally squeeze past and glance down at the path, looking like Toad, in his goggles, there was no sign of them. Ah well, they would be back that afternoon, to regale him with stories of their day. With a light heart he continued his chipping away at the plaster and sawing on the unwanted laths. Perhaps he might find a note, or an old newspaper. But then he had had enough of old newspapers for the time being. He need not have worried: his DIY yielded nothing more exciting than the skeleton of a long-dead mouse and a few desiccated bluebottles.

Slowly the opening grew in size and, once he had reached the lines that he had drawn on the wall to mark its outline, he stopped and laid down his hammer and chisel. There it was: a new doorway. Strange how different it made the two rooms look; his bedroom appeared larger now, and so did the bathroom. With great ceremony he stepped from one to the other and then back again, several times, as if to convince himself that he really had achieved his aim.

He went downstairs to get a breath of fresh air and to make

a cup of coffee. As he crossed the kitchen he saw them coming down the garden path – Alex and Anne. The child waved, and Alex shouted: 'We won't disturb you; we're just off. See you this afternoon.'

And with a smile that melted his heart yet again, the two of them turned and walked hand in hand down the path and out into the lane.

By lunchtime he had managed to fit the new jamb in place and to plaster around it. He congratulated himself on both his speed and the efficiency of the job, running his hand up and down the new timber with pride. He would not hang the door today; he would do that when the plaster had gone off properly and the whole thing had settled. He had taken the old plaster, and the laths, down into a corner of the garden, carrying them in an old tin bath. Now he would clean up properly, though he knew that for days, and maybe weeks, there would still be dust settling on furniture and on every surface.

As he folded up the last dust sheet and made to go downstairs to make coffee, from out of the corner of his eye he caught sight of a figure walking up the stairs. They must have come back early. But when he turned there was no sign of anything. He shook his head. It must have been a speck of plaster in his eye.

Down by the chalk stream, the fresh air was especially welcoming. He opened a bottle of beer and sat down on the grassy bank. He would lunch alone today, down here, and think about them. But his reverie was broken by a voice he had not heard for some weeks.

'Can I come down? Are you at home to visitors?' Harry swung round and saw the figure of Pattie Chieveley, gamely picking her way between the dog roses that threatened at every moment to remove her clothing.

'Hello!' Harry was genuinely pleased to see her.

'You haven't been round for a while, so I thought that if the mountain couldn't come to Muhammad . . .'

Harry rose to his feet and went to greet her. 'I'm sorry; I've been so tied up with . . . this place and—'

'I know, dear; don't you worry. I quite understand.'

Harry put his arms around her and gave her a big hug.

'Oh, careful dear, I'm not as strong as I was.'

Harry grinned. 'You? You're as strong as—'

'Now don't say "as strong as an ox", dear, or I'll begin to think that Ted's home cooking is beginning to take its toll.'

'Ted? Cooking? Are you serious?'

Pattie smiled, and then Harry noticed that her eyes had filled with tears.

'Hey! What's the matter?' Without waiting for an answer he put his arm around Pattie's shoulders and led her back up to the garden, sitting her down in a comfortable chair by the kitchen table.

'There you are. Would you like a coffee?' he asked. 'Or something stronger?'

'Coffee would be fine, dear, thank you.'

Harry went about the coffee-making quietly, casting a glance at Pattie now and then, but unwilling to press her.

After a few moments she said, 'Well you've made it very nice, Harry. Very cosy.'

'Do you think?'

'Oh, yes. Most men are not very good at "cosy". They can do "macho" – is that what they call it? Masculine. But not cosy. In a masculine sort of way.'

Harry grinned. 'I'll take that as a compliment.'

'You should be very pleased with yourself. And you haven't been here very long at all, have you?'

'Three weeks.'

'Gosh,' said Pattie. 'What a lot you've accomplished in three weeks.'

'Yes,' murmured Harry. 'What a lot . . .'

Pattie noticed the preoccupied look. 'I won't keep you,' she said, sipping her coffee.

Harry came back down to earth. 'No. I mean, don't worry. It's lovely to see you and I'm not doing anything in particular – not now. I've just finished knocking through a doorway upstairs. From the bedroom to the bathroom.'

'Oh?'

'So that – you know – if I have guests . . . well, a guest, we don't have that . . .'

'Polite "after you" on the landing?' asked Pattie.

'Exactly.'

'Just like you,' she said. 'Very thoughtful.'

'I try,' said Harry. 'But enough about me and my house. How are you . . . and Ted?'

'Oh, muddling on, you know.' And once more she began to look troubled.

'Is everything all right?'

'Not really.'

Harry said nothing, but looked at the rather crumpled old lady sitting in front of him. Pattie did not really do 'crumpled'. Or 'old'. She was a woman of advanced years but one who kept herself in pretty good order and whose general demeanour was perky rather than world-weary.

'Is it Ted?' asked Harry.

Pattie nodded.

'Not well?'

'It was gradual at first. I mean, when you last saw him, what . . . a couple of months ago . . . he was all right, most of the time. Just occasional lapses . . .'

'Lapses?'

'Of memory. A bit forgetful. He'd go to the fridge and stand with the door open wondering whether he was there to put something in or take something out.'

'Well, I do that,' said Harry.

'It's got worse. Sometime he sits in his chair and he's clearly . . . well, somewhere else.'

'Do you think it's anything to worry about? I mean, anything serious?'

'I'm afraid so.' Pattie took another sip of coffee. 'He's been for tests. He doesn't know what for – just that they were routine; you know, a check-up. Something that all men his age have to go through.'

'And?'

'The doctor called me in on my own the following day. He's suffering from dementia. He's got Alzheimer's disease.'

Harry sat down beside her thinking 'not another' but asking, 'What's the prognosis?'

Pattie turned away and looked out of the window towards the garden. 'Not good. I have to keep a close eye on him.'

'So you can still leave him at home on his own?'

'Sometimes. He can be fine for a while – often for a few days at a time – and then he'll just be . . . well . . . sort of absent. Somewhere else in his head. He'll sit in his chair and not really be with me. He mutters, too. Things I can't make out. Says things that bear no relation to what we have been talking about. Inconsequential things.'

'Do you think you can carry on looking after him?'

'For now. While he's like this. But they've warned me that

he might change quite quickly. That his behaviour will be different.'

'In what way?'

'Well, they've said he might become violent, and if he does that . . . he'll have to go into a home because I won't be able to manage him.' Pattie finally dissolved into tears. 'Oh dear, Harry; forty-seven years we've been married and it has to end like this . . .'

Harry put his arm around her shoulders and gently rocked her as she sobbed. 'Oh, Pattie. If there's anything I can do . . .'

Pattie lifted her head. 'I don't think there's anything anyone can do. It's just one of those things. But the saddest thing of all is that the Ted I know is gradually disappearing, and one day he'll be gone altogether.' She managed a brave smile. 'You've no idea how dreadful that is, Harry. No idea at all.'

29

The Old Mill, Itchen Parva
19 June 2010

Like many of the Upper Class
He liked the sound of Broken Glass.
Hilaire Belloc, 'About John', *New
Cautionary Tales*, 1930

'You know, he really was a prick!'

Harry was surprised at Alex's outburst, especially since Anne was within earshot.

'Who was?'

'That Carew bloke. The one who goes around in his Range Rover as though he owns the place.'

'I've seen it parked outside his house. It's not a Range Rover, it's a Porsche Cayenne.'

'Well, there you are: even worse then.'

'And he does own the place – well, a few cottages. And the bit of land the fete was on.'

'Just because some distant ancestor used to live in the Manor House here – when we had one, it doesn't mean that he can stomp around the place like . . . like . . . Lord Muck.'

Harry handed Alex a glass of red wine and tried to suppress a smile. 'Why so angry though?'

'Because he backed into me and then told me it was my fault for being so close.'

'Oh, I see.'

'And now I shall need a new headlight and all he got was a scratch on his Range Rover's—'

'Porsche's—'

'Porsche's bumper! Stupid little—'

Harry cleared his throat and nodded in the direction of Anne who was having a particularly in-depth conversation about the afternoon's events with Mr Moses.

Alex stopped mid-tirade.

Harry looked at her and grinned.

She took a playful swipe at him with her free hand and said, 'Oh, I'm sorry. What a waste of energy. Stupid man – no wonder he's divorced. Who could put up with that sort of attitude?'

'Oh, in my experience there are some women who are quite drawn to it . . .'

'Well, I'm not one of them. And another thing . . . oh, sorry. I'm just cross about my headlight, that's all.'

'So tell me about this, er . . .' He lowered his voice and mouthed the word 'prick'. 'I've seen him driving through the village but I don't know much about him.'

'He's some distant relative of the old lord of the manor.'

'Didn't know we had one.'

'We don't any more. Or a manor house. But there used to be one – at Withercombe. There's nothing much there now, except a few old cottages.'

'So what happened to the manor house?'

'There was a big fire there in the 1950s.'

'Destroyed?'

'Not completely; but that was the time when nobody wanted rambling old houses and so they pulled the rest of it down. Used the stone to build a lot of local walls. The one outside my front garden was built from it.'

'I wonder if there's any in my garden?'

'Oh, I shouldn't think so. You're house isn't smart enough.'

Harry shot her a look, then saw the smile stretching across Alex's face. 'Cheeky blighter,' he countered. 'Anyway, tell me about this . . . er . . . merchant banker.'

Alex flopped on to the sofa and Harry perched on the arm of the one opposite. 'Sir Miles Carew?'

'Sir Miles eh? Very "lord of the manor".'

'Funnily enough I think he is a merchant banker. The real sort. Works in the city anyway. Has one of those new houses outside Alresford – you know, on the Cheriton Road.'

'Smart.'

'Showy,' retorted Alex.

'That sort, is he?'

'Oh, you know. Bit of a hooray Henry. Not that there's anything wrong with that. Some hooray Henrys are quite fun, but he just throws his weight about. The rumour is that he claimed the title through some legal wrangle. It didn't come straight to him. Anyway, that's just gossip, and I really don't care for that.'

Alex looked thoughtful for a moment, as though she were admonishing herself for saying such a thing, then she continued, 'But he's not very nice to people. Old Mrs Smart went up to him with a collecting tin for the local hospice and he pretended he didn't have any money on him.'

'Maybe he didn't.'

'Well, five minutes later I saw him buying his son who's home from Eton or Harrow or somewhere, a pile of cheap DVDs from one of the stalls.'

'Now there's nothing wrong with Eton or Harrow. I know of some very nice prime ministers who went there.'

'No, but there's something wrong with you if you can send

your son there and can't spare an old lady a fiver for a good cause.'

'Very true.'

'He's unkind. And he's just . . . well, when he looks at you he's one of those who seems to be undressing you, you know?'

'Oh dear.'

'And he never looks you in the eye; always talks to your breasts.'

Harry spluttered on his wine and stood up. 'If there's a red wine stain on your sofa now, it was your fault,' he said, mopping at his chin with his sleeve. 'Anyway, how was Anne?' He looked across at the child, still deep in conversation with her stuffed dog. 'Did she have a good time?'

'Yes,' said Alex, and for the first time her voice sounded more relaxed. 'She just loves animals, and there were lots of them there – chickens and quail; even alpacas and sheep. Oh, and the local beagle pack. All she wants now is a real Mr Moses . . .'

'Maybe you should get her one.'

'With her at school all day and me out at the day centre? I know it's not full time, but the dog would be here on its own a lot and that wouldn't be fair.'

'I could look after it.'

Anne looked up. 'I said that Harry wouldn't mind.'

Alex looked across at the girl and frowned. 'I thought you were playing with Mr Moses.'

'I am. But I can still hear.'

Alex looked at Harry with a long-suffering expression. 'What am I to do?'

Anne cut in. 'Let me have a dog.'

'One day, sweetheart, but not just yet. Let's get a bit more settled and work out what we want and how we can look after it.'

'But if Harry can help . . .'

'Harry has only just moved in and it wouldn't be very fair if we asked him to look after our dog straight away, would it?'

Harry made to protest but, before he could say anything, Alex had put a finger to his lips and raised her eyebrows in warning. 'Maybe one day,' she said.

'Soon?' asked Anne.

'In a while.'

The child sighed and went back to playing with Mr Moses.

'Anyway, how did your day go? Do you have an en-suite bathroom now?'

'Well, I have a hole in a wall. A very neat hole, but just a hole. En suite sounds a bit grand for a cottage.'

'Can we come and look?'

'Of course.'

Alex turned to Anne. 'Do you want to come and see Harry's en-suite bathroom?

'What's on sweet? Anything to do with pudding?'

Harry laughed. 'Not exactly. It's a bit boring really. Just a doorway between the bedroom and the bathroom.'

Anne turned to the stuffed dog. 'What do you think, Mr Moses? Shall we go and have a look?' She turned back to Harry. 'Mr Moses says that would be very nice.'

'I see what you mean,' said Alex. 'It's just a hole. But a very nice hole. And it does make a difference.'

Harry walked through from the bathroom to the bedroom and then back again. 'See? Luxury!' Then he looked around. 'Where's Anne?'

'Anne?' Alex called her daughter. There was no reply. 'Anne? Where are you poppet?'

Harry went back into the bedroom and looked around. He could tell at a glance that the child was not there. Then he went into the spare bedroom. Anne was standing against the far wall, her face as pale as chalk, clutching Mr Moses tightly to her chest.

Alex was at his shoulder. 'What's the matter, sweetheart?'

The child did not answer, but continued to gaze straight ahead of her.

'Aren't you feeling well?' asked Alex. 'Come on, let me take you home.' She walked across the room and put her arm around her daughter. 'Goodness, you're cold.' She rubbed Anne's upper arms to improve the circulation.

Harry asked brightly, 'Don't you like my alterations?'

Anne shook her head.

'Oh dear,' said Harry. He looked rather crestfallen and Alex made to console him. 'I'm sure she thinks they're very nice really. It must be the candyfloss from the fete. She did eat rather a lot of it. The woman selling it was a bit insistent.'

Anne shook her head. 'The lady,' was all she said.

Alex took her hand and led her down the stairs and into the garden. Harry followed. Anne clutched tightly at Mr Moses, unwilling to release her grip. Once they were in the garden, the colour began to return to her cheeks and the sun came out from behind a cloud.

'That'll warm you up,' said Alex. 'It's been a bit of a chilly day, that's all.'

Anne shook her head. 'It was the lady.'

'Which lady?' asked Alex. She was crouching down in front of her daughter now and looking into her eyes. 'The candy-floss lady?'

Anne shook her head vigorously.

'Which lady then?'

Anne pointed towards the cottage. 'The white lady. In there.'

30

72 Godolphin Street, Portsmouth
16 April 1816

> We read that we ought to forgive our enemies; but we do not
> read that we ought to forgive our friends.
>
> Cosimo de' Medici, 1389–1464

The pounding in Anne Flint's chest was a direct result of her believing that this was the end of her escape from Lavallier; that when the door that was slowly opening finally revealed the identity of her visitor, she would see his evil face and know that all was lost. She was convinced now that within a few days she would be on a ship bound for the ends of the earth and that all that was familiar to her would be lost forever.

Her feelings when the figure emerged around the edge of the door caused her to emit a cry of relief. It was, indeed, a man, but not the one she had been convinced had followed and found her.

'Well, well! If it isn't Anne Flint,' he exclaimed.

She gazed upon the form of Frederick Carew with wide-eyed incredulity, eventually managing to blurt out, 'Master Frederick!'

'You remember me?' he smiled at her.

'Why yes, sir. Of course!'

'And what on earth are you doing here, Anne? So far away from home.'

The words came flooding out. 'Oh, sir, please do not be angry with me. I thought I was to be a lady's maid and so agreed to go with Lady Eleanor and Mr Lavallier but there was the most dreadful accident and Mr Lavallier took me with him on his horse and brought me to Portsmouth and tried to get me to sail with him to the West Indies but I escaped and—'

'Stop, stop!' Frederick Carew raised his hand – the one that did not contain the bumper of red wine – and bade Anne slow down and repeat the entire story. Carefully he lifted the tails of his green velvet coat and lowered himself on to the chair in the corner of the room. Perched on the edge of her bed and tugging nervously at the sleeve of her gown, Anne related the events of the day – a day which seemed to have started at least a week ago, so eventful had been her last few hours.

Frederick listened attentively, occasionally sipping at the glass in his hand. His attention did not waver and never once did he raise an eyebrow, which would have suggested to Anne that he did not believe her version of events.

'And now you are here,' was all he said at last.

'Yes sir.'

Frederick took another sip of his wine. 'And have you a plan? What do you propose to do?'

'To return to Withercombe as soon as I have the money to pay for my carriage fare.'

'I see.' Frederick smiled.

She had forgotten just how winning was the smile of Sir Thomas Carew's younger son. For a brief moment she was kneeling at a grate once more, looking up as he crossed the room through the enfilade of doors, and blushing as he winked at her. He was still as dashing as ever. Still as handsome, with that rich hank of fair hair that would keep falling over his pale blue eyes. How the housemaids gossiped about him. How handsome he looked when he returned from hunting; his cheeks with their high colour and his breeches spattered with mud. She thought that perhaps then he looked more hand-some than ever. Even Mrs Fitzgerald would sometimes colour up as he addressed her and flashed her that amazing smile. And now here he was, sitting opposite her, as close or even closer than he had ever been before, talking just to her, giving her his undivided attention. She was mesmerised by those eyes, the colour of a summer sky. How wonderful it felt to be the object of his concentration, even for just a moment.

'It is good fortune that you bumped into me then, is it not?' he said, draining his glass.

'Oh, yes, sir! Such good fortune.'

'But the story you tell me is not one that will cause you to be favourably received upon your return to Withercombe, is it?' The smile faded now, and Master Frederick looked more serious.

Anne's hopes, having been raised momentarily, were dashed again by Master Frederick's accurate apprehension of her circumstances.

'No, sir.' She hesitated, then asked, 'Do you think you could explain it for me, sir? To Sir Thomas, and Mrs Fitzgerald? So that they would not scold me but would understand that what I done were a stupid thing and that I had learned my lesson? I won't ever do it again.'

'I could try, Anne. But there is the question of the death of Lady Eleanor. That cannot lightly be explained away. There is likely to be a lot of ill feeling. Grief. Tragedy. People are often swayed in such circumstances.'

'Sir?'

'They will find it very hard to take you back, Anne. Your actions, though not responsible directly, were in some way entwined with the loss of Lady Eleanor Stockbridge. Her father is very important and influential in the county.'

'Oh, but Master Frederick, it were none of my doing! I only did what I were bid.'

Frederick took a sip of his wine and smiled indulgently. 'That may be so, Anne, but you could see how others might view the situation differently, in the light of those disastrous and tragic consequences.'

The relief that Anne had felt on encountering a man who seemed to promise salvation was rapidly evaporating.

'It cannot be denied that, seeing as you are the only person who has born witness to these events, your testimony will be questioned very closely. I do not like to suggest such a thing, Anne, but a scullery maid is not always considered the most reliable of characters. Lord Stockbridge might find your version of events less than convincing.'

'But I was not just a scullery maid, sir. I was allowed to clean the grates and—'

'Yes, I know that your position was in some ways unusual, that Mrs Fitzgerald was preparing you for other duties – such was her trust in you – but that nicety might be lost on Lord Stockbridge.'

Anne felt the tears spring unbidden to her eyes. 'What am I to do then, sir?'

Frederick Carew thought for a moment, then he rose. 'Would you grant me a moment's leave, Anne?'

Anne nodded and sniffed back the tears. As her master's son left the room, she lay back on the bed, her head reeling. Disaster had been imminent a few minutes ago, then her hopes were raised in the most unexpected manner, only to be shattered again when Master Frederick heard her story. It was only then that it occurred to her to wonder what on earth he was doing in the house of Old Phoebe and Mr Pontifex.

31

72 Godolphin Street, Portsmouth
16 April 1816

We do not look in our great cities for our best morality.

Jane Austen, *Mansfield Park*, 1814

Anne was gazing at herself in the clouded looking glass. Not through vanity, but as some way of searching her soul and her mind and seeking for the truth. But what sort of truth? The truth about herself? To discover the kind of person she was, or the kind of person she feared she was to become? She took the cloth beside the washstand and rubbed at her lips and cheeks to remove the rouge. Somehow it only seemed to heighten her colour even further. She looked down at the gown that covered her young body – a gown made for someone far in excess of her own years. Fearfully she wrapped her arms around herself, as if to protect her virtue, and as she did so the door opened once more and Old Phoebe entered, smiling broadly and showing, again, the few teeth that remained in her head.

She was carrying a tray. 'Here we are, dear. Look what I've brought you. A nice bumper of wine!'

Anne backed away and shook her head. 'No. No thank you.'

Old Phoebe sighed, then she rested the tray on the corner of the chest of drawers, lifted up her skirts and deposited her not inconsiderable weight on the edge of the bed. Out of the corner of her eye, Anne noticed the voluminous layers of lace and calico beneath the cloak, in varying shades of off-white. Phoebe looked across to where Anne was standing and then patted the space beside her. 'You come and sit here.'

Anne felt reluctant to conform to the old woman's wishes, but the room was so small that there was little alternative but to do as she was bid.

As she lowered herself tentatively on to the coverlet beside the old woman, Phoebe took her hand and patted it. 'I know what you are thinking, my dear.'

Anne looked at her pleadingly, but seeing that her entreaties were having no effect, she averted her eyes.

'But there are some things in life that we must needs do if we are to get on.' Oblivious to the horror that was spreading across Anne's face, the old woman continued. 'I recall when I was your age. Oh, yes, I was once. And I had such high hopes. I, too, was to be a lady's maid in a grand house . . .'

Anne shot her a brief glance.

'Yes, dear. Just like you. But I realised that we cannot always have what we want, just when we want it. Sometimes we have to compromise. Or use our feminine wiles to get what we want. Do you know what "wiles" are, Anne?'

Anne looked straight ahead, not at the old woman, and shook her head.

'They are what we ladies have to use if we are to get the better of men.'

Anne began to shake, at which point Phoebe took Anne's right hand in both her own and squeezed it.

'Master Frederick says he will help you to get back to Wither . . . Wether . . . wherever it is you are from, but I do think he will need a little encouragement to do so.'

Anne sat quite still now.

'What has happened is very serious, and it would be

unreasonable, would it not, to expect Mr Frederick to put his own reputation at risk just to save yours? And so, what I suggest you do is, when Mr Frederick returns, you show him just how grateful you are for his help.'

Anne looked at her pleadingly. 'But how can I do that? I have no money.'

'Bless you! Mr Frederick has no need of your money. He has plenty of that himself. No, what Mr Frederick needs is for you to be kind to him. Nice to him.' The old woman looked at the young girl sitting next to her. 'You do understand what I mean Anne, do you not?'

Anne shook her head, and the old woman could see that her ignorance was genuine. She lay down Anne's hand on the coverlet and turned to face her.

'When Mr Frederick returns, he will ask you to sleep with him.'

A look of incredulity spread across Anne's face.

'And before you sleep, he may ask you for certain signs of affection.'

Anne did her best to apprehend. 'Like . . . kissing?'

'Yes. Like kissing. And holding you.'

'But Mr Frederick is the master's son. If I were to be found doing that, I should be dismissed. Mrs Fitzgerald would not approve of such—'

The old woman cut in. 'Mrs Fitzgerald is not here now. This is a different household. We do things differently here. And Master Frederick is very handsome, is he not?'

'Oh, yes but—'

'Then I do not think you should worry. You are a very beautiful girl, Anne. You will be very successful, of that I am sure.' Old Phoebe rose from the bed. 'I shall go now. Take a sip of your wine; it will make you feel better – put a little colour in those pale, soft cheeks. Master Frederick will be back directly. You will be nice to him, Anne, will you not?'

Anne nodded gently, and as the old woman closed the door behind her, she fought back the tears. She dug her nails into the palms of her hands and felt a tremendous sinking feeling in the pit of her stomach. Her heart beat so loudly that she could hear it above the murmurings from downstairs. Quickly she got up from the bed and walked to the chest of drawers. She lifted the bumper of wine from the tray and took two large gulps. Its fiery taste burnt the back of her throat, and as she swallowed she felt the warmth spreading through the rest of her body. She might be young, and she might be inexperienced, but she would not let the hand of fate dictate her future. From somewhere deep inside her, she must now find reserves of strength that she had, until this moment, never had need to call upon. But she would find them. Somehow. She would try to survive the next few hours, and then never again would she be forced to do anything against her will.

The gentle tap at the door startled her. She took another sip of the wine, dabbed at her lips with the sleeve of her gown, put down the glass and said in as clear and steady a voice as she could, 'Come in.'

32

The Old Mill, Itchen Parva
19 June 2010

Children and fools tell the truth.

Sixteenth-century proverb

When Alex had put Anne to bed, she sat with Harry under the old Bramley apple tree down by the chalk stream. Side by side they were, like Darby and Joan, thought Harry. His thoughts turned to Pattie Chieveley, and Ted, but he still did not like to bring up the subject. Instead he asked, 'Will Anne be all right?'

'Oh I should think so,' said Alex, topping up his glass from the bottle sunk into the long grass at her feet. 'Just something in her imagination, I should think. She saw such a lot of things at the fete today. It was more like a country fair really – lots of animals – and she probably just had a bit of an overload. You know what she's like with things that crawl, fly or scamper.'

'A proper country child,' offered Harry.

'I suppose so. She didn't have much of a chance when we were in Southampton, but since we came here she's really taken to it. You know she's pressing wild flowers?'

'No. How lovely.'

'Between sheets of newspaper under the rug between the sitting room and the kitchen. She's got quite a collection now. We have to sit down and look them up in a book, and then she writes their names underneath them in her spidery little hand. Not bad for a seven-year-old.'

'Perhaps you should get her a dog.'

'Not just yet. Eventually. When I get my life sorted.'

Harry looked at her quizzically.

'Sorry. I didn't mean—'

Harry broke in, 'You could get her some chickens. They don't take much looking after. A small coop and a run, that's all. You can get one that you can move around the garden. She can feed them in the morning before she goes to school, and again in the evening. It would be good for her. Give her something to look after.'

'I suppose . . .' murmured Alex.

'Silkies. She'd like those. They're like balls of fluff.'

'I'm not sure she's into balls of fluff.'

'Marans then. Cuckoo Marans. Now they're sturdy blighters. Or Welsummers – lovely brown eggs.'

Alex grinned at him. 'You're beginning to sound like *Poultry World*. How come you know so much about chickens?'

'Oh, we had a neighbour who used to have them when I was a kid. I got a few quid for collecting the eggs.'

'Well, well, well. I never thought of you as a poultry farmer.'

'Oh, there are lots of things about me that you don't know . . .'

Alex looked a little uneasy.

Harry realised immediately the implications of the remark and made to put her at ease. 'Like the fact that I can recite the entire list of the Kings and Queens of England from 1066 to the present day.'

Alex raised her eyebrows. 'You can't.'

'I can.'

'Go on then,' she said, disbelievingly.

'Ready?'

Alex nodded.

Harry took a deep breath and began:

'Willy, Willy, Harry, Ste, Harry, Dick, John, Harry Three.

'One, two, three Neds, Richard Two, Henry Four, Five, Six, then who?

'Edwards Four, Five, Dick the Bad, Harrys Twain, Ned Six the Lad.

'Mary, Bessie, James ye ken? Charlie, Charlie, James again.

'William and Mary, Anna Gloria, Four Georges, Will Four and Victoria.

'Edward Seven next and then came George the Fifth in 1910.

'Ned the Eighth soon abdicated, then George the Sixth was coronated.

'After him came Liz the Second, and with Charlie next it's reckoned.

'That's the way our monarch's lie, since Harold got it in the eye.'

Alex threw her head back and laughed. 'You are a silly man.'

'Silly but brimful of fascinating information.'

She leaned forward and squeezed his hand. 'And extremely good company.'

'You think so?'

'Oh I do. The best company since I don't remember when . . .' She paused and looked away.

Harry squeezed her hand back. 'You can talk about it, you know. Whenever you want. I might be a mine of useless information but I'm also a good listener.'

'Oh, I think you've proved that already. And I don't want to get all maudlin. Not tonight.' She looked up at the sky. 'The weather's improving. Sunday tomorrow. That'll be nice.'

'Do you want to . . . I mean . . .'

'Why don't we go for a picnic? I'll show you where the old Manor House was. That nasty bit of work's family seat.'

'I thought you'd want to forget about him.'

'Oh, I have already. But the spot's nice. Withercombe. There's only a few cottages there now, but the views across the water meadow are good.'

'What will we do for food?'

'Well, I did take the precaution of buying a few bits at the fete – local cheese, home-made pâté, bread and pickle – that sort of thing. Only if you're interested. You might prefer to carry on with your en-suite arrangements.'

Harry gave her a withering look. 'Don't be silly. I just didn't want to—'

Alex leaned forward and kissed him on the lips. 'It's a bit late for that, isn't it?' she said.

33

72 Godolphin Street, Portsmouth
16 April 1816

Il faut, parmi le monde, une vertu traitable.
(What's needed in this world is an accommodating sort of virtue.)

Molière, *Le Misanthrope*, 1666

Frederick Carew stood just inside the door of Anne Flint's room, a half-drained bumper of red wine in his hand. His coat and waistcoat were unbuttoned, and the stock at his neck hung loose. Anne thought she detected, for a moment, a look of nervousness upon his face. But the moment quickly passed, and he smiled that disarming smile of his that ordinarily reduced her, and the rest of the female household, to jelly. On this occasion it only served to quicken her resolve. Realising, instinctively, that she must somehow survive this encounter, Anne stood up, smiled back at him and asked, 'What do you require of me, sir?' (She wondered at the wisdom of this remark, but determined that she would not play a completely passive role. She had learned, after all, that where men are concerned, it is important not to let them have everything their own way. Why, if she had allowed Sam his way, she would have been behind the hayrick last harvest, and heaven alone knows what that might have led to. No, she knew, in spite of her innocence, that somewhere deep inside her were these things that Old Phoebe called 'wiles'. She would need all of them if she were to endure the next few hours.)

Frederick cleared his throat. 'I gather Old Phoebe has explained the situation to you?'

'She has, sir.'

'And that it will be extremely difficult for me to argue your case?'

'Yes, sir.'

'But that, nevertheless, I am prepared to make some endeavours on your account.'

Anne nodded.

And what Frederick Carew said next surprised her.

'You are very beautiful, Anne.'

It was not at all what she had expected, and her colour heightened, even through the remains of the rouge.

'Perhaps you do not realise how beautiful.'

Anne stood frozen, unable to move. No one had told her before that she was beautiful. Sam had told her she was 'presentable', but that seemed a grudging comment, and one that was probably only offered to get him somewhere closer to her person. To persuade her to go and kiss him behind the stables or down by the chalk stream.

Frederick Carew took the few steps necessary to approach her. She could feel her heart beating in her chest again. That heart; it was a wonder it was beating at all after the events of this extraordinary day. Frederick put down his glass upon the chest of drawers and raised his right hand to her face, gently stroking her cheek with the backs of his fingers.

He did not speak now, but with his left hand pulled at the ribbon that held the silken cloak about her shoulders. Loosened of its ties, the cloak slid silently to the floor and Anne stood before him in nothing but the translucent chemise in which Old Phoebe had dressed her.

Ordinarily she would have cowered in embarrassment, but

this was no ordinary moment in no ordinary day. She would see this through; she knew she had to do so if she were ever to retrieve her own life. Drawing on strengths she hardly knew existed, she managed to smile a gentle smile and to avoid wrapping her arms around herself to hide her near nakedness.

Frederick took off his coat, then his waistcoat, and lay them on the chair, gazing at Anne all the while. Then he stepped up to her and took her in his arms, pressing his lips to hers.

Anne could feel the fire within herself, and the fierce heat of Frederick's body. As their bodies parted for a moment, she thought that she might stop breathing, but before she had a chance to think further he took hold of the chemise in both hands and deftly lifted it above her head until she stood before him completely naked.

'Oh Anne,' he murmured 'you really are quite, quite beautiful.' Delicately he traced the outline of her curves with his right forefinger and leaned forward again, feathering her lightly freckled shoulders with soft and gentle kisses.

Anne arched her neck away from him, and then felt a novel sensation of freedom infusing her entire body. It came over her in a great wave that took her completely off guard. She knew that she should really be fighting this man, for she was now instinctively aware of what he wanted. But she could not; something was holding her there, daring her to go on. Now she was breathing more heavily, and so was Frederick, his hands exploring her soft young body's graceful curves. Her heart beat faster and faster, her mouth was open now, she was almost panting with the thrill of it all.

The thrill! It was a thrill, though in her heart and bones she feared it should not be. Suddenly, she pulled away from him, gasping for breath. Then, without taking her eyes off him, she slid quickly between the covers of the bed.

Frederick, too, was gasping for breath. She thought for a moment that he might be angry, but then he smiled. It was not, she was relieved to see, a wicked smile, but one of excitement and desire. She might have been forced into this situation against her will, but she was determined that it would not break her spirit. Perhaps it was wicked; perhaps it was foolhardy; but this was where she was and she would need every ounce of guile and determination to endure it. For the very first time in her young life, she felt the merest sensation of power. She could either submit, whimperingly, to Frederick Carew's advances – for there was, indeed, fear in her heart: fear of the unknown, fear of ruin – or she could try, somehow, to rise above the feminine feebleness that he would be expecting and to channel her feelings so that instead of being weakened as a result of this encounter, she was strengthened by it. Not that she was able to articulate these feelings; they remained just that – feelings. Instincts. Intuition or, as Old Phoebe would have it, 'wiles'.

Frederick took off his breeches and then his shirt. His body was, as the ladies of the household had suspected, a paragon of muscle and sinew, thanks to the exertions of hunting and field sports (and now, suspected Anne, from other exertions as well). Without pausing he slid in beside her, and the events of the next few hours were to transform the rest of Anne's life.

It was daylight when she awoke. There was no clock in the room and so she had no idea of the time, save that there was little noise coming from the street below. Silently she slid from the bed, easing out from under the sleeping Frederick's arm. He stirred slightly and, fearful of waking him, she stood quite still. But when she had satisfied herself that he was still fast asleep, she hurried across to the window and lifted the drapes just a little. It was a clear spring morning and Portsmouth had been freshly rinsed by a shower of rain. She could not smell the acrid tang of settled, dampened dust, thanks to the tightly closed window and the stagnant atmosphere of the tiny bedroom, but the prospect of doing so made her heart leap. She could see the gilded hands glinting on a church tower several streets away: it was half past five o'clock.

She thought quickly. The rest of the house would be asleep at this early hour, surely?

Without making a sound, she slipped on the chemise. But where were her clothes – the ones in which she had arrived? Carefully she slid open the drawers of the chest. 'Be there, please be there!' she thought. The two upper drawers were empty, save for some faded hanks of cloth. She closed them. Master Frederick stirred a little and murmured something inaudible. Anne froze. Then his breathing fell back into a steady rhythm. She opened the larger of the two drawers at the bottom of the chest and – joy! – there was her cloak. The other revealed her dress and undergarments. But where were her boots? She could hardly travel barefoot. Anxious now, she dressed as quickly and as silently as she could and then tiptoed to the door. She glanced back at the bed; he was still asleep and breathing heavily. Then she caught sight of his coat upon the chair, and the corner of his pocket book just visible in the inside pocket. Could she do it? Should she do it? Would he still speak up for her to Sir Thomas and Lord Stockbridge? There was no guarantee that he would do so at all, regardless of her future actions. Perhaps it had all been just a ruse to get her to . . . well, she had done that now and would have to take her chance. No. She could not afford that chance. If Master Frederick had used it as an excuse simply to have his way with her, where would she be then?

She eased the pocket book from its resting place and opened it. Three five-pound notes nestled inside it. She could not take those. A country girl carrying such a large amount of money would arouse much suspicion, and she did not want to be thought a thief. That she was not. But she must have some means of paying her way. Coins. Where were his coins? She felt in the pockets of the coat. Success! A purse! She would not take it; but just a modest amount of the contents – a single gold sovereign, four shillings and eight pence three farthings. That should be enough to get her on her way. Perhaps he would not even miss them. The feebleness that she had felt originally – that she did not know her way to Withercombe, or even to the place where she could board a coach – now seemed but a small inconvenience. She was still here. She had survived her ordeal of the night before. Master Frederick had been gentle with her, at least, and though she felt changed forever by what had happened down by the chalk stream and now under Old Phoebe's roof, something deep inside her told her that if she buckled now, then that would be the end of her. She would not whimper. She would not cower before the son of the master of the house. For if she did, what would her life be worth?

As she returned the purse to the pocket of the coat, she noticed something underneath the chair. Her boots! She picked them up and once more made for the door. As she turned the handle Frederick stirred again, and this time she heard him murmur, 'Anne!'

Not pausing to see if he had woken, she slipped through the door, closed it behind her and padded quickly down the stairs in her bare feet. Reaching the front door, she then saw the next obstacle in her way. Three large bolts. She put down her boots and set to work. She could grasp the bottom two, and slid them silently to one side. But the uppermost bolt – of black and grimy cast iron – was beyond her reach. Fearfully, she looked about her in the dark and shadowy hallway, lit only by the weak rays of sunshine glinting through the fanlight above the door. In the shadows, beneath a coatstand laden with cloaks and blankets, stood a mahogany hall chair with a battered and faded coat of arms upon its back. Quickly she lifted it up and stood it against the door, then reached up and grappled with the bolt. It was stiff, but applying all her strength she eventually managed to pull it free. It shot back against the metal stay with a sharp crack.

Swiftly now she replaced the chair and reached for the doorknob to effect her escape. As her hand began to turn it, so another hand lay upon her own. Not that it was much of a hand at all. A spare and bony claw it was, more birdlike than human. Anne turned, to see the form of Mr Pontifex beside her. He was grinning and chuckling to himself. 'Are you going somewhere, Anne?' he asked. 'So early in the morning?'

34

Mill Cottage, Itchen Parva

20 June 2010

Still round and round the ghosts of Beauty glide,
And haunt the places where their honour died.

Alexander Pope, 'To a Lady',
Epistles to Several Persons, 1735

There was plenty to keep Harry awake that Saturday night: his developing relationship with Alex being uppermost in his mind. Try as he might to back-pedal, to tell himself not to expect too much too soon, it was difficult not to look ahead, to think of what might happen – of what he wanted to happen. It was both ironic and sad that what was potentially the most enjoyable prospect in his life for a long time was clouded by the knowledge that Ted Chieveley would soon cease to be the father figure that he had, over the years, become. And then Harry felt ashamed; ashamed of dwelling on how the loss of such a man would affect himself rather than Pattie Chieveley. Harry had known him for five years. Pattie had been married to him for close on fifty. What must it be like for her – watching the man she had loved and been exasperated by, cajoled and cosseted for four decades gradually disappearing before her very eyes? And that the cruel twist of fate that had caused this trauma was the same as the one that had created the only barrier between himself and Alex. Coincidences. Life was full of them, and not always happy ones.

He turned over and tried to sleep, but there was a coldness

about the room that chilled him to the bone. It was June, for heaven's sake, the weather should be warming up now. And it had not been a bad day; the sun had come out eventually and the forecast for Sunday, as Alex had remarked, was a good one. Why, then, did he feel frozen to the marrow?

The doorway. It must be the new opening from the bedroom to the bathroom. The door was not yet in place and he had clearly created a draught. And yet he could not feel any air movement, as such, just a stupefying iciness in the atmosphere. Old houses: that's what it was. They always said that the thick walls in old houses kept them warm in winter and cool in summer. It was just that he was not used to it. He had come fresh from a modern apartment block with all mod cons, where the walls were as thin as tissue, the better to hear the goings-on of your neighbours, to an old house with walls almost two feet thick – external ones at least. It stood to reason that it would feel cooler.

He sat bolt upright in bed. Why? What had disturbed him? There was no sound to speak of. He looked around him in the room, lit by the faint shafts of moonlight. Nothing. Silly. His mind was obviously whirring; full of thoughts of Alex and Pattie and Ted. And Anne Overton. He would see her today – along with her inseparable companion, Mr Moses. Perhaps today he would get to know her a little better. He had taken things slowly so far. Did not want to put her off – to become one of those instant 'uncles'. He smiled to himself, remembering young Palmer's retort to a classmate who had confessed that he did not like his new 'uncle' Darren. 'We had him,' said Palmer. 'He were rubbish.'

Harry would do his best not to be rubbish.

The remains of the Manor House were, as Alex had suggested, just that. There were a few low walls, but they disappeared into the hummocky banks of green velvet above the river. A hundred yards away three or four cottages – once simple dwellings for artisans and ostlers – sat tidily inside their white picket fences, done up now, with shutters and window boxes and pretty front gardens replete with hollyhocks and marigolds, snapdragons and tobacco plants.

'Is this it?' asked Harry.

'Yes,' replied Alex. 'I told you there wasn't much.'

'Was it very grand?'

'Apparently. There was a stable block and parkland around it. The river ran through it – there are the water meadows.' Alex pointed to the chalk stream snaking away into the distance.

'How old was it?'

'Well, I think it must have been Elizabethan – with additions probably.'

Harry shook his head. 'How on earth could they have knocked it down?'

Alex sat down on a grassy knoll just across from the cottages and glanced across to where Anne was lecturing Mr Moses on the banks of the chalk stream. It was an idyllic spot: rolling Hampshire countryside dotted with clumps of oak and ash trees, the distant sounds of sheep chivvying their now muscular lambs, and little traffic noise to disturb the peace and calm that pervaded a scene which, but for the absence of the big house, had probably not changed for a century or more.

'Oh, there was a time – in the Twenties and Thirties and Forties – when nobody wanted to be lumbered with such monstrosities. We think of it as a criminal act now, but at the time they saw it as . . . well – pragmatic, I suppose. Who was going to look after these big, old damp houses that cost a fortune to keep warm and watertight? What with dwindling family fortunes, death duties and the like. And so they went. Hundreds of them. Did you know that between 1920 and 1955 we lost an average of thirteen large country houses a year?'

Harry looked surprised. 'And I thought I was the one with a mind for useless facts.'

Alex shook her head. 'They're not useless. They keep us informed.' She looked across to the faint tracery of ruins. 'They teach us a lesson – not to let it happen again.'

Harry sought to lighten her mood. 'It could have been worse, of course.'

Alex regarded him quizzically.

'Old what's-his-face could have been living here – Sir Miles Carew. Just how impossible would he have been then?'

Alex grimaced. 'Yes, there is that, I suppose. We should be grateful for small mercies; but all things considered I'd rather have had a large manor house lived in by a small prick rather than a small house lived in by a large one.'

Harry laughed. 'You really have got it in for him, haven't you?'

'Does it show? Sorry, I shouldn't let it get to me. Anyway, he probably wouldn't have been living in it anyway.'

'How so?'

'Well, he's only a distant relative of the old squire's. Some far-off cousin or something. He just lords it as though he were the direct descendant of God. But he's only a pale shadow, really.'

'Talking of shadows,' said Harry, 'do you believe in ghosts?'

'What on earth brought that on?' asked Alex.

'Oh, just yesterday . . . when Anne said she saw something at Mill Cottage . . .'

'Oh, I wouldn't worry about that. She was probably just a bit tired.'

'Only last night . . . well, it's probably nothing but . . .'

Alex waited for a moment and then said, 'Go on.'

'Well, there was this . . . I can only describe it as coldness . . . in my bedroom.'

'You haven't got any central heating and it was a clear night,' said Alex matter of factly.

'No, it was more than that. There was a real chill about the place. An icy chill. Not a draught; the air was quite still, but really . . . well . . . cold.'

Alex sat upright. 'I've heard of this happening before.'

'What do you mean?'

Alex looked thoughtful, then she said, 'It would make sense, wouldn't it? With what Anne said yesterday. About a woman in white.'

Harry laughed. 'I didn't see a woman in white. I've read it – the Wilkie Collins book – but I've not seen her . . . unless . . .' Harry shook his head to dispel what he considered to be unworthy thoughts.

'No, but Anne thought she did. And why on earth would she say that if she hadn't?'

Harry looked down towards the streamside where Anne was showing wild flowers to Mr Moses. 'Well, she has got a vivid imagination.'

'Imagination, yes. But she's not fanciful. She doesn't make things up – not in a deceitful way. I thought it was just tired-ness, but she really did seem to think she'd seen something in your cottage. She was as white as a sheet.'

'Oh, and there was the voice,' added Harry.

Alex looked confused. 'What voice?'

'Well, when I was knocking out the doorway, I was sure I heard you shout my name, calling goodbye. But you weren't there when I looked out of the window, and then you really did say "goodbye" later. Odd. I never gave it a second thought at the time but . . .'

'There is a theory, you know . . .'

'What sort of theory?' asked Harry.

'That spirit manifestations occur when the dwelling they inhabit is disturbed in some way.'

'Like me knocking a hole in a wall?'

'Exactly like you knocking a hole in a wall.'

'So I've disturbed the spirit of the place?'

'Probably someone who lived there once. Or who died there.'

Harry looked uneasy. 'Sinister . . .'

'Not necessarily. It could just be confused. Making its presence felt.'

'I've never thought of you as believing in ghosts.'

'I'm open-minded. It wouldn't do to say that I don't believe in something just because I've never experienced it, would it?'

'No, I suppose not.'

'So do you believe in them?' asked Alex.

Harry sighed. 'I'm rapidly thinking I'm going to have to.'

35

72 Godolphin Street, Portsmouth
17 April 1816

Always, Sir, set a high value on spontaneous kindness.

Samuel Johnson, 1709–1784

Edwin Pontifex could see the terror in Anne Flint's eyes as he grasped her hand on the knob of the door. 'Are you leaving us so soon?' he asked.

Anne could not answer, but looked into the rheumy eyes of her interlocutor hoping to see some kind of compassion. There was none in evidence. Her mind raced. She could not be stopped now. If she did not escape, then she would be condemned to a life of servitude so shockingly different from and far more terrifying than the one from which she was fleeing.

'I must go,' was all she could stammer. 'I must—'

'But Mistress Phoebe will be expecting to see you when she rises, which will be – ' he pulled out a small, slender pocket watch from the faded black bombazine waistcoat that wrapped up his crooked body – 'within the hour.' He looked pensive, then slipped the watch back into its pocket. He had his back to the door now, blocking her way. 'And what of Mister Frederick? Will he not be disappointed that you have left? Is he not about to make amends for your earlier misdeeds?'

'They were not misdeeds! Not mine . . .' exclaimed Anne.

'But may be perceived as such, as I understand?'

'Yes, but—'

'Then that is the way it shall be. You will find it very difficult to regain your old position. Things change, Anne. The world does not stand still. We can never go backwards. In spite of Mr Milton's ruminations, paradise can never be regained. But then you did not think it paradise, did you, Anne? Which is why you found yourself here. A house of pleasure, yes, but such a long way from paradise.'

Pontifex tilted his head so that he appeared even more lopsided than usual. Anne could see the thin, wispy strands of pewter-grey hair catching the early morning sunshine that glimmered through the fanlight above the door. He stood there, silhouetted, clad entirely in black, from the stockings and knee breeches to the swallow-tailed coat and the waistcoat, all except for the once-white food-stained stock at his scrawny neck. All around him, dust motes floated like celestial bodies in the air, and he stood with his arms outstretched like a spider at the centre of its web, intent on capturing its prey.

'I would rather you stayed with us, Anne. You see, Mistress Phoebe will be very cross with me when she discovers that I let you go without saying goodbye to her.' He flashed her a smile, showing off the decaying graveyard that passed for his dental inheritance. 'She gets very angry with me when things do not go according to plan. I really would rather you stayed.' Pontifex stretched out a scrawny arm towards the hallway, urging Anne to walk that way rather than through the door and out into the street. He was not a strong man; she could simply have pushed him aside and run away, but something made her hesitate. There he stood, half crouching in the shadows, his expression a mixture of fawning obsequiousness and veiled threats. She saw him now for what he was – not a menacing spider but an acolyte at the court of Old Phoebe. A dogsbody like herself.

'Why should I stay?' she said at last. 'So that I can be like you?'

Pontifex looked bewildered for a moment, then wounded by the cruelty of her candour.

She continued: 'I am young. I have a life ahead of me. I will not be held back, not by the likes of you and Old Phoebe. I may have been bad, I may have done wrong things; but it is not that I am bad, just that . . .' She was lost for words now; knowing how she felt but somehow unable to articulate her feelings.

'Circumstances got the better of you?' offered the crooked man.

Anne nodded. 'Yes; circumstances . . . that is all.'

Pontifex nodded thoughtfully. 'And you think that running away from here will let you escape a terrible future in a disreputable house, and that when you get to wherever you are going then life will be fine once more and that you will meet the man of your dreams and live happily ever after?'

'I know I cannot hope for that. But I can – I *must* – hope for better than this.'

The old man looked crestfallen. 'What about old Pontifex? What is to become of him?'

'Do not try to turn me from my will. You have had your life and chosen what to do with it. Mine is just beginning and I will not be . . .' She sought for the word and finally it came '. . . diverted. No. I will not be diverted.'

The words echoed around the empty hallway, causing Pontifex to raise his crooked finger to his lips, encouraging her to speak more softly. 'And what will you do for money,' he asked, 'to escape from this – ' he looked about him – 'this den of iniquity?'

'I have sufficient for my needs.'

Pontifex regarded her quizzically. 'But when you came here yesterday you had nothing. No coach fare. Not a farthing for a piece of bread.'

Anne looked nervous. 'I found some.'

Pontifex nodded. 'In the pocket book of Mister Frederick?'

Anne could feel the coins in the pocket of her coat. Now she withdrew them and held them out in her hand. 'One sovereign, four shillings and eightpence three-farthings. I done my sums.'

'A good night's work,' confirmed Pontifex.

At this Anne threw the coins at him and they clattered from his cowering form on to the bare floorboards at his feet. 'I ain't for buying. I took them for my coach fare, that was all. Master Frederick had his way with me; I only wanted to go home.' There were tears in her eyes now: tears of anger and frustration. In a world where she had done her best to please those whom she had served, last night making the ultimate sacrifice, it seemed that no one would take her for what she was: an honest, simple girl who wanted a better life than the one dealt to her by the unfeeling hand of fate. She knew that she was not wicked – though after the events of the night she would have to work harder convincing herself of that – but only that she must somehow make progress in a world where endless drudgery seemed the only certain prospect.

Fighting to hold back the tears that would only blur her vision, Anne now elbowed Pontifex aside and made for the door. At that very moment a voice boomed from upstairs, 'Mr Pontifex? Is that you? What is the commotion?' Old Phoebe had been woken by the disturbance and made to discover its origins.

Anne's hand was on the doorknob now, and again she felt the bony claw grasp it. In desperation she turned to push

Pontifex away once more, but saw that he was holding out his other hand towards her.

'You were right not to steal, Anne. It can only lead to trouble, sooner or later. Here: take these.' He lifted up Anne's hand and dropped into it four silver crowns. 'They should help you to get home.' He gave her a flicker of a smile and added, 'Without causing too much suspicion.'

Anne did not speak but her wide-eyed expression showed both her astonishment and her gratitude.

'Mr Pontifex!' the strident voice echoed again down the stairway and across the hall.

'Now go,' he said, opening the door on to the street.

The morning light flooded in, so strongly that the old man had to shield his eyes. Anne, too, was dazzled by its brilliance, and the heady aroma of morning air, horse dung, sea salt and reawakening life. She turned as she reached the top step. 'Thank you!' she murmured. 'Thank you so very much. I shall . . .' She paused for the briefest of moments. 'I shall never forget you.'

Pontifex smiled and shook his head. 'Best that you do, my dear; best that you do.' And then she heard footsteps coming down the stairs behind him, and the rustle of petticoats. Without a backward glance, she ran down the steps and away through the carts and the carters, the sailors and the street urchins in the direction of what she hoped was the coach to Winchester.

'Oi, miss,' shouted one of the sailors. 'Fancy a good time?' But she did not hear, for her thoughts were on the future and what it might hold.

36

The Streamside

20 June 2010

We wove a web in childhood,
A web of sunny air;
We dug a spring in infancy
Of water pure and fair;
We sowed in youth a mustard seed,
We cut an almond rod;
We are now grown up to riper age –
Are they withered in the sod?

Charlotte Brontë,
'Retrospection', 1835

'Do you remember when you were like that?' asked Alex.

'Oh yes. Sometimes I think I still am like that,' confirmed Harry.

'Me too.'

They were watching Anne, lost in her own little world with Mr Moses, down by the banks of the stream. At this moment she was oblivious to them and everything around her, except for that which was a part of her present, intimate world. A look of intense concentration was upon her face as she picked first one wild flower, then another, and showed them to her canine companion, identifying them one after another in her clear little voice: 'This is water figwort. Can you see its tiny pockets? And this one is water mint. Here you are Mr Moses: smell it. Isn't it lovely?

Mummy says it's good with roast lamb. I'm not sure about that.'

'Do you worry about her?' asked Harry.

'Doesn't every parent? Perhaps I worry more than most. I worry about her crossing the road, about getting on at school, about . . . well . . . just about everything, I suppose. I worry more than anything if she'll grow up a balanced child. With a sense of proportion. Fairness. With a sense of values.'

'Like yours?'

'I suppose.'

They were leaning back against the trunk of an old oak tree, each at an angle, so that they spoke without looking at one another; talking and almost thinking out loud.

'Do you want her to have what you had as a child or something different?' asked Harry.

'I'm not sure. Some of the things I had. Loving parents. Well, parent in my case. A happy home. I'd quite like her to have siblings. One day . . .' Then she quickly changed the subject. 'What about you? What would you wish for a child?'

'Security. Knowing that when you came home everything would be the same as it was when you left. That life would not change too soon, too suddenly. That your parents would be happy with each other – and with you.'

'Forever?'

'Forever.'

'That's a bit of a tall order nowadays, isn't it?'

'I guess.'

'So was your childhood secure?' asked Alex.

'It was in that I knew we wouldn't starve. My parents stuck together for as long as they could – for my sake, I suppose – but I knew that they weren't happy. I picked up on little things: cross words that were more than minor irritations. Absences that were not due to legitimate causes. I knew that something was wrong. I'm not sure that it was a good thing that they clung on for so long. But then when is a good time to break up? Before the child can understand what's going on, so that it never knows what it's like to have both a mother and a father; or later on, when it has supposedly grown up enough not to need them?'

'Did it scar you – emotionally?'

Harry thought for a moment. 'I'd like to say "no", but that wouldn't really be true. It made me wonder if I could have done anything to stop it.'

'But how could you? It was their relationship, not yours.'

'But I was a part of it. It knocked my confidence.'

Alex looked at him sympathetically.

'It's a funny thing, confidence,' Harry continued. 'You see people who have it in spades – like old whatshisname, Miles Carew – and you wonder where the hell they get it from. And then there's old muggins here who has to grope for every ounce of the stuff. Pathetic really. Lack of confidence is something I wouldn't wish on anybody. At best it's debilitating, and at worst a crashing bore. People tire of it, assume it's some kind of affectation; but in reality it's a pain in the arse.'

'Nature or nurture?' asked Alex.

'Nurture, I think. It's like an incurable disease contracted early in life.' He thought for a moment, then said, 'Oh, I don't know; perhaps you are born with it. One thing I do know is that it never goes away.'

'Does it affect your . . . relationships?'

'Only when push comes to shove. When everything's going well it seems to fade away. Then when things start to go wrong and you're powerless to do anything about it, it comes roaring in at you and you realise it has just been waiting to pounce.'

'Is that what happened when Serena left?'

Harry nodded. 'Like a raging tide engulfing its victim. Like I said: pathetic.'

'Not really. It just shows that you're a sensitive soul.' She smiled at him. 'I rather like sensitive souls.'

Harry laughed. 'That's a relief. You seem to have found one here. Sensitive to mood, sensitive to changes in atmosphere, sensitive to . . . ghosts?'

'Of the past?'

'I hope not. Time to move on.' He looked at Alex meaningfully. 'At the right pace, I mean.'

She leaned around the tree and kissed him on the cheek. 'Go and talk to Anne while I get the picnic ready.'

Harry got up and ambled down to the bank of the chalk stream where the child was playing. She looked up as he approached, squinting at him in the noonday sun. 'Mr Moses likes the smell of mint.'

'That's good,' said Harry, dropping down on the grass beside her. 'So do I.'

He put out his hand and stroked Mr Moses on the nose. 'I'm sure you'll have a real dog one day.'

'Oh, Mr Moses is real; it's just that he's different real. You can't take him for walks or feed him.'

'So what sort of dog would you like – when you get one?'

'Don't mind.'

'Large or small?'

The child thought for a moment. 'Small. Then he wouldn't get in Mummy's way or be big enough to knock me over. I like Mrs Armstrong's dog but he's a labrador and a bit excitable. Sometimes he can barge into you and it really hurts.'

'Who's Mrs Armstrong?'

'My teacher. She's very nice. She likes walking in the countryside. She knows about wild flowers, too.'

Harry watched as Anne gathered up her buttercups and clover, plantains and water mint into a bunch. She was a pretty child, her red hair glinting in the sunshine. She had about her an air of intense concentration; of preoccupation, as though in her own world she had found safety and security. Then she surprised him by asking quite clearly and levelly, 'Do you like Mummy?'

He hesitated for a moment, then said, 'Yes. I like her very much.'

'Enough to marry her?'

The hesitation now was rather more profound. 'Well . . . who knows what might happen? But I like her very much.'

Anne was looking him straight in the eye now. 'But you'd need to love her to marry her?'

'Yes. Of course.'

'Do you? Do you love her?'

Harry looked thoughtful and then asked gently, 'What would you like me to say to that?'

'I'd like you to say that of course you love her.'

'You wouldn't mind?'

Anne shook her head.

He found it hard to suppress a smile. 'Well, then, you won't be disappointed when I tell you that I do.'

'Good.' She turned back to Mr Moses. Then, having considered her next question, she looked at Harry again and added, 'Are you in love with her? Because that's different, isn't it?'

At this Harry did his best not to look either surprised or discomfited. He said nothing for a few moments and then confirmed, 'Yes. Yes, I am.'

Content, the girl returned to her flowers, but Harry made to attract her attention once more.

'There is one thing,' he said.

Anne looked up.

'I want to keep it a secret just a little bit longer.'

Anne nodded. 'OK,' she said. 'I can keep a secret.' Then she picked up Mr Moses and walked up the grassy bank towards her mother.

37

Portsmouth
17 April 1816

Enough, if something from our hands have power
To live, and act, and serve the future hour . . .
William Wordsworth, 'The River Duddon', 1820

In spite of the early hour, the streets of Portsmouth were already astir, for sailing ships begin their voyages according to tides, not clocks. Gathering her cloak about her, anxious that it should catch on nothing and impede her progress, she wove between the ever-increasing confluence of humanity. Tars with shiny broad-brimmed hats swarmed over the streets, weaving their way, with bags on shoulders, between horses and carts, carriages and costermongers towards the burly vessels, packed bulwark to bulwark along the quayside, each straining at the thick ropes and hawsers, anxious to be away. As anxious as she herself. She glimpsed the names of today's collection: *Hotspur* and *Black Swan*, *Gay Buccaneer* and *Dauntless*, each with its own figurehead jutting out from the prow – a bare-breasted mermaid, a pirate with a scimitar between his teeth, a sailor shielding his eyes and a maiden swathed in a swirl of hand-carved muslin. Each bound for who heaven-knows-where; just like herself. Everywhere there seemed to be parallels with her own situation – the unpredictability that lay in front of her seemed quite overwhelming.

She pushed on through the melee as the street cries fell upon her ringing ears: 'Hot pies!', 'Carry your bags, milady?',

'Fresh watercress!'. Why would anyone want watercress at six o'clock in the morning? thought Anne. But the housekeepers and mistresses were out early for the freshest of produce, the better to impress the master of the house.

'Lemons! Oranges! Fresh from Spain!'

How she would love an orange right now. She could not remember the last time she had tasted one. And then she realised how hungry she was. Neither could she remember the last time she had eaten, having, the night before, declined Old Phoebe's offer of bread and cheese. For a moment she wondered what Mr Pontifex was saying to the old woman right now. How would he explain that he had let Anne go? But she could not dwell on such things.

She slipped her hand into the pocket of her cloak to check on the safety of the four crowns. They were still there. She would break into one of them to eat, for already she was feeling light-headed. But an orange would not suffice. She bought from a sturdy youth with a tray of hot pies and felt herself salivating at the prospect. Although he raised his eyebrows at the sight of a whole crown, he gave her the four shillings and eleven pence change, along with a bright smile and the injunction to, 'Enjoy it, miss.'

Anne found a corner, vacant of passers-by, against a warehouse wall; there a stone bollard, pushing up between thick coils of sisal, provided a welcome seat. Putting the crisp pastry to her lips, she tilted back her head and savoured the warm and nourishing liquor as it ran over her tongue. Eagerly she devoured both pastry and meat until, within the space of two or three minutes, there was nothing but a few crumbs on the cobblestones to betray that it had ever existed. For a few moments she sat quite still, feeling the strength returning to her body.

She needed a plan. What would she do? She could not go straight back to the Manor House, assuming that she would be able to work out how to get there. There was little likelihood of her being accepted with open arms. And there would be questions. All kinds of questions: about Eleanor, and Mr Lavallier – if they knew of him. She began to panic, but then admonished herself. Panic would be unproductive: there was no point in 'getting herself into a lather', as Mrs Fitzgerald would have said. She must approach the matter sensibly.

A coaching inn. That was what she needed to find. She could not remember, in the fear and excitement, where the carriage from Winchester had deposited her and Lavallier. But if she could locate a coach, journeying through the streets of Portsmouth, she could follow it to its destination and board a carriage there for the return trip. Yes, that was what she would do. The crowds were becoming so thick that the carriages were compelled to travel slowly – if she walked briskly, she could just about keep up with one, provided she did not trip over her skirts. Eleanor had been slightly taller than her, and she needed to gather her cloak about her so as not to impede her progress.

She saw coaches now, but they were travelling in different directions. Which were coming into town and which departing? She looked about her for inspiration. Standing outside The Fountain Inn she saw a man reading a newspaper. 'Excuse me, sir . . .'

The man lowered his paper and peered at her over the top of his spectacles.

'Please could you tell me which coaches is coming into town and which is going out?'

The man – perhaps in his late sixties, portly and clearly well-to-do since his coat was well cut and his top hat freshly brushed – pondered for a moment, endeavouring to reconcile the courtliness of the young woman's dress with her apparent lack of the finer points of grammar. But, sensing a maiden in distress, he smiled at her regardless and indicated that those coaches travelling in a northeasterly direction from this particular spot would be entering the town, having deposited their passengers on the quayside, and that they were the ones most likely to be travelling to . . . where was it she wished to go?

'Winchester, sir.'

'Now there is a coincidence; for I myself am bound for Winchester and will be happy to escort you to the coach. Do you have a ticket?'

'No sir,' confirmed Anne. 'But, I do not want to be any trouble. I am happy travelling alone.'

The man shook his head. 'I think that inadvisable. Portsmouth is full of blackguards and drunken sailors, even at this early hour. Better that you are in company.' And then, seeing Anne's discomfort, he added, 'I can assure you that I will make no demands upon you in terms of conversation or any other matter, for I have my paper and do not wish to impose.'

The man had a kindly face and a warm smile, but Anne was anxious not to encounter any further strangers on her so far too-eventful journey. 'Oh, no, sir. It is just that—'

'But you have no ticket, you say?'

'No, I do not. Not yet.'

'Why then, come inside. This is The Fountain Inn. Coaches for Winchester depart from here; there is no need to travel on foot any further.'

Anne thanked the gentleman and gave a little bob before entering The Fountain Inn and purchasing a paper ticket from the clerk behind the coaching desk. He hardly looked at her, which came as a great relief, and said nothing as she handed over an entire crown to pay for her journey.

'The Regulator leaves at eight o'clock, miss,' he said. 'You can wait in there – ' he indicated a small room to the side of the tap room – 'or else take the air and come back at half past seven o'clock when we starts loading luggage.' He looked up from his ledger and took in the fact that Anne would not be needing to load any luggage. 'Five minutes to eight o'clock then,' he muttered, and went back to his ledger.

That was it; she had done it. She had booked her passage as far as Winchester. During the course of her journey back, she would have to work out what to do on her arrival. Where to go and who to see. For the life of her she had absolutely no idea.

She spent the better part of two hours outdoors rather than confine herself to the stuffy little room with hard wooden benches to one side of the beer-stained taproom. She had had enough of confinement to last her a lifetime, and while the docks at Portsmouth hardly ranked as the great outdoors, the salt-laden sea air, mingled, admittedly, with the aromas of maritime industry – hot tar and canvas, sodden rope and horse dung, smoke and rotting fishes – smelled finer to her than any perfumed salon could do. The old gentleman was true to his word. Apart from ensuring that she was not bothered by sailors or tradesmen, hawkers and urchins, he kept a discreet silence, engrossed in his paper, while Anne sat upon a wooden bench hard against the sea wall.

Soon the coach arrived, and once the passengers had been disgorged – anxiously and excitedly looking about them and endeavouring to locate the ship that would transport them to foreign climes – and their luggage had been handed down to eager porters salivating at the prospect of a generous tip in

pounds, shillings and pence from those who would, like as
not, have no further use for the coinage of their sovereign
country, the coach was swept out and made ready for the
return journey. When the tired and sweating horses had been
changed to cries of 'Next pair out!' and the postboy doffed his
hat to indicate that all was ready, the old man held out his arm
to escort Anne across the cobbles, helping her up the two
steps into the coach, ensuring that his own large trunk was
safely stowed, and solicitously enquiring as to whether or not
she was comfortable in the corner seat, with her back to the
horses (safer, he suggested, in the event of any unforeseen
hazards). Having confirmed that she was perfectly happy, he
took off his hat and carefully placed it on the seat beside him,
before smiling again at his temporary charge and resuming
the scrutiny of his *Daily Examiner.*

The two of them were quite alone inside the carriage on the
first leg of their journey as far as Fareham, since the rest of the
passengers occupied the cheaper accommodation up top. But
the old man had to put down his paper for much of the journey, since the roughness of the road made reading impossible.
It was wide enough to take six coaches abreast, but Mr Telford
and Mr Macadam had yet to make their presence felt.

To the sound of a yelping horn they drew to a halt outside
The Red Lion and her companion turned to Anne and said,
'We shall have company now, I suspect.'

The old man took out his pocket watch and checked the
time. 'Not too long now. We should be there for luncheon.
And I have to admit that I shall be ready for mine. My brother
will send his chaise to meet the coach at Winchester. Perhaps
I might be able to offer you passage should you be travelling
in the same direction?'

'Oh, no. I am not sure . . .'

'It really will be no trouble, should you care to tell me in which direction you are to travel onwards.' Then the old man paused and smote his knee. 'But forgive me, I omitted to introduce myself. My name is Nicholas Stockbridge. Brother of the earl. Perhaps you have heard of him?'

38

The Old Mill, Itchen Parva

20 June 2010

Kind jealous doubts, tormenting fears,
And anxious cares, when past,
Prove our hearts' treasure fixed and dear,
And make us blest at last.

John Wilmot, Lord Rochester, 'The
Mistress: A Song', 1647–1680

'Can I get her some chickens then?' Harry asked Alex, once Anne had gone to bed and the two of them were alone in the kitchen.

Alex gave him what is often called 'an old-fashioned look'. 'Oh . . . go on then. But not too many. We do like an egg or two, but not until they're coming out of our ears.'

'Great! I'll have a scout round and see what I can find. Four should be enough. Shall I get a cockerel as well?'

'No thank you! I do like the occasional lie-in on a Sunday morning and I don't want to be woken at the crack of dawn by a screaming bird!'

'Er . . . right. No cockerel, just four chickens.'

'But what about a hen house? Don't we need a coop or something?'

'Just leave it all to me.'

'But it will cost quite a lot—'

'Hey! Did you hear?' admonished Harry. 'I said, leave it all to me. A present for Anne. It's time she had something alive to look after.'

Alex frowned. 'Mr Moses is alive to her.'

'I know, but looking after a stuffed dog is not the same as looking after—'

'Unstuffed chickens?'

'Quite. They'll be good for her; show her what real animals need – regular care and attention.' Then he saw the look of concern on Alex's face. 'Not too much, though; that's why chickens will be perfect, and at least they produce something – unlike a rabbit or a guinea pig. And hamsters die if you breathe on them. Oh, and chickens don't bite.'

'No,' agreed Alex, 'but they peck.'

'Dirt and grass, not humans. Well,' reflected Harry, 'not very often.'

'They could have your eye out,' countered Alex.

Harry looked at her and saw that she was laughing. 'Do you remember when your mother used to say that? When you were playing with anything remotely pointed: don't do that, you'll have your eye out! But nobody ever did. Disappointing really.'

Then he noticed she had gone quiet. 'Oh, sorry. Did I . . .'

'No. It's nothing. I lost my mum quite early that's all. Brought up by dad. She never had the chance to offer me any advice – about sharp objects, puberty or . . . men.' Then she saw Harry's discomfort. 'Oh, don't worry! I got over it years ago. Had to. The wounds have mended. I've had others to occupy me since then.'

'Like losing James?' It came out unbidden. For so long it had been the elephant in the room, and now he had let it loose, thoughtlessly.

'Yes.'

It was too late now to retract. 'You never mention him.'

'Don't I?'

Harry shook his head. 'Not that I'm being critical, it's just—'

'An observation?'

'Yes. I don't want to pry or anything . . .'

'No. You ought to know. Come on, let's take a bottle down to the stream. It's warm enough outside, and I can hear Anne from there if she needs me.'

They strolled down the garden in silence, Harry nervous as to what he was about to hear, wishing that he had not brought up the subject, and Alex wondering how best to explain things.

An old wooden table and two chairs sat underneath one of the willow trees, and Harry noticed that its branches had been trimmed to make a kind of green umbrella above their heads. A little jam pot of buttercups sat in the centre. 'Anne's,' said Alex, by way of explanation for the crudeness of the arrangement.

'S'lovely,' said Harry kindly.

Alex poured them each a glass of the cool white wine and leaned back in her chair. 'You didn't read about it in the paper then?' she asked.

'No. Well, not originally.'

Alex looked at him questioningly.

'Rick found an old one the other day and showed it to me.'

'Oh. I see.'

Harry made to explain. There was a hint of anxiety in his voice. 'He just came across it. What he really found – in his grandfather's chest – was an advertisement for the sale of this place. As I told you, his family used to own it – years back – and his grandfather had cut it out and kept it. The story of your . . . court case . . . was on the back. It was just weird. An odd coincidence.'

Alex said, 'I saw the advert when I read the paper. I thought that at least some good might come out of the whole sorry mess. I took it as a sign, I suppose. A happy coincidence; a pointer as to where I should go and what I should do. You know: when God closes a door he opens a window, that sort of thing. I wanted to move away from the city, bring up Anne in the country, away from all the people who would have their own preconceptions – misconceptions – of what happened. I – that is I mean, we – just wanted a fresh start. It was really quite dreadful.' She took a sip of her wine. 'Here seemed as good a place as any, and, when we saw it, everything just fell into place; well, as much as anything could back then. Life seemed so disjointed that I could hardly think straight. I just had to get away quickly, that was all, or I think I might have gone mad.'

Harry waited for a moment and then asked, 'So who suggested that . . . well, that you had a hand in James's suicide?'

'Some old biddy who used to dote on him. He used to handle her affairs – legal affairs – after her husband died. She didn't like me at all. Used to call James up at every hour of the day and night. Got very shirty when I answered the phone and suggested to her that it would be kinder to call him in business hours between Monday and Friday. But she had a bit of money and knew a few important people and so assumed that meant she could call whenever she wanted.'

'Were she and James – well, you know . . . ?'

'Oh, heavens no! She was far too old, not at all his type, and whatever else James was, he was faithful.' She looked thoughtful and then added, 'Apart from just the once.'

Harry paused with his glass halfway to his mouth. 'Just the once?'

'Oh dear, you really are getting the full works tonight, aren't you?'

'That's all right. I don't mind.'

'We'd been married about four years. We were both quite busy. That was the problem I suppose – two career-minded people who love each other but don't have enough time to work at their relationship. She filled the gap. Was there when he needed her – well, they worked for the same firm; shared an office. The irony was that James and I met there, too, but it was unwritten company policy that married couples didn't work together in the firm, so James remained with Walker, Payne and Geery and I moved out to work on my own. Mainly doing legal aid cases.'

'Brave,' offered Harry.

'Someone has to do it. It seemed important. James used to specialise in probate and advising old ladies on their investments and I used to battle for the voiceless. Not because I was noble, but just because . . . well, it needed doing.'

'So . . . ?'

'Oh, he had a fling, then she went off with another of the partners and he realised what a fool he'd been. That she was just using him as a leg up – as well as a leg over. But it woke me up, too. Made me realise that we couldn't both work at the rate we were doing and that it would be better if I stayed at home.'

'Wasn't that a bit tough? A bit hard on you?'

'It was my choice. And I didn't stagnate. I did odd bits of work from home – just to keep the little grey cells going – and then Anne came along and I was happy to be a mum. Simple as that. There was no great sacrifice involved. I'm not one of those career women who thinks that bringing up a child is dreary and boring. It's every bit as challenging as the law – just different, and very rewarding.'

'So how long was it before . . . ?'

'Before James's illness started? About four years after Anne was born. It was little things at first – lapses of memory. Disorientation. Suddenly he'd be absent . . . I mean, he'd be here but his mind would be elsewhere, and not in that way that it is when you're concentrating on something else. He'd just be vacant, and then come back. It quite quickly became evident that it was something serious.'

'Did he know?' asked Harry.

'Not at first, no. And then when he did realise I'm not sure that he really took it in. The progression was fairly rapid in the early stages. And then came the worst bit of all – the personality change.'

Alex took a large gulp of her wine and put down the glass on the table. 'He started to get violent. Lashing out for no apparent reason. I can tell you that a thirteen-stone man can't half pack a punch. I used to lay witch hazel in by the crate, until I got better at dodging. But that's when I really started to worry. I was afraid he might hurt Anne. I thought it would really be best if he went into a home, but I just couldn't bring myself to do it.'

'So what happened?'

'Before I could work out what to do for the best, he took his own life.'

'At home?'

'Yes. That's when I realised that he must have known what was happening. That he didn't feel he could go on.'

'And Anne?'

'She went into herself for quite a while. Became very self-reliant. She still is, I suppose. But I worried. Bottling things up is not a good thing – especially for a child. It can lead to all sorts of problems.'

'But how could anyone think that you were involved with James's death? I mean, for it to come to court?'

'Oh, James's client was very persuasive, and once the police were involved they have to satisfy themselves that there are no real grounds for prosecution.'

'So why did they prosecute?'

Alex shrugged. 'Who knows? Wheels within wheels. Perhaps she was a personal friend of the chief constable. But I can tell you that it was the most dreadful thing that's ever happened to me. I've never felt so desperate before or since, and it's only now that I'm beginning to get myself together again.' She smiled at him. It was a rueful smile. 'I can tell you; you're taking on a real basket case here.'

Harry reached across the table and squeezed her hand. 'Oh, I don't think so.' Then he asked 'How did he . . . I mean, what did he use . . . ?'

'Sleeping tablets. I came home with Anne and found him. I'd been at school with her all day and he was sitting in a chair with the pill bottles beside him.'

'So you had an alibi anyway?'

'Not exactly. I came home at lunchtime on my own to check that he was OK.'

'And that was enough?'

'Enough to make them think that it was possible that I'd helped him.'

Harry picked up his glass and got up from his chair, walking over to the stream. Then, without looking at Alex, he asked, 'Do you think it's ever acceptable to help anybody to end their life?'

Alex stood up and walked over to him. 'No. I don't.'

He turned to look at her now. 'Not even when you love them more than anyone else in the world and you're watching them suffer, knowing that it will end in a painful death?'

'No, not even then. It is the most unspeakable thing. It is

agonising, more painful than I can begin to tell you, and the most heartbreaking experience in the world next to losing a child. But I don't think we can ever play God. Not under any circumstances.'

Harry turned away again and looked out across the stream, gazing silently into the middle distance.

Then she asked, 'You just had to be sure, didn't you?'

39

Winchester

17 April 1816

God moves in a mysterious way
His wonders to perform;
He plants His footsteps in the sea,
And rides upon the storm.

William Cowper,
Olney Hymns, 1779

The coach was quite full now, having taken on a party of six at Fareham for the second half of the journey to Winchester. Anne was agitated and, as a result, fidgety; playing with a loose button on the leather seat until it came off in her hand. She slipped it into her pocket and hoped that it would not be noticed. The sky was darkening as they reached their destination and, as the coach pulled into the yard of the Royal Hotel, there was much commotion.

Luggage was unloaded, ostlers came and unhitched the steaming team, passengers disembarked from up on the box and inside the coach, assisted by the postboy between his customary shouts of 'Next pair out!' and the potboy, the man who swept the courtyard and the chambermaid who happened to be passing.

The old man turned to instruct Anne to follow him and that his brother's chaise would be happy to deposit her at her ultimate destination, should it be anywhere along their route to Hatherley. But she was not to be seen. She had vanished as quickly as the dew on a June morning. The old man shrugged and said, 'Bless my soul!', then he went into the hotel to enquire as to the whereabouts of his transport.

The landlord explained that the earl's chaise had been delayed. A horseman had come to apologise; some family problem had meant that the household had been thrown into disarray. The old man frowned. His brother was a man who prided himself on his efficiency. Ah well, there would like as not be some perfectly simple explanation. He strode into the hall of the hotel and ordered a pint of ale. He would sit and read his paper until the earl's chaise arrived. It was odd. Very odd, but then these were odd times.

Anne used the confusion of disembarkation to slip into the shadows, and from there edged her way out of the courtyard and on to the street. But which way to go? She leaned on a low stone wall, overgrown with ivy and hop, some way from the hotel, and looked to left and right. Seeing a man walking towards her she was at first fearful that it could be her coach companion come to find her, but this man was clad in a different coloured coat – he was in dark blue, not the honey colour that Nicholas Stockbridge had been wearing. He walked with a determined step and Anne lifted her arm to attract his attention and asked, 'Excuse me, sir. Could you be kind enough to point me in the direction of Withercombe?'

The man smiled and lifted his hat. 'Of course. When you come to the end of the street here, you will find that the road forks. Take the right fork, and then after a mile take the left fork. Keep straight along that road and it will lead you, eventually, to Withercombe.'

Anne made a small bob and said, 'Thank you.'

The man raised his hat once more, then a look of concern

crossed his face. 'But it is seven miles. Surely you are not to walk all that way?' He looked up at the sky. 'It will likely rain before too long.'

Anne smiled, and her relief was palpable. 'Thank you, sir. I shall not mind the rain, now that I know I am on the right road.' And with that she turned and walked off in the direction that had been pointed out to her. The man watched her go and shook his head. The distant rumble of thunder confirmed his suspicions that, on the balance of probability, the young woman was in for a soaking.

She had gone little over a mile – just past the right fork – before the heavens opened. She was clear of the city now; even the cathedral tower was no longer visible. The high road had now become a track, wide enough for only a single coach – not that many came this way – and there were occasional passing places for farm carts and teams of horses. The gently rolling Hampshire downland to right and left, emerald in its spring livery, seemed to be nudging her on, and then she saw the river. Her river. The chalk stream, the River Itchen, snaking its way across the meadows; dividing and reuniting, whispering its way over its pebble bed, snaking through flag irises and rushes, teasing the long wands of willows that trailed across its shimmering surface and singing now with the sound of rain. The acrid tang of freshly moistened earth came to her nostrils. It made a welcome change from the smell of the city, laced though it was with salt air. This was the smell she was used to. The smell of the countryside: of crushed grass and bruised leaves, of river water and early morning rain.

She did not mind the rain at first. It refreshed her and seemed to be washing away the shocking events of the night before. For they were indeed shocking. She had felt brave at the time; determined to survive the ordeal placed before her. But now, in the cold and rain-soaked light of day, came the terrible dawning of reality. Her joy at seeing the familiar river once more was tempered with the bitter gall of harsh truth. That only yesterday she had witnessed the death of her one true friend (Sam did not count; Sam was Sam and he was different). She had been run away with – and she had, had she not? It was not of her own free will, was it? Not after the dreadful accident? The escape from the evil Lavallier – and he was evil, was he not? Falling into the clutches of Old Phoebe and Mr Pontifex – but she could not feel too much ill will towards Mr Pontifex, for it was he who had allowed her to escape. And as for the night and Master Frederick . . . It was at this point in her recalling of the events of the previous twenty-four hours that her emotions overcame her and she collapsed sobbing on a fallen tree trunk by the banks of the river, as the rain beat down upon her once fine clothes – Eleanor's once-fine clothes – and upon the surface of the spinning waters. What was to become of her? Where did she think she was going? And what would happen when she got there? Did she really think that they would welcome her at the Manor House with open arms? The news of Eleanor's death would surely be known now, and her own disappearance in some way linked with it. They must have found her body down by the river. And her own book. Her book! It would be lying near Eleanor's body, for that was where she had rested it when they were changing clothes. In the rush to mount the horses and be away, she had not picked it up and transferred it into the pocket of her new garment. She had hastily pulled it from her own pocket and forgotten to pick it up. Her book and Eleanor's body . . . the words kept turning over and over in her mind.

Perhaps Mrs Fitzgerald would understand. Would help her. But Mrs Fitzgerald had clearly been exasperated by her recent actions. Why else would she have lectured her the previous morning and forbidden her from going out? And yet she had defied her and taken off without asking. 'Without', as Mrs Fitzgerald would say, 'a by-your-leave.'

The truth. That would be her only salvation. She would ask to see Sir Thomas and tell him exactly what had happened. Tell him about Lavallier, and how she was taken against her will. Tell him that she had escaped his clutches in Portsmouth and spent the night— But no! How could she confess that she had lost her maidenhood to Master Frederick? It was unthinkable! And she could not tell only part of the story, for she was sure to be found out. She had, after all, taken Master Frederick's money. But then she had returned it, hadn't she? So she had proved her honesty. It was she who had been wronged, all along. First by Lavallier, and then by Master Frederick. But who would believe that? Would a father take the word of a housemaid against that of his son? It was out of the question. Banishment would then be Sir Thomas's only recourse. She had brought disgrace on the family and would spend the rest of her life in the workhouse.

Oh, why had she done it? Why could she not have realised that her life at the Manor House was a fortunate one? That Sam was her sort of boy and not some dreamt-of highwayman who would whisk her away? She had indeed been whisked away, and look where it had led.

On she trod, with faltering steps. She could feel the rain penetrating her clothes now. The cloak, though capable of repelling a light shower, was not intended for heavier weather. Soon she would be soaked through, and already the weight of the saturated garment was beginning to tire her. She stood up, determined to carry on. Just ahead of her was a wooden finger post, pointing the way to somewhere. She must read it and reassure herself that she was on the right track. Then she trod upon the hem of her cloak and fell headlong on to the muddy track. She struggled to her feet under the weight of the sodden fabric and bowed her head to deflect the torrential rain that beat down upon meadow and tree, river and rivulet. The whole world seemed to be engulfed in water now. So hard did the rain fall that it bounced up from any surface that offered resistance. Anne fought to draw breath without sucking in a portion of the deluge. Eventually she reached the sign and read the two names – one village to the right and one to the left. Shielding her eyes, the better to make out the script, she read 'Martyr Worthy' to the left and 'Alresford' to the right. There was no mention of Withercombe. But Withercombe was small. Not large enough or important enough to have a sign of its own.

Which fork to take? Was it right and then left? Or left and then right? Which was nearest to Withercombe? Martyr Worthy or Alresford? In the midst of the deluge she found it difficult to recall. There was a large oak tree ahead; she would rest underneath it and get her breath back in the hope that she might also be able to gain her bearings. Think! She must think . . . and remember the man's instructions.

Had she turned to the right or to the left at the last fork? Right! She had turned right, because she had noticed the milestone and it had said 'Winchester 1 mile, Portsmouth 30 miles'. She could remember that quite clearly. So she must now turn to the left.

She stepped out from under the oak tree, her head bowed against the rain, and pushed forwards in the direction of Alresford. She had walked just a few hundred yards before her head began to spin and the ground to rise upwards. Within a few moments the rain had ceased, but by that time Anne was no longer aware of the vagaries of the weather. They found her beside the track, looking for all the world like a pile of discarded clothing.

40

The Manor House, Withercombe
21 April 1816

From this amphibious ill-born mob began
That vain, ill-natured thing, an Englishman.
Daniel Defoe, *The True-Born*
Englishman, 1701

Jacob Palfrey had been every bit as troubled by Anne's disappearance as Sam the stable lad, though he did not, for the sake of his own dignity, give much away to his friend. Sam, however, continued to finger the copy of *The Highwayman's Bride* that nestled in the pocket of his jerkin, as though it might, somehow, give up its secrets. But yield them it did not.

Jacob found him this April morning, mucking out the horses. Sam looked up from his menial task and enquired, 'You be not working this morning then?'

'Father is gone to Winchester with cloth. I cannot work the mill alone.'

Sam scraped at the dung that clung to the floor of the stable. 'So you are of a mind to come and bother me?'

Jacob nodded.

'Well, I have no time to stop. The master is to go by carriage to see Lord Stockbridge at noon and I must ready the horses.'

Jacob looked about him. 'I see no horses.'

Sam stood up and stretched his aching back. 'They be tethered by the coach house.' He nodded in the direction of the end of the stable yard. 'Ready for harnessing.' He put down the long-handled shovel and picked up the wicker basket of dung, walking out of the stable and round to the back of the building where he added it to the steaming heap of straw and equine ordure.

Jacob followed him. 'No more news?'

'Not until the master returns.'

'You think then we shall know more?'

'Only if he cares to tell Mr Jencks of any developments.' Having emptied the basket, Sam walked back to the stable and hung it from a hook on the wall, before crossing to the coach house to harness Leger and Alderney. Jacob followed him like a spaniel.

'You can help me pull this out if you have nothing else to do,' instructed Sam, indicating the pole at the front of the chaise that nestled, gleaming, in the end coach house along-side the larger monogrammed carriage that was used for 'state' occasions. There had not been one during Sam's time here – the last time the coach had been out had been in '89 for the service celebrating the recovery of the old king's health when Sir Thomas felt that some show of grandeur would be appropriate. Sir Thomas had been in his thirties then, and newly married; those were times when he was more carefree, more showy, said Mr Jencks, who had himself been a lowly stable lad at the time. Nowadays, on almost every occasion, the smaller chaise was considered perfectly adequate.

The two horses tossed their heads as Sam fastened bits and bridles, collar harnesses and traces. Looking on at this strange and confusing arrangement of leather and brass that Sam handled with a deftness born of habit, the miller's son could not but be impressed, though nothing on earth would have caused him to acknowledge the fact. His own understanding of horsemanship stretched no further than harnessing his father's cob, Nobby, between the shafts of the simple cart that took their cloth to market.

Now the horses were fully attached, Sam stood back to check that all was in place, and caught the merest hint of a smile on Jacob's lips. It quickly vanished, but for Sam it was enough; he had received the silent compliment and it lifted his spirits.

At the sound of footsteps and general commotion at the archway that led from the Manor House to the stables, Jacob melted into the shadows and left his companion to hold the horses' bridles while Mr Jencks and Sir Thomas crossed to the chaise. Sir Thomas, cane in hand, had on his best tailcoat and Timothy Jencks his day livery; this was an outing of some note, clearly.

'Sam,' acknowledged Sir Thomas. 'All ready?'

'Yes, sir,' confirmed the boy.

The baronet mounted the chaise with some considerable effort and heaved himself around until he was comfortable. The horses shifted their weight a little and blew heavily. Timothy Jencks stepped up to the box and took the reins. 'Just hold for a moment, Sam,' he instructed. 'We have another passenger.'

Sam looked questioningly at the groom.

'Master Frederick is home and he is to accompany the master.'

There was no time for any further questioning (not that Sam would have made to ask anything in the presence of Sir Thomas) since at that moment, across the yard, strode a fair-haired young man, dressed in a long green coat and carrying in his hand a tall hat and a pair of yellow leather gloves. He nodded at Sam as he leapt up the step with far greater agility than his father. 'All right, Sam? Still here then?'

The man winked at him, and Sam felt embarrassed and surprised that the baronet's son should have remembered his name. Master Frederick had been up in London at his uncle's chambers for almost a year now, and Sam doubted that he would ever return. What could have brought him back to Withercombe; a young man whose love of the town and all it had to offer was well known? He had left under something of a cloud; some kind of disagreement with his father, by all accounts. And yet he was popular with the staff, especially the ladies, who blushed whenever he came into a room – Anne included. This was a courtesy visit, obviously. Either that or he had come to ask his father for money. That was what all sons of rich gentlemen did; it was well known.

Sir Thomas coughed loudly, and Master Frederick was dissuaded from any further conversation with the stable lad. Instead he nodded resignedly at Sam and sat down opposite his father, who took his cane and tapped smartly upon the polished woodwork, at which signal Timothy Jencks urged the horses forward. They trotted smartly out of the stable yard and away down the drive in the direction of Lord Stockbridge and Hatherley.

With the stable yard empty once more, Jacob Palfrey emerged from the shadows and looked down the drive in the direction of the cloud of dust kicked up by the chaise and the two horses. 'Bless me,' he said. 'I did not think to see him again.'

By the end of the day, Sam had further news for his friend. At the Bluebell Inn, over a half-pint of ale, Sam told Jacob all that he knew. It did not take long. The crumbs of gossip that

Timothy Jencks let drop were few in number; they did not concern Anne, which was a disappointment to them both. The story was that Lady Eleanor had been going to elope with a man called Lavallier. A man who had, since that day, completely vanished. Just like Anne.

41

St Jude's School, Winchester

21 June 2010

Sunt geminae somni portae, quarum altera fertur
Cornea, qua veris facilis datur exitus umbris;
Altera candenti perfecta nitens elephanto,
Sed falsa ad caelum mittunt insomnia Manes.

There are two gates of Sleep, one of which it is held is made of horn and by it easy egress is given to real ghosts; the other is shining, fashioned of gleaming white ivory, but the shades send deceptive visions that way to the light.

Virgil, *Aeneid*, Book VI, 29–19 BC

'Only three weeks to go, thank God.' Rick dumped a heap of exercise books on the table in the staff room and took from Harry's proffered hand the mug of coffee that was waiting for him. 'Christ, you look knackered!' was his secondary remark.

'No. You mean "thank you for the coffee", I think.'

'That as well. But you do look knackered. Not sleeping?'

'Not much, no.'

Rick grinned. 'All loved up?'

'No! Haunted.'

'What by? Fear of the future?'

'I'm not sure. But not that. Something. Someone . . .' Harry slumped down in a chair and Rick saw the expression on his face.

'You're not kidding, are you?'

Harry shook his head. 'Nope. There's something going on in that house of mine and I don't know what it is. Cold winds. Draughts. I've never really thought much about ghosts – or poltergeists – but I am beginning to . . .'

'Is it menacing then?' Rick leaned forward, eager for any crumb of excitement in a day that had so far yielded nothing more eventful than three detentions and a potential exclusion order.

'No. At least I don't think so. It's just . . . well, a presence I suppose.'

'Nothing visible?'

'No. Well, not most of the time. I did think I saw something out of the corner of my eye when I was knocking a hole from the bedroom to the bathroom to make a new doorway. And I thought I heard a voice, too, calling my name. But nothing since then.'

Rick looked sceptical. 'Are you sure you're not being a bit fanciful? I mean, you have got a lot going on in your life at the moment – new house, new relationship – I mean, it's not surprising that you're not sleeping. It could just be cold feet, you know?'

'At the moment it's cold everything,' replied Harry, frowning. 'And I'm not fanciful. There's a real chill about the cottage – upstairs anyway – and it wasn't there before. And Alex's little girl, Anne, she was convinced that she saw something. A lady, she said; a lady in white.'

'Well, well, well. Sounds like a ghost to me. Perhaps you'd better have it exorcised.'

'Oh, for goodness' sake. This isn't a movie!'

'No! I'm serious. You can have things like this . . . sorted out.'

'Who by? Spencer Tracy or Trevor Howard in a cassock?'

'There was a piece in our parish magazine—'

Harry looked incredulous. 'You read your parish magazine? Now I've heard it all.'

'Not me. Rachel. Tilly goes to Sunday school . . . Anyway, there was this piece written by a local vicar, apparently every diocese actually does have somebody whose job it is to go to houses or . . . buildings . . . or whatever and deal with, you know, visitations. It's something the church does and they do it more often than you'd think.'

'Well, that's a relief.'

'So you'll do it then?'

'I mean it's a relief to know that it's not my imagination.'

Rick took a large gulp of the coffee. 'More common than you'd think. I'd seriously consider it if I were you. That way you might get some sleep at night. Or at least if you didn't sleep it would be due to doing more exciting things.'

'Cheeky bugger!' said Harry.

'Language Timothy: not in front of the head of RS.'

Harry turned to see Deirdre Tattersall sitting on the other side of the staff room reading a magazine. She was frowning at him – Central Casting's version of a religious education teacher – her straight dark hair cut into a neat bob, Dame Edna glasses on the end of her nose, her body encased in a tweed skirt, powder-blue jumper and pearls.

Harry mouthed, 'Sorry', and turned back to Rick.

'So what's the latest?' asked Rick.

'If you're going to ask for a progress report every time we meet, I'm going to stop seeing you,' said Harry.

'Just interested, that's all. Just keen for you to be happy.' Rick patted Harry on the knee.

'If you keep doing that,' warned Harry, 'the head of RS will get the wrong idea.'

'Nah, she's reading *The Tablet* now. Totally engrossed in Popedom.'

'Anyway, we spoke about the newspaper clipping. Eventually.'

'And you're happy that she was innocent?'

'God! You make it sound as though she's a mass murderer!' At this Deirdre Tattersall looked up.

'Keep your voice down,' retorted Rick. 'I was only asking.'

Harry lowered his voice to a whisper. 'Well of course she was innocent. It was some jealous old biddy who had a crush on James – her late husband – apparently. Just muck-raking.'

'Evil old cow!'

'Yes. Really put Alex through it.'

'And the house? The Old Mill? Did she know it was in the same paper?'

'Yes. She saw the advert, too, apparently, when she was reading the piece about the case. Thought it was divine intervention.'

'There's quite a lot of divine intervention in your life at the moment, isn't there?'

'Rather too much if you ask me,' confirmed Harry. 'You've heard about Ted Chieveley?'

'Yes. What a bugger.' He looked over his shoulder. 'Sorry Deirdre.'

Deirdre looked up from *The Tablet* over her streamlined blue glasses and offered a weak and insincere smile.

'Bit of a coincidence, that happening to Alex and now to Ted. History repeating itself.'

'There's a lot of it about,' said Harry. 'Everybody seems to know someone with dementia in one form or another. Do you think it's always been as bad?'

'I suspect so,' said Rick. 'You can't blame it all on aluminium saucepans. Or was it copper? I think the thing is nowadays we just have names for everything. What was the title of that Alan Bennett play? The one about the Surveyor of the Queen's Pictures? Anthony Blunt – the gay bloke who was a spy?'

'What are you talking about?' asked Harry exasperatedly.

'The play about him . . . its title: *A Question of Attribution*. I've told you before.'

'What's that got to do with Ted?'

'What I'm saying is that I reckon we've always had these problems – diseases and the like. It's just that in the old days they used to give them different names – vague ones like dropsy and 'the ague' and all that sort of thing. Now we call them specific things – Parkinson's disease, Hodgkin's lymphoma, Alzheimer's, that sort of thing. Fancy having a disease named after you. What an accolade. It's as if we invented them all, but I bet really they've always been around. It's just a question of attribution. And finding a cause. And, as far as that goes, we're as much in the dark as we always were, aluminium saucepans or no aluminium saucepans.'

'Have you finished?' asked Harry.

'Yes, I think so.' Rick drained his mug and got up to go. 'Oh, I almost forgot. I've been delving around a bit more in my grandfather's trunk. Just a tick . . .' He walked over to the row of lockers arranged along one wall, pulled open the door of the one marked 'R. Palfrey, Mathematics', and withdrew from the top shelf a small and battered book which he tossed casually in Harry's direction. 'Here you are,' he said. 'Some kind of notebook. Kept by one of my ancestors. Jacob Palfrey, I think his name was. I haven't really had much of a chance to read it, what with taking Tilly everywhere lately, and by the evening I'm too knackered to keep my eyes open. The writing's a bit hard to fathom, and to be honest I'm happier with *Motor Cycle News*, but you never know, there might be something interesting in there. It'll give you an insight into a prominent local family.' At this he grinned, picked up the pile of exercise books and staggered through the doorway.

As he passed Deirdre Tattersall he said '*Motor Cycle News*, Deirdre. That'd put hairs on your chest.' And then, under his breath when he was confident that he was out of earshot, 'If there aren't any there already . . .'

42

Mill Cottage
24 April 1816

For secrets are edged tools,
And must be kept from children and from fools.
John Dryden, 'Sir Martin Mar-All', 1667

'I still think we should have told the squire,' confirmed William Palfrey. ''Twill not be long before he finds out and then we shall be in trouble.'

Agnes Palfrey bestowed upon her husband what was known, even in the reign of King George III, as an 'old-fashioned look'. With a note of impatience in her voice she addressed him: 'And what then? What do you suppose would have happened? What could squire have done that we have not?'

The miller shook his head. 'There is trouble here. Much trouble. They has been looking for yon maiden for a week now. Vanished, she has, they thinks. In to thin—'

'Oh do stop, William. 'Twas you who found her, I admit, but 'twas both of us who gave her shelter. And we cannot know for certain who she is . . .'

'That we do woman. 'Tis the maid from the Manor House as sure as sure. Clothing of a lady and hands of a housemaid. 'Tis plain to see.'

'And a human being for all that. When you found her she had hardly a breath left in her body. Of course you did right by bringing her here. Any Christian would have done the same. Tell the squire? There will be plenty of time to tell the squire once we know she is well enough. The fever is passing now. It has been a week. A long fever. But she is mending, slowly. We must build up her strength, and then she can answer the questions she will surely be asked.'

'And if we are discovered?'

'If we are discovered we will explain that we have done what anyone with plain decency would have done – brought a stranger back to life from the brink of death. And that is no crime. We are not harbouring a criminal. Just a young girl who fell foul of the nature of others. Look at her. Does she seem evil? Does she seem wicked? She seems to me to be a young girl the like of which we could have had ourselves, had we not been blessed with Jacob. No; when the time is right she will face the consequences of her actions, whatever they were. It is not up to us to judge; it is up to us to do our Christian duty. With that and calves' foot jelly and a steady supply of broth, she will regain her strength. We are far enough away from the Manor House to keep the matter from those who live and work there.'

'They will find out, mark my words.'

'Not if we keep our peace. They do not come this way; they has no reason to.'

'And what of Jacob? And the stable boy at the Manor – Sam?'

'Jacob has been told that should he breathe a word of what has occurred here to anyone at the Manor House then he can consider that there is no longer a roof over his head at the Mill. He sleeps there; you and I live here. He need not venture over our threshold until there is reason to do so.'

At this the miller shrugged and left the room, mumbling to himself. He was not happy, but he was wise enough to know that should he cross his wife, his life would be even more uncomfortable than if he were to cross the squire. The squire could deprive him of his job. A scolding wife could deprive him of the will to live. He went back to the mill and his hammers, but even the sound of their rhythmic thumping, and the roar of the water through the sluices, could not erase from his mind the worry of his discovery.

He had been journeying back from Winchester with an empty cart, alone this time. Jacob had been left behind at the fulling mill to oversee the latest batch of cloth. The rain was so heavy that his head was bowed low under the oilskin that kept out the worst of the weather. But even so, the wind blew the rain into his face until it ran off his chin in a steady rivulet. The sodden horse, head bowed as low as that of her master, could do little more than plod steadily into the teeth of the storm. At the Martyr Worthy junction, he noticed what at first he thought was a large rock at the side of the road. But then his familiarity with the route alerted him to the fact that there were no rocks or boulders on this road and that the grey-black heap upon the verge must be a bundle of discarded clothing. Irritably he pulled on the reins and stopped the horse, who did not even try to pull at the lush grass as the rain pelted down. Instead, she stood as still as the rock that he had at first thought he had seen.

Alighting from the cart he walked over to the bundle and pulled at the cloth, starting when his actions revealed a pale and rain-washed face. Swiftly he lifted up the crumpled body, weighing no more than the clothes themselves it seemed, and carried it across to the cart. He was far from certain that the young girl – for it was a girl, he could see that now – was alive, so cold did the skin of her cheek feel to the back of his hand.

If she were breathing it was very shallowly, for he could not detect any form of life.

He laid her gently in the cart, immediately behind the box where he sat and where she would be sheltered from the rain, pulling over her the tarpaulin he kept to protect his cloth from foul weather. Whipping the reins across the horse's back, he travelled now at a brisk trot in the direction of the mill, the horse sensing the urgency and not protesting at what would previously have been regarded as unseemly haste, given the foul weather.

Agnes Palfrey had been quite clear what they should do. While most would have sent for the doctor, it was her opinion that such an action would, in all probability, lead to problems, not to say expense. If this young girl was who they thought she was, then taking her up to the Manor House and exposing her to the squire and Mrs Fitzgerald would, like as not, result in serious consequences. The girl had a fever. But Agnes Palfrey had sat with enough of her relations to know what to do in the case of a fever. She was here. She would minister. William could complain all he liked, but the girl was young and healthy – if a little frail – and would, with God's help, come through. It seemed more important to the miller's wife that the girl was treated with kindness, for although Agnes Palfrey was regarded by many locally as a tough old battle-axe, she was, at heart, a woman of devout Christian principles, and these manifested themselves in all the ways of God. The seven deadly sins were anathema to her and the Ten Commandments her rules of life. She lived by her catechism, but never lost sight of the fact that human kindness was at the heart of life and that many weaknesses could be forgiven if they were accompanied by generosity of spirit. It was lucky for Anne that of all the people who could have found her by the road, she had chanced to be discovered by the husband of a woman who was, above all, pragmatic and humane.

Seven days after they had found her, Anne opened her eyes and took in her surroundings. Agnes Palfrey was by her side at the time. At first came the disorientation, then the fear, and finally the insistence on rising, dressing and going on her way. This sequence of events was rapidly quashed by Agnes who, sensing the likelihood of such a reaction, had taken care to remove all traces of Anne's clothing, so that all she had to protect her modesty was the cotton night-dress in which she had slept.

'But how long . . . ?' asked Anne feebly.

'A week. Seven long days you have been here.'

'But where . . . ?

'The cottage. At the mill. The fulling mill. I am Mrs Palfrey. My husband William it was who found you. Lying by the Winchester road.'

Anne's eyes began to fill with tears as the realisation of her plight flooded over her.

'Now, now. There is no need for that.'

'Oh but, Mrs Fitzgerald—'

'Mrs Fitzgerald will be told when the time is right. At the moment there is no need for you to worry. We need to build up your strength and get you on your feet again. You have taken water and a little broth, but calves' foot jelly and wholesome food will have you mended in no time.'

'Does anyone know I am here?'

'No one except William and myself, and my son Jacob who has been sworn to secrecy.'

'But he knows Sam, the stable boy and—'

'And should he breathe a word to anyone, he knows that the

wrath of his mother is akin to the wrath of God; but God is safely in his heaven and I am closer to hand. He will tell no one.'

Anne flopped back on to the pillow and murmured, 'I fear I have been very wicked. I do not know as I shall be forgiven.'

Her face was white, and her auburn hair framed it so that it seemed to have been carved from alabaster.

'It is the way of the world,' said Agnes softly, 'that pretty young girls is taken advantage of.' She was speaking to herself as much as to Anne, and she wondered what might have befallen this young maid, so innocent and unworldly, lying there before her like a broken china doll. She would keep her peace, for the time being, and help the young girl to mend. How often she had prayed, when younger, for a daughter. And then Jacob had come along and she had known in her heart that she would have no more children. She had lived in a household composed completely of men for her entire married life. More than twenty years it was now. It would be a change to have the company of a young woman. And then she chastised herself for such thoughts. The world was as the Lord intended, and there was no sense in wishing for anything other.

At the Manor House, Sam listened daily for news of Anne. He could not understand why none was forthcoming. Mr Jencks mentioned the subject not at all; not since the day that he had taken Sir Thomas and Master Frederick over to see Lord Stockbridge. They had all returned with faces as long as a week, and nothing more had been said.

Even Jacob had stopped coming round to see him now. He had no idea why. Normally Jacob enjoyed the sport of baiting Sam, knowing that he was fond of Anne. He would tease him about her; suggest that she had not been the pure young girl that Sam had taken her for. Now he must have grown tired of the pastime. Soon the summer would come and there would be other distractions for Jacob. But for him, Sam, nothing would erase from his mind the memory of Anne. And nothing would stop him from wondering what had happened to her. He would never forget her, and the little book with its silly title would live safely in the box beneath his truckle bed as a reminder of times past.

43

Mill Cottage, Itchen Parva
21 June 2010

Into his diary, each day,
He poured his heartfelt thoughts;
His heart, alas, doth beat no more,
We read a life, of sorts.

Eleanor Chatfield,
'From Cradle to Knave', 1938

Was it, wondered Harry, because he now had better and more fulfilling things to occupy him than tracing his ancestry and researching the lives of the saints that they had assumed less importance in his life? The very phrasing of the question in his mind seemed to highlight the truth. It brought him up short. Almost made him laugh out loud at the absurdity of the comparison. How on earth could he possibly compare the two? Surely the reason that he had become so obsessed with the past was because for the last couple of years he had nothing to speak of in the way of a future. How could the past possibly be as important as the present? Or the future? And then he heard his own voice resonating across the classroom of his mind: 'The past informs the present and allows us to put our lives in context.'

Well, maybe. But with the end of term rapidly approaching, the future loomed large in his mind and context seemed irrelevant. What sort of future? With Alex? Doing what? It was not lost on him that having failed in a marriage with one lawyer he was heading speedily into a relationship with another. Yes, but

Alex and Serena were like chalk and cheese. They were both lawyers, yes. They were both women. To suggest that all lawyers were the same was to suggest that all women were the same. A pointless parallel. The relationship must be allowed to develop at the right speed. This was his inner voice of reason, as distinct from the other inner voice that rashly urged him on, regardless of the consequences.

Sighing heavily, he flopped into a chair by the kitchen window and looked out over the botanic garden that passed for a lawn. Time he got down to sorting out the garden as well, except that he rather liked it the way it was. Enjoyed the overgrown loucheness of it all – the natural abundance. He chuckled as he remembered the story of the vicar leaning over the white picket fence and saying to the gardener who was bent double pulling the weeds from a border overflowing with flowers, 'Isn't it wonderful what God can do in a garden?'

And the gardener replied. 'Yes; but you should have seen what it was like when he had it to himself.' God definitely had the upper hand in Harry's garden.

He leaned back in the chair and closed his eyes for a moment. 'God, grant me a better sleep tonight,' he muttered. 'Free of nature's icy grip.' It must be nature really, mustn't it, rather than supernature? Only people with overly vivid imaginations were in touch with that side of . . . whatever it was. He opened his eyes and glanced up the stairs, then he started. A glimpse of something white. Leaping from the chair he ran to the stairs and bounded up them two at a time to the landing. Nothing. Not even a breeze, though the long net curtain at the landing window did seem to be moving. It was his own slipstream that had caused it, dashing past at such a speed. Of course. Stupid. He must have caught it out of the corner of his eye and thought it was moving. He was tired, that was all. Suggestible. There was absolutely no sign of any lady – in red, white or blue. Lack of sleep had started him hallucinating. Well, if not hallucinating, then making his imagination more vivid.

He showered and changed, then went to the phone to call Alex. But there was no reply. He felt slightly deflated. He'd been unaware that she was going out, and then he checked himself. She did not have to tell him every time she wanted to leave the house, every time she was out with Anne. They had a life of their own. But the very thought of that filled him with a hollow sadness now, however unreasonable he told himself he was being. He wanted to know what she did now. When she did it. And who with.

His mind went back to their conversation of the day before. She had believed that he had accepted her version of events, hadn't she? But then what had been the last thing she'd said when she had explained the circumstances surrounding her husband's suicide? *You just had to be sure, didn't you?*

Hadn't there been a note of distress in her voice? Disappointment at the fact that he had pursued the matter; questioned her too deeply about where she was when James took his own life and on her feelings about assisted suicide. But he had only been curious; had only wanted to understand her more. It was all a part of getting to know her. But supposing she had misread it; had thought that he was questioning her honesty? What then?

She would have been hurt. She would have felt a sense of betrayal, that the man she was in a relationship with now (and they were in a relationship, weren't they? Surely he need not doubt that . . .) had needed to make sure that she was not capable of helping her husband to die. And what if she had been? Was it really so dreadful to help the person you loved most in the world to escape the pain of a slow and agonising death? Was it the work of a wicked and evil person to ease the

burden of a loved one, knowing that their subsequent departure from this world and absence from your life would leave
you feeling so wretched as to be unable to carry on? Surely
that was not selfish? Quite the opposite.

But who was he to sit in judgement? How dare he pass
an opinion on the rights and wrongs of a situation in which
he had never found himself and, God willing, never would
find himself. His thoughts turned to Pattie and Ted
Chieveley, now going through the same situation themselves. He would go round and see them at the weekend.
Though what he could say or in what way he could possibly help, he had no idea. He thought of Pattie and Alex
being in the same situation. What would Pattie do, compared
with what Alex had done?

He flopped into the chair again. Such introspection was
getting him nowhere. Alex would be back soon – Anne would
have to be put to bed – and then he would slip round and see
her. He would reassure her that he was there for her, come
what may. The past was the past and they both needed to
move on. Could they move on together?

He drummed his fingers on the chair arm, and then remembered the little book that Rick had handed to him in the staff
room. He went and pulled it from his school bag – a leather
pannier filled with books and forms that would soon be a part
of his past. What a relief it would be to unpack it for the last
time, and to discard the accretions of umpteen years of scho-
lastic life before moving on to . . . what?

'Here we go again,' he thought. 'Round in circles without
getting anywhere. What I really need is to not think for a while.
To take life as it comes. To work out gradually where I want to
go and what I want to do rather than panicking.' Easier said
– or thought – than done. But he would try. He would

endeavour to proceed rationally and at a sensible pace in terms of both his relationship and his working life. For now . . .

He opened the covers of the small, faded notebook. It was covered in a kind of rough felt, not the usual leather or card of old books. On the inside front cover he read: Jacob Palfrey – His Book. 1815. The Mill on the Itchen, Hantshire.

The writing was in an angular hand. Not exactly spidery, but difficult to read, nonetheless. The spelling was, in some cases, highly original (the schoolmaster in him would take some erasing) and the first entry was typical of such notebooks:

1815
Christemas day – Cold and bitter. River frozen at hedges. With father and mother to church. Mother say fine sermen. To me dull. Home for goose and pudding then out. Hard walking in snow and ice. Geese on field. Watercress beds frozen over. Gorse in bloom – kissing in season.

Harry had forgotten that old saw. His mother had told him it when he was young. The joke being that, whatever the time of year, the prickly gorse bush was always capable of sporting a few bright yellow flowers. Their aroma surprised him as a child – they smelt of coconut macaroons. He read on:

Boxing day – To Manor House for meet. Snow and ice still on groun but non so cold. Houns giving much tong. Walked four hour after houns. One fox to ground. One catched. Sam say he kissed scullery maid under misseltoe yesterday. She clout him round ear. Serve him right. He say I be jelous. No maid here to kiss. Pushed him over in snow and telled him that

scullery maid looking for better than he. Know the girl. Pretty
and good spirit. Name of Anne.

27 December – Thaw setting in. Dripping trees. Father starts
milling again as river thoring. Do not care to work today. Too
much ale on Boxing eve. Father not pleased with me. Says
must shape mysel. Mother say nothing. Only four days of year
left to see out.

The diary made Harry smile, though so far there was nothing
of significance within its covers. What was he hoping for?
Revelations? Unlikely. But he would carry on over the next
few evenings – dipping into it and deciphering the scrawl. The
sentiments might be of a mundane nature, but it was interesting that they had been written almost two hundred years ago
by the then miller's son, and close by, too. It would also reignite
the interest, put to one side over the last few weeks, in his
ancestry. There was still, deep down, a need to know.

Quite why it niggled away at him he did not understand.
There was nothing rational about it. He was not so rooted in
the past as he had been before he met Alex and yet, when he
cared to admit it to himself, that quest for understanding, for
knowledge of his forebears was still there. Perhaps it was just
natural curiosity, or the fact that having got as far back as
Merrily Flint in 1816, he did not want to leave it at that. The
mysterious Merrily Flint. It was the name as much as anything
that drove him on. He would solve the puzzle. One day.

It was a quarter to eight now. He called Alex again but there
was still no reply. He climbed the stairs to the bedroom. He
needed to fit an architrave to the doorway and had still to
measure up and order the door itself. He must get on. There
was no room in such a small cottage for a standard size;

Harry's narrow bathroom door would have to be bespoke. He pulled out the tape measure; he would be lucky if it could be 2 feet wide, rather than the customary 2 feet 6 inches.

He jotted down the measurements on the back of an envelope and turned to go back downstairs; the cold air that surrounded him as he did so was almost palpable and he gave an involuntary shudder.

'What is it?' he found himself asking out loud. 'What do you want? Who are you and why are you here?'

He did not expect an answer and was not disappointed when none came. But he did feel rather sick in the pit of his stomach. Having checked every room on the first floor for open windows, and finding none, he went downstairs again without a backward glance and poured himself a large Scotch. The fire that burnt its way down his throat and into the core of his body had the desired effect of settling the fluttering feeling. It also cleared his mind of what he realised deep down were irrational thoughts.

Standing at the bottom of the stairs, he looked up them towards the landing and declaimed in a loud voice: 'White lady, pink lady, lady in red, lady of the bloody lake, fast lady, foxy lady . . . will-o'-the-wisp . . . whoever you are – you are perfectly welcome to stay here. I mean you no harm and I am very happy to live with you. Just stop making the place so bloody cold.'

He took another slug of the Scotch, draining the glass, and muttering to himself, 'What is it with me and women?'

By nine o'clock there was still no sign of Alex, and Harry was beginning to tell himself that she was clearly engaged in something that she had omitted to tell him about. It did not matter. He was not her keeper. They had a relationship, yes, but it should not be so stultifying that either of them should have to give up their individuality or feel that they could not do something on the spur of the moment without seeking the permission of the other.

Having brought in some timber from the outhouse, he set to and began to construct the architrave around the bathroom doorway, trying to take his mind off the largely imagined situation. By eleven o'clock it was in place, and he had managed to fill in around it roughly with plaster. The dust filled his nostrils and, having washed his trowel and float, he went out into the garden with a glass of beer to inhale a lungful of clear air.

He would wander around to the Old Mill, just to see if she was back. He wouldn't bother her if she were there. It was too late now, but he just wanted to be sure that she was home safely. He could see a light in her window. So she must be in. Was her car in the drive? Yes it was. But parked alongside it was another. It was the sort of car he would never have expected to see there. It was a Porsche Cayenne.

44

Hatherley

22 April 1816

Forgiveness to the injured does belong;
But they ne'er pardon, who have done the wrong.
John Dryden, *The Conquest of Granada*, 1670

'Good morning, Sir Thomas.' A nod. 'Sir.' Another nod – one for each of the visitors. It was the second time in a week that the squire had reason to call on his distant neighbour, and he had scant hopes that on this occasion the atmosphere might be more congenial than on the last, for he feared that the information his younger son had to impart would be little better received than the tragic news he himself had delivered some six days earlier. The house steward ushered Sir Thomas Carew and his younger son, the Honourable Frederick, into the spacious black-and-white tiled hallway. 'If you will just wait here, sir, I will see if his lordship is ready to receive you. He has, as you can imagine, had many sad arrangements to make of late.'

'Of course.' Sir Thomas nodded his courtesy and the steward retreated into the library, closing the heavy mahogany door behind him. The two men stood in silence now. The air was filled with the scent of lily-of-the-valley – Sir Thomas noticed a large bunch on the marble-topped hall table where a sturdy bracket clock ticked sonorously. By way of avoiding any dialogue with his son, the squire stepped forward to examine the timepiece and to check against it the accuracy of his own pocket watch, the assumption being that the earl – an exacting gentleman – would be a stickler for punctuality and that the horological masterpiece of – the squire peered more closely for the name of the clockmaker – Mr Joseph Knibb would be more reliable than his own more modest possession. Satisfyingly, there was barely half a minute between them, and the squire slipped his half-hunter back into his pocket and patted it securely in place.

The minutes ticked by. Master Frederick was clearly more discomfited than his father, for he paced up and down the hallway, past a large and elaborate gilt mirror in which he checked the neatness of the stock at his neck and the fit of his waistcoat on more than one occasion. In one hand he grasped a silver-topped cane, and in the other his fashionable beaver hat. Sir Thomas tolerated the peregrinations of his son for as long as he could, and finally snapped, 'For goodness' sake, Frederick: either stand still or sit down, but cease this incessant route march.'

At almost that exact moment, the door of the library opened and the steward declared, 'His lordship will see you now, sir . . . sir.' With a modest bow he held open the library door and ushered in the two uneasy gentlemen, having taken from them their walking canes and headgear.

Frederick would rather have held on to either or both, since they gave him something to do with his hands, but he reluctantly relinquished them and thrust both his hands behind his back and under the tails of his coat, once the courtly bow to Lord Stockbridge had been executed.

Both men were relieved when the earl bade them sit opposite him on a gilt sofa, while he himself perched elegantly on the front edge of a matching fauteuil. It took just a few seconds for Frederick to notice that this was a room furnished with taste and rather more style than the Manor House. Here sporting trophies – the heads of stags and hares, wild boar and foxes – did not thrust forward from every wall as though they had left the adjacent room at high speed. Instead there were elegant torchères and display cases, a preponderance of furniture by Mr Chippendale and gilt-framed portraits of more finely boned and finely dressed men and women than those that graced the rough plaster walls of the Manor House, where each and every one resembled a monument to a diet of game and root vegetables.

Lord Stockbridge came straight to the point: 'I gather that you have some information concerning Lady Eleanor?'

'We do,' confirmed Sir Thomas. And then, clearing his throat, 'Or rather my son Frederick has information. He had the good fortune to encounter someone who had witnessed the events and could offer him a first-hand account of the tragedy.'

'Really?' The earl leaned forward, eager for reliable information.

'Yes, sir.' Frederick hesitated.

'Do go on,' encouraged the earl.

'It seems that Lady Eleanor was to . . . er, well . . . that she was to . . . elope with a certain gentleman.'

The earl held Frederick's gaze. 'I suspected as much,' he said. 'Headstrong girl. Would not be told. Would not wait. Do you know the identity of the gentleman in question?'

'I do, sir. His name was Roderick Lavallier.'

'Damn the man!' Lord Stockbridge half rose from his seat and then sat down again. 'Absolute rogue. A blackguard if ever there was one.'

'You know him then, sir?' asked Sir Thomas.

'By reputation. I am happy to say that he is not of my acquaintance and that I will have absolutely no converse with him. He is a charlatan and a mountebank. Eleanor would not be the first young woman to fall foul of his attentions. And now she has paid the price.'

'Sadly it would appear so,' confirmed Frederick.

'But this man Lavallier: do you know of his whereabouts?'

'He is, as we speak, sir, bound for the West Indies. He was endeavouring to spirit Lady Eleanor away with him when she unfortunately fell from her horse and dashed her head upon the stones of the riverbank. You know of the tragic consequences.'

'But she was a fine horsewoman.' The earl was speaking almost to himself now. 'Rode to hounds from an early age. But fate takes a hand in the lives of even the most competent of horsemen and -women. Oh, but how could she get herself entangled with such a brute?'

Sir Thomas interjected. 'The folly of young love, your lord-ship. The folly of young love . . .'

'It would appear so. But tell me, young man, how came you by this information? You say that you encountered someone who had seen the occurrence at first-hand?'

Frederick replied very calmly. 'I did, sir. I was playing cards in Portsmouth – at Lady Rattenbury's. Seated at the table was a gentleman who had been riding by when the tragedy happened. He witnessed the entire scene, and saw exactly what transpired. The horseman and -woman were riding at some speed along the riverbank. Their journey was clearly of some urgency, for they were making a fair pace. The two horses were, it seemed, a stallion and a mare, and the stallion was taking a considerable interest in the mare.'

'Foolhardy combination,' murmured Sir Thomas.

Frederick made to continue. 'On a particularly treacher-ous stretch of ground – quite close to the riverbank – Lady Eleanor's mare was bitten on the neck by Lavallier's stallion

– a savage attack by all accounts – and it reared up in fright. Lady Eleanor did her best to rein in the mare, and she had, it was thought, succeeded, but then the stallion lunged at his quarry yet again and the resulting action was too much for her ladyship, who was thrown to the ground and whose head was—'

'Yes; yes, I understand.' Lord Stockbridge interrupted to save himself from having to hear, yet again, the gory details of his daughter's demise. 'But why did this fellow – the one you met at cards – not dismount and go to Eleanor's assistance?'

'By all accounts he saw Lavallier galloping off, once the tragedy had occurred and, thinking to apprehend the man, rode in pursuit but, alas, the stallion was too fast for the gentleman's own mare and he outpaced him after less than a mile.'

'And did he not then return to Lady Eleanor, as any gentleman should have done, to offer her assistance?'

Frederick cleared his throat. 'He did, sir. But by that time Lady Eleanor's body . . . Lady Eleanor was no longer there, and neither was her horse. The gentleman assumed that Lady Eleanor must have recovered from her fall – however severe – and journeyed home.'

Looking at his father for approval, and receiving a curt nod of assurance, Frederick leaned back on the sofa and concluded, 'That is all I know, sir.'

Lord Stockbridge let out a heavy sigh. 'Well, at least we know the story now. And what a tragedy it is. Oh, headstrong girl . . . but she was always such. And this damned fellow Lavallier, where is he now? On the high seas, free to press his attentions on some other unsuspecting heiress.'

'I fear he will not be doing so,' said Sir Thomas.

'And how can you be sure?' enquired the earl.

'The ship upon which Lavallier was bound for the West Indies was called the *Leviathan*.'

The earl regarded him curiously. 'But he will be too far away to be arrested now,' he complained. 'Even knowing the name of his vessel. And by the time he reaches foreign shores, in several months' time, there is no knowing where he will fetch up. The West Indies comprises several islands – farther from each other than we find ourselves from France. To discover one particular Englishman out there, in lands noted for the richness of their bounty and therefore attractive to all manner of British speculators, would be the very devil of a task. I am quite sure that once he sets foot in that colony, he will be beyond the reach of the law and the constabulary.'

'We shall not be in need of the law, or the constabulary, Lord Stockbridge, for the Almighty himself has taken care of matters.' Sir Thomas reached into the long pocket of his tail-coat. 'I have here a copy of today's *Examiner*,' he said, with a portentous note in his voice. 'There is a report of a ship capsizing at sea in a terrible storm off Cape St Vincent. All hands were lost. The ship was the *Leviathan*.' He proffered the newspaper and leaned back silently.

'Bless my soul,' said the earl. 'If ever there was a case of divine intervention . . .' He scrutinised the paper most carefully and then asked, 'May I?'

'Please do retain it, sir, for the one crumb of good news to come out of this sorry state of affairs.' Sir Thomas coughed and adjusted his grey wig, which had slid slightly to one side due to the dramatic delivery he had employed during his revelation.

'Well, gentlemen, I thank you for the information you have vouchsafed to me, though I cannot pretend to have more than a strange satisfaction as a result of these revelations.'

Lord Stockbridge slipped the paper on to the table beside him and thought for a moment. 'We have accounted then for this Lavallier, but what of your maid – the one who exchanged costume with my daughter? Is there any news of her?'

At this Sir Thomas looked uncomfortable. It was Frederick who made to answer:

'It seems that he took the maid with him to Portsmouth, but it is unclear whether or not she boarded the ship with him.'

'How so?' asked the earl.

'The gentleman who witnessed the accident thinks that he may have caught sight of her there.'

'But is there nothing more definite than that? Nothing which can prove with certainty that this girl is alive and still on these shores?'

'Alas, no, sir.'

'But was the girl a party to the whole sorry business, or simply swept away by Lavallier against her will.'

'We cannot be certain,' said Frederick, with an unusual air of gravity, 'but it may well be the former.'

Sir Thomas interrupted. 'It seems I may have been mistaken as to the girl's nature, milord. If the situation is as my son reports it, then I fear she may well have had a hand in all this. I fear, also, that we shall never see her again.' Sir Thomas shook his head repeatedly. 'A sorry, sorry affair. All I can do, milord, is offer my deepest sympathy and regrets. Frederick told me of the news just yesterday, and I decided that we must journey to you without delay and apprise you of the situation.' Sir Thomas rose to leave.

The earl got up from his chair. 'Well, Sir Thomas, I thank you for your promptitude.'

Frederick, following the earl's lead, rose also.

'Then we shall be on our way, sir,' said Sir Thomas, 'and

detain you no more. I am sure that such tragic circumstances have resulted in many tasks which, while proper and necessary, are inclined to—'

'Just so,' interrupted Lord Stockbridge. 'Just so.'

As they collected their hats and canes from the steward in the hall and made to take their leave, Lord Stockbridge addressed Frederick rather than his father. 'Should you encounter again the gentleman who witnessed the events of last week at first hand, perhaps you would be good enough to ask him to come and see me here at Hatherley, for I would very much like to hear the unfolding of events from his own lips.'

Frederick smiled his most winning smile and, with the fingers of his right hand, pushed the fair fringe from his eyes. 'I will indeed, sir. Though I fear it unlikely, for I believe he, too, was sailing for foreign parts.'

45

St Jude's School, Winchester

22 June 2010

The man who makes no mistakes does not usually make anything.

Edward John Phelps, 1822–1900

Harry did not really feel like talking to anybody at break time on the Tuesday morning. He was sitting quietly in a corner, catching up on his marking, when Rick walked in and said brightly, 'Morning all!' He was answered by a few desultory murmurs from various corners – notably the art group – and by a sour nod from Deirdre Tattersall who, having gleaned everything of interest from *The Tablet* was now thumbing through *Private Eye*.

Harry said, 'Morning', quietly, without looking up.

Rick made his own coffee and slid into the seat next to Harry. 'What's up this morning?' he whispered. 'It's like a mortuary in here.'

Harry answered without looking up, 'Just getting on with work, that's all.'

'Oh,' said Rick. 'That sort of morning. Sorry I asked.' He took a sip of his coffee.

Harry closed the topmost exercise book and said, 'No, I'm sorry. Just a bit weary, I suppose. Up late last night doing DIY.'

'Mmm,' said Rick. 'I've heard it called some things in my time, but that's a new one.'

Harry let slip a rueful smile. 'I wish,' he said.

'Oh dear. Lover's tiff?'

'Not exactly.'

'What then?'

'Oh, just . . .'

'Come on, out with it.'

Deirdre looked up from her reading.

'Keep your voice down,' said Harry. 'I don't want the entire staff room to know about my private life.'

'I should think they're fascinated. Harry Flint, the man who keeps himself to himself, revealing the sordid and intimate secrets of his nights of lust—'

'Do you mind? Anyway, I am not having nights of lust.'

'That's a shame. If you're not having them this early on in a relationship, there's not much hope later on. You have heard the parable of the marriage, haven't you?'

'What?'

'It says that if you put a coin in a jar every time that you make love during the first year of your married life, and if you take a coin out every time you make love for the rest of your marriage, then the jar will never empty.'

'Yes, well, that's as maybe, but I'm not married, so it doesn't count.'

Rick looked sympathetic. 'So what's happened to love's sweet idyll then?'

'I'm not sure.'

'I feel a but coming on.'

'We don't live in each other's pockets, and I know I shouldn't be feeling like this but . . . well . . . Alex didn't get in till late last night. I don't know where she'd been, and she didn't call, but when I went out at eleven o'clock for a stroll, guess whose car was in the drive next to hers?'

'Can't think.'

'Marcus Carew's.'

'Sir Marcus Carew? The gay divorcee? The old bloody lecher?'

'The same.'

'Bugger me. You don't think she's having a—?'

'I don't know. I mean, I wouldn't have thought so. She was absolutely incandescent about him a few days ago. Said he was an arrogant prick.'

'Oh, well, I should think she's bound to be having an affair with him then. You know what women are like. The ones they hate, they come round to loving in the end. It was just the same with me and Rachel. She couldn't stand me at first. Couldn't bear to be in the same room.'

'I know how she feels,' murmured Harry.

'No – seriously. But I won her round in the end. Maybe that's what Marcus Carew's up to. I mean, Alex is an attractive woman. She's not going to be single for long. If you want to be in there, boy, you'd better pull your finger out. Never mind all this "take it easy, let's not rush things" sort of stuff. If you don't get a move on, that old bugger is going to nick her from right under your nose.'

'But that's ridiculous,' protested Harry. 'She really can't stand him. You should have heard her going on about him – about how he always mentally undresses her when he's talking to her.'

'She's noticed then. And you mean to tell me she's not flattered? Come on! Lovely as Alex is, she's a woman, and women like to be noticed.'

Harry looked nonplussed. 'But Alex always says what she means . . .'

'Alex says what she thinks you want to hear. I'm not saying she's leading you along, but you can't expect her to be totally frank with you, can you? Not yet. I mean, what sort of commitment have you made to her? Nothing. You've just admitted to her that you like her a lot . . .'

Harry raised his eyebrows.

'Well all right,' Rick conceded, 'I don't know the precise details of your joint conversations, but from what you tell me there's an agreement not to rush things; to see what develops. All I'm saying is, you've no hope of anything developing unless you do something positive to progress things. Hell, I'm not for rushing in, but if you're as keen on Alex as you seem to be, then strike while the iron's hot. Offer her something more definite than "let's see how it goes". I don't know any woman who'd find that much of a commitment. And with old Carew showing an interest, she might just think that she'd be better off there.'

'That's absurd! There is no way she'd—'

'Don't you be so sure. Stranger things have happened. Alex is a single woman with a young child to bring up – education and all that sort of thing. Her child is the most important thing in the world to her. The one constant. Carew's not short of a few quid. When she starts weighing things up, who's the better bet for the future of her child: a baronet who works in the City, or a soon-to-be-out-of-work teacher with no job prospects and a pile of shit for a house?'

'When you put it like that . . .' said Harry weakly.

'There's a danger of complacency here, Harry. You need to assert yourself a bit more and show her that at the very least you see a future ahead of you. At the moment you're just the sweet guy next door who's very nice to her. But it's not going to be long before she wants more than that. Needs more than that. If Marcus Carew is sniffing around there, then your warning bells should be ringing.'

As if to emphasise the point, a very loud bell did at that point ring, and the various members of staff got up from their chairs with a marked sense of reluctance, it being only three weeks to the end of term.

Before any of them could leave the staff room, the door opened and a familiar figure walked in, wearing a suit and tie and carrying a briefcase under his arm. Ted Chieveley smiled brightly and asked, 'Where's my first lesson?'

At first there was a stunned silence. No one really knew what to make of it. Perhaps it was a joke. The old headmaster had come back to say hello and this was just a light-hearted jest. But something in his eyes told them that this was not the case. Those who knew of Ted's condition (and they were relatively few, Pattie having been circumspect in her spreading of the sad news) had expressions of foreboding; those who did not were simply thrown by the unexpected sight.

It was Deirdre Tattersall who broke the silence. 'Headmaster,' she said softly. 'How lovely to see you again. Won't you come in and sit down?'

From her slightly theatrical and gently patronising tone, it was clear that she was one of the few who understood the situation. 'Can I get you a cup of coffee?'

'That would be nice,' replied Ted. He had a faraway look in his eyes, and now clutched his briefcase to his chest as if to protect the contents. Looking up at Deirdre, he said, 'The results. I have the results. Here in my briefcase.'

'Splendid,' responded Deirdre. 'You just sit down here and I'll make you a nice cup of coffee.' She shot Harry a look that said 'get help', and Harry made to leave the room to call Pattie and tell her of her husband's whereabouts. He did not need to, though, for as he reached the door, Pattie came into the staff room.

Harry could see the concern etched into her face, but she attempted to make light of the situation. 'Ted! There you are. I've been looking for you. I was getting worried. You went off without saying where you were going.'

Ted looked up from the chair, still clutching his briefcase to his chest. 'Did I? It's very important that I take care of the results. I've just come to put them in the safe.'

Pattie walked over to him. 'Well, you're here now. You can hand them over and then we'll go home, shall we?' She bent down and made to take the briefcase from him, and it was then that a change came over Ted's demeanour.

'No!' he said loudly; snatching the briefcase away from her. 'No, you can't!' And then, swiftly and with no warning, he brought the case down so heavily on Pattie's head that the old woman reeled for a moment, then keeled over sideways and crumpled to the floor. Rick leapt forward, attempting to save her from the full impact, but his progress was impeded by the coffee table and Pattie's head hit the linoleum-covered concrete floor of the staff room with an ominous thud.

A collective gasp from the room was followed some minutes later by the arrival of two paramedics, who moved swiftly to Ted's side and took an arm apiece. Harry instantly relieved one of them, indicating that he would be better employed attending to Pattie, who was now lying quite still on the floor.

Harry, under instructions from the other paramedic, firmly but carefully eased Ted out of the chair and across the room. He was weeping silently now, the crisis having passed and an awareness of his actions having dawned. Harry spoke softly and encouragingly. 'It's all right, Ted. Pattie will be fine. We'll just get you both to hospital and then you'll be all right.'

'Yes. Yes . . . I didn't mean to,' sobbed Ted. 'I didn't mean to . . .'

Rick was standing over Pattie, watching as the senior paramedic attempted to resuscitate her. The rest of the staff were now grouped in a corner, watching silently as their former headmaster's wife lay quite still on the floor. It was Deirdre Tattersall who took the lead and marshalled them all. 'I think we'd better return to our classrooms, ladies and gentlemen. The bell has gone.'

The staff did as they were bid. Only Deirdre and Rick remained, watching with concern as the paramedic continued in his endeavours. Repeatedly he applied pressure to Pattie's chest and repeatedly he listened for signs of breathing. Then, after several minutes, he stopped and sat back on his haunches, looking up at Rick and Deirdre who were standing side by side.

'She's breathing,' he said. 'But only just. She's had one heck of a blow to her head. We'll get her in and have her X-rayed. I can't think she'll be going anywhere for the next few days. But then neither will her husband.'

46

Mill Cottage
27 April 1816

Liars ought to have good memories.
Algernon Sidney, *Discourses Concerning Government*, 1698

Slowly Anne Flint mended. Agnes Palfrey was careful not to ask too many questions of her, but to let matters unfold slowly so that the girl felt secure and safe once more. Anne would sit for much of the day on an old fallen tree down by the river, gazing at the gently rippling water. Agnes wondered for how long a fifteen-year-old girl could sit without saying anything, without a need to share her troubles, but gradually concluded that Anne's introspection was a part of her recovery; a way of learning to deal with what had happened and to straighten things out in her mind. Whatever had befallen her on her brief adventure, it was clearly of such gravity that the girl had been deeply disturbed. She would speak of it when she was good and ready. Or maybe, just maybe, she would not.

William Palfrey went about his business with similar circumspection. He had made his feelings clear about the girl's presence at Mill Cottage and now remained silent on the subject. It was Jacob who had the greatest difficulty in keeping his own counsel, for much as he teased Sam about his liking for the girl, he knew in his heart that the youth cared for her and was troubled by her disappearance. It was this, rather than any willingness to spread gossip or share confidences that led him early one morning to accost his friend on the banks of the chalk stream.

Sam had already mucked out the stable and was allowed half an hour's idleness with a crust of bread and an apple – a late-stored pippin that was more wizened than he would have liked but nevertheless of reasonable flavour. He was biting into it absentmindedly when Jacob flopped beside him.

A light breeze was stirring the willow wands, and so Sam did not hear Jacob's approach. When Jacob sat down heavily alongside him, he started a little and almost choked on the pippin. 'You made me jump!' said Sam, accusingly.

Jacob smiled. 'Should have been listenin' out then. What you doin'?'

'Nothin' to speak of. Finished my chores and eatin' my apple. Mr Jencks says I can 'ave a set by the river.' Then he looked thoughtful. 'What you doin'? What brings you up here?'

Jacob hesitated. He knew that what he was about to say might result in all manner of consequences, and he could not predict Sam's reaction.

'What be the matter? Why d'you look so sheepish?' asked Sam.

'That business with Lord Stockbridge's daughter . . .'

Sam stopped chewing, his face frozen at the prospect of news that he somehow dreaded but which he was nevertheless eager to hear.

Jacob continued: 'News has come.'

'What sort of news?'

'Have you heard nothing from Mr Jencks?'

Sam shook his head.

'It seems that some foreigner – Laval or something – was to run off with the earl's daughter. They was to meet up by the river and elope.'

'Well?'

'They meets up all right, but then it all goes wrong. She falls off her horse and hits her head. Falls stone dead at his feet. He gallops off with Anne. Takes her with him.'

Sam turned to face Jacob square-on now. 'Takes her where?'

'No one knows. 'Cept that he's been lost at sea in a ship. Foundered off Cape St Vincent. Dead he is. Dead and gone.'

'And Anne? What about Anne?'

Jacob realised the cruelty of keeping Sam in the dark any longer. 'You are not to tell a living soul, promise me that?'

'Cross my heart, I promise,' said Sam, gesturing to his chest and with a look upon his face that was a mixture of eagerness and fear in equal proportion.

Jacob looked about him to make sure that they were quite alone and then said, 'She is with my mother at Mill Cottage.'

Sam leapt to his feet; a look upon his face of such relief and joy that it quite took Jacob by surprise. 'Then I must go and see her. Is she well? What does she say? How did she escape?'

Jacob shook his head. 'You must not go and see her. You must not tell a living soul what I 'ave telled you. I only tells you to put your mind at rest.'

'But the master . . . does he know?'

'Nobody do know except my mother, my father and me. My mother swore me to secrecy and if she do find out that I telled thee, I shall be banished. Or worse . . .'

'But—'

'I only tells you so that your mind is at rest. I knows you was worried. I could see, like. But until my mother says, we cannot tell a soul.'

Sam flopped down on the bank. He sat for a few moments, staring at the water and then asked, 'How do you know all this?'

'Father talked to Mr Jencks.'

'But Mr Jencks ain't said nothin' to me.'

''Tis not general knowledge. They wants to keep it to themselves. But Mr Jencks hears things in the chaise on the way to Lord Stockbridge, and he tells my father.'

'Who did know then? Who did find out this information?'

''Tis from Sir Thomas's son – Master Frederick. He did meet a man who seen it all 'appen. The man tells Master Frederick and Master Frederick and Sir Thomas goes to Lord Stockbridge and tells him.'

'And they knows about Anne?'

'They knows she was there, and that the Laval man rides off with her. But they know not where she is now, or even if she be alive.'

'But how can you keep it secret from them? They will find out. The mill is only a few mile from here.'

'No one comes to the cottage. No one from the Manor. You is the only one outside the family who knows where Anne is.' Jacob reiterated his warning: 'You must promise me that you will not tell a soul.'

Sam nodded eagerly. 'I promise.'

Jacob got up to go.

Then Sam asked, 'When can I see her?'

Jacob shook his head. 'You cannot. I have gave my word to my mother. If she do find out I broke it then . . .'

Sam looked crestfallen. To know that Anne was alive was the best thing he could have hoped for, but to be unable to see her was the cruellest of blows. She was but a few miles away, but for all that she might as well be at the other side of the world. As Jacob wandered off towards his horse and cart, Sam tried to convince himself that he must abide by his word. He would have no difficulty in keeping the knowledge to himself, but somehow he must try to catch a glimpse of Anne. Somehow.

Five miles is a long way to walk, especially upon uneven ground. But that evening, when his duties were done, Sam excused himself from the stables and wandered off in the direction of the river. He had with him a willow wand that he had fashioned into a primitive rod. Attached to it was a length of stout thread that he had begged off Mrs Fitzgerald, and tied to the end of it a bent pin. He would catch a trout for tomorrow's meal, he told Mr Jencks. The groom cast Sam a look of pity. He meant well, but his chances of catching a trout with such a primitive arrangement were less than hopeful. Timothy Jencks knew the ways of trout and their disdain of bent pins; there was no hope of success with the kind of arrangement that Sam clutched in his hand. But it did not seem to bother the lad, who left swiftly after eating little of his supper. Strange. He usually wolfed down whatever was on his plate, and more besides if he could get it. He must be sickening for something. The groom paid little heed, and went back to filling his clay pipe with tobacco.

Checking that he was well out of sight of the Manor House and the stables, Sam stowed his rod behind a hedge, tucking it into the welter of cow parsley and campion so that it was invisible from view. Then, staying close to the hedge for as long as he could, he walked downstream in the direction of the Fulling Mill. For an hour and a half he walked, more confidently now that he was clear of his home, past the spot where he had found Anne's book, past twists and turns in the river where the water ran swift and deep and then chatteringly over pebbled shallows, until eventually the distant rooftop of the mill hove into view, sheltered, as it was, by alders and willows.

The sound of the mill race grew louder as he approached, and his heart beat faster. He stuck close to the trees now, trying to remain in the long evening shadows as much as was practically possible, though from time to time great cushions of brambles forced him out into the open. But his shirt was a dull green and his leather jerkin brown; he would not stand out and, if he were careful, he would be able to approach closely without being seen. If he could just get a glimpse of her, that would be enough. To see for himself that she was well and had survived her ordeal. He could not hope to speak to her – that would be too much to ask; but he would endeavour to get close to the mill and peer through a window, perhaps to see her in the candlelight, for dusk was beginning to fall now and soon it would be dark.

Slowly he edged towards the mill. A bevy of rooks took flight from a nearby poplar; fluttering about like sooty rags in the evening air, and cawing their disapproval at being disturbed. Damn. He had tried to be quiet but no one can be quiet enough for birds. As if to prove the point beyond doubt, a blackbird darted from a clump of brambles, its clarion alarm call making him start and causing his heart to beat faster yet.

He stood still for a moment to catch his breath and to plan a route across the rough grass to the window of the mill, which he could see clearly now, illuminated by the gentle glow of freshly lit candles.

There were hazel bushes scattered about the edge of the copse, and hawthorn and elder. They were dense enough to give him cover, and the sweet smell of the may blossom – just beginning to open – lay thickly on the air. The headiness of its perfume and the nervousness he felt at the prospect of sighting her made him light-headed.

For a few minutes he stood silently in the evening shadows,

quite confident that he had not been seen. And then, at the moment when he least expected it, a voice in his ear almost made him jump clear of the ground.

'Sam! What you be doing here?'

It was Anne! She stood there in front of him as clear as day. Anne! Looking just like she always had. But there was something different about her. She had only been gone eleven days, but she had about her face a kind of weariness. It was not the sharp and vital expression he was used to. There was nothing of the teasing, head-tossing look that he had come to take for granted. He found it impossible to speak, and she could see upon his face the look of disbelief.

She sought to reassure him: 'It is me,' she said. 'Anne. I am here but you must not tell anyone.'

Sam shook his head, still speechless.

'Why did you come?' she asked. 'How did you know?'

'J-J-Jacob,' he stammered. 'Jacob told me.'

'He will be in such trouble,' said Anne.

Sam quickly made to defend his informant: 'He made me promise not to tell. I shall not. I shall not tell a soul.'

Anne nodded. 'I know you will not.' She smiled at him kindly, with a look that melted his heart.

'Oh, Anne,' he said. And then the words came flooding out in a torrent that had been held back for days. 'I were that worried. I knew not what had happened to you. Where you had gone. And then we found the body – with your clothes on it. I hardly knew what to think. At first I thought it were you. Then I saw it were not. Then you had disappeared and nobody did know where you were. Where has you been, Anne? Where has you been?'

Anne shook her head. 'I cannot say. Not yet awhile. But I am back, and glad to be so.'

'Will you come back to the Manor?' asked Sam eagerly.

'I cannot. Not yet. Maybe not ever. I know not what the future holds for me, Sam. I have been ill used. I am not the Anne you knew ten days ago.'

'Eleven,' corrected Sam. 'I been counting.'

Anne smiled again. She had spurned this callow youth but a fortnight ago; had spurned him for the last two years. How she regretted that now. For he was indeed young – as young as she and every bit as innocent as she once had been – but he meant well and it was clear that he thought much of her. How she had taunted him, and yet he still had feelings for her. How could he still care for her after what had happened? Were he to learn the bitter truth, then he would be on his way with never a backward glance, of that she could be sure. She bowed her head, for the feeling of shame that she had become so used to enveloped her once more.

Sam spoke again. 'It do not matter, Anne. It do not matter what happened on the road. I will still look after you.'

'Do not say that, Sam. Not until you knows. And I cannot tell you yet awhile.'

There was the sound of a latch being lifted on a wooden door. Anne glanced back at the mill and a worried look crossed her face. 'You must go, Sam, before you is discovered.'

Sam stood, rooted to the spot.

'Promise me you will say nothing?' asked Anne.

'I promise.'

'Now be gone.' And with that Anne walked swiftly across the rough grass to the door of the mill. She looked back at him only briefly before she closed the door behind her, but it was enough to let Sam know that she had been glad to see him. He would never let her down. Not ever.

47

The Old Mill, Itchen Parva

22 June 2010

The more I see of men, the more I like dogs.

Madame Roland, *Notes and Queries*, 1908

The sadness that Harry felt when he went home on the evening of Pattie and Ted's disastrous encounter was of a depth he had not experienced since Serena's departure. He had, to all intents and purposes, lost two people who for the last five years had become his adopted parents. Pattie would warn against his excesses, often with no more than a 'do you really think so dear?'. And Ted. Dear Ted, who offered guidance when it was asked for – and when it wasn't, but always with Harry's best interests at heart. They had . . . well . . . just been there. Often that was enough. A kindly man. A gentle man, with a gentle wife who now . . .

Harry dropped his bag on to the kitchen table and went in search of a stiff drink. Why hadn't he been to see them more frequently of late? That way maybe he could have seen the way things were going and done something to help. Pattie had said there was a danger that Ted might become violent, but Harry had not expected it to happen so quickly. It was barely two months since his condition had been diagnosed. Could the change really have occurred with such rapidity? Maybe it was something to do with the drugs they had given him? But such conjecture was fruitless. What had happened had happened, and there was little point in recriminations, even those aimed at himself.

For the first time now he could completely understand how Alex must have felt when James had gone through the same sort of character change. Nothing had prepared him for the alteration he had observed in Ted's behaviour. It had come like a bolt from the blue: the transformation of a dear and cherished friend into . . . what? And Alex had lived through this nightmare with the man she loved most. The father of her daughter. The agony must have been unbearable. And he had not exactly been the most understanding friend to her of late. And now . . . ?

He flopped down on a chair at the kitchen table and gazed at the amber fluid in the glass, as if seeking inspiration. He took a fortifying gulp and felt the liquid burn into his throat. It would be good to talk things over with someone. Well, one particular person. But he would not go round. He hadn't the energy, and, anyway, what was the point? If, as Rick suggested, Marcus Carew was making a play for her, then let him. If that was her kind of guy, then so be it. And to think that only a few days ago she had called Marcus a prick! How quickly things change. '*La donna e mobile*', thought Harry. Maybe that was his problem: a complete lack of understanding of the opposite sex.

The tap on the kitchen door broke in on his self-absorption. 'Can I come in?'

In truth he had half expected her to come round. She was probably going to make some excuse about being busy for the next few days. Taking Anne out. Saying that she did not want to see him. Well, he would cope. He had managed without a woman for the last two years and there was no reason why he could not carry on doing so.

She saw his expression and the glass that he cradled in his hands. 'What on earth's the matter?'

Harry explained the events of the afternoon as Alex sat opposite him, listening intently as history began repeating itself. He looked up as he got to the end of the story.

'So there you are. So many things change in such a short space of time.'

'Yes. Yes, they do.' She thought for a moment. 'What will you do?'

'Nothing I can do. Ted will be taken into care. Pattie will be in hospital for a while – I don't know how long. All I can do is go and see them. I don't suppose it will be long before Ted doesn't recognise me, but I'll still visit him. As often as I can. I should have been to see them more than I have, then maybe things might not . . .'

She interrupted and laid her hand on his. 'It wouldn't have made any difference, you know. There's no way you can stop it.'

'I know. I just feel—'

'Guilty.'

'Yes. For not doing more for them, and for not realising just how tough it must have been for you.'

'Oh, don't go there. There really is no need. And there is absolutely no point in feeling guilty. It achieves nothing. I can tell you that from experience.'

Harry nodded and took another gulp of the whisky. Then he said, 'I'm sorry; I didn't ask you if you wanted one.'

'No, thanks. Not at the moment.'

'No,' he said. 'No, of course not. Other things to do . . .'

She looked surprised. 'No. I just don't fancy a drink, that's all.'

'Oh. I thought maybe you were going out. With him, you know . . .'

Alex looked puzzled. 'With who?'

'Carew. The man whose Porsche Cayenne was parked outside your house at eleven o'clock last night.'

Alex half laughed. 'What?'

'Well it was, wasn't it? And there's me thinking that you thought he was a prick. How wrong can you be?'

Alex was taken aback by Harry's unexpected attitude. 'Well, very wrong as it happens.'

'Mmm?' Harry drained his glass and stared at her. The self-pity was beginning to take over.

'Yes, his car was parked outside my house last night and, yes, he was inside with me. But only for about ten minutes.'

'At eleven o'clock?'

'Yes, at eleven o'clock. Because I'd taken Anne to another bloody sleep-over before I went to the school to help them with a fund-raising evening at which Miles Carew was present and at which I told him in no uncertain terms that he owed me some money for the repair to my car headlight that he had smashed and which was not my fault at all. He went home to get his chequebook and then came round and handed it to me in person. All of which would have been quite laudable had he not tried to grope me in my own house – stupid me for letting him over the threshold – and quite frankly I could have done with you there to see him off, but as you weren't around I had to manage for myself which I've been quite used to doing for a couple of years now, thank you very much.'

There was a rising note of anguish in her voice, and Harry could see the tears in her eyes. He sprang up from the table. 'Oh God! I'm so sorry. It's just that Rick was going on today about how I'm so slow and how Carew would be getting in there and—'

'What is it with you and Rick? When are you going to stand

on your own two feet and make your own decisions? What does Rick know about me?' She was shaking with anger now.

Harry made to put his arm around her, but she pulled away and turned from him.

'I thought we understood each other better than that,' she said.

'So did I,' said Harry contritely. 'It's my fault. It's just been such a bloody day and things build up and . . . this house and . . .'

She turned to face him. 'You can't go on blaming things on this house. You loved it when you came here . . .'

'And I love it still; it's just that . . . it doesn't seem to love me.'

'Well, you haven't really given it a chance, have you? You've only been here a month. You need to get to know the place better, then you'll get the feel of it. It's just the same as with people. Like love at first sight. There's an initial attraction, but if that isn't built on then the whole thing falls apart.'

Harry looked into her eyes: 'Is that what you think has happened to us?'

Alex met his gaze. 'Not as far as I'm concerned, no. But I could do with a bit of proof.' She turned her head away and he walked towards her, cradling her in his arms from behind.

'I'll give you the proof whenever you want,' he said. 'And I'm sorry for getting hold of the wrong end of the stick, for listening too much to a mate with a vivid imagination, for not being patient enough with my house and for not—'

'Enough,' said Alex gently. 'Enough.'

He turned her round to face him, lifted up her chin with his hand and kissed her gently on the lips. 'I'll try not to cock things up again. And if I do, you have my permission to throw me over for Sir Miles Carew and go off with him in his Porsche Cayenne to wherever he wants to take you.'

Alex smiled gently. 'Not very likely.' Then she said softly 'Let's just keep going, shall we? We've a summer ahead of us and it would be nice to enjoy it.'

Harry kissed the top of her head. 'Yes,' he said. 'It would.'

Alex squeezed his hand. 'I'll have that drink now,' she said.

48

Hatherley
30 April 1816

You may tempt the upper classes
With your villainous demi-tasses,
But Heaven will protect the working girl!
Edgar Smith, 'Heaven Will Protect the
Working Girl', 1909

Lord Stockbridge was at supper in the dining room at Hatherley. There were but two of them at the table, and while it might have been more sensible to have taken their repast at a smaller board in the library, it seemed to the earl that any vestige of normal life that could be clung to was a comfort. In the old days, when the house was full of voices and children and a wife, this was where they had dined. When alone he would, indeed, take his meals in the library, usually in front of a roaring fire. But since his brother Nicholas had returned from Italy, he had reverted to the old arrangement, the one concession being that they dined at one end of the long, polished board of mahogany rather than having to shout at each other along its entire length. The silver was still arranged down the centre and the candelabra still burned brightly, but there was, in Lord Stockbridge's heart, a darkness that no flame could penetrate.

The earl's brother had had the great misfortune to arrive on the very day that Eleanor's body was discovered, and so had been bound up with the tragedy from the very start. Lord

Stockbridge had taken great pains to keep Nicholas informed of every development, and as the cheese and port arrived on this particular evening, they fell once more to talking about the events surrounding that fateful day, as indeed they had for the better part of two weeks.

Their conversation on this particular evening surrounded the revelations of Frederick Carew some three days previously.

'I find it a curious coincidence,' said Nicholas, 'that young Carew encountered the very man who saw the tragedy unfolding.'

'A coincidence, but a fortunate one,' said the earl. 'For without his information, we should have remained in the dark as to the precise nature of Eleanor's death.' He took a sip of port. 'Though I cannot, in truth, claim to gain much in the way of solace from such revelations. It was a sorry business. I dread to think what Charlotte would have made of it. Had she still been alive, I am sure that Eleanor would not have been so headstrong. A girl needs a mother more than a father, I have come to believe. To curb her excesses. To say "no" perhaps with greater frequency than I have done myself.'

'You castigate yourself too much, brother. All young women are headstrong nowadays, whether they are in the charge of their mothers or their fathers. Eleanor could not have wanted for a better parent. She was always a girl of forthright opinion, and of such determination that it would have taken wild horses to have dragged her in a direction in which she had little intention of travelling.' The earl's brother then realised the infelicity of his analogy and made to apologise for it.

'It is of no matter,' said Lord Stockbridge. 'I am beyond being wounded further.'

Nicholas cut himself a large piece of Stilton and proceeded to peel back the skin of one of the figs that he had brought with him from Italy. He offered the silver dish that held them to his brother, but the earl shook his head and took another sip of port.

'Are you well acquainted with the Carew family?' asked Nicholas.

'I am acquainted with the father,' confirmed the earl. 'I have little knowledge of the sons. One I believe is in the militia, and the other a lawyer. They return home but rarely. The boy Frederick – the one who came here with his father: he is the lawyer, as I understand it, though I confess he has little of the bearing I would expect of someone embracing such a profession. The third son would no doubt have gone into the clergy, had there been one, and Sir Thomas would have consulted me as to a living for the boy. In that circumstance we might have become better acquainted. But a third son was there not, and so Sir Thomas must content himself with two sons in the same way that I must now content myself with two daughters.'

'You have no personal knowledge of either son then?' asked Nicholas.

'None,' confirmed the earl.

'I see.' Nicholas considered for a moment and took a bite of the fig. Then he said: 'While I have no knowledge of the elder son – the one who serves in the militia, I do have some knowledge of his younger brother. I rather wish I had not been absent when he and his father came to visit you, for I would like very much to have listened to his story. And perhaps to have questioned him further.'

The earl looked surprised. 'I was not aware—'

'I had resisted saying so. I hardly wanted to add to your discomfort, since the information he imparted has given you some little peace of mind. But it seems the boy has something of a reputation with the ladies.'

'How so?'

'Oh, the usual thing. A little too free with his attentions.'

'And how came you by this information?'

'I was delayed a little in Portsmouth. Certain business transactions to be completed after my arrival from Italy, and some problem with my trunks and valises. How such chattels can go missing with such regularity, I cannot comprehend. But since I had business to undertake with the shipping line, it mattered not. I chanced to spend one or two evenings in the company of what passes for Portsmouth society. It seems that Master Frederick Carew has not endeared himself to Portsmouth hostesses on account of his reckless gambling and ... er ... dalliances with the ladies.'

'But, sir, every young man has "dalliances with young ladies". That is hardly a reason to ostracise him from society.'

'Brother, the kind of ladies with which Master Frederick has dalliances are not the sort one would want to boast about. Neither is he discreet. His conduct has resulted in his being declared unwelcome at more than a handful of households in that city. I am not sure that I would be inclined to believe all that he says. He has the reputation of being – how shall I put it? – a romancer.'

'Indeed. Well, that is as maybe, but he is certainly an habitué of Lady Rattenbury's, for that is where he learned of the events concerning Eleanor. From the gentleman who witnessed them at first hand.'

'At Lady Rattenbury's you say?'

The earl nodded. 'I remember distinctly.'

'But that cannot be,' contradicted his brother. 'There must be some mistake.'

'No. No mistake. I remember quite clearly that he informed me – while he was here, in the presence of his father – that he had encountered the gentleman who had witnessed Eleanor's accident at Lady Rattenbury's.'

'Then, brother, you have been most grievously ill informed.'
The earl sat back in his chair. 'I do not understand.'

'The very house where I was apprised of Master Frederick's
lack of popularity with Portsmouth society was that of Lady
Rattenbury. It was she herself who told me. The lady might
well have exaggerated Master Frederick's fondness for the
tables and for ladies of dubious repute, but she most certainly
did not exaggerate her own opinion of him. She will not have
him in her house.'

49

Winchester

26 June 2010

Your children are not your children.
They are the sons and daughters of Life's longing for itself.
They came through you but not from you,
And though they are with you yet they belong not to you.

You may give them your love but not your thoughts,
For they have their own thoughts.
You may house their bodies but not their souls . . .

Kahlil Gibran, The Prophet, 1923

This particular Saturday morning, Harry had found Anne surrounded by felt-tip pens, colouring in the shapes of a book of animals at the kitchen table of the Old Mill. 'Do you like colouring?' he had asked.

'Yes. Very much.'

Their brief conversation had been interrupted by Alex, who came downstairs at such a speed that Harry thought she might take off.

'Oh, are you going somewhere?' he asked brightly.

'If I tell you, you have to promise not to laugh,' she said.

'Try me.'

She frowned at him and then said, 'I have to go to the optician's in Winchester. The words are starting to run together when I read.'

'Ha!' he said.

'You said you wouldn't laugh!'

'I said, "Try me." You tried. I failed.'

'Come on sweetheart,' she said to Anne. 'This is going to be very boring for you, but you'll just have to sit and wait while Mummy has her eyes tested.'

'But I'm colouring,' responded Anne, without looking up from her work, pushing her tongue out through the corner of her mouth the better to execute a particularly tricky shape.

'I'll tell you what,' said Harry, 'why don't I come, too, and while your mum is choosing the most wonderful pair of specs that will make me appear more handsome than ever, I'll take you to see the best bit of colouring that's ever been done.'

Anne looked up. 'Where? In Winchester?'

'Yup.'

'I don't believe you.'

'It's true. And if it isn't the best bit of colouring in you've ever seen, then I'll buy you . . . ooh, what . . .'

'A dog?'

'Ah, well, maybe not a dog but . . . some chickens?'

Anne frowned. 'You can't take chickens for a walk.'

Alex and Harry glanced at one another. 'She's not wrong,' said Harry. 'Anyway, is it a deal?'

Anne thought for a moment and then put down her felt tip and said, 'OK, it's a deal.'

'I do hope you know what you're doing,' cautioned Alex.

'Oh, I know,' said Harry.

They split up by the Butter Cross, Alex going off in the direction of her express optician's, and Harry walking with Anne through Great Minster Street into the Cathedral Close.

'But you said we were going to see a colouring book,' complained Anne.

'And so we are.'

'But this is the cathedral,' she said as they walked towards the west front.

'I know.'

'But they don't have colouring books in the cathedral. I mean, I know they have some in the cathedral shop, because Mummy bought me one, but they're not exactly special. Nice. But not special.'

'Has anybody ever told you that you are very polite?' asked Harry.

Anne looked at him with a curious expression, as though he were some kind of foreign object that she had not encountered before.

'Anyway, the colouring book I am going to show you is far better than those.'

'Can I have a go with it?'

'Er, no. I don't think that's a good idea, really. But you can have a very close look at it.'

'Oh.'

'No, really. You won't be disappointed.' Harry lowered his voice. They were in the cathedral now and Harry guided Anne towards the narrow staircase that led up to the library.

'What's a trif . . . a trifor . . . ?' asked Anne, scrutinising the sign.

'A triforium?'

Anne nodded.

'It's a sort of gallery – a kind of arcade. Look, you see, the arches holding up the roof? But they don't start until we're above the ground.'

'It's like Harry Potter.'

Harry looked bemused. 'I'm sorry?'

'The train. The Hogwart's Express. Where it goes over those big arches.'

'Oh, you mean the Settle to Carlisle viaduct!'

'No! The Hogwart's Express. I thought you knew about things.'

'Yes, well I know about some things but not about everything.'

'Mmm,' said Anne. 'I hope this isn't going to be a disappointment.'

'So do I,' muttered Harry under his breath.

'I heard that.'

This child is seven going on twenty-seven, thought Harry. Still, having gone through what she has, it's hardly surprising that she's had to grow up so quickly. But there were still childhood traits about Anne, in spite of a vocabulary that was in excess of her years. Her thumb would slip absently into her mouth as she gazed about her at the towering arches. And she would hum softly to herself when she was having a good time, or eating food that she particularly enjoyed, quite unaware that she was doing so.

At the top of the narrow, twisting stairs, Harry pointed to the doorway that led into the small room.

'In there?' asked Anne.

Harry nodded.

'It doesn't look much.' And then she walked through the door and saw the four volumes of the Winchester Bible, lying under the glass cover, their illuminated letters glowing from the ancient pages.

The child gazed silently at the work before her, and slowly walked along the length of the cabinet, peering at each of the four books that dwarfed her small frame. When she reached the final volume she looked up and said softly, 'I suppose this means that I don't get my dog?'

Harry shrugged. 'I guess.'

'It's beautiful. When was it coloured in?'

'You guess.'

'It must be a long time ago. A hundred years?'

'Nope.'

'Two hundred years?'

'Nope.'

'Five hundred?'

'Nope, nope, nope.'

'How many then?'

'Eight hundred and forty years ago.'

Anne's eyes widened, 'No!'

'S'true. It took one man fifteen years to write it and six men all that time to paint the letters.'

'How do you know they were men?' she asked.

'Well, because in those days it was the men who did this sort of work, not the women.'

'Did the women stay at home and do the washing and the cooking?'

'I suppose so.'

'Not very fair.'

'No,' agreed Harry. 'Not fair at all. But today, if they were making another one, perhaps they'd let you have a go.'

'No. I don't think so. I'm not as good as all that,' admitted Anne. She walked down the length of the glass case again, and this time Harry could hear her gently humming to herself. He had to bite his lip to avoid telling her that this was why he had become a teacher; because of those rare and fleeting magic moments when you could open a child's eyes to something unexpected. Especially when it involved history. The trouble was that it seemed to happen so infrequently nowadays. Maybe he had just been teaching for too long. But this particular feeling – the one he had right now at this very moment – was what gave him the greatest lift. Not telling a child something, not *making* it learn, but just leading it to something which would capture its imagination and in which it could then lose itself. Maybe this is what he should do in the future. Stop teaching ungrateful adolescents and turn his attention to the young. It seemed so obvious, really. Primary school teaching. Oh, but wouldn't they drive him nuts with their runny noses and their short attention spans? Wasn't Anne really a cut above the norm? Yes; he supposed that she was. But the prospect of such a challenge lifted his spirits and that was something that had not happened in a long while. He would give it further thought. After all, male primary school teachers were valued for their rarity. They were a unique breed. The prospect made him smile. Yes; he would seriously think about it.

With unusual brightness he asked, 'Shall we go now?'

Anne nodded.

'But you did enjoy it?'

Another nod.

'And it is a good colouring book, isn't it?'

'Yes,' she said. 'But you're really a bit of a cheat, aren't you?'

'What do you mean?' asked Harry, concerned.

'Well, you knew that I'd have to say yes, didn't you?'

'I didn't know. I just hoped that you'd enjoy it as much as I do.'

'Mmm,' she murmured.

They were walking through the retrochoir behind the altar, when suddenly Anne grasped Harry's hand and stood quite still. He could feel her body trembling.

'What's the matter?' he asked.

Anne simply stared at the wall ahead. Harry looked in the direction of her gaze and saw a stone carving let into a niche in the wall. It was palest grey, almost white, and of a robed woman, except that it lacked a head.

'The lady,' murmured Anne.

'She seems to have lost her head,' said Harry lightly.

'The white lady,' continued Anne.

'Oh. You mean at the cottage?'

Anne nodded.

'And she didn't have a head?' asked Harry.

'Yes,' said Anne softly. 'She did have a head, but her dress was like that.'

Harry regarded the monument. 'Ecclesia,' he murmured.

Anne stood rooted silently to the spot, and Harry noticed that her face, lacking any colour at the best of times, seemed now to be paler than ever, emphasising the light dusting of freckles on the alabaster skin. Her auburn hair seemed to shine all the more.

Harry sought to reassure her. 'Her name is Ecclesia. She was the personification of the church.' Then, remembering her tender years, 'She was a lady who represented the church and all it stood for. The long dress would be her robes.'

'Robes . . .' murmured Anne.

'Yes; they wore long dresses from ancient times right up until – oh, about a hundred years ago.'

'Like the white lady.'

'If you say so.'

Anne turned to him. 'Is she still there?'

'Well, I don't know; I haven't seen her.'

Anne looked disappointed, and Harry didn't want to give

her the impression that he did not believe her. 'But I have – well – felt her presence,' he said.

'What do you mean?'

'Well, the house feels cold a lot of the time.'

'Like the wind?'

'A bit. But more than that; a sort of atmosphere.'

Anne continued to gaze at the statue. 'She was carrying something,' she said.

'What sort of something?'

The child didn't answer, but gazed, almost mesmerised, at the figure of palest stone.

'Shall we go and have a drink and wait for Mum then?' asked Harry.

It was a second or two before Anne answered. Then she said, absently, 'If you like.'

They passed the altar and were walking down the side of the cathedral towards the west door. Harry asked her, 'What about you? What would you like?'

Anne stopped in her tracks. 'Do you really mean that?'

'Well, yes, but not if you say "a dog": that wouldn't be fair.'

'Mummy says life isn't fair.'

'No. I don't suppose it is. The thing is, we just have to make the best of it.' He began walking again, Anne by his side, deep in thought.

As they walked out of the west door, the sun appeared from behind a cloud and flooded the Cathedral Close with light.

They made their way back to the Butter Cross, then Anne said, 'You asked me what I would really like.'

'Yes, I did.'

'But you didn't let me answer.'

Harry stopped. 'Oh, I'm sorry.'

'Well? Ask me again.'

Harry smiled and asked, indulgently, 'So what would you really like?'

'I'd like you and Mummy to get your act together.'

For the first time in a long while, Harry was lost for words.

50

The Manor House, Withercombe
1 May 1816

Have patience, heart. Once you endured worse than this.
Homer, *The Odyssey*, Book 12, 8th century BC

Sir Thomas Carew understood that the matter was serious when Lord Stockbridge sent word that he would call upon his neighbour on the morning of 1 May at 11 o'clock and that he would expect to find both the baronet and his son in residence. Upon receiving the message, Sir Thomas immediately summoned a servant to fetch Master Frederick to him that instant.

Some twenty minutes later, in a state of dress that Sir Thomas regarded as less than complete, but which he let pass, bearing in mind the likely gravity of the ensuing conversation, his younger son stood in front of him, wearing upon his countenance a look of such innocence that his father was wont to doubt his own misgivings.

'Lord Stockbridge has sent word that he will be here at eleven. It is now – ' he took his half-hunter from his waistcoat pocket and squinted at the dial – 'a quarter past ten o'clock. You will be properly dressed and waiting upon me within thirty minutes, Frederick.'

'Father?'

'His lordship has asked specifically to see us both.'

'But why is that? I had understood that our interview last week had been conclusive.'

'Not so, apparently.'

Frederick shrugged. 'I have no more information that I can pass on.'

'That may well be the case, but his lordship was quite insistent upon the matter, and is to bring his brother Nicholas with him.'

'His brother.'

'Yes. He has recently returned from Italy. I gather he spent a few days in Portsmouth. Perhaps you encountered him at Lady Rattenbury's or some other house during your recent stay?'

At this Frederick looked uneasy, and shifted his weight from one foot to the other.

'I cannot say that I recall.' He pushed the blond fringe from his eyes and turned to avoid his father's gaze.

'No matter. I am sure we will discover the true nature of his lordship's enquiries within the hour.'

Had Sir Thomas known at this juncture the precise nature of the facts he would discover before luncheon, then he would have treated his younger son to a more robust dressing-down than the lad had encountered in many a year.

Behind the stables, at the other end of the social spectrum, Sam was attempting to bring a pile of equine ordure under control: an operation known in common stable-lad parlance as shovelling shit. 'One day,' he told himself, 'one day I shall be the groom and some other fool will do this.' And then he was brought up sharply not by the voice of Mr Jencks, but of that of his conscience, reminding him what effect such thoughts of self-improvement had had upon Anne.

How he missed her. He had, as she had entreated him, stayed away from the Mill Cottage, but it had been four days now, and four days is a long time when the heart of a young man yearns for the company of his girl. Not that she was his girl. Or not that she admitted to it. But maybe, if he persisted, she might just come round to his way of thinking. He was sure that she was not to blame for Lady Eleanor's death; that was something he most certainly could believe without an ounce of doubt. Nor was he as eager as Jacob to find out precisely what had happened. It was enough for him that she was safe; though he did worry as to how long she could remain at the Mill Cottage without being discovered.

Tossing aside the long-handled shovel, he checked that Mr Jencks had gone about his duties. Two of the servants were laid up with colds, and Timothy Jencks had been summoned by the master to wait on in the house through luncheon. It was a task the groom loathed with a passion, and Sam knew that he would be in a foul temper on his return, but that would not be until half past two o'clock at the earliest. If Sam were sharp about it, and ran most of the way, he could get to the Mill Cottage and back again before he was missed.

He checked his jerkin pocket. Safe in the knowledge that he had what he needed, he retraced his steps of four nights before and made his way along the river. In little less than an hour he saw the roof of the mill and his heart began to beat faster. What if she were not outdoors? What then? He could not knock on the door and give away the fact that he knew of her presence. But it was a fine May Day morning, and Anne loved to be outdoors. Surely she would not be cooped up inside on such a day as this, not unless she were a real May gosling?

His suspicions were vindicated by the sight of a slender figure sitting on a fallen tree trunk by the river. Silently he snaked his way through the bushes that fringed the copse, and came into her vision only when he had reached the end of the fallen tree.

'Sam! You startled me!' she said. And then, 'You promised not to come.'

'That I did not,' said Sam, defiantly. 'I promised to tell no one that you was here. And that I have not – will never – do.'

Anne smiled at him and then a worried look crossed her face. 'But what if you are seen? Mrs Palfrey is in the house baking bread. She may well come out at any minute for a breath of fresh air.'

'If she do, she do. I ain't afeared.'

Anne was flattered by his bravery. Somehow he looked more grown up to her than he used to. She could no longer see any sign of warts; just a sturdy youth of reasonable looks who seemed to want to look after her. She should be grateful really. But now it was too late for that—

Sam interrupted her thoughts. 'I cannot stay, for I will be missed, but I brought you something.'

Anne looked at him enquiringly.

Sam slid his hand into the pocket of his jerkin and pulled out a small purple book.

Anne caught her breath. 'Where did you find that?'

'By the stream. The day after you left. I went looking for you and found it on the bank.' He passed it to her and she took it from him, running her hand over the spine and reading once again the words: *The Highwayman's Bride*. And then she bowed her head and began to cry.

'Don't,' said Sam, anxiously. 'Don't cry, Anne. I thought you would be happy to have it back.'

Anne nodded her head. 'Oh I am, but then I am not. It was the start of all my troubles. Dreaming of something different.

Something I thought I could find, but that I now know all too well that I cannot.'

Sam sat down beside her on the fallen trunk and nervously ran his hands over the surface of the bark-free timber. Washed and silvered by years of weathering it was. Smooth to the touch. Then he tentatively lifted up his arm and put it around her shoulders. She made no move to resist, but sobbed gently until he could see her tears running down the front of his jerkin.

'It will all come out all right,' he said. 'I am sure of that.'

Anne shook her head and dried her tears on the sleeve of her cotton dress – a dress worn by Agnes Palfrey in her younger days, and preserved in a trunk with sprigs of lavender for a time when it might 'come in again.'

'No, Sam. Life will not be the same again. It cannot be. But I must make the best of what is left.'

'Where will you go? What will you do?' asked Sam, wanting so much to add, 'And can I come with you?' but being too afraid of a refusal to dare go there.

'Mrs Palfrey has a sister. In Devon. I shall go there for a while.'

'But Devon? That be miles and miles away.' He looked wounded, and she took pity on his evident pain at her planned departure.

'Only for a time. Until this has calmed down. Until I has been forgiven.'

'But forgiven for what? It were not your fault, were it?'

'No. It were not. But I were there and I must pay for that. And for other things.'

'What other things?'

'Things I cannot – will not – tell you, Sam. Forgive me.' She stood up from the fallen trunk. 'Thank you for my book. It was kind of you. I am sorry that it made me cry. It was just that—'

'I know. It upsets you to have it back.'

'No. Not just that. It upsets me that I did not know what I had until I turned my back on it.'

Sam looked confused. He was anxious now. Anxious to get back before he was missed, but anxious, too, to make his peace with Anne and discover when he could see her again.

'Can I come back?' he blurted out, his face a picture of youthful ineptitude and profound agony.

Anne shook her head. 'I must go from here. 'Tis not your fault. Not your fault at all. 'Tis mine. And I am deeply sorry.' She leaned forward and kissed him gently on the cheek, and by the time that he was aware of what was happening, she had disappeared from view.

Sam only just managed to get back to the Manor House in time for Mr Jencks's return to the stable block. Far from being in his usual foul temper after such duties, today he had a glint in his eye. As if he had been party to some news that he could not wait to share. But it would not be shared with Sam. Sam was too young to understand the ways of the world. Mr Jencks's news would have to keep until that evening in The Bluebell. Then, within a few hours, it would be round the village. He should have felt pangs of guilt at being disloyal to his employer's son, but Master Frederick had always been a little shit: driving his horses too hard, and expecting Timothy Jencks to clean up after him without so much as a 'thank you'. The groom had seen it coming. It was about time Frederick had his comeuppance. And talking of which, ''Ave you not finished on that heap yet? There must have been more muck than I thought if it had taken you that long.'

Sam did not reply; he just kept shovelling. He took off his jerkin, since this was warm work, and hung it up on a wooden post. As he paused to roll up the sleeves, he looked at the leather of the shoulders and noticed the salt marks of her tears. They were marks that stayed on the jerkin until it finally fell apart several years later.

Inside the Manor House, Sir Thomas was directing a final valediction at his younger son. 'And when you have packed, you can summon Mr Jencks, who will take you – and all your trunks and valises – to the Royal Hotel in Winchester. From there you will go—'

'Father; I am old enough to go where I please.'

'That's as maybe, but you will not darken these doors again. I am only grateful that your mother is residing with her sister. I shall explain to her upon her return . . .'

'You will not tell Mama, I pray you!'

'I shall explain to her that you have been called away and that I am uncertain as to when you will return. Should you manage to find employment in foreign parts, in a land whose morals are more in tune with your own, then you will receive a small allowance to keep you there. And I say "small". I shall expect a letter from you when you are settled.'

For the first time, Frederick Carew's face bore a look of some contrition.

'Father, there is one thing that I did not reveal to Lord Stockbridge.'

Sir Thomas's face bore a look of horror. 'Not more revelations, I beg of you!'

'The servant girl, Anne. The girl who gave me the information. The girl I met in Portsmouth.'

'Yes?'

'I have reason to believe that she may be being given shelter nearby.'

Sir Thomas sat down heavily on a sturdy oak chair. 'And how do you come by that information?'

'I listen, father.'

'Yes: that I have come to realise. And in the most unfortunate places.'

'Do not be hard on her, Father. I am quite convinced that she had no part in the affair, but was just an innocent pawn.'

'So you have told us. It would have been kinder, would it not, if you had spoken up and spoken truthfully at the outset, instead of weaving some yarn which has led to considerable distress for many parties.'

Frederick shrugged. 'Ah, well, Papa. Water under the bridge now.'

'Get out!' said Sir Thomas softly.

'When I have—'

'GET OUT OF MY SIGHT!'

Frederick did not argue. His father was a large man, and he was not above striking his son, even though his offspring might be taller than he was. Frederick bowed curtly from the waist, and mutely left the room.

Sir Thomas thumped his fist on the table. 'Mrs Fitzgerald! Mrs Fitzgerald! Damn her, where is the woman?'

A shuffling sound outside the door betrayed the presence of the housekeeper, who entered rather too quickly to have convincingly made the journey from her quarters.

'Yes, sir?'

'You heard all that, I presume?'

'I'm sure I don't know what you mean, sir.'

'Come, Mrs Fitzgerald; you have worked for me for long

enough to be aware of the fact that I understand your modus operandi . . .'

'Oh, but sir, I would not dream—'

'Enough, Mrs Fitzgerald. Make your enquiries, and discover the whereabouts of this girl will you? Anne.'

'Of course, sir. I think I know where to begin.'

'She will need help, I dare say. And shelter. She will not find me lacking in compassion. I have a son whose treatment of her has fallen far short of the standards that I would like to think should be upheld in this family. It is time that at least one member of this family showed her some kindness.'

Sir Thomas was speaking as a gentleman; it was a description which, to his considerable chagrin, was unlikely to be applied to his younger son.

Frederick sat in the back of the chaise as Timothy Jencks drove him to Winchester, cracking the whip with more than a little relish, since he was glad to see the back of a lad for whom he had little time and even less respect.

The matters of which Frederick had apprised his father, Lord Stockbridge and his brother Nicholas were only partially complete. While he had given detailed information of the events of the fateful morning when Eleanor had come to grief, as related to him by Anne, leaving out not a single fact, Master Frederick had been somewhat vague concerning the precise location of their meeting and the means by which it had come about. It seemed sufficient for the three gentlemen's needs that he should explain that he had bumped into her in Portsmouth, recognised her as being one of his father's household staff and, having observed her apparent distress, had listened while she poured out her story. That the encounter had occurred purely by chance the three senior parties had accepted. Why should they not? That much was perfectly true. When he had opened the bedroom door at 72 Godolphin Street and found her sitting on the bed in front of him, he was taken quite by surprise. That the girl had taken flight and given Frederick the slip was true also. And it seemed quite unnecessary to relate any details concerning the precise location of their encounter, or that portion of it which took place after dark. Such information could only lead to embarrassment for both parties.

He was quite certain that the servant girl would not mention it herself. He had been sure of that at the time, too, for he had learned long ago how to differentiate between a reluctantly compliant servant and one with manipulative and malicious intentions. Of course, were the maid to create difficulties, then his own rank would ensure his emerging the more believable party. But in this case his confidence would not be misplaced. That much had been proved already. After all, she had left his funds intact, in both his purse and his pocket book. Were she to be the sort of girl who would capitalise on such an encounter, she would have already done so. No. It was clear that the girl was to be trusted. He could be on his way with no pricking of conscience. While he might not have behaved exactly as his father would have wished, he could now rest assured that all loose ends had been tied up. He was, after all, a man of the world, and certain things were to be expected of such members of society. All he had to do now was plan his next move and decide where to go next.

Frederick's arrogance and self-assurance, while typical of his set, blinded him to one particular consequence of his actions. It was an obvious one. And one that was to have more lasting repercussions than any of the others.

51

Mill Cottage
Christmas Day 1816

Our birth is but a sleep and a forgetting:
The Soul that rises with us, our life's Star,
Hath had elsewhere its setting,
And cometh from afar . . .

William Wordsworth,
'Ode: Intimations of Immortality', 1807

Anne Flint gave birth to her son on Christmas Day. The baby was a month early coming and, despite the diligent ministrations of Agnes Palfrey and Mrs Fitzgerald, the child's mother gently slipped away from them. It was, for the two women who had seen many comings and goings in their lives, the calmest and most serene of deaths, and also one of the most heart-rending.

Ice held fast the wheel of the mill that winter; snow and biting wind tightened their grip on the river and the water meadows for two whole months. The ice seemed to creep into the heart of Sam, too, as he sat outside the Mill Cottage on that fateful day, knowing that he should not be there, but certain that he could be nowhere else.

Mrs Fitzgerald had gone to her old friend the miller's wife almost immediately after the squire had sent word to find

Anne, in early May; for the miller's travels to and from Winchester resulted in his picking up crumbs of information on all manner of movements and events. Somehow it came as no surprise to discover the girl in the care of Agnes herself, though when she asked herself why, Philomena Fitzgerald could come up with no answer. That it was ordained that way, was enough to assuage her curiosity.

There was discussion of Anne's return to the Manor House, but when it became clear that she was with child, such thoughts were banished. Agnes would care for her at Mill Cottage and that was an end of it. Mrs Fitzgerald would share the load as much as her household responsibilities would allow.

It astonished Anne that not once did either woman admonish her. There seemed to be some tacit agreement between the two of them that the situation was accepted and they must make the best of it. At first Anne found this unnerving; and then, as time passed, she became deeply grateful to the two women who shared their mothering duties. In this role she saw quite a different side to the Mrs Fitzgerald she had known of old.

But then Mrs Fitzgerald was also aware of a change in Anne. No longer the flighty, irresponsible child she had once been; at sixteen – the age she passed midway through her pregnancy – she seemed to have been overtaken by some strange sense of knowing. It manifested itself in a kind of all-consuming calm. At first it worried the housekeeper, who suspected that Anne had undergone some kind of mental epiphany, and not for the better. But as the weeks went by, she took Anne's state of mind for what it was – in essence a rapid growing up; an awareness of burgeoning responsibility. Parental responsibility.

As to the identity of the child's father, neither Agnes Palfrey nor Philomena Fitzgerald made any reference to it. Anne wondered if they suspected the truth. Master Frederick had, after all, been banished from the household at the very moment of her own return to Withercombe, but she herself would give nothing away. She kept her counsel; the baby was to be hers and no one else's. There were moments when the conversation seemed to be steering in the direction, but when it did, then Anne would lightly change the subject and no one saw fit to press her.

On hearing the news of Anne's pregnancy, which spread as fast as such news does in small communities, there were rumours. There always are. But nothing was substantiated.

Sam knew not what to think. At first he was angry; angry at Anne giving of herself so freely. But it was Jacob who reasoned with him that such might not have been the case. And then a kind of revulsion crept over him, to be followed by sympathy, and then an overwhelming feeling of sadness at his loss. Anne had made it clear to him on that day when he had returned her book that she would see him no more. But he would never give up thinking of her; never give up believing that one day she would be his. She would come round and learn to like him – maybe love him, if he were patient, if he were always there. And on that fateful day, when he was there, at the very end, the tears that fell from his eyes were of a heat and number that might have melted any frozen river.

They had not let him in the house during the birth. Said that it was no place for a boy. Jacob and his father had gone to the mill to play cards in front of a roaring fire. Sir Thomas, in spite of this being Christmas Day and he and Lady Carew being at home, had released his housekeeper for what he clearly regarded as a more important duty. His wife, unaware of quite all that had transpired the previous spring, accepted the absence of her housekeeper with rather less good grace, but sufficient resignation to allow Mrs Fitzgerald to commandeer the chaise and to ask Jencks to battle through the snow and ice to drop her off at the Mill Cottage when events took that premature and unexpected turn.

Sam sat on the fallen tree trunk until his body was as cold as the dead and icy timber beneath him. And then he heard the cry; the small and agonising cry of a baby. His heart leapt. He ran as fast as he could to the door of the cottage and beat on it with his fists; already the tears were running down his face. It would not matter. He would care for them both – Anne and the baby. He could help; then she would see how much she meant to him.

He knew at once when he saw Mrs Fitzgerald's face. Knew what had happened. That she had gone from him; gone from them all. The housekeeper put her arms around him and rocked him as he howled, failing to staunch her own tears which coursed down her cheeks and disappeared into the rough weave of her linen smock.

''Twas quiet,' she murmured. 'She slipped away. There was no pain . . .'

Sam looked up at her accusingly. How could there be no pain? She had died giving birth. It was known as the keenest of pains, even to men and boys.

Seeing the disbelieving look, the housekeeper made to console him. 'Peaceful at the end. She saw the baby. Held him in her arms. Gave him a name.'

Between the heaving sobs that wracked his body, Sam asked haltingly: 'What is he called? What did she call him?'

Philomena Fitzgerald smiled and said softly: 'Merrily. She called him Merrily.'

The youth held her so tightly that she felt she would

almost stop breathing. And then she said to him: 'Anne said that I was to tell you she was sorry. She was sorry that she let you down.'

Sam gazed at her disbelievingly. Mrs Fitzgerald nodded. 'I think she realised in the end, Sam. Realised just a little too late.'

52

Mill Cottage, Itchen Parva

17 July 2010

Our ancestors are very good kind of folks; but they are the last
people I should choose to have a visiting acquaintance with.
Richard Brinsley Sheridan, *The Rivals*, 1775

The combination of a lifted burden and fear of the unknown
left Harry slightly light-headed at the end of term. There was
the expected presentation on the final day in the school hall,
where he had been surprised at the level of enthusiasm shown
by the boys when he went up to receive a rather smart laptop.
It quite took him aback. He made a brief acceptance speech,
doing his best not to sound like Mr Chips, and then went to
pack his bag.

Rick put his head around the door of Harry's classroom.
'That it then? Galloping off into the sunset?'

'Sort of.'

'So when will I see you?'

Harry shrugged. 'Around.'

'Well don't leave it too long. We're off camping in the
Dordogne. Can't say I'm looking forward to it. I'd rather be
in a nice little hotel on the Riviera, but that's teachers' pay
for you.'

Harry smiled. 'Your choice,' he said softly.

'What about yours? Made any decisions?' asked Rick.

'Yes.'

'Well?'

'I'll keep you posted.' Harry picked up his bag, slapped Rick on the shoulder and walked out of St Jude's for the last time.

He had hoped that Alex, Anne and he would be around on that first day after the end of term. His first weekend of real freedom. But the two of them were in Bournemouth for a couple of days. Anne had been asked by her school friend to stay in the family's apartment by the sea for a whole week. She had been nervous about going, and so Alex had agreed to stay for the first couple of nights. It was rather an anticlimax. He had determined to launch himself into the rest of his life without a backward glance, but without Alex – and Anne – he somehow felt deflated. They had become, he realised, a part of his family.

He would busy himself until their return. Potter about in the garden a bit – bring some order to the chaos and surprise them with his mini-makeover – and start sorting out his books in the outhouse, where they had lain unloved in their boxes since the day he had moved in.

And the diary. In the evening he would delve more deeply into its pages. It had lived on his bedside table for the last couple of weeks, and he had dipped into it from time to time, but it seemed to contain little of real import, and when you had read about one bolt of cloth going to market, and another ne'er-do-well being hanged for stealing a sheep, even if you were possessed of a deep and abiding fascination for local history, you could be forgiven for losing interest.

On the Saturday night, having spent the day in the garden, mowing paths through the long grass, cutting back brambles and pruning wayward apple trees, he poured a glass of wine and opened the felt-backed book yet again.

The entries had begun on Christmas Day 1815 and had now reached April of the following year. It was around this time that the entries became more interesting. Jacob Palfrey was clearly enamoured of a girl called Anne. Harry smiled at history repeating itself. Though Harry's Anne was clearly younger than the girl Jacob wrote about, there were similarities – both, it seemed, had auburn hair and freckles – and both were clearly capable of winding men around their little finger.

It transpired that Jacob lived in the Old Mill, in the attic, but that his parents lived in Mill Cottage. Harry suddenly realised that the book in his hand was, of course, a history of both their houses – Alex's Old Mill and his own place. In the confusion that had surrounded his life of late – of leaving school, of Pattie's injury and Ted's decline, of the developing relationship with Alex and the confusion of his feelings – he had missed the really obvious. As well as being Rick's history, that of the Palfrey family, this diary contained something of his own history now – of the house in which he had come to live. That was the first revelation, and a minor one as it turned out. As he read on, the story began to unfold. Of Jacob's friend, Sam – a stable boy at the Manor House – there were asides: 'Beat Sam with the horse shoes' and 'Caught a trout today. Sam catched naught.'

Harry began to build up a picture of the two lads and their youthful rivalry; wondering what they looked like, who was the taller, who was fair and who was dark. And then, as the months passed and winter turned into spring upon the faded pages, the story became much more compelling, the entries longer and more detailed. Harry sat entranced, reading of the death of Eleanor Stockbridge and the fact that she had been clad in Anne's clothing. The story of

Anne's disappearance began to unfold. Between the lines, Harry could detect Jacob's anxiety – and also Sam's – at her absence. Although Jacob wrote of him briefly, and most often in scathing terms, it was clear that Sam felt Anne's absence, if anything, even more acutely than his friend.

After a few days, Anne had clearly come back and, in spite of the fact that she seemed originally to have worked as a maid in the Manor House, on her return she stayed here in the Mill Cottage with Jacob's mother and father. There was no further explanation of the death of Eleanor Stockbridge, apart from the suggestion that she was eloping with a man called Lavallier and had fallen from her horse. Anne's part in the story remained a mystery.

There was mention of the squire – Sir Thomas Carew – and occasional references to his son. It was clear that Jacob was not enamoured of the man, for he described him variously as 'that blagard Maister Frederick' and 'yon Frederick'.

(It amused Harry to think that, two hundred years ago, the ancestor of Miles Carew had been held in similar regard by those living in the Old Mill as Miles himself was today.)

Harry wondered now if the maid Anne and the miller's son Jacob were destined to become man and wife, with Anne being accommodated in Mill Cottage rather than the Manor House. What other explanation could there be for her relocation? Throughout all of this, Anne's surname remained absent from the pages.

Then there were further comings and goings with Frederick Carew and his father, the former clearly leaving the household under a cloud. But the entries became erratic at this point. Like all youths who begin a diary, thought Harry, the initial good intentions wear thin, and with the greater distractions of spring and early summer, Jacob Palfrey obviously had better things to do than painstakingly fill in an account of his daily life which had clearly returned to the humdrum and mundane. Even Jacob now seemed weary of recording the weekly journeys to Winchester with bolts of cloth. The adventure seemed to have ended almost as rapidly as it had begun. How frustrating.

Harry flipped forwards through the few remaining entries, and noticed that the final one was more comprehensive. A valediction at the end of the year? Making up for earlier omissions? An assuaging of guilt at being a poor diarist? Well, the lad was only a miller's son. Not exactly a Samuel Pepys. What had Harry expected?

With little expectation of anything approaching a revelation, he read:

Christmas day 1816. Anne Flint has her baby. Father and I playing cards in mill. Mother and Mrs F in cottage helping her. Sam say he not go away but set by river on log crying. When father and I comes to see, mother tells us of Anne's death. She were only sixteen and I feels dreadful. Jencks comes for Mrs F. and takes news back to squire. Hope Master Frederick do rot in hell. Think he father though Anne never say. Anne do lie in upstairs bedroom of cottage at front. Baby in room next door. She to stay there until she be buried in three days time. Mother say she will care for baby. I know not what to think. Sam Overton do not speak. Father say he will get over it and that time heels. Hope same for self. Very low in spirits. Baby do not cry much. Anne gave it name before she die. Say it to be called Merrily. May God protect us in the coming year. Amen.

Harry gently closed the book and put it down. Such a small
and insignificant volume, but one that had answered questions that he had been asking for years. They had lain,
undiscovered, in Rick's grandfather's trunk for goodness
knows how long. What were the odds against that? And of
so many ends being tied up? For the first time Sam's
surname had been mentioned: 'Overton.' It would be too
much of a coincidence for Sam to be related to Anne,
wouldn't it? There was, after all, the village of Overton
nearby. He had to pinch himself to believe that it were true.
Why had these things not been spoken of before? Maybe
the book seemed like just another old diary, littered with
dreary day-to-day goings-on. To Harry, to open it and read
it seemed such an obvious thing to do, but clearly no one
else had either bothered or made the connections. But then
if their name was not Flint, or Palfrey – or Overton – why
would they? And if Rick's grandfather had kept it locked
away all these years . . .

Further conjecture seemed pointless. He had found the
mother of Merrily Flint, and her name was Anne. And Anne
had been loved by Sam Overton. The family connection
continued. He sat back in the chair and closed his eyes, and
gradually the fog began to clear. The ghost in the room
upstairs. It was carrying something, said the seven-year-old
Anne. Yes; of course it was. It was carrying the baby from
whom it had been separated by death. The baby was Merrily.
The knocking of the doorway from one room to the other had
reunited them.

Harry opened his eyes. Why was he being so fanciful?
How could any of this be proved? Wasn't it just what Rick
would have called 'A question of attribution'? Maybe it was,
but it was Harry's attribution, at any rate, and one that made

complete sense. He had been searching for months for his roots. Now he had not only uncovered them, but found that by some strange serendipity he had bought the very cottage in which they had been put down, and maybe even fallen in love with someone whose ancestor had been in love with his own. How weird was that? No: not weird. Comforting, that was what it was. Ordained. Meant to be. He had been guided here by a force or forces unknown. Why should that be so odd? Why, in a world of microchips and messages being sent by satellites through the airwaves, should something as old and established as intuition and fate be thought absurd? It made perfect sense. That, he told himself, was why history was so satisfying. Why it 'informs the present and allows us to put our lives in context.' He would never have to tell it to a classroom of boys again, but it heartened him to prove it true for himself.

So that was that. He knew his roots and he had come back to them. And in the house next door, having returned unknowingly to her own roots, was someone he would be happy to spend the rest of his life with. It had been barely a couple of months since they met. Wasn't this rather rushing things? He had already rushed into a previous relationship, and look where that had got him. But somehow this time it seemed completely different. Deeper somehow. He could tell that now; could remember that feeling with Serena and compare it with the way he felt about Alex. There really was no contest. It was not given to Harry to feel confident on anything like a regular basis, but on this particular topic there was not a shred of doubt. He just hoped that she would feel the same way.

But something niggled him about the revelations he had just uncovered. There was one fly in the ointment in this ancestry thing. He went to his new laptop and connected to the internet.

Half an hour later he had the information he needed. Tomorrow, Alex would return, and when she did he would, as Anne had instructed, 'get his act together.'

53

The Old Mill, Itchen Parva

18 July 2010

Let other pens dwell on guilt and misery. I quit such odious
subjects as soon as I can.

Jane Austen, *Mansfield Park*, 1814

Alex returned on the Sunday, and with her came Anne. The
child had quite enjoyed her day in Bournemouth, she said, but
had informed the assembled company that she would not be
able to stay any longer because they had to go home to see
Harry who would have some news for them. It was quite
important, she said.

Alex had done her best to persuade her that she was being
silly, and that many arrangements had been put in place so that
she could spend a week by the sea, not just a day. She explained
that it would be both rude and inconsiderate if Anne were to
return home immediately. To all this the child listened attentively, and then apologised quite fulsomely to her hostess, while
explaining at the same time that it was quite impossible.

In the end they gave in, and Alex and Anne returned – the
mother baffled, and the daughter content.

When, that evening, Harry proposed in the sitting room at
the Old Mill, Anne was listening upstairs with Mr Moses. She
took in the situation and then whispered to him, 'There, I told
you so.' Neither of the parties downstairs heard her, though
both knew that their love for one another was in some way
enhanced by a small child who seemed sensitive to the kind of

feelings and atmospheres that more experienced and supposedly sophisticated adult minds are inclined to overlook.

'I know it seems sudden,' confessed Harry. 'I mean, I know we've only known each other a couple of months . . . but the thing is . . .'

'It feels like longer,' said Alex. 'Almost as if we've known each other all our lives.'

Harry could hardly believe what she said. He told Alex all that he had gleaned from the diary – of Sam Overton and Jacob Palfrey, of the other Anne and all the things that had befallen her. Well, almost all. He did leave out one name, for fear of spoiling the story. Alex listened silently and, at the end, said: 'How astonishing. Sam Overton and Anne Flint. Now we know two Annes. And both of them auburn. Such a coincidence. It's almost as if you've come back to where you were meant to be; that we've all come back to where we were meant to be. The ghosts have been laid to rest.'

'Not quite,' said Harry. 'There is still the question of Merrily's father.'

'Who do you think it was? Will you ever know?'

'Not for certain. It was only a rumour . . .'

'A rumour?'

'Yes. Nothing was ever proved.'

'But?'

'I've been doing a bit of digging on the internet. It seems that the most likely candidate was one Frederick Carew – younger son of Sir Thomas Carew, baronet: the local squire who lived in the Manor House.'

'Oh heavens!'

'Now the thing is, that both Frederick Carew and his elder brother Edward *decessit sine prole mascula*.'

'You are talking to a lawyer, you know.'

'And . . . ?'

'Died without male issue.'

'Correct.'

Alex's face took on a look of dawning horror. 'You don't mean . . . ?'

'Well, as you said some time ago, Sir Miles Carew has dubious claims to the title, since he was a very distant relative. However, thanks to the internet, and various fascinating websites, I have been able to trace my direct line of descent from Sir Thomas which, no doubt, a DNA test will prove.'

'So you are the rightful heir to the Carew baronetcy?' Alex murmured gravely.

'With one flaw.'

Alex brightened. 'Of course! You're illegitimate!'

'I most certainly am not. But Merrily was.' Harry adopted a heavy judicial tone and clutched at an imaginary pair of lapels to make his legal point: 'And so, regrettably my dear Alex, I have no legal claim on the title and therefore to my profound regret I shall not be able to make you Lady Carew.'

'Thank the lord for that!'

'You can say that again,' said Harry. 'Fortunately I shall continue to abide by George Bernard Shaw's dictum.'

'Which is?'

'Titles distinguish the mediocre, embarrass the superior, and are disgraced by the inferior.'

'Quite right, too.' Alex laughed; a laugh of relief and of contentment. 'I don't think we need anything else,' she said.

'Neither do I. I won't bother with the DNA test. What's the point? I've found out all I need to know. I think my family can rest in peace now – every last one of them. And we won't inform Sir Miles for fear of undermining his confidence, though you can keep it at the back of your mind the next time he makes a pass at you.'

'So it's our secret?' asked Alex.

'Ours alone. Mind you, I can't wait to tell Rick when he comes back from France. He doesn't know that our family association goes back two hundred years.'

'Do you think he cares?' asked Alex.

'Oh, I think deep down he's a sensitive soul. He just doesn't like to show it.'

'Not like you.' She said the words softly, putting her head on his shoulder.

'No. Too sensitive for my own good, me.'

'Like someone else I know,' said Alex, casting a glance upstairs.

'Well, as you say, we have everything we want now,' said Harry, stroking the back of her head.

And then a little voice cut through the stillness.

'Not quite,' it said. 'We still haven't got a dog.'

Both Alex and Harry laughed as Anne walked down the stairs, trailing Mr Moses behind her. She came over to the sofa and squeezed her small, pyjama-clad body between them.

'Do you believe in happy endings?' asked Harry.

Anne looked thoughtful. 'Not always,' she said. Then she brightened and looked directly into her mother's eyes. 'But I do believe in happy beginnings.'

Perhaps ghosts believe in happy endings, for there were no further disturbances at the Mill Cottage, and the atmosphere in the upper rooms became increasingly warmer. But then, after almost two hundred years of being alone, I suppose Anne and Sam had finally been reunited. In a funny sort of way.

Acknowledgements

I am enormously grateful to John Matthews, H.M. Coroner for the Isle of Wight, and to Tim Kent for furnishing me with details of the way in which mysterious deaths were handled in Georgian times. I also owe thanks to Richard Wilkin who gave me information on various people's experiences of hauntings during his time at English Heritage, and to Jo Bartholomew, the librarian at Winchester Cathedral, for patiently answering my questions on Bishop Morley's library. Stephen Dick of Holybourne Rare Books has furnished all manner of information via our Saturday morning conversations – along with Tim Kent – in his treasure trove of a bookshop, and my editors Rowena Webb and Isobel Akenhead provide the kind of encouragement that all novelists dream of. To them all I express my profound thanks; they make the telling of stories even more of a pleasure.